THE FABLED OCEAN

TALES FROM THE DEEP

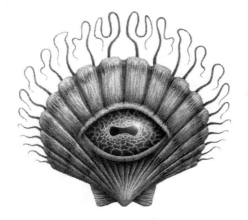

THE FABLED OCEAN

TALES FROM THE DEEP

J. S. WEIS

Holy Mackerel Enterprises LLC

HOLY MACKEREL ENTERPRISES EDITION, NOVEMBER 2023

Copyright © 2023 by J. S. Weis

All rights reserved under International and Pan-American Copyright Conventions. No parts of this publication may be reproduced, stored in a retrieval system, or transmitted in any form or by any means, electronic, mechanical, photocopying, recording, or otherwise, without the prior written permission of the copyright owner. This book is sold subject to the condition that it shall not, by way of trade or otherwise, be lent, resold, hired out, or otherwise circulated without the publisher's prior consent in any form of binding or cover other than that in which it is published and without a similar condition including this condition being imposed on the subsequent purchaser. Under no circumstances may any part of this book be photocopied for resale.

This book is a work of fiction. Names, characters, businesses, organizations, places, events, and incidents either are the product of the author's imagination or are used fictitiously. Any resemblance to actual persons, living or dead, events, or locales is entirely coincidental.

ISBN 979-8-9891990-0-6

Cover design & illustrations by J. S. Weis

www.jsweisart.com

For the walrus named Freya. The real one.

Contents

STORY 1
Eighty

The Room (3)
Twoskins (7)
Sister (11)
Forty-Two Seconds (18)
FIRE-FIRE-FIRE! (23)
Very Special (31)
New Toys (36)

Down the Tubes (44)
Practice Makes Perfect (50)
Striking Gold (55)
Mr. Zoloto (63)
The Sand that Trembles (66)
A Room without Walls (70)
Déjà Vu (78)

STORY 2
The Holy Mackerel

Behold! (85)
A Humble Fish (91)
The Good Word (97)
Miracle or Illusion? (100)

Second Coming (104)
The Shepherd & His Sheep (109)
Paradise (115)
Salvation (124)

STORY 3
Vorvan the Scarred

An Auspicious Birth (135)
So Many Questions (144)
The Disappearing Sun (155)
Of Elders and Urguds (160)
How to Eat a Clam (167)
Little Fish, Big Fish (174)
A Tragic Flaw (183)
Freyland (190)
The Orphans (198)
Sommersand (203)
Soulcatcher (210)
High Helligdom (219)
Vintersang (227)
Zver the Striped (231)

Spring Storms (238)
Aftermath (243)
All the Busy Birds (248)
Hunger (254)
The Grim Look (256)
A Blossom in the Darkness (262)
Blow, Slurp, Spit (270)
Bottomless (273)
Sorrowstone (279)
Red-Eyed Shadows (287)
Just a Push (291)
A Place Beyond Digging (299)
A Fire to the North (304)

Epilogue

Answering the Call (313)

Preface

The first in a series of books, *The Fabled Ocean: Tales from the Deep* follows the adventures of marine creatures as they navigate a crumbling world order. There are three stories in total, which I tend to think of as self-contained planets that share the same solar system, each composed of their own unique atmosphere and stylistic elements. I highly encourage taking breaks between them to reset your mental palette.

Why sea creatures? Well, despite growing up far inland, I've always been curious about the blue blanks on the map. Scientists often declare we know more about the moon's surface than the deep ocean, and this extreme environment guards some of the last true wilderness on earth. New species are still being discovered on almost every dive and most biologists theorize that life originated near hydrothermal vents. If there's any mystery left to us in the age of Google Maps, then it surely has to be at the bottom of the sea.

I also enjoy learning about different sensory organs and how they might filter a creature's unique experience of the world. Do dolphins dream in sonar? What would it be like to *see* with an octopus's skin? Obviously, I can't know what life is like for anything other than a human, but whenever science didn't get in the way of the plot, I tried to keep one toe in reality. However, take this claim with a grain of salt. Some of the animal protagonists speak English, which is just as silly as tap-dancing bananas.

Speaking of absurdity, I worked as a visual artist prior to writing *The Fabled Ocean*, and the inspiration for the central characters came to me after painting an odd Christmassy mackerel and an octopus wearing a football helmet (both of which you can see at jsweisart.com). One day, for some inexplicable reason, I followed a harebrained impulse to create scenarios explaining these visions, and this book developed as a result. Hope you enjoy it!

Eighty

STORY 1

1
The Room

A spotless, white room lies just beyond the glass. It measures twenty feet by twenty feet. No pictures hang on the walls and nothing hints at an outside world, except for the equipment that softly ticks, burbles, and murmurs. The room gives an impression that everything inhabits its proper place, happening at its precise time, as if every great mystery had already been solved and the solutions were stored neatly in a box somewhere.

Despite this impression, a curious inhabitant lives there, one whose very nature compels her to wonder, right down to the tips of her eight arms. Her name is Eighty and the room represents her entire universe. She wants to understand her role in the family of things, but she doesn't know where to begin. She doesn't even know what a question is—not as such—but in its place, she finds an impulse to shed light on darkness, to flip over stones and see what lies underneath.

Eighty achieved consciousness just three weeks ago and a luster of newness still imbues her surroundings. She's barely the size of a green pea, so even the smallest things appear monumentally grand to her. Bright rectangles shine down like suns, power lights twinkle like faraway stars, and as far as Eighty knows, her tank holds the only sea that's ever existed. It also contains a single mountain, a desert, and a black sky holding three tubular moons.

Caves honeycomb the mountain, and while she could technically sleep in any of its chambers, Eighty prefers the one closest to the top, where it's possible to survey the whole dizzying world.

"EIGHTY"

Down below, a desert sprawls away from the mountain until it terminates into four transparent barriers. She tried and tried to get past them, but it seems as if the water has magically hardened into an impenetrable wall. There's also a fifth barrier buried beneath the sand. She discovered this by spending an entire night digging, heaving aside granules the size of boulders, just to satisfy her curiosity.

A tube sticks out of the desert, siphoning away detritus, but a fine mesh blocks the hole, so there's no danger of getting sucked inside. Near the surface, another tube spouts clean-tasting water along with a steady stream of bubbles, most of which are bigger than Eighty. She tries to grab them for fun, exploding the spheres of gas into smaller ones, but the majority race to the surface and dissipate. She wonders where they go, but this liminal zone is so inhospitable to her that it might as well be outer space. She can briefly lift herself above the waterline by suctioning onto the glass, but it's much harder to breathe and her body feels like it's made of stone. Thus, the three moons remain tantalizingly out of reach for now, but she dreams of exploring them someday.

Time moves like clockwork in the room. Every twelve hours a click signals the transition between light and dark. This happens instantly—just the blink of an eye—and being a nocturnal creature, Eighty awakens to the click of moonlight. Then she stretches a bit on the stoop of her den, looking down at the crags, chasms, and sandy valleys that make up her home. Then it's time for breakfast.

She hunts all over the limestone mountain. Coralline algae encrust some of its porous surfaces in pink plates, and the rest has been colonized by a bewildering array of invertebrates. Clusters of zoanthids fan out like giant flowers, each displaying concentric rings of dazzling color. Vast communities of coral polyps fan out from their holes, each at a neighborly distance, plucking zooplankton that happen to drift by. Taken altogether, they've created a maze of fleshy branches, semi-sentient trees, and living shadows. It's a veritable jungle, and Eighty is the queen.

After feasting on a creature even tinier than herself—a copepod, for instance—she likes to stroll through her miniscule kingdom, taking stock of its other inhabitants. Here and there, skittish worms weave through the undergrowth, wriggling back into a crevice at the first sign of trouble. It's much easier to spot snails barging through the canopy, since they're big, sluggish, and sport a wide variety of striking shells. Eighty likes to push and prod them, testing for reactions, but the snails tend to ignore her. It's only when she nibbles their fleshy parts that they're spurred to retreat inside their mobile fortresses.

The tank also hosts chitons, sponges, starfish, and lots of other critters. Some consume microscopic organisms. Others break down waste into its constituent particles. In this way the circle of life appears to be a tidy affair, but despite the constant bustle, Eighty feels quite lonely. She's grown increasingly bored of munching away the hours and starts to crave an adventure of some kind—danger, even—anything to break up the humdrum of her secluded mountain existence.

To occupy her insatiable mind, Eighty contemplates the objects outside her tank, but without the possibility of physical interactions, she can only guess at their significance. There are so many puzzles to solve: How do the suns make light? What are the strange shapes on the screens? How did water get in the tank? And for that matter, how did she? Eighty has a few hunches, especially pertaining to the last two questions, and both have to do with the door.

As far as Eighty is concerned, the silver door is the most spectacular object in the entire universe. It has a bracket-shaped handle and a small rectangular window on top, but its less tangible properties are what make it so special. Everything in existence seems to have come through the door first, as if it were the womb of creation, where substances incubate until they're perfectly formed. The answers to life's big questions must lie on the other side, so Eighty spends a great deal of time staring at the window.

"EIGHTY"

Of all the marvels that have paraded past the glass, heads are her favorite so far. They come in a variety of shapes and sizes, but all have a pair of eyes, an odd protuberance above their mouth, and two rows of teeth guarded by plump pieces of flesh. Some have pink skin, others brown, and most have tufts of hair that help her distinguish between individuals. The heads generally rush from one place to another, but two will pause on occasion and flap their mouths at each other. Their lips appear to dance over their teeth, tightening, twisting, and pursing together. Eighty finds this behavior endlessly fascinating.

2
Twoskins

A semi-familiar head stops in front of the window, one with a stubbled jaw and combed-back dark hair. When he pushes the door open, Eighty discovers how wildly different he appears from what she'd imagined. To begin with, his head looks absurdly small in proportion to the rest of his body, which is roughly a hundred thousand times bigger than hers. Instead of eight arms, he only has four and uses the bottom two for walking rather than swimming. Two layers of skin cover him. One is tight and tan, the other floppy and blue. A badge clipped to his floppy skin reads:

```
Manuel Blanco
   Aquarist
 231-Q15-48
```

Daunted by the giant's sheer magnitude, Eighty scurries into her den and peeks out for further assessment. She notes his broad shoulders and muscular arms with pictures on them, including a winking mermaid, an eagle clutching an anchor, and a kraken attacking a ship. Eighty doesn't know what any of these things are, but there's something familiar about the kraken—a kindred spirit of sorts—albeit much more ferocious than her.

"*Cómo estás?*" he asks, stooping to peer inside the tank. "Good, I hope. My name is Manny and I'll be taking care of you this evening. If you need anything at all, don't hesitate to ask."

He makes a point of blinking one eye, then tightens his cheeks to bend his mouth and bare his teeth. They're slightly different shades of white, some tinted yellow or blue, as if they'd been knocked out and replaced at separate times. He's so scary-looking that Eighty starts to think of him as Monster, not so much with words—a wholly foreign concept—but with feelings.

Monster unlatches a portal in the sky-lid and Eighty flees deeper into the mountain, certain she's about to be gobbled up. Instead, he extracts a dropper's worth of the sea and squirts the contents into a machine. Symbols pop up on a screen, one of which causes him to scowl. Monster fiddles with the equipment below the tank, pours an unidentified liquid into the area where the pipes go, and adds a few stumps of dead coral.

He whistles absentmindedly while attending to these tasks, stopping only when dissatisfied. Then, once the offending issue has been resolved, he starts back up again, cycling through the same series of notes. What are the noises for? Are they dangerous? To Eighty, whistling sounds like charged particles flying through the air, and she wonders whether Monster truly wants to eat her.

"That should do," he says, closing a panel below the tank. "Well, that's all for today, but I'll be back soon. We're going to be best buddies, you and me. *Linda noche, Ochita.*"

Monster opens the door and disappears into the unknown.

As Eighty winds down for bed the next morning, a different head pushes a supply cart through the door. She also has two skins: One is tight and bronze, the other floppy and beige. Eighty guesses this double-skinned trait might be common to all giant creatures with tiny heads and starts to think of them as twoskins. Her badge reads:

```
        Maya Walker
          Janitor
        713-J40-51
```

The janitor has a svelte figure, black curly hair, and a gold nose ring. Eighty watches intently as she takes a stick from a rolling bucket, presses the water out, and pushes the stringy end across the floor until it shines with moisture. Then the janitor taps a device in her ear, which emits a steady tick, and begins to bob her head with the beat. At one point she kicks out a leg, spins around, and talks to the end of the stick, repeating sounds in a funny way. The more the janitor does this, the more Eighty associates her with the behavior of rhythmic movement, and though she has no idea what dancing is—let alone its purpose—she essentially thinks of this twoskin as the one who dances.

After finishing with the bucket and stick, Dancer wipes down surfaces with a cloth. It makes a squeaking sound: *Whaaa-Uh! Whaaa-Uh! Whaaa-Uh!* Dancer eventually makes her way to the tank and spritzes the glass with a lurid blue solution. Then she moves the cloth in a circular fashion, leaving behind streaks of liquid that swiftly evaporate. Eighty emerges from her den, feeling more curious than afraid.

"There you are, sweetheart," Dancer says, splaying her fingers on the glass. "I was hoping to see you."

Eighty approaches cautiously, this speck of a creature, darting from shell, to pebble, to shell again. Then she musters the courage to touch the other side of the glass and in response, Dancer makes a face similar to what Monster had done the previous day, the one where they show their teeth. Although Eighty doesn't understand the significance of a smile, she's fairly confident it's not a threat display.

Dancer wipes off her fingerprints and chirps, "Right as rain. See you in a week!"

From then on Monster and Dancer visit on a regular basis, talking to Eighty as they perform their perplexing duties. She ultimately

"EIGHTY"

gets used to their colossal size, then craves their company, which she prefers over her simple-minded tankmates. Not only are twoskins more interesting, but Monster and Dancer treat her as if she were the star of the room, around which everything else orbits. It's an electrifying feeling, and Eighty just can't get enough. She even tries to summon them with her mind, looking longingly at the window, as if desire had its own gravitational pull. But she quickly realizes that they control her fate—not the other way around—and this power dynamic makes her eager to please them on some fundamental level.

3
Sister

Eighty puffs up from a pea to a grape, which is precisely big enough to puncture a shell, so she eats all the snails. It couldn't be helped: They were too tasty! But now that snails are extinct, a primitive form of regret takes their place, and she starts to miss them a little.

By her sixth week of consciousness, Eighty has explored the tank ad nauseam, so she turns her attention inward and examines her own physiology instead. To start with, she's extremely flexible and squishy, except for her parrot-like beak, which determines the smallest hole she can fit inside. As a game, Eighty likes to challenge herself to squeeze into ever-tighter crevices and empty shells, the latter of which she finds rather cozy. She even pretends to be a snail a few times, taking pains to match their drowsy pace, and soon concludes that their lives spent grazing algae must've been terribly boring. Whatever she is, it's better than being a snail.

The most shocking anatomical revelation comes while tracking a shrimp, when one of her arms attaches to a rock and transitions to a mottled brown. She's changed colors before, so that isn't surprising, but then her skin turns bumpy to match the texture. This makes her camouflage that much more convincing, and even she can't tell where her body ends and the rock begins. Astounded, Eighty stops hunting to study her arms, as if to ask, *What else are you capable of doing?*

Each arm has two rows of suckers and they're constantly in motion, fiddling with anything in their vicinity. This can happen without her full awareness, let alone consent. In fact, the more Eighty gets to know them, the more distinctive her arms become, especially the front four, who seem to respond to particular moods. Put another way, if she feels threatened, a specific arm will confront the challenge. If she feels inquisitive, a different one will probe the object of interest. Thus, Eighty comes to think of them as Brave, Explorer, Hello, and Fidget.

As a consequence of their individuality, her arms can be willful and bicker with each other on occasion. For instance, if Explorer were to pick up an old shell, Fidget may try to snatch it away. This could lead to a squabble that Eighty has to mediate, sometimes by enlisting the support of her other arms. It's exasperating at times, but for the most part, she's happy to parent her extended family of limbs, however dysfunctional they might be.

During her fifth week of consciousness, a new creature appears outside the glass: one half her size with skinny legs, a glossy black body, and a red mark on its underside. Eighty spots it rappelling down a translucent line that magically unspools from its rear end. The bizarre animal fastens the thread to a pipe, scampers up to the skylid, and descends to a different spot on the pipe.

Up and down.

This way and that.

Over and over.

Until an intricate structure forms. Then the creature secretes a droplet and flicks the thread, spreading tiny beads of fluid down its length, which glitter under the light of the three moons. The sight bewitches Eighty, whose eyeballs have been pressed against the glass the whole time. Then she notices that the creature has eight arms just like her, and though the concept lies well beyond her grasp, she vaguely thinks of this new creature as Sister.

Because they're so similar, she wonders if Sister also struggles to get her arms to obey the simplest commands. Then Eighty takes the next logical step: Maybe she can do things that Sister can. After all, she'd been ignorant of her skin-sculpting powers until recently. As an experiment she starts to mimic the way Sister moves—or tries to, anyway—but walking is trickier than it looks. First of all, her arms are nearly impossible to straighten out, partially due to their lack of bones and partially because Fidget insists on coiling into a useless spiral. On top of that, coral polyps keep wandering into the path, forcing her to stop and bat them aside. After several frustrating attempts, she abandons the enterprise and shoots Fidget a disgusted look, as if it were all his fault.

Eighty decides that learning to walk isn't important—at least, not compared to conjuring her own magic thread—though she's not exactly sure how to test this ability. Perhaps it's similar to excreting waste, so she squeezes the same muscles to see if something else will come out, but only pees a little. Then she tries an adjacent muscle group, but the effort doesn't result in any thread, just a queasy stomach. This all comes as an utter disappointment.

The next night yet another species appears, and this one can swim through the air. Eighty follows it with her eyes—around, and around, and around—as it buzzes between surfaces for no apparent reason. The creature eventually rams headlong into Sister's home, where it spasms desperately and snaps several threads. Seeing this, Sister scurries over from the sky-lid and bites down with her fangs, causing its wings to sputter a few more times before giving out. Then her legs deftly unspool a gauze-like secretion, wrapping its body into a mummified egg with ghostly pink eyes.

Eighty has no sympathy for the winged creature. It should've made up its mind where to go, then gone straight there. Instead, it crashed into Sister's home and made a mess of things. Being so careless, she thinks of it as Stupid.

◆

"EIGHTY"

Something rises from the darkness and skulks toward Eighty. Its presence seems sinister, but she can't tell what it is, even as the spindly shadow gathers her up. She tries to fight back, but Brave won't respond—none of her arms will—as if some rudimentary neural connection had been severed.

Eighty gradually dissolves into a puddle of goo. The sensation is warm and not altogether unpleasant, but scary nevertheless. Then her eyeballs detach from her body. One spins in a circle while the other stares straight ahead, and the incongruous visual information makes her woozy. The spinning one eventually stops and watches the other drift farther and farther away. *Goodbye forever*, they seem to say.

Eighty jolts awake and verifies all her body parts are there, stretching each arm and groping around her eyes. She's never had a dream before—or none that she could recall—and wonders why her mind would make up such a horrifying scenario for no good reason. She tries to calm herself, but something still feels amiss, like a crucial task has been left undone. That's when she remembers to check on Stupid.

On her swim up to the sky-lid, she sees something trembling in the distance and tries to hurry, not wanting to miss whatever was happening. Then the butchery comes into sharper focus: Strands of thread flex as Sister jockeys herself into position. The gauze has been torn open, and she's slurping the juices out of Stupid's head. Eighty watches as its body slowly crumples into an empty husk, a rather gruesome sight, and her skin starts to crawl. But something else clicks. It seems that she shares another trait with Sister: They're both cunning killers.

No more Stupids appear for a week, then Sister vanishes. Eighty searches every inch of the sky-lid that falls within her line of sight, becoming more distraught the longer it takes. Did Sister go through the door? But how? Only twoskins are powerful enough to push it open. And what's that spot down there? A strip of metal runs along the base of the tank, creating a thin shelf, and there's a dark shape teetering on the edge.

Eighty dives to the bottom and finds Sister lying upside down with her arms folded across her belly, as if clutching at an invisible wound. *Is she hurt?* Eighty flails around, trying to get her attention, but Sister doesn't seem to notice.

Over the next couple of days, Eighty eventually acknowledges that Sister won't be waking up again, but spends time with her body anyway. She has no idea why—whether out of mourning, or habit, or curiosity—but deep down she hopes Sister will be revived by some miracle. Nothing happens, of course, except that her corpse gradually desiccates until Eighty can no longer bear to look. Sister brought a little enchantment to the room and now that she's gone, it feels lonelier than ever.

Dancer pushes a supply cart through the door. This usually happens in the morning, a few minutes after the rectangular suns click on. Today is no different: She comes in right on cue, greeting Eighty in her customary fashion.

"Hello, sweetheart," she says, flashing bright white teeth.

Feeling a little sleepy and quite depressed, Eighty can only muster lukewarm interest in their routine, but then Dancer does something truly horrifying: She stuffs Sister's body into a wad of tissue paper.

"Yuck," she says, scrunching up her nose. "I absolutely detest spiders, crawling around in the dark, scheming at God knows what. Not to mention these beasties are especially dangerous—and I should know! My brother got bit by one putting on his trainers. Can you believe it? He nearly lost a toe."

Then, if that wasn't bad enough, Dancer destroys Sister's home with one swipe of her hand.

"Ah, much better. Don't you think?"

Any goodwill for Dancer evaporates in an instant, and Eighty justifies her sudden reappraisal with some harsh comparisons. To begin with, Sister created an object of exquisite beauty and Dancer just wrecked it. Sister was also better at walking, because she never spun around in pointless circles or wiggled her hips in an inefficient manner. And if those contrasts aren't enough for outright rejection, Dancer's skin is dreadfully dull, not shiny like Sister's had been. Nor does it change color like Eighty's, who can essentially pick whatever outfit she wants, each hue tailored to a different mood. Generally, there's pale for fear, bright for excitement, and darkness for anger.

Eighty rushes to her den, totally heartbroken, and mourns Sister anew. Dancer taps on the glass before she leaves, attempting to say goodbye, but Eighty refuses to come out. Instead, she turns the blackest of blacks, her new shade of choice for Dancer.

Over the course of a rather uneventful month, Eighty balloons from a grape to an orange, during which time, her intellect not only keeps pace, but it outstrips her physical growth. She identifies more causal relationships, in particular that events tend to follow a seven-day cycle. For instance, Dancer pushes her cart through the door every third morning. Eighty knows this because she's been keeping track with pebbles, one for every night. When she gets to the seventh, she adds a bigger pebble to a different pile and starts over with the small ones.

Eighty is ambivalent about her newfound powers of observation. The advantages of knowing precisely when things happen are apparent, but it also takes the shimmer out of life, causing time to crawl by at a snail's pace. In fact, the more she understands, the more her tank becomes a stale block of water, suffused with a stifling sense of predetermination.

To fight the malaise, Eighty tries to stay busy. She swims laps around the desert, having sadly outgrown her jungle strolls. Other times she searches for a new star, but never finds one, because there are exactly twelve—forever and always, it seems. She squeezes inside things, or practices her camouflage, or plays games with her arms. She stares at the window when all else fails, hoping a big surprise will rescue her from the tedium, but nothing comes of this either, except that her eyes get bleary.

Her resentment toward Dancer smolders for a while, then it gradually cools, and now Eighty is counting the pebbles until her next arrival. There are two, soon to be three, which will mark the four-week anniversary of Sister's desecration.

The following morning Dancer pushes a cart through the door, and Eighty peeks out of the den to observe. The same as always, her hips sway back and forth as she dusts, mops, empties bins, and wipes down surfaces. Despite the vast gulf separating their genetic lines, Dancer's joy translates in some form, and Eighty finds this trait hard to dislike. The last embers of her anger seem to extinguish, leaving nothing but an urgent need to make peace.

When Dancer finally gets to the tank, Eighty emerges blushing her prettiest pink, meaning: *All is forgiven.*

"Oh, sweetheart, I've missed you!" Dancer declares cheerfully. "This might sound a bit daft, but I thought you were mad at me. Isn't that funny?"

4
Forty-Two Seconds

Eighty wakes up to discover an oblong ball, and all three of her hearts skip a beat. Being roughly the dimensions of an orange, she finds the pineapple-sized object intimidating. It could be aggressive for all she knows. Also, it snuck inside her tank undetected. But how? And what else is happening while she's asleep? Perhaps all sorts of queer phenomena fill the bright hours.

Brave nudges the ball, causing it to wobble, and Eighty darts back to her den. A few moments later a single eyeball pokes out to scan for danger. The ball hasn't given chase. Nor does it appear to be a trap, and nothing seems to be watching her. The ball is simply there. But why?

Over the course of the evening Eighty prods, flips, nibbles, and scrutinizes every aspect of the ball. Its tapering shape and pointy ends are interesting, as well as its primary material: a dense, rubbery substance which tastes faintly bitter. It's definitely not food and doesn't appear to have been alive at any point. She wonders why the twoskins would create such a peculiar thing—if they did, in fact—though that thought occurs so often that it's hardly worth noticing. Yet this particular circumstance strikes her as different somehow, and Eighty has a vague suspicion that something *wanted* her to find the ball. But whatever its significance, Eighty quickly becomes enthralled by the ball and has trouble imagining life before its arrival only a few hours earlier.

◆

A new pair of twoskins enter the room. They look nearly identical: black shoes, black pants, black hair, white coats, pale faces, cherry lips, placid expressions. Eighty has seen glimpses of them through the window, but they've never opened the door. Their badges read:

```
Dr. Hana Yoon
  Sr. Trainer
  197-T20-50

  Lucee Yoon
    Trainer
  247-T35-50
```

Only their haircuts are different: Lucee wears her hair in a bob that bounces as she moves. Hana has hers in a ponytail that swishes back and forth. Thus, Eighty thinks of them as Bounce and Swish.

Swish removes the sky-lid and places a two-foot diameter ring in the tank. It's painted black with a gold pinstripe corkscrewing around the tube. Swish takes the ball and puts it through the hole in the ring. Once it comes to rest on the other side, Bounce drops a ghost shrimp into the water. The tiny crustacean is completely transparent except for its eyes, heart, and the yellow eggs clustered between its swimmerets.

Dinner has been served.

Eighty instantly turns the color of sand and scurries from one position to the next, stalking her prey like an overcomplicated cat. Oblivious to its imminent demise, the shrimp loiters in the corner and taps at the glass with its antennae. Once Eighty gets close enough to pounce, her eyes jump around in a few last-second spatial calculations. Then Explorer shoots out and reels it in. *CRUNCH!*

Swish and Bounce repeat this pattern until it becomes clear to Eighty that she gets a treat whenever they put the ball through the ring, like a magic spell that summons food.

♦

"EIGHTY"

The following night, Swish places the ball near her den and the ring on the opposite side, then reattaches the sky-lid. But she doesn't put the ball through the ring as Eighty has come to expect. Instead, the twins stand around poking at screens, occasionally flapping their mouths at each other. It's all gibberish to Eighty, who wishes they'd complete the magic spell already so she can eat. What gives?

Figuring they expect a new behavior from her, Eighty paws at the ball, monkeys with the ring, and tosses a few shells around. But nothing seems to satisfy the twin's mysterious preconditions for breakfast. After a few hours of this, she's run out of ideas and her hunger intensifies to utter privation. She stares plaintively at the twins, and Hello hangs out near the portal like a beggar, pleading for the smallest shrimp they could spare.

"Don't look at me like that," Swish scolds, denying her even a crumb of sympathy. "You have to work for your meals now. No more freeloading."

The twins pack up their things and as they exit the room, Eighty jams into the corner nearest the door, convinced they've made a huge mistake. She waits the rest of the night, but food never comes, and the next day passes without so much as a snack. She attempts to sleep, but tosses and turns while her stomach grumbles, demanding that she fill it with something. Then an epiphany strikes like a bolt of lightning, and her eyes pop wide open. Of course!

"We're back," Bounce announces that evening. "Hopefully you've had a good, long think."

"Yes. Show us your bright ideas," Swish adds, sounding a tad more skeptical.

The twins set up the same scenario as the previous night, and Eighty immediately sets to work on her plan, one more easily conceived than executed, she soon realizes. Because the ball is pineapple-sized and therefore too heavy to pick up, she tries pushing at first, but it keeps veering off to the side. It snags on rocks, bumps against the glass, or spins in pointless circles. It goes everywhere except toward her goal. The setbacks grow more and more frustrating, but hunger is a powerful motivator, and she eventually learns to apply equal pressure on both narrow ends. Using this technique, the oblong ball rolls straight into the lower curve of the ring, where she rotates one of the pointy ends toward the opening. With half her arms pushing against the sand and the other half attached to the ball, Eighty heaves with all her might. The ball stands on its nose for a moment, then topples through the hole. *SUCCESS!* Her skin flushes magenta, certain a treat will materialize any second.

"Not bad," Swish concedes, nodding at her sister. "Give her the puzzle box."

Bounce opens a cooler and retrieves an olive-green crab with brown spots. It's a typical dinner, except for being locked inside clear cubes of descending sizes, each one nested within the other. Also, they appear to be fastened shut by different mechanisms. Eighty eyes the contraption inquisitively and as soon as the Bounce opens the portal in the sky-lid, Explorer reaches out to grab it.

"Let's see how long this takes you."

As Eighty holds the puzzle box the room melts away and touch becomes the only sensation that matters. Her dominant mind liquifies into the neural network of her arms—nine intelligences in total—all working toward a common goal. That is, all except for Fidget, who interferes so often that a pair of her back arms are forced to restrain him.

Explorer twists, jostles, and pulls each fastener, hunting for just the right combination of actions. Meanwhile, the crab brandishes its claws as a warning, but the bluff offers little, if any, deterrence. Eighty soon solves the last mechanism and snatches the crab, sinking her beak into its carapace like a pickaxe. The meat tastes even sweeter than usual and with the puzzle safely solved, her back arms release Fidget, who promptly dances around, victorious.

"EIGHTY"

"How long?" Swish asks.

Her sister taps the screen in her hands. "Forty-two seconds."

"Just remarkable."

"Should we tell Schröder?"

"Yes. As soon as possible."

5
FIRE-FIRE-FIRE!

Eighty quadruples in size from an orange to a cantaloupe, and her life settles into a new routine. She eats, sleeps, solves puzzles, and plays with the ball—night in, night out—until it starts to feel like the same old thing, and the interminable boredom sets in.

One day Monster enters the room at his usual time and says with a smile, "How's my *burbujita* this evening? That's what my *abuela* used to call me when I was little like you." Then he extracts a water sample to test, making up jingles to fill the silence:

"Keep flying higher bubble,
Don't worry 'bout no trouble,
Cause you're my little bubble,
I'll be there on the double!"
[cue cheerful whistling]

Monster finishes up his normal duties, but instead of leaving afterwards, he gives her a mischievous look. "We're not supposed to do this, but I won't tell if you don't."

He taps a screen and the shiny eyes that monitor the tank go dead. Then Monster lifts the sky-lid and dangles his fingers in the water, but doesn't attempt to touch her. Eighty intuits that she's supposed to make the first move, but feels a little bashful, since she's never touched a twoskin before. Hello, on the other hand, doesn't seem to care. He creeps toward the surface, sidles up to Monster's hand, and loops around his pinkie. It tastes like sweat, motor oil, charcoal, and a trace of cumin—all exotic flavors to Eighty, who lights up with fascination.

"EIGHTY"

"Believe it or not, you eat better than I ever did," Monster begins to confide. "I grew up dirt-poor in a very scary place where only *bichotes* could afford shrimp and crab. I once lived off peanut butter for a week straight. *Buddy's Nutty Butter • You'll go nutz for this stuff!* Twenty-five percent real nuts, that's what the fine print said.

"Anyway, we couldn't afford a Christmas tree, but every year my abuela—Sofia, the one I mentioned earlier—she would scrape together money to get me a pass to the aquarium. Said it would keep me off the corners. I thought it was pretty lame to be honest, but I went to make her happy. Then a funny thing happened. After spending so many hours there, wandering around, avoiding my homework, something changed in me. Stupid as it sounds—and believe me, everybody laughs at this—I imagined myself in the tank, swimming around with the fish. They just looked so peaceful, it kinda made me jealous, cause shit was hitting the fan everywhere else . . . But that's another story for another day. Anyway, the staff sort of became my second family. Even gave me a job helping in back. Only grunt work to start, but things snowballed from there . . ."

While Monster jabbers away, Eighty inspects a cut near his fingernail, puzzling over its metallic flavor and his overall intentions. The gentle giant seems to be seeking a connection of some kind, and this rekindles the memories of lonely nights, trying to decipher the world all on her own. She begins to sense a deeper companionship between animals is possible and once this concept takes hold, Eighty can't bear the idea of things going back to the way they were.

". . . Anyway, the point I'm trying to make is that the aquarium had lots of exotic animals from all over the world, but *pulpos* were always my favorite. I've cared for dozens over the years, so trust me when I say there's something special about you—that you aren't like the other zombies here—and I'm going to figure out why."

Monster gives her a broad grin, disentangles his hand, and relatches the sky-lid. Eighty wishes their interaction would continue, but there's no way to communicate her desires. All she can do is sucker onto the glass as Monster crouches down to eye level.

"Ochita," he whispers, almost mournfully. "They're going to do something awful tomorrow. I wish they wouldn't, but I can't stop them. Just try to be brave."

The aquarist turns the shiny eyes back on, dims the lights, and vanishes through the door.

The next evening Swish pushes a cart into the room and locks the wheels. A small tank sits on top—empty, except for water—and a few items rest on the shelf below. Swish completely removes the sky-lid, lays it to the side, and flits her fingers along the surface.

"Come on, I'm not going to hurt you."

Remembering her pleasant experience with Monster, Eighty wraps around her hand eagerly, hoping to get a treat out of the exchange. Swish's fingers taste more sterile than Monster's—like astringent chemicals and soap—and their texture is smoother, especially the red paint on her nails.

"Good girl. Up you go."

Swish lifts Eighty out of the water for the first time in her life, and an exhilarating rush of cool air sweeps over her skin. Then Swish places her in the small tank, snaps the lid shut, and leaves the room. Several minutes pass and the compact space starts to make Eighty increasingly nervous. She's never been in another tank before and looks at her old one with a newfound appreciation, as if she'd just landed on the moon and were gazing back at Earth.

A different twoskin enters the room, wearing glass circles over his eyes and a long white coat. Eighty has never seen him before, not even through the window. The badge clipped to him reads:

```
            Dr. C. F. Schröder
      Director of Research & Development
                005-D10-45
```

"EIGHTY"

His posture is hunched, and his complexion is akin to a pale cheese webbed in blue veins. Deep wrinkles cover most of his face, except for his exceptionally smooth scalp, where the ceiling lights are flaring across his liver spots, like a speckled egg dipped in oil. Eighty notes this and starts to associate him with shininess.

Shiny plops down on a swivel chair and adjusts its height while rolling toward her tank. He does this in a perfunctory way, as if it's happened a million times before. He reaches for a thick black glove on the middle shelf, pulls it onto his right hand, and unsnaps the lid.

"It happens to all of us," he says, attempting to corner her. "We're children for a few carefree years, then we have to grow up and face the music."

Eighty dodges the glove, ducking back and forth, but there's nowhere to hide, so she inhales water and squirts his face. She's never lashed out at a twoskin before and immediately feels anxious about the repercussions, but rather than an outburst of anger, Shiny calmly blots the drips with his coat sleeve.

"You're only prolonging the inevitable," he lectures while wiping his glasses.

Then, with surprising reflexes for such a withered creature, he reaches out and grabs two of her arms. Seeing no other recourse, Eighty twists around to bite wildly at the glove, but it's too tough to puncture.

Shiny pulls her out of the tank, pins her against the table, and pokes around her mantle with his ungloved hand. A ring adorns one finger and Eighty notices the cold rigidity of the metal. His touch makes her feel like meat on a butcher's block. There's no give to it, no empathy at all. Eighty thrashes around to free herself, swatting instruments off the shelf, and they go clanging to the ground.

"Hold still!"

Shiny stretches for a syringe that's been knocked to the floor, picks it up, and stabs her with the needle. A drop of blue blood swirls in the barrel before he plunges its contents into one of her three hearts. Eighty writhes in terror, but her strength soon wanes and she goes limp, feeling utterly betrayed.

Buzzing lights overhead.

"Get it prepped."

The scuffle of fabric and clinking instruments.

Life is so delicate compared to oblivion.

Just a bubble floating over deep, black water.

Eighty wakes up in her tank, disoriented and panicky, with the residual anesthesia making her feel like she's wearing a stranger's skin. She scans the room: It appears empty besides the usual humming equipment, but something still seems off, as if the world were only pretending to be normal when, in fact, its continuity had secretly been broken. She tries to glue her memories back together again—to tell a story about what happened—but the fracture between then and now is too deep.

Eighty curls up in a ball and stays in her den for the remainder of the night, seesawing between restlessness and exhaustion, until Dancer comes to tidy up the next morning. Unlike most visits, the janitor doesn't wiggle around or sing to the stick. Instead, she peers inside the den, seemingly aware of yesterday's ordeal.

"Keep your chin up," she urges. "It may not seem that way now, but I promise we're not all bad. You'll see."

A little later that morning, Eighty eventually nods off and sleeps like the dead. No dreams. Just a sea of darkness.

When the twins enter the room the following evening, Eighty is uncertain of whether Swish conspired with Shiny. She turns corpse gray reflexively—a sign of distress—and wonders if some friends are actually enemies, sort of like the trap Sister made to catch Stupid, or how she camouflages herself to stalk a shrimp, pretending to be something that she's not.

Eighty hides, wary of some unforeseen treachery, but Swish only puts the ball and ring inside the tank. Meanwhile, Bounce powers off the three moons and affixes a red light to the outside of the glass, drowning the room in a crimson glow. Then the twins leave Eighty to mull over the puzzle, quietly observing her with screens in their hands.

Eighty hasn't eaten in a day and despite her misgivings, there's really no other choice but to trust the twins again. They're her only source of food, after all, doling it out as they see fit, so Eighty may as well get on with satisfying their arbitrary conditions. The sooner she does, the sooner they'll be on their way. Moreover, the puzzle doesn't seem that unusual: The red light might be novel, but everything else makes sense, so she emerges from her den to do exactly what she's been trained to do: Push the ball through the ring.

ZAP! FIRE-FIRE-FIRE!

A burning sensation scorches through her body, coming from everywhere at once, as if her own blood had caught fire. All her muscles lock up and she can't move. Then the pain ceases as abruptly as it began, and Eighty scrambles to locate the source, with each arm hysterically inspecting the other's skin. A few seconds later, Explorer finds an incision at the base of her head and tugs at the stitches.

ZAP! FIRE-FIRE-FIRE!

The pain burns hot and bright for a moment, then stops, and a coppery taste trickles into the water. Eighty dimly recognizes this as the flavor of her own blood. But *why*? Why is she bleeding? If she knew the word, it would be screaming through her thoughts. Instead, there's only panic, and a feeling that her world is unraveling—that nothing can be trusted—so Eighty retreats to the safety of her den, eyeing Swish warily from the rocks.

"Yes, there's something new inside your body," Swish explains matter-of-factly. "It's called a painmaker and from now on, that area is strictly off limits. The sooner you accept this, the better."

"Do you ever feel bad for them?" Bounce asks.

Swish shrugs her willowy shoulders in response. "At first, but every animal must obey a set of rules to survive, including us. And, unfortunately, pain is the best teacher. You only have to touch a hot skillet once for that lesson to last a lifetime. The scar too." She holds up her palm to show Bounce the angry red mark.

"Yeah, I remember. Mom lathered you up in that ointment she swore by, the one that stank like a dumpster fire. What was the herb in it?"

"*Angelica sinensis*, I think. But that smells like licorice on its own, so it must've been another ingredient."

"You're such a nerd, Hana! Not the Latin name."

"Oh, you mean *dong quai*?"

"Yeah, that's it."

As the twins continue chatting, Eighty begins to suspect some form of parasite has infiltrated the wound. If that's true, then the den won't offer her any protection. Nothing could. The parasite would go wherever she goes, tormenting her like a vicious shadow, and this realization makes her desperate to get it out. So, she gathers all her courage to try once more.

ZAP! FIRE-FIRE-FIRE!

Her head is a puzzle box, booby-trapped with electricity. It hurts so badly that she wants to rip out all her organs: hearts, gills, viscera, and every last scrap of fascia until she finds the culprit.

ZAP! FIRE-FIRE-FIRE!

Eighty fumbles with the sutures, but can't control her muscles, so she lets go and the burning finally stops.

Three times is enough to make one rule abundantly clear: Don't touch the wound! But how to solve the food puzzle? Eighty already tried pushing the ball, which led to her discovery of the electric parasite in the first place, but just to be absolutely sure, she dares one more attempt.

"EIGHTY"

ZAP! FIRE-FIRE-FIRE!

"Ah-ah-ahh," Swish chides. "Not when the red lights are on."

Bounce bites the corner of her lip. "God, it's so hard to watch."

"Hard, but necessary. And they pick up the rules quickly enough. Okay, it's time to switch."

Swish nods at her sister and Bounce taps a screen to turn off the red lights. Eighty notices the three moons glowing softly again, but remains frozen in place, paralyzed with indecision.

"Should we give her a hint?" Bounce suggests.

"No. She'll figure it out on her own."

Eighty recognizes the twins expect her to do something. That much is obvious, or they would have fed her by now, but she doesn't want to risk angering the wrathful parasite again. Brave, however, isn't as afraid. Without her initial awareness or permission, he begins to creep along the sand, camouflaging until he gets within range, then taps the ball. No shock. Brave taps it again, and still nothing happens. Eighty notes this and, feeling reassured, the rest of her emerges from the crevice to push the ball through the ring.

"Good girl," the twins say at exactly the same time, in exactly the same way.

Bounce drops a shrimp in the tank and while devouring her hard-won reward, Eighty notes a caveat to the magic food spell: Never touch the ball when the red lights shine! Or very bad things will happen.

6
Very Special

Eighty hits another growth spurt, ballooning from a cantaloupe, to a watermelon, to a giant pumpkin. Now she can swim through the ring and hold the ball at the same time, but that's the only benefit of bigness as far as she can tell.

With aching nostalgia, Eighty recalls when the anemones and coral towered over her like a jungle canopy. Back then, her mountain home still had an aura of majesty, but now it's shrunk to a mere rock, and the glass narrows with each passing day, threatening to suffocate her. There's no one around to reassure her of what's normal, and she struggles to quell the monstrous feeling of having outgrown the world. She longs to curl up in a simpler time—to be small once more.

The twins enter the room, followed by Monster, who's pulling a handcart holding a plastic barrel. He puts on a heavy glove, unfastens the sky-lid, and tries to coax Eighty out of a crevice.

"Hey, Ochita. Any chance you'll make this easy on me?"

But Eighty has no intention of doing that, because the last time a glove touched her, the parasite got inside. She clings to her former mountain and when Monster tugs a little harder, she squirts his face, sending rivulets down the tip of his nose.

"Should've seen that coming," he half-says, half-spits. "Can't say I blame her."

"Regardless, she must be corrected," Swish insists, deadpan.

"Is that necessary? Let her warm up to us again. Or maybe we can give her a shrimpsicle. You catch more flies with—"

"There's no time for that. We have seven more transfers tonight."

"But shocks should be a last resort. They're highly sensitive, intelligent creatures. If you give them an incentive, they'll figure it out."

"They're also highly engineered, so she doesn't really experience distress the way we do. Think of her as a puzzle-solving jellyfish."

"How can you be so sure? It's not like they can scream."

"I don't have time to explain the science to you," Swish says tersely. "And if you don't have the stomach for this job, we'll find someone else."

Monster gives her a defeated look. "Okay . . . But for the record, I hate this."

"Cover your eyes, then. Go ahead, Lucee."

Bounce taps the screen in her hand.

ZAP! FIRE-FIRE-FIRE!

Eighty instantly contorts with pain, though she's still lucid enough to put cause and effect together—that twoskins control the shocks with their screens. This deals yet another blow to her trust in them, but before she can fully process the implications of this revelation, Monster hoists Eighty out of the tank and deposits her in the barrel. Then he seals the top, tilts the handcart, and off they go.

Eighty can't see through the opaque plastic, but she's convinced they've traveled through the door, triggering memories of all those aimless hours spent staring at the window. Journeying into the womb of creation had always struck her as an impossible goal, but now that it's finally happened, she's a little surprised there's no transcendent rapture, not even a tingling of some kind. Rather, the world seems to grow less magical by the minute.

The barrel stops rolling forward, leans back, and comes to rest.

An electric motor starts to whine, and there's a new sensation of speed as they pass beneath a cyclical buzzing sound.

"I don't care what that ice queen thinks," Monster says. "This must be very scary, but I promise it'll be worth it." Then he starts whistling a sunny tune.

Trapped in the dark, Eighty can't tell how far they've gone, but it feels like a long way—many times the length of the room. Then the motor cuts out, footsteps approach, and the barrel leans back. Eighty hears the wheels rattling over metal, followed by an upward sensation and a droning sound, then the rattle of metal again. The lid pops open, flooding the barrel with light, and her pupils shrink to slits. Monster bends his head over the top, haloed in a luminous circle.

"We're here! *Tu casa nueva.*"

He grabs the rim, slowly tipping the barrel, and water gushes over the side until Eighty pours out with the dregs.

The lurching motions, sloshing, and strange noises have made Eighty's head swim, so when her eyes come into focus, she hardly trusts them, the sight is so astounding. She had no idea the world held so much space. The room looks four times as big as the last one, and though it contains familiar equipment like pumps, filters, and monitors; everything is scaled up to a ridiculous size. There are also new structures, including a platform elevator and a metal catwalk running along the upper perimeter of the tank. That's where Monster is leaning on the handcart, looking down at her.

"Pretty cool, eh?"

Eighty spreads her arms and spins in a circle, relishing the freedom of movement. Then her skin flashes lemon, apricot, lava orange, ruby, and rose—all the way through the rainbow.

"*Feliz navidad,*" he says with a grin.

After taking a moment to calm down, Eighty starts to study her new home in greater detail. She notes a massive rock looming over an entire corner and just like the old one, there are plenty of holes for a den. It's also covered in a kaleidoscope of invertebrates: huge emerald anemones, little strawberry ones, ochre stars, and colonies of gooseneck barnacles with armor-plated heads.

A gentle current runs through the tank, made visible by marine snow blowing from side to side, where several tubes branch into the wall. The small ones have a plethora of screens, filters, and gauges attached to them. A couple bigger tubes are wide enough to swim through, but a ball valve blocks the entrance. Otherwise, Eighty would try to see where they lead, more from a spirit of inquiry than a desire to escape, since that would imply she knows of a better place to go. However, it's equally true that she possesses the talents of a natural-born escape artist and the tank has no lid, so Eighty tries to hoist herself up to the catwalk. But as soon as Brave hooks onto the edge, Eighty gets zapped and drops back into the water, where she looks at Monster for an explanation.

"Sorry, I bet that hurt. It's an electric fence. Whatever asshole designed this thing must've had a dog."

Then the twins walk in holding their ever-present screens, and Monster nods at them while taking the platform elevator down.

"Like watching a baby eat sugar for the first time."

"Yes," Swish replies indifferently. "Are the skimmers fixed?"

"Yeah, checked them again this morning. Apologies for the delay, but we had to close off the sump from the main system. Need anything else?"

"Not at the moment, thanks. See you at the next one in fifteen minutes."

The twins return the following night, pushing a cart loaded with mystifying objects, including a knobby black sphere, a pink pyramid with white polka dots, a blue cube covered in a fingerprint texture, and a dodecahedron, each facet of which had a different neon hue.

Happy in her new and improved home, Eighty is feeling more

receptive to surprises and watches with rapt attention as Bounce pushes the cart onto the platform elevator. Meanwhile, Swish takes out a laser pointer and wags a red dot over a sandy patch. Eighty has never seen a laser pointer before.

"Let's spread them out in this area," Hana instructs.

Bounce picks up a long pole with a crook on the end and hooks a small metal ring attached to the black sphere. She lowers it into the tank and repeats this sequence until all the objects are resting on the bottom. Then Swish points the laser at the blue cube covered in a fingerprint texture, but Eighty doesn't know what that signifies and fails to react.

Swish waves the laser dot in erratic circles. "Come on, think!"

Eighty swims over and tentatively prods the blue cube, looking back at Swish for validation, but her expression remains impassive. They clearly want something new, so Eighty does what she always does, experimenting by trial and error until inspiration strikes and the solution suddenly becomes obvious. She flattens against the top of the cube, calibrating her pigment to exactly the same shade of ultramarine. Then her skin bunches up in whirling creases to match the fingerprint texture—and poof! She completely vanishes. Bounce reaches into a tub and drops a crab into the tank.

"How long?" she asks.

"One minute and thirty-seven seconds," Swish reports.

"She's special, right?"

"*Very* special."

7
New Toys

The camouflage exercises intensify over the coming nights. The twins point at a series of objects in quick succession, which Eighty must sprint to match, and if she fails to go fast enough, they remind her to hurry with a little zap. The drills are strenuous and by the end of practice, her skin feels like an old rubber band that's worn out its stretchiness, but she soon learns to transition through shapes, colors, and textures at breakneck speeds.

"Congratulations, you've mastered camouflage!" Bounce declares one evening.

"Okay, let's calm down," Swish counters. "The really hard part comes next."

"I bet she figures it out in two nights."

"You do realize that's *half* the norm, right?"

"You do realize you're *condescending*, right?"

Anger flashes across Swish's face, but then her characteristic restraint returns. "I've been doing this a long time, so one might conclude that I know what I'm talking about. And I got you this job. And I'm your boss at work, *not* your sister."

"Yes, yes, and I've thanked you a million times already... Look, all I'm saying is that she's impressed us so far, so it stands to reason she'll do it again."

Bounce grabs the ring and makes her way to the platform elevator. Eighty, who's quite hungry at this point, has been watching them flap their mouths with growing impatience, knowing there won't be any food until the ball goes through the ring.

"All right, she gets two nights. What are we betting?"

"Dinner."

"Restaurant or homemade?"

"Noodles. From scratch."

"I haven't made those in years, but . . . okay, deal."

Bounce is now holding the ring over the tank. It's black with a gold pinstripe, the same as always, but instead of splashing when she lets go, the ring gradually lowers itself and stops in the middle of the water. Eighty is perplexed by this and starts to fiddle with the object in her usual fashion. But when she tries to pull the ring down to the bottom, it won't budge an inch, as if it were bolted into empty space. She finds this very intriguing, but her curiosity can wait until after dinner.

Then, as Eighty attempts to swim through the ring with the ball, something truly curious happens: The ring moves out of the way, seemingly under its own volition. She questions her perception for a moment, then tries again and again, but the ring evades her each time, dodging left, right, up, down, sideways, and flat. She even feints one direction only to move in another, but no matter how cunning her deception, Eighty can't swim through fast enough. The ring has acquired a mind of its own, one more clever than hers.

She doesn't eat that night, not a single scrawny crab leg.

On the second evening of the exercise, Eighty chases the ring around for an hour or so, then gives up in exhaustion. Meanwhile, her wily opponent hovers just a few feet away, as if to taunt her, which is infuriating. She flings the ball in anger, only this time the ring doesn't move and the ball passes through the center. Eighty stares in disbelief.

Bounce slow claps on the catwalk. "I knew it would be today."

"Don't gloat," Swish snaps.

"Remember, I like lots of fish sauce, just like Mom's."

"Feed her already, or the association will pass."

With a big grin, teeth and all, Bounce tosses a substantial reward in the tank. Eighty still doesn't know what a smile really means, but nothing bad has followed one and three crabs count as a feast, so she infers that the twins must be very pleased, which makes her happy in turn.

"Good girl," Bounce says pertly. "I always believed in you, unlike my sister."

Swish rolls her eyes. "You're so unprofessional."

The ring becomes increasingly agile over the next month, adjusting to Eighty's skill level as her accuracy improves.

Then the twins give her a new ball with extra oomph. It's still oblong with tapered ends, but this one has a clear front and back, the latter of which has short fins and a circular guard protecting a small propeller. When Eighty throws the new ball, it makes a scootering noise and bubbles spurt from the back as it arcs toward the target. This doesn't necessarily make it easier to score, but at least she can take shots from farther away.

More exercises follow.

Using a system of winches, the twins lower kettlebells and platforms of varying sizes into the tank. Eighty has to place a kettlebell wherever the twins point the laser, and some of the weights are so heavy that her arms feel close to ripping in half. What's worse, the twins often direct her to put the kettlebell right back where she got it only seconds before. More than any other, she grows to hate this seemingly pointless exercise, though she doesn't have much choice. It's the drills or starve.

The twins have totally suspended any supplemental feedings by this point, and every morsel now comes with strings attached. On top of that, there's no guarantee that she'll exhibit the necessary behavior, and the bar keeps rising higher each day. It's all she can do to keep one step ahead of her mental fatigue, which compounds with every single mistake and the lack of calories that signifies. After one particularly long string of failures, Eighty gets so ravenous that when no one is looking, she devours the gooseneck barnacles—*all* of them.

Eighty hides as the twins enter the room that night, presuming she's in big trouble. She didn't think to conceal the evidence until it was too late.

"Holy shit!" Bounce exclaims on her way in, absorbing the scale of the slaughter. Mangled carcasses are scattered across the entire tank, dangling from rocks, littering the sand, and jamming up filters. "Looks like a bomb blew up in there."

Swish shakes her head. "Will you look at that? Ate every last one. Well, this is entirely unacceptable."

"What should we do?"

"Correct her behavior."

"How?"

"Like you would any dog. Point at the mess, give her a shock, tell her she's been a bad girl."

"Do I have to? She looks pretty guilty to me," Bounce says while peeking into Eighty's hidey-hole. "*See!* She's already white."

"That's just a reflex we couldn't engineer out of them. And you're starting to sound like Manuel . . . And that's not a good thing."

"You mean *Manny*. He prefers Manny."

"I don't care what he prefers. Listen to me, both of you need to start taking your job more seriously. Despite appearances, this place isn't a game. There's a lot of money tied up in what we're doing, and wherever there's lots of money, there's lots of risk. I need to know you understand that. Now, discipline her."

Bounce reluctantly points the laser at a limp body, which does vaguely resemble a goose's defeathered neck. Eighty notices the red dot swirling around the evidence, and Bounce notices her noticing.

"Bad girl," she mumbles, then briefly zaps Eighty, who shrinks deeper into the hole.

But Swish isn't satisfied yet. "No, Lucee. Longer and louder, like you mean it."

"Fine! Bad girl! Bad girl! BAD GIRL!" she cries, administering a sustained jolt with each repetition, but Eighty already understands what she did wrong and wishes they'd stop.

"Okay, good enough. Now call someone to clean up the mess."

After that, Eighty never so much as nibbles any of her tankmates, but despite the severity of her punishment, she doesn't hold it against the twins. They set the rules, for better or worse, and it would be like blaming a drought on the same gods you depend upon. The best she can do is dance and pray they'll make it rain. Thus, she learns to accept her austere existence, adapting to the constant hunger and even growing to appreciate the clarity it provides. Eventually, just the hint of food is enough to spring-load her reflexes, readying them to snap into action, because she can't afford to miss a single opportunity.

It's a clean feeling. A good feeling.

One evening Monster and the twins enter the room pushing a cart loaded with more strange equipment. They look similar to football helmets, including a grid of bars where a face would normally go. Some are white plastic and look rather banged-up. The others are black and sleek, with an odd patina shimmering over the surface.

"Look, Ochita. New toys!" Monster says, gesturing toward the bulbous objects. "Get ready to have some fun."

Swish snorts and gives him a derisive look. "I'd tell you not to anthropomorphize, but it doesn't seem to do much good."

"Is there a thaw in the air? Pretty soon you'll let me whistle."

"Not a chance. You're a terrible whistler."

"That, or you don't have the constitution for music." Monster raises a single eyebrow, as if it were a question.

"Don't push your luck."

"But she likes it when I whistle."

"She's not a pet."

Monster throws up his hands. "Okay, you win. No more fun. Zero, zilch, nada. And if I see someone else having fun, I'll shock the pants off them. Happy?"

"Can we get started already?" Bounce interjects on her way up the elevator, white helmet in hand. "I don't want to miss dinner, and I'm too hungry to listen to this garbage."

"Fine," Monster and Swish reply together.

With that, Bounce drops the white helmet in the tank, and Eighty begins to scrutinize its properties. The helmet is very smooth and hard, but not too heavy, so it's easy enough to pick up. She tries to gnaw on it, but can't get her beak around the domed part. The bars, however, are a different story and she spends a good deal of time mouthing them from various angles. It's strangely satisfying and like a dog with a chew toy, she drags the helmet around, merry as can be, until Monster knuckles the glass to get her attention.

He takes a stuffed animal from the cart—a squid with googly cartoon eyes—and shoves it into a helmet. Then Monster turns the cavity toward her to show that it's completely tucked inside. Eighty immediately grasps the lesson, but execution is another matter. Her arms cooperate at their discretion, so wrangling them into a tidy ball is no easy feat. The first time she attempts to squeeze inside the helmet, Fidget insists on dangling out of the face guard for no apparent reason other than stubbornness, so Swish points the laser at him and gives Eighty a zap. Blasted Fidget! But with concerted willpower, she eventually reins him in and starts to get the hang of the sheltering technique.

Swish nods at Monster. "Show her what the helmet is *really* for."

"Gladly."

Monster takes a black helmet from the cart and places it on the ground. Then he picks up a hefty kettlebell, squats over the helmet as if he'd just laid an egg, and drops the weight. In the split-second of impact, a shield of light flickers over the surface and the helmet deflects the blow without so much as a scratch. Swish tells him to repeat this action until sweat rolls down his forehead and his kraken tattoo ripples angrily over his bicep.

"Good enough?" he suggests, panting a little.

"Perhaps . . . Throw it in and find out."

Monster shrugs and lobs the helmet over the side. Then all three of them line up shoulder-to-shoulder to observe what happens next. Before it has a chance to sink, Eighty catches the helmet and appears to contemplate her next move. Then she starts to whack things in the tank—the glass, rocks, and her camouflage toys—a shock of light crackling with every blow. This is fun, Eighty thinks.

"I have no idea what genes you fiddled with, but it's a wonder any of this makes sense to her," Monster says. Then he comments at a lower volume, "It barely makes sense to me."

Swish looks at his reflection in the glass and explains, "The training regime has a cumulative effect. Every ingrained behavior adds a piece to the puzzle. She'll know what to do when the time comes."

"How long have you been a trainer again?"

"None of your business . . . again."

Bounce smiles and shakes her head. "Sunshine, meet your rain cloud."

Monster stays behind after the twins leave that morning. He approaches the tank on the lower level, glancing furtively at the door, and puts his palm on the glass.

"It's good to see you happy," he says, sounding a bit more solemn than usual. "I know you won't understand what I'm about to say, but I'm going to say it anyway. People—maybe most of us—we end up doing things we don't want to. My Grandma Sofia used to say, '*Mijo*, if you sleep with dogs, you're gonna wake up with fleas.' Well, I'm covered in the fuckers now. But I really needed the money, same as everybody else, I guess."

Eighty doesn't understand Monster, of course, but she does detect a strain in him and wonders what's the matter. In a gesture of empathy, Hello suckers onto the opposite side of the glass, doing his best to line up with Monster's fingers.

"She's asked me to join them—the fucking *nelves*—can you believe it? Dumb as their name is, I want to help. I really do. It's just that other people depend on me, and I'm no hero to be perfectly honest. Where I come from, you don't stick your nose someplace it doesn't belong. Surviving is hard en—"

The door cracks open and Monster instantly pulls his hand away from the glass.

Swish leans into the room. "Are you coming, Manuel? We have a meeting at seven."

"Yeah, just thought I saw a crack in the acrylic. Maybe from the helmet."

"That would be *quite* unusual. Did you?" Swish asks, eyeing him mistrustfully.

"No. Seems okay, I guess."

"Let's go, then. Dr. Schröder hates when we're late."

She closes the door, and Monster hurries shortly after.

8
Down the Tubes

The twins direct their assistants to remove everything from the tank but the sand, rocks, and the critters attached to them. Eighty is glad to watch the kettlebells go, but not her camouflage toys. She wonders whether she's being punished for some trivial infraction, despite her best efforts at obedience. She really is trying to be good, but when the assistants attempt to take her ball, that's a bridge too far. She pops the ball out of the net and runs away with her prized possession until the shocks convince her otherwise.

She changes her skin to a glum blue-gray in protest, but quickly becomes sidetracked when Swish taps her screen, opening the ball valves that block the two big tubes on opposite sides of the tank. Maybe they're about to play a new game, Eighty supposes, so she swims over to see where they go, but the holes are impenetrably dark. A grinding noise reverberates from far away, possibly another valve opening, but it's hard to tell. Then she hears a dull rumble, getting louder each second, like the roar of swelling thunder. Whatever it is, it seems to be charging toward her. Eighty backs away from the opening and prepares to make a run for her den.

Water blasts out of the hole, propelling her into the middle of the tank, where the other tube instantly starts to suck her backwards. Explorer seizes a spike of rock, then Brave gets a hold of it, and Fidget helps too. They all fight valiantly against the current as it hurtles across the tank, but before Eighty can pull into a crevice, Swish zaps her into paralysis. The twoskins will always get their way, she thinks, while stoically watching her last sucker come unglued. Then the rocks rush away, and the tube swallows her whole.

A whoosh of speed.
Complete and total darkness.
Sharp turns. Centrifugal force.
Dashes of light.
More turns.
More dashes of light.
Then, an overwhelming brilliance.
Like flying into the center of the sun.

The tube spits Eighty into a tiny cylinder and a ball valve closes behind her. Grains of sand swirl through the water, including a few dismembered anemone tentacles. Glaring lights beam down from the ceiling without mercy and if there are shadows at all, they're scarcely more than hairlines. She's used to a nocturnal ambience, and her eyes recoil in pain; but once they come into focus, she sees a vast room containing many rows of compact tanks, each connected to two tubes that elbow into the floor.

A small motor whirs as an arm unfolds from the tank's cap, unsheathing itself like the sinister appendage of an insect. There's a black eye at the end, which lowers and pauses for a moment to make tiny calibrations. It shoots her with pinpricks of red light, scanning from top to bottom, then rotates to a different position and scans from another angle. Symbols flicker onto a black screen, opposite a three-dimensional likeness. Finally, the arm folds back into the cap, transforming into a seamless shape once again.

Eighty starts to ponder the significance of this, when she's distracted by a ball valve opening in an adjacent tank. The water appears to boil as bubbles race from tube to tube. Then something big spews out, catching against the exit grate, and her reality falls apart in an instant.

She can barely fathom that another eighty is just a few feet away, so close there's no mistaking the truth of it. Hello instinctively reaches out to touch the glass, but the second eighty doesn't reciprocate. Then that tank's mechanical arm swings out to scan

Eighty-2, who turns a smooth, spiritless gray in response. After it tucks away, her eyes dart around the room nervously, searching for danger perhaps, or some sign of what comes next. This instigates the original Eighty to look around too, but she doesn't see anything especially concerning.

Though Eighty may not conceive of it in exactly this way, the embryo of an idea forms—that they could be allies and protect each other from this nameless threat. The problem is that she doesn't know how to communicate with her own kind, not even the simplest ideas, let alone future intentions; so she does what comes naturally and tries changing colors, aiming for the prettiest ones she can think of—rainbows, elaborate swirls, and dancing rings of light—but nothing seems to alleviate Eighty-2's anxiety.

Another eighty shoots into a different tank.

Then another one.

And still more come.

The duplicates keep multiplying until all the tanks are occupied and the situation becomes profoundly disorienting, like staring at a reflection, of a reflection, of a reflection, in a house of mirrors. Eighty can't tell what's real anymore and dissociates from the moment, worrying that her sense of self had been an illusion all along.

The door swings open on the far side of the room, and Eighty braces for another psychic bombshell. Instead, Swish walks through the door and holds it ajar for Shiny. Eighty hasn't seen them together, but ever since the electric parasite invaded her body, she'd suspected them of having some form of communication. She's essentially forgiven Swish by now, but the sight of Shiny triggers the memory of his pitiless touch, putting her on edge.

Their shoes clop softly against the buffed concrete floor as Shiny and Swish move from tank to tank, pausing in front of each one for a discussion. Shiny mostly keeps his arms folded across his chest, while Swish pokes at the consoles, causing holographic diagrams to explode out of the panel. They're laden with anatomical data, which she deftly manipulates, paring away or adding various biological systems.

They stop in front of Eighty-2, who's still cowering in a corner. "And this one?" Shiny asks, pointing a crooked finger.

"G-Seventy-five. A legacy variant. One of the first batches with boosted hemocyanin for faster oxygen uptake, but saturation levels have improved across the board since then. As far as cognition, this one tested in the bottom ten percent."

"Terminate the lineage. No need to waste time on a dead end."

"Understood."

They move onto Eighty. Just behind her reflection in his glasses, Shiny studies her with ice-gray eyes, which appear about as cold and calculating as his touch had been. "So, this one is *special*?" he says, smirking faintly.

"Yes. She's much faster than the others. Brilliant really."

"Which variant?"

"N group. Specimen eighty. Cleaves at chromatophore sequence 3p14. Papillae 12q5. Nervous system 17q22—"

"Excellent," Shiny cuts in. "Take a sample for further study."

"Shouldn't we set her aside? Since she's so unusual."

"No, the investors wouldn't be happy."

"But she's—"

Shiny waves his hand dismissively. "I said no, Dr. Yoon. We'll simply iterate. Remember, they're just stepping stones. Don't get so attached that you lose sight of the bigger picture."

"But surely we can divert a few resources toward a potential discovery. Look at these developed areas around the vertical lobe." She points to the anatomical diagram hovering in the air, then zooms in on a central mass with two bean-shaped attachments. "There's something unique about this one's cognition, like . . . like a hyperawareness. She's processing things differently, but I need time to prove it. Isn't that worth pursuing?"

"*Hyperawareness*?" Shiny repeats, raising his bushy eyebrows, each hair sprouting in its own errant direction. "Need I remind you that's not the focus of our research?"

"But—"

"My decision is final and we're moving on. Understood?"

"Yes, Director."

Sidetracked by an unlatching noise, Shiny and Swish glance at the door as Monster walks in, but they don't acknowledge him with anything more than a slight nod. He approaches them holding a cup, his bicep looking absurdly unnecessary for such a puny item, and Shiny appears even frailer by comparison. It's obvious that Monster could physically dominate the other twoskins, but shows them deference instead, and Eighty finds this social dynamic puzzling.

During a lull in their conversation, Monster says, "Just so you're both aware, we need to flush the system again."

"And when will you be done?" Shiny asks curtly.

"Three days. Maybe four."

"Keep it to three."

"Yessir."

Monster goes on to report water quality statistics, as well as upcoming maintenance, but none of the information seems to interest the other two. Shiny and Swish continue scrolling through Eighty's data with their backs turned to him until Monster does something unexpected: He drops his cup, splashing a brown liquid everywhere.

"Damn! Must've bumped one of the tanks," he says sheepishly.

Shiny sidesteps a steaming puddle and inspects the stains on his pants, picking up the fabric at the knees to get a better look. His hand gestures toward the cuffs, as if to say, *Look what you did!*

"We've talked about this," Shiny seethes. "No drinks in the lab!"

"My apologies. Won't happen again."

Shiny shoos him away. "Go find someone to clean up this mess."

"Yessir, right away."

Monster obediently hurries through the door and closes it behind him, taking care to make as little noise as possible.

Shiny turns to Swish. "Why did we hire him again?"

"You sat in on the interview. Manuel was the most experienced candidate we could find on such short notice. Plus, the aquarium staff gave him glowing reviews."

"Then, what's going on with the system?"

"I don't know . . . It's unusual."

"Well, he'd better figure it out. We have deadlines to meet."

Once Shiny and Swish finish their assessment, they dim the lights and close the door.

Eighty has been anticipating this moment and changes colors again, hoping to attract the others' attention before the trainers return, but they're too busy hunting for a way out to notice. She waves her arms around, then shimmies and shakes, as if performing an exotic mating ritual for the first time—and poorly, it might be added. She even clicks her beak against the glass, though this makes her look quite deranged, but nothing seems to work. If the other eighties happen to glance up at all, their eyes swiftly skip to the next thing, like she was a plain old rock or something equally dull. They seem totally devoid of emotion, which baffles Eighty, who's still stunned that she isn't alone. Something must be wrong with them, she concludes.

Dancer opens the door, her standard bucket and mop in tow. The wheels echo as they roll across the floor, and once she's done mopping up the liquid that Monster spilled, Dancer does something strange herself: She stands in front of each tank and touches her headphones, then moves onto the next a few seconds later. When it's her turn, Dancer winks at Eighty and says, "Hang in there." Then she rolls the bucket out of the room and turns off the lights, leaving Eighty to her fruitless attempts at socializing.

9
Practice Makes Perfect

The following evening Eighty gets sucked into the tubes again. She considers grabbing onto something, but doesn't resist, since that would only get her shocked. Instead, she attempts to count the turns and their direction, speculating that it might be useful information at some point, but it's hard to keep her bearings, twirling in the dark.

The tube discharges Eighty into a new tank—the biggest one yet—maybe twenty times the size of her home. It's entirely empty except for the other eighties, eight in total, and most remarkable of all, no dividers separate them. Eighty could tap Eighty-2 on the head if she so dared, but the red lights are on, warning them to stay put. Outside the tank, Shiny and the twins loiter around at ground level while several assistants take the platform elevator up to the catwalk. They're pushing carts that hold shiny silver spheres the size of pumpkins. The acronym *D.O.T.* is stamped across their surface, and the words *DYNAMIC ORB TRAINER* are printed below.

While awaiting instructions, Eighty recalls her disappointment from the previous night and wonders whether her kind is supposed to communicate by touch. The very second this notion crosses her mind, Hello goes rogue, wandering off to make a friend, since Eighty-2 is so close and the opportunity may never present itself again. When the inevitable zap comes, Eighty rubs the back of her head and gives Hello a look that says, *Never do that again!*

"I think we're ready," Bounce alerts her sister.

"Okay, everyone, eyes on me!" Swish orders the crew. "I want grid formations reset as soon as a play is completed. We key this behavior to three flashes of red light. And watch out for too much contact. This is the first time they've shared a tank and some may react strangely. Don't hesitate to shock them if things get out of hand. Ready? All right, release the DOTs."

The trainers throw the metallic spheres over the tank, where they levitate for a moment, then slip into the water, moving optimally and without hesitation, just like the ring. The DOTs line up in a three-by-three grid on the far end, guarding the goal. Then a trainer tosses a ball in the tank and as it drifts to the bottom, Eighty battles the urge to throw it through the ring, though the effort makes her skin crawl, as if little crabs were pinching every nerve ending.

The red lights turn off and everything in the tank dashes for the ball at once, including the DOTs, which advance so silently that Eighty misses this crucial bit of information. Moments later, one slams into her side and pushes her all the way to the glass, pinning her in place, where the polished sphere reflects her squirming limbs as they fumble to break free. Meanwhile, the ball pops out of a cluster of bodies, and a distinctly muscular eighty launches it through the ring. The red lights flash three times, cuing them to return to their side.

"Reward the team!" Bounce shouts up at the catwalk.

The trainers fling nine crabs into the tank, which the eighties snatch up and greedily devour.

"Which one was that?" Shiny asks Swish.

"K-Fifteen."

"Very promising."

Though they're generally emotionless, the other eighties still signal excitement at food by turning red, but not K15. Despite having scored a goal, she appears just as tempestuous as the moment Eighty first laid eyes on her. Dark blues and grays storm across her skin, interrupted by the occasional burst of electric purple. Thus, Eighty thinks of K15 as Gloom.

"Okay, good job, everyone," Swish barks at the room. "Let's try that again."

As practice continues, Eighty realizes that the DOTs will pursue whoever holds the ball, so it's advantageous to make lots of quick passes. Moreover, it doesn't appear to matter who scores the goal. All of them get fed regardless, so they might as well work together; and this aspect of the game pleases Eighty on a subconscious level, since cooperation feels like a language of some kind, however rudimentary. Not that this clicks right away, since the eighties have never interacted before, and some pick up on strategy much faster than others. They're still woefully awkward, but the nascent promise of teamwork is there.

Just one incident spoils the mood. It happens close to the end of the night, when Gloom throws a shot and Eighty-2 accidentally gets in the way. The ball deflects toward the bottom and bounces into a cluster of DOTs, which means the play has ended, and they have to reset their starting positions. Up to this point the other eighties have avoided Eighty-2, who's plainly dim-witted, but her incompetence seems to enrage Gloom. While the others continue the next play, Gloom grabs Eighty-2 and bites off one of her eyeballs, shearing through the soft flesh with her powerful beak, like scissors through gelatin. Blue blood spurts into the water, turning purplish as the red lights come on.

"Hey, what did I say? Pay attention!" Swish yells at the catwalk.

A second later Gloom goes completely rigid, like a dead spider with rigor mortis slowly sinking to the bottom. Eighty can tell the punishment is more ferocious than anything she's endured.

Swish turns to Bounce in anger, a vein ticking just behind her alabaster temple, and asks, "Who's responsible for K-Fifteen?"

"Gorman."

"It's Gorman's last day. Notify him after practice."

A trainer hooks Gloom with a pole and brings her to the surface, where another one awaits with a net. Working in tandem, they lift

Gloom out of the water—the strain written across their faces—and place her in a barrel, then slap the lid closed. Meanwhile, two other assistants struggle to fish out Eighty-2 as she flops around listlessly, apparently on the verge of death.

"Well, that was certainly fascinating," Shiny remarks to Swish. "Let's tinker with the K variant, shall we? Dial down some of the aggression, but not too much." There's a morbid glint in his eye.

Swish points at Gloom's barrel. "What should we do with her?"

"Recoup our expenses. I know someone."

"Who? Not Mr. Z—"

Shiny cuts her off. "*Who's* not important."

They never see Gloom or Eighty-2 again, and life becomes a blur of nightly practices, so many that Eighty loses count. The trainers introduce new equipment and techniques, dialing up the challenges, both in terms of strategy and their physical toll. The DOTs forgive nothing, and if Eighty takes her mind off the game for a second, they make her pay dearly. It's a grueling schedule, and by the time the tubes deposit her home, she crawls to bed and crashes asleep.

At first, Eighty hopes that practice will provide an opportunity to socialize, but a few nasty shocks make it clear the trainers don't want her fraternizing between plays. However, amid the chaos of a scrum, their suckers sometimes linger to taste each other's skin, or their eyes might lock for a fraction of a second. But even so, Eighty senses a barrier between them, not unlike the glass of a tank, keeping their inner worlds separate and isolated. Her only real companion is Monster and she marks the days between his visits, fixating on the door whenever his scheduled time approaches.

One evening as Monster arrives, she twirls around with excitement, then turns bright magenta. The same as always, he tells Eighty that she's been a good girl and makes up little songs for her while completing his chores. Then he lies flat on the catwalk and reaches his arm into the tank. It's all part of their normal routine, except that when Eighty holds his hand, she detects a faint difference in his standard residues—something akin to a hormone, as if fear had a flavor.

"I've been meaning to talk to you," Monster begins soberly. "You're just so damn curious, and I know you want to make friends, but tomorrow will be a very dangerous day. The others will rip you apart if they get the chance, believe me, and the sad fact is, this place doesn't give a shit whether you live or die."

Eighty senses his affection as Monster gazes down at her, exactly what she's been yearning for from the others. She wishes he'd stay forever, but Monster always leaves too soon, and this thought makes her skin turn a pouty blue.

"Ah, don't give me that face. Let's say I could get you out of here, which I can't, but let's pretend. Where would I take you? I can't just dump you in the ocean—you'd get eaten alive—and my shithole apartment doesn't have a bathtub. And even if it did, my water ration wouldn't cover it."

Monster pauses to let the gears crank in his mind, then gives her a weary look and continues, "I don't think you appreciate how hard you are to take care of—all the special equipment you'd need. Even if the aquarium wasn't closed, that's the first place they'd look. Honestly, it probably wouldn't matter where I went, the league would hunt me to the ends of the earth. Those stupid nelves don't stand a chance... Fuck! You don't understand any of this! Just know that I'm sorry—I'm very, very sorry. *Soy un cobarde*."

Moisture builds around the corner of his eyes and a clear liquid drops in the tank. Explorer stretches to taste it, identifying trace amounts of fatty oils and proteins. Eighty senses him preparing to leave, and Hello hangs on that much tighter.

"Please, be careful," he says softly.

10
Striking Gold

One, two, three...
Ten, eleven, twelve...
Forever counting dashes of light.

By this point Eighty has been sucked inside the tubes so many times that she can differentiate between training facilities, but it's taking longer than usual to arrive at a destination, and the series of turns feels unfamiliar.

Several minutes of rushing along.
Stop. Wait for a valve to open.
Water whooshing through another tube.
Moving again. Stop.
Whoosh of water. Move again.
Suddenly, an open room. Huge—no, gigantic.
A sapphire cube floating in the velvet darkness.
She's headed toward it. Closer. And closer still.
SPLASH!
The roaring of a thousand little bubbles.

Eighty takes a minute to orient herself, noting her teammates are already there, all eight of them. Hello raises up in a gesture of recognition, ever-hopeful to make a friend, but the others have never responded in kind and tonight is no exception. Instead, they're staring straight past her, apparently tense, so she spins around to see what's spooked them.

Nine other eighties are floating in the distance, total strangers, trapped inside a sapphire cube that resembles their own. The tank's glow mottles over a pool just below, but she can't find the edges, so it gives the impression of being limitless. Eighty can hardly fathom so much water exists and as her attention drifts closer to her own team, she realizes they're hovering over the exact same pool. White sand covers the bottom, and large polygonal ridges break up the space into a series of peaks and valleys. Each facet of these structures is decorated with a unique pattern, including zebra stripes, fingerprint grooves, pink polka dots, rainbow gradients, knobby grids, and much, much more. They resemble her camouflage toys, but mashed together and scaled up to the size of actual marine ridges.

As her vision acclimates, Eighty looks up and discerns an oddly concave sky. Its latticework appears to curve into a dome with a hole at the center, as if they were inside the nucleus of a gargantuan, mechanical eye. Two rings start to plummet out of the darkness: One is teal and silver. The other is black and gold—her team's goal—just the sight of which is enough to make Eighty salivate.

The rings pass in front of service platforms on the short ends of the pool, where a pair of unusual twoskins face each other. Both are wearing masks, fins, and vests with hoses running up to their mouths. They step out like mirror opposites and plunge into the tank, launching ripples over the placid surface to clash in the middle. Assistants push carts up to the pool's edge and hand them helmets, which the divers randomly distribute across the polygonal ridges.

Eighty is amazed that twoskins can swim, because they've never gotten in the tank with her, despite their many interactions. But then she sees them gracelessly frog-kicking, as well as the extravagant number of bubbles they make, and speculates this might be the reason why they don't play the game themselves. Perhaps eighties are simply more beautiful to watch.

On their last trip to the bottom, a diver places a ball in a sandy clearing at the center of the tank. This incites the teams to crowd against the glass, provoked by the prospect of dinner, like a beehive jabbed with a stick. Eighty can empathize. She hasn't eaten for a day, at least, and her stomach feels as if it's about to cave in on itself.

All of the sudden, Eighty detects movement in the periphery, and her pupils dilate into shiny moons, startled by the crescents of light reflecting off watch faces, cameras, screens, and goggles. A vast crowd is peering at her from the shadows, sitting in tiered rows that ascend toward the dome's upper reaches. Though darkness obscures their true numbers, it's a staggering amount of twoskins and once again, she can scarcely believe the world is big enough to hold so many of one thing.

Something flits by Eighty and makes a wide arc over the audience. It reminds her of Stupid: the flying creature that Sister ate. Then the strange object boomerangs back and stops a few feet away, glassing her through a solitary black eye. The lens refocuses and bands of light roam over her body, just like the scanners from the bright room. A monumental hologram of Eighty appears above the pool, her every wrinkle captured in preternatural detail.

Then the one-eyed drone zips away and her image disappears, replaced by an elaborate font, spelling *Gold Strikers*. A tail loops down from the *s*, sweeping backwards to underscore the words, and flames explode from behind the luminous graphic as it rotates to face different sections of the audience. They erupt into chants, stomps, cheers, and boos; and the dome positively throbs with vibrations as other symbols flash above the pool:

ゴールドラッシュ

淘金热

ЗОЛОТАЯ ЛИХОРАДКА

A spotlight projects onto the floor outside the tank, revealing a sunken marble platform with cracks webbing through the semigloss finish. Statues flank the penumbra—mermaids, krakens, sea gods, and other mythical beings—all frozen in poses of combat.

Except for a few throats being cleared, the audience falls silent as a pair of shoes clop through the darkness. They echo around the dome before emerging in the spotlight—sandals, in fact—attached to yet another kind of twoskin, dressed in white robes that shimmer as he moves. His disembodied head appears above the pool, giant and olive-skinned, wearing a gold wreath atop his platinum hair. After a dramatic pause, the announcer's voice soars over the dome, sounding self-assured and grand. Eighty has never heard anything so loud and immediately starts to think of him as Noisy.

"Greetings, ladies, gentlemen, and the gen-fluid. I'm Hadrian Populi the third, or just plain old Hadrian to my friends. And we're all friends here, aren't we?" Noisy suggests with a wink. "Welcome to our new aquarena! And how about that SupraScreen display? It sure is magnificent."

Color nebulas spiral above the aquarena, gradually forming the words, *Sponsored by HOLY MACKEREL SEAFOOD • A Taste of Heaven*. Then a gleeful winged fish jumps over the letters and splashes into nothingness. The spectators slap their hands together, clearly delighted, until Noisy's face replaces the graphic.

"Thank you, thank you. We think so too . . . Well, folks, I know you've traveled from all over the globe to be here tonight, so let me assure you, we're in for a real treat. Not only are the Tridents and Gold Strikers last year's finalists, but this season's competitors are faster, stronger, and smarter than ever before. In short, dear guests, you're witnessing the dawn of a new era in zoosports."

Noisy holds for the applause to die down, then continues, "Yes, indeed, our octoballers are the finest of their kind, honed by the most skillful trainers on earth. We also guarantee that they're one hundred percent ink-free, so you won't miss a moment of action. And, of course, we've engineered them to be fearless, so don't lose any sleep on their account. Our champions are no more capable of distress than one of our famous tako dogs, available at a vendor near you."

Noisy stops to chuckle at the Suprascreen, where a cartoon octopus is simultaneously juggling tubes of meat, dicing toppings, and squirting condiments into a bun.

"They're tasty, all right . . . Okay, folks, the match is about to begin. You only have one more minute to place your bets and just remember, even if today isn't your lucky day, at least the T-shirts are free, courtesy of Holy Mackerel Seafood. Let's give them a big round of applause! Our staff too—they work so hard—we mustn't forget about them!"

The spotlight shifts to the service platforms, where a contingent of trainers take a bow. Eighty recognizes most of the ones on her side from practice. She doesn't see Bounce, but Swish is standing there, though not in her most familiar form. Instead of a white coat and black slacks, she's donned an elegant gold dress that accentuates her hourglass figure. Her eyes are done up like a cat's, and rather than being tied in a ponytail, her glossy black hair cascades down past her shoulders.

Just after the clapping dies down, pumps kick on inside the service platforms to drain the holding tanks. The octoballers rapidly pancake into a few inches of water, then the bottom drops away and Eighty plunges into the aquarena amid a cloud of bubbles. A wave of panic washes over her, and she quickly turns to the spectators, whose silhouettes seem to rise endlessly toward the ceiling. She's never played the game against another team before—only the DOTs—nor has she performed in front of so many twoskins. It makes her feel like a microscopic larva again, dropped into the big blue world, entirely without explanation.

She spots Monster in the audience, and his presence brings her a modicum of comfort. He's urgently pointing at something behind her, and Eighty wheels around just in time to find an opponent on the verge of tackling her. She scoots away, scot-free, and dashes toward the center of the aquarena.

Scanning ahead, Eighty spots what looks like a hundred worms pinned to a single hook. In fact, it's one of her teammates buried beneath a pile of bodies, including Gloom, unseen since she killed a clumsy teammate months ago. The other tank was so far away that Eighty hadn't noticed her, but now that she does, a twinge of dread spikes her blood pressure even higher.

Suddenly, the ball flicks from the scrum to a Gold Striker, who snaps it to Eighty, who struggles to stay clear-headed. Reality seems lucid, but also faraway, as if it were happening to someone else, and the world starts to blur around the edges. Out of the optical fog, an opponent swings a helmet by the face guard, which Eighty only narrowly dodges. Then her spatial awareness surges back and she sees a clear path to the ring. All she has to do is throw the ball—right now! But before she has a chance to act, two Tridents loom up from behind a ridge, blocking her shot.

In a split-second, Eighty ducks behind a polygonal boulder, pulls the ball beneath her webbing, and matches the zebra stripes. As her outline dissolves into the pattern, the Tridents blow by her position and scour the wrong area. More opponents show up to join them, but Eighty remains invisible except for her two swiveling eyeballs. Then, when the next opportunity presents itself, she pops up and hurls the ball toward the open goal. The Tridents realize their misjudgment and chase after it, but the ball torpedoes straight through the ring, leaving an elegant trail of bubbles behind the assisted propulsion. Most astonishing of all, Fidget threw the scoring shot, who seems just as stunned as Eighty and forgets to dance around for once.

Red lights flash three times, and the teams return to their positions while one-eyed drones pan across the audience, displaying their reactions on the SupraScreen. Some applaud or lean over to joke with their giddy companions. Others work themselves up into a furor, their hands flying up to ask, *How could this happen?* One particularly upset patron chucks a tako dog at the glass, splattering ketchup everywhere, and is immediately escorted off the premises by burly ushers.

Meanwhile, the SupraScreen replays the goal in super-slow motion, showing how Eighty torqued the ball into a graceful spiral. The hologram sails across the darkness and into a row of delighted spectators, whose smiling teeth glow as the phantom of light passes through them.

"What a spectacular shot! Like threading a needle," Noisy raves, stirring up another round of applause. "Okay, folks, at this time we'd like to open up a lightning round. You have until the start of the next play to make an additional wager, which will automatically enter your name into our Bonus Bonanza."

Half the audience illuminates while tapping the screens next to their seats and as the jackpot climbs higher, a diver strides into the aquarena to reposition the ball at the center. On the way back, he discreetly stashes something in a mesh bag, then flutter-kicks to a ladder and flops his gear on the service platform. Drooping from the cinched end of the bag, Eighty spots a lifeless arm belonging to the teammate who passed the ball from the scrum. Eighty guesses that Gloom is to blame, but she doesn't feel much of anything beyond that—or if she does, it's only the dimmest recognition of the game's deadly consequences. She's simply too hungry for anything to be real.

"The Gold Strikers sub H-Seventeen for F-Ninety," Noisy says.

H17's hologram pops onto the SupraScreen, as well as stat lines listing her weight, max deadlift, straightaway speed, camouflage scores, and throwing accuracy. Then a valve opens and water begins spouting into the Gold Strikers' holding tank. A few moments later, H17 vomits out of the tube and splats into a shallow pool. She struggles to orient herself—to buffer the shock of what's happening—but without bones, she's just a frightened puddle of muscle. Finally, the bottom drops away and H17 splashes into the aquarena.

Trainers toss crabs to the Gold Strikers, and Swish—smiling for once—throws one directly at Eighty. It isn't nearly enough to satisfy her appetite, but she's still relieved to have something in her belly. Meanwhile, the Tridents leer with jealousy from across the aquarena, none with more hostility than Gloom, who paces back and forth until her temper boils over. She starts to jet toward the Gold Strikers, but the trainers quickly zap her into submission, and Gloom staggers back to her side while Noisy narrates.

"Wow, look at that passion! One thing is for certain, I wouldn't get between K-Fifteen and the ball. No siree, Bob. Not if I wanted to keep all my fingers."

The red lights flash three times to signal the next play, and the rest of the match blurs into a cyclical pattern of exertion, fear, and triumph. Eighty scores another goal near the end, and the Gold Strikers win four to three, but Gloom's death-stare is her most vivid memory from the night. If it weren't for the trainers keeping her in check, Eighty would've been torn limb from limb, and while being sucked through the tubes, she feels grateful to be going home in one piece.

11
Mr. Zoloto

Monster visits Eighty the next night. She's too tired to greet him with much enthusiasm—no prismatic hues or frolicking limbs—but she's glad to see him all the same. He usually performs his tasks right away, but this time he bounds up the catwalk stairs and dangles his arm over the tank; and when Hello suckers onto his hand, she tastes the unmistakable relief on his skin.

"I could barely watch, Ochita, but you did amazing last night. I was so proud. And that deserves a treat, don't you think?" Monster says while fishing something out of an ice cooler. "*Mira!* I brought your favorite, shrimpsicles!"

Without letting go, Eighty takes the delicacy from his other hand, and as soon as the ice touches her radula, her skin starts to pulse rose-colored waves of approval.

He grins from ear to ear. "*De nada.* Just keep up the good work."

Something clicks in Eighty after her first match against the Tridents. Virtually overnight, all that strenuous training comes into crisp focus, if not quite logically, then on some emotional level. She feels infused with purpose, almost divinely so, as if the universe had just opened its treasure trove of secrets and revealed her sparkling, true essence: This is what she was born to do. She's an octoballer.

Over the coming months, the Gold Strikers steamroll through opponents, beating the Abyss, Frostbites, Hammerheads, Harpoons, Moby-Dicks, Nemos, Sea Serpents, Typhoons, and Tsunamis. They absolutely crush the Scallywags, seven to zero, and Eighty sends the crowd into an uproar when she deflects the ball off an opponent's helmet, straight into the goal. In fact, she becomes the Gold Strikers' scoring machine, executing tough plays with surefire precision, though never in a conceited way. At her core, she regards herself as a collective of arms, so Eighty draws little distinction between her identity and the team's. This makes her just as likely to pass the ball as to take the shot; but putting ego aside, the plain truth is that Eighty shoots better than anyone.

Yet, something else beyond skill sets Eighty apart from her teammates. Whereas the others play out of habit, she plays for joy, and in spite of the stiff punishments and not-so-occasional deaths, Eighty learns to love the game. She even admires its beauty: an especially graceful spin, or a dizzying series of passes that zigzag past their defenders. Those moments make her happy, and the game becomes so pervasive in her consciousness that she dreams about it nearly every night.

During practice one day, an unusual twoskin enters the training facility. His jowls bulge from a cream-colored sweater and a thick gold chain hangs from his nonexistent neck, but Eighty first notices the prominent belly hanging over his belt. Thus, he becomes Gut in her mind.

Gut is followed by a pair of brawny twoskins in immaculate gray suits, black shoes, black sunglasses, and black shirts with the top buttons undone. They stand next to the door in exactly the same way, one hand cupping the other over their groin. Shiny is by himself at ground-level, and a couple trainers are up on the catwalk, but they're too far away to hear the ensuing conversation.

"Mr. Zoloto, nice to see you," Shiny says, though he doesn't look so happy.

"How's slimeballs doing today?" Gut asks in a thick accent.

"Very well. They're a formidable team."

"Good. This is good." Gut turns to the tank, appearing lost in thought, and the longer the pause draws out, the more Shiny seems to squirm in his skin. Then Gut continues, "How you work with such ugly things? Give me heebie-creepies."

"I'm used to them, I suppose, and they have so much to teach us. They're the key to a revolution in genetic advances, not to mention medical and material engineering applications."

Gut grunts in response. "Don't even have mothers, but have face only mother can love. Unless, maybe, you are mother?" He laughs and slaps Shiny on the back, causing him to readjust his glasses. "Oh, and that one you sell me. I like her. She may not have backbone, but she have balls, eh?"

Shiny gives him a skittish grin. "Ah, yes. Very funny."

"But enough of jokes. We talk business now. Good team is good, of course, but *too* good is bad. Would be nice if they lose, your team. Very nice. By two points would be best for you." He looks at Shiny with a knowing expression, and his smile has vanished. "Splicing in human . . . *tsk, tsk, tsk* . . . very illegal, doctor. Would be shame for you if authorities find out. Understand?"

"Yes, I understand."

"This is good."

12
The Sand that Trembles

The tubes again.
Valves open and close.
Always rushing forward.
No surprises there.
But then a new sound.
Growing louder each second.
EIGHTY! EIGHTY! EIGHTY!

A tube ejects her into the sapphire holding tank and after the bubbles scatter, Eighty hears the crowd chanting her name—only she doesn't know that it's her name. Even so, their excitement rings out clearly, and the dome feels supercharged with anticipation.

She searches the audience for Monster, who's usually close by, reassuring her with his familiar face, but not tonight. However, she does recognize Gut from the previous evening, watching from the row closest to the aquarena. He buys something off a vendor and shoves it into his mouth: a red tube on a white pillow with ribbons of sauce. His subordinates sit to either side, stony-faced in dark glasses.

The SupraScreen shoots off an extravaganza of holographic fireworks, booming so loud the water shakes. It startles Eighty at first, but then she marvels at the spectacle of light. It appears the twoskins can do anything, and though her intuition tells her otherwise, Eighty sometimes wonders if the trainers imagined her into existence—and voilà! So she became.

As the last explosion fizzles overhead, Noisy makes his grand entrance, always Eighty's favorite part of the show. The words are a total mystery, of course, but she can still sense the magnetism of his voice, attracting the attention of so many others. It comes across like some form of mind control, and she finds his power fascinating.

"Greetings, zoosports fans of all colors and creeds," Noisy's disembodied head begins. "Thank you for being here, and welcome to Octobowl Fourteen! What an exciting season it's been: razor-thin wins, high-scoring games, and the biggest cash prizes in the league's history!"

The audience claps as the SupraScreen displays the jackpot, rolling into place as if someone pulled the lever on a slot machine, accompanied by cheerful casino-style sound effects.

"Tonight, we bring you a rematch between bitter rivals. Scoring on teal and silver, we have the powerhouse Tridents, led by the mighty K-Fifteen. No joke, folks—that bulldog is capable of tearing an opponent to shreds in the time it took me to finish this sentence. Good thing we've got pros standing by to put a muzzle on her."

Noisy chuckles as the jackpot fades away, and a three-pronged spear materializes on the SupraScreen, waves swelling and crashing behind it. Then the Trident logo is replaced by a golden pickaxe with shiny coins raining down from the sky.

"The Gold Strikers will take aim at black and gold, led by the masterful N-Eighty, who's such a dead shot that she could hit a minnow between the eyes at fifty yards. She broke all kinds of records this season—rushing, passing, goals, you name it—and as you well know, the Gold Strikers remain undefeated, having dished out the Tridents' solitary loss. Honestly, it's a storybook ending to an amazing year, so I'm pretty excited. How about you?"

Noisy holds for applause, but they don't seem to satisfy him, so he ramps up the volume. "Come on, we can do better than that. I can't hear you! Don't sit on the sidelines! Make the dome thunder! Dream big and place those wagers!" His voice resounds from up high like a deity perched on the clouds, whipping the crowd into a frenzy. "Now that's more like it. Betting will close in one minute.

And never forget, you have to play to win!"

As the teams take their positions, Eighty scans the crowd: Some twoskins are wearing black and gold—a familiar color scheme by now—others wear teal. Some are holding up handmade signs. One reads, *Strikers Struck Again!* Another says, *Stick a Trident in Them, They're Done.* But there's no Monster. He's never missed a match before, and Eighty suspects that something might be wrong, but her spiraling worries are abruptly curtailed by the red lights.

The match begins and true to form, the Gold Strikers pass the ball around like a pinball machine—zip, dazzle, bang! Eighty makes a phenomenal shot, flying through the arms of several defenders to ricochet off the glass into the ring. The Tridents and crowd are dumbfounded alike, and Noisy's gigantic mouth goes slack-jawed after watching the replay. "How on earth did she do that?"

The red lights flicker three times, signaling the octoballers to return to their sides, where only the Gold Strikers get crabs. Gloom glares from across the aquarena, brewing up a tempest of malevolent colors, warning of the pain she'll inflict should they attempt to score again. Eighty is intimidated, but not unduly so. The trainers have always kept a protective eye on her, and she's never been seriously injured, just the minor bites and bruises of a typical game.

The next play begins and both teams race toward the center, where Eighty reaches the ball first. But before she can dart away, several opponents corner her against a polygonal rock formation. There's nowhere else to go, so she tucks inside a nearby helmet, hoping a teammate can get close enough for a handoff. Instead, with mounting panic, she watches through the face guard as her nemesis plows through the surrounding scrum. Gloom soon grabs the helmet and whacks it against the ridge, causing its energy shield to crackle over and over again. Eighty gets increasingly woozy from the burst of concussive blows. Then something truly unexpected happens.

ZAP! FIRE-FIRE-FIRE!

Eighty hasn't disobeyed a rule.

ZAP! FIRE-FIRE-FIRE!

But she's being punished as if she had.

ZAP! FIRE-FIRE-FIRE!

The shocks keep escalating until they're unbearable and Brave slackens just a bit, giving Gloom an opportunity to grab him. Brave fights to keep his grip on the ball, but Gloom yanks him taut with staggering force. There's a searing sensation as the flesh tears. Then the pain rockets into agony until, at last, Eighty feels the pressure release.

The helmet careens down the ridge, knocking against cheetah print, then herringbone, then embossed squiggles, all the way to the sandy bottom, where it pitches to the side. Through the bars of the face guard, Eighty watches Gloom sprint away with Brave still coiled around the ball, blue blood streaming in his wake. Eighty tries going after him, but quickly slumps over, too weak to move.

On the Suprascreen above, giant holograms tackle each other as Gloom barrels through the melee to score. "What a beast!" Noisy shouts, and the crowd explodes into riotous thunder. Eighty can feel their enthusiasm vibrating the sand, all those tiny grains trembling at their feet, while blood continues to gush from her grievous wound. But it doesn't hurt too terribly. Not really.

With the last bit of her strength, she turns to face the audience, hoping to find Monster—to glimpse his stubbled chin and know that he cares. Instead, she finds Gut again, leering from the front row. He flashes Eighty a malicious grin as her eyes start to glaze over. Then she slides into unconsciousness, and the roar fades to silence.

13
A Room without Walls

Her eyes open gradually. Something is wrong, the water doesn't taste right—has a sterile quality—as if all the organic molecules had been scrubbed out. Then she remembers the aquarena and the awful game, but worst of all, that Brave is gone. The memory punches Eighty awake, and her skin drains of pigment until it's as pale as moonlight. One by one, her remaining arms touch the cauterized stump where Brave used to be, slowly coming to terms with their injured reality: That now, they only number seven.

She closes her eyes again.

She's not ready for the next thing to happen.

Not yet . . .

Once her grief ebbs a little, Eighty surveys the dimly lit room. She sees power lights flickering here and there—the stars of her youth—as well as several rows of cylindrical tanks. Bubbles climb up the glowing columns and scatter around peculiar shapes, which bear a resemblance to eighties, but not exactly. Some have ten arms or more, looking gnarled as the branches of a desert shrub. Others have far less and their appendages terminate into corpulent nubs. A few have growths erupting from their skin, clusters of beaks or suckers where they don't belong. One aberration Eighty can't even begin to decipher, but they all have one feature in common: Their eyes are shut, as if they'd embarked into a shared nightmare, never to return.

Stainless steel shelves line the walls, holding hundreds of jars.

They contain juvenile specimens suspended in a yellowish liquid, all of them malformed in some way. The jars are labeled with a series of numerals: A3-60-4320, B8-47-8493, and so on. Eighty doesn't know what these symbols mean, but with an acute sense of foreboding, she acknowledges that some stones weren't meant to be overturned. Whatever this place is, she shouldn't be here.

Eighty hears a faint clicking as a door swings askew on the far side of the room. She shrinks into the corner of her tank, attempting to camouflage herself, but there's nothing to match and she can't turn transparent. Instinctively, she summons Brave to protect her, then winces, realizing he'll never answer again.

Dark figures slink through the doorway, wearing masks that cover everything but their eyes. A slender silhouette directs the others to fan out and unlock the tanks' access panels. They spritz the sensors with spray bottles, and the lights go from red to green, then the tops slide open. A big, broad-shouldered shadow moves between them, pouring white pellets into the tanks, which causes the water to violently hiss, spit, and fog over. The specimens soon blanch a milky white as their molecules fall apart, dissolving into gelatinous spittle and even more grotesque forms.

The figure with the pellets approaches her tank and Eighty holds perfectly still, like a fawn cowering in the grass as a lion approaches. Fidget starts to tremble, and Eighty does her best to steady him as the access panel swings open with a delicate, mechanical buzz. It's the last obstacle between her and the white pellets. She just hopes death will come swiftly, but instead of melting her into goo, the masked face says, "Don't worry, Ochita. We'll get you out of here."

Eighty knows that gravelly voice! With indescribable relief, she reinflates from the corner as Monster reaches his hands into the tank. "You've gotten so heavy," he groans while lifting her from the tank. Then Monster holds her to his chest, letting the water soak his clothes and drizzle onto the floor, but he doesn't appear to mind.

"EIGHTY"

Another figure rolls over a handcart with a barrel, and Monster eases Eighty inside, but Hello entwines around his wrist, refusing to let go.

"We can play later," he gently scolds her while peeling off her suckers. "It's not safe here."

"Time's a-ticking. Let's roll!" the slender figure barks.

Seconds later the room illuminates, and an ear-splitting alarm suddenly goes off. *AHHH! AHHH!* A spinning beacon starts to flash red light across the walls and shelves of hideous specimens. Because they're red, Eighty wants to hold still reflexively, but then someone shouts, "Run!" prompting Monster to slap the lid closed. The handcart jerks to an angle, and Eighty soon feels the wheels vibrating over various floor textures.

K-thunk, K-thunk, K-thunk.
A hollow drum sound as the barrel bangs into a wall.
Twoskins yelling.
Doors slamming.
Glass breaking.
Blasts ring out.
POP-POP-POP!
Thip . . . thip . . . BANG!

Something shoots through the barrel and two holes materialize on either side, stabbing a spear of light into the darkness. A voice yelps close by, followed by a thud and a metal object skidding across concrete. Someone wails in pain, but it isn't Monster, who's still gasping for breath and cursing to himself.

More doors. More running. Echoing in a hallway.
"Hey! Stop!" *orders a stranger.*
"Fuck you!" *Monster roars.*
The smack of bone connecting with meat.
Then a body crumpling to the floor.
"Shit, sorry man. Fuck!"
Heavy breathing.

"Hope he's not dead."
Heavier breathing.
"He's probably dead."

A door slams shut, muffling the alarm, and the spear of light retreats from the barrel. An electric motor powers up and whirs closer. A voice yells, "Load 'er up!" Eighty feels the barrel tip and rise into the air, then jostle against metal. Her head is swimming, and she turns pea green from the nausea.

Ratchet sounds.
Two thumps from a palm.
"Let's go!"

The tires screech around a series of tight turns until they hit a straightaway and scream to full speed. Meanwhile, Eighty sloshes around in the barrel, trying to absorb the whiplash of movement and new information. She's more scared than she's ever been: more than after the twoskins installed the painmaker and shocked her for the first time; more than being dismembered by Gloom in the aquarena; more than waking up in the nightmare room, surrounded by her mutant kin. Everything is changing too quickly, and she yearns for the sanctuary of her den, but a part of her recognizes that it isn't safe to return—that she no longer has a home.

Straps flapping in the wind.
Air whistling through the bullet hole.
An endless procession of fears.
Then the motor slows down and cuts out.
A bell chimes from far away. Lapping water much closer.

Feet hop up on the truck bed and slide the barrel to the edge, then lower it to the ground. The handcart is rolling again, but the floor sounds different from before, creaking and hollow underneath. "Over here!" a voice shouts. The barrel angles steeply backwards and the wheels rattle over heavily-textured metal. Then it lurches down a couple steps, rolls a few seconds more, and comes to a complete stop. The lid pops open and Monster leans over the rim.

"Here we are. Safe and sound."

Then he disappears and Eighty finds herself gazing up at an impossibly high ceiling, scintillating with pricks of light. Explorer reaches out to touch them—a tendril of curiosity grasping at distant suns—but they're too far away. Instead, he tastes decay in the air and its pungent mix of bewildering molecules.

Monster returns, wiggling something in his hand. "Look what I got," he says.

Explorer eagerly grabs the ball, and Monster snaps the lid shut, leaving her in the dark once again. But Eighty wants to know what's happening, so she suckers onto the barrel, lining up her eye with one of the bullet holes, and gets her first glimpse of an incomprehensible new world. The room has no walls, and strange vehicles surround them, floating in a dark pool so massive that it seems to stretch into infinity.

An engine starts to chug below her, vibrating the barrel, and the boat sputters into an open channel. Eighty watches the wake fan out behind them, where it laps against a mind-boggling assortment of oddities. Further ashore, there's a tall plant with green fronds that rustle in the breeze. Next to it, a lamppost casts a bright circle onto the pavement below, where several four-wheeled vehicles are squealing to a stop. Twoskins spill out of the doors, run onto the docks, and point their arms at the boat. Yellow flashes burst from their hands, and sounds sting the air.

"Get down!" someone yells.

POP-POP-POP!

Thip . . . dink . . . PANG!

But nothing hits the barrel.

A few seconds later, Gut steps down from a large truck and waves off his subordinates. Then they unload something from the bed: a sleek gray shape with wings and lots of blinking lights. A propellor starts to spin, but before Eighty can see what it does, the boat speeds away, and Gut's toy recedes in the distance.

They're skipping over the waves now, and Eighty relocates to the opposite hole, where she sees about a dozen masked figures chatting, coiling rope, and stowing gear. She can't tell whether they're janitors, aquarists, trainers, spectators, divers, or an entirely new kind of twoskin, but all of them are black from head to toe with N.E.L.F. stenciled across their backs. Whatever their intentions, Eighty feels confident they don't mean her harm, because Monster is there and she trusts him implicitly.

Several figures remove their masks and Eighty immediately recognizes Dancer, who's shouting, "Gorman! Hey, Gorman! Get your head out of your ass and collect batteries. We can't have them tracking us." This induces the NELFs to pull screens out of their pockets and remove a small component, while Dancer continues barking orders, "Everyone else, screw your eyes into the sky. That Raptor will cloud-hop until it's close enough to fire. We need to microwave it before we're fish food." Then Dancer turns to Monster and in a quieter voice, she says, "Hey Manny, let's get that painmaker out. I need you to hold her still, okay?"

"Can't it wait until port?" he asks with upturned eyebrows.

"Too risky. If that drone gets within range, it'll scramble her brains. They don't want their dirty little secret getting out."

"All right . . . She's going to be scared out of her mind, though."

"I know, but we don't have a choice."

Dancer rifles through her cargo pocket, pulls out a surgical kit, and jabs a needle into a vial, extracting the liquid within. "I'm sorry, sweetheart," she says to Eighty. "You're going to feel a little pinch." Then Dancer pricks the base of her head and drains the syringe.

Eighty squirms in agitation while they wait for the anesthetic to kick in, and Monster strokes the back of her mantle until it goes numb. "*Shhh.* Everything's going to be fine," he whispers.

Dancer grabs a scalpel from the kit and takes a deep breath. "All right. I'm a bit rusty, and it won't be easy with the waves knocking my hands around, but here goes nothing. Hold her up, please . . .

yeah, just like that . . . and keep her as steady as you possibly can."

Monster nods. "Singing calms her down, so I'm going to do that, but no comments about the lyrics. She doesn't care if they're bad."

"You can recite the bloody national anthem for all I care, just as long as it works."

As Dancer begins the incision, holding up a wad of gauze to catch the blood, Monster sings:

"Keep flying higher bubble,
Don't worry 'bout no trouble,
Cause you're my little bubble,
I'll be there on the double!"

"Rhyming bubble with bubble. Absolutely brilliant," Dancer says distractedly.

"Everybody's a criti—"

"Gotcha, bugger!" she interrupts, triumphantly holding up a blood-smeared silver disc with two wires poking out. "Such a wicked little thing. How would you fancy having one of these stuck in your head? Anyway, just have to sew her up now."

"Hear that, Ochita? Almost done!" Monster says cheerfully. Then he makes a contemplative face and asks, "You think she gets that we're helping?"

"Maybe," Dancer mumbles as she rips open a package with her teeth, exposing a curved needle. "She's got some of us in her, but there's no telling how she connects the dots. Anyway, you know her best. What do you think?"

Monster searches for the right words, then hesitates to say them. "Um, this might sound crazy, but when she looks at me, sometimes I see a little girl trapped in there. It's kinda freaky."

"Yeah, well, that's why we're all here. The world needs to know what Schröder's been up to. Now we can prove it."

While Dancer stitches her up, Eighty tries to take her mind off the unpleasant tugging sensation, so she looks over Monster's shoulder at the unfolding city skyline: the cloudscrapers, bridges, superfreighters, and pleasure yachts; the centipedes of transport pods winding through buildings; the holographic advertisements projected onto every inch of sky. Coming from such a compact world, Eighty can't begin to comprehend the vast distances between things, that so many miles could separate two objects. She only knows that it's beautiful—all those glittering jewels of light—just like the web Sister made a long, long time ago.

Eighty sees something spark out of a nearby cloud, lighting up its pearl-gray belly. Explorer extends to touch the dot of light, only to realize that he's made the same mistake twice.

"Last one," Dancer says, snipping the suture just as electricity starts to arc across the painmaker's wires. She looks up at the sky in dismay. "Shit! What's that? Hawkins, what is that?"

The dot gains on them quickly, getting bigger and brighter by the second, swelling into a fireball against the night.

"Shoot it! Shoot it!" Dancer screams repeatedly.

"I can't!" howls the NELF named Hawkins.

"What do you mean, 'you can't'?"

"A bullet fried the antenna."

"Everybody, jump! Right n—"

BOOOOOOM!!!

Terrified faces launch into the dark with breathtaking force, mixing with seawater, shattered plastic, and shards of glass. The boat explodes below them, like an angry phoenix spreading its wings, and the flow of time slows to a drip. It seems Eighty has an eternity to panic.

Falling...

Forever...

And ever...

Then the world comes rushing back.

Wreathed in smoke and flames.

14
Déjà Vu

Orange blurs crackle in the darkness.
Green ribbons sway left, then right.
Silver streaks vanish and reappear a few feet away.

Eighty is reborn atop the waves, delivered into a broken world, already damaged herself. She's missing an arm, cut and bruised from the fall, and her eyes won't focus. Explorer gropes for the glass out of habit, but only finds debris snowing down: ash and embers, bits of rope and paper, monstrous hunks of melted plastic, and a clump of someone's singed hair. A fire rages across the water's surface, rolling over huge swells, and smoke infuses the sky with its acidic tang.

Eighty dives to escape the inferno, careful to avoid the plumes of foul-tasting chemicals, until everything becomes quiet and peaceful again. Her eyes take a moment to adjust, but once they do, she sees an underwater forest bathed in flame light. Kelp stands sway in the current, and schools of fish are meandering through their golden green blades. On the seabed below, her larval mountain appears to have multiplied, covering the bottom of the world in its entirety. She recognizes some of the creatures—sea stars, zoanthids, anemones, and algae—but the majority are completely new to her.

Eighty pursues the fish, having never encountered one before, but they shy away from her advance, as if repulsed by a negative charge. She gives up and inspects the slower animals instead, gingerly poking a sea cucumber, then a flamboyantly decorated nudibranch, then a spiny purple urchin. The more she explores, the more Eighty feels intoxicated by a profound sense of homecoming. Yet, at the very same time, the universe seems to expand in all directions, like a star exploding in her consciousness. She nearly falls apart at the vastness of it.

The anesthetic is wearing off and while examining the sore spot at the base of her head, Eighty detects the parasite's absence. Being freed of its wrath comes as a glorious relief, but then Fidget starts to shake, and she suddenly recalls that Dancer and Monster were on the boat—that they could've been killed in the explosion. She swims around in a frenzy, flipping over whatever wreckage she has the strength to lift, until a thicket of kelp parts down the center, and an oblong shape appears in the gap. It's the ball!

Eighty picks it up, closing her eyes to savor its familiar form. If only this were a terrible dream, she might awaken in her tank at any minute, everything back in its rightful place, but no such luck. Rather, when she opens them again, there's something else in the distance: a body lying in a shaft of light, one with curly dark hair and a tiny glint on their nose. Her stomach wrenches into a knot, but Eighty can't turn away.

She dashes over and suckers onto Dancer's cheek, which smacks of diesel smoke and much more faintly of floral lotion. Explorer investigates her tight corkscrews of black hair while Hello tugs at the gold nose ring, causing her nostril to flare and snap back as soon as he lets go. If Dancer were alive, this would be the most intimate moment they've shared together. But she's gone.

Not knowing what else to do, Eighty curls up on Dancer's chest and loses track of time, drifting into a kind of emotional hibernation. She's motionless except for her siphon, softly pulsing water past her gills, and everything becomes simple. There's no use in fighting it: The future will be whatever it's meant to be. Several minutes pass, or maybe it's hours.

A throbbing stump where Brave used to be.

"EIGHTY"

The suddenness of loss is the hardest part.
Always one change after another.
What's next? A pang of hunger answers.

Between the onslaught of stimuli and her long slumber in the nightmare room, Eighty completely forgot about food. Her last meal was a single crab tossed into the aquarena, seemingly a lifetime ago, and where her stomach should be, she finds an aching hollow begging to be filled. But there are no rings in sight, no trainers to teach her the rules of this place. And even if there were, without the game, what purpose does she serve?

Still on Dancer's chest, gazing up at the fiery wreckage of her former world, Eighty gets her first taste of absolute freedom, and the uncertainty this brings is awful beyond measure. It makes her yearn for home once more—for the straightforward clarity of glass walls and a tight lid on top, shielding her from chaos—although that door seems to be slamming shut. But while she understands some changes are permanent, just like a mutilated crab cannot be made whole again, there's one last thing she's not ready to give up on. Not if she can help it.

Eighty keeps searching for Monster and stumbles upon many more dead NELFs, crepuscular and serene in the fading light, though none belong to her faithful caretaker. She even braves the surface, winding her way through the maze of hellish flotsam—all those myriad compartments gargling dark water, blood, and oil—but nothing comes of this either.

Finally, with all other possibilities exhausted, Eighty turns away from the flames and contemplates the boundless shadow past the kelp forest. She guesses that both food and Monster must be hidden in its secret expanse—danger too, though she's less afraid of that, than solitude. So, with hunger and loneliness driving her onwards, Eighty tucks the ball in her arms and ventures deeper into the room without walls, hoping against all odds that her friend has survived, wherever fate deigned to toss him.

The Holy Mackerel

STORY 2

1
Behold!

The moon casts its tattered reflection across a calm bay. Occasionally, the quiet is disturbed by a dog bark carried out to sea—*woof, woof, woof*—the sound reverberates through space and stillness, then dies over the water. It's coming from a town at the mouth of a river, where boats idle in their slips and FOR LEASE signs hang in the storefront windows. An old Ferris wheel has stopped spinning for the night, tracing a black circle across the indigo sky. Near the ride's main entrance, a Macky's Shack seafood restaurant is lit up in neon, buzzing like an electric insect.

At the end of the pier, a few vagrants snore on benches, draped in grungy blankets or worn coats, their hole-infested socks poking out from underneath. Having made their living off the thankless ocean, they've retired from fishing to crawl inside a bottle, trading one form of hardship for another. One of them turns, scratches his beer gut, and farts. A sign next to him says, SUPER MODEL—*Out of Work*. Another scruffy man relieves himself directly into the ocean, his golden stream catching the light of a streetlamp. Once these men were young and full of promise, but just like the town, their big dreams have long since shriveled on the vine. Nowadays, success is measured by making it from one morning to the next.

In the shallows close to the pier, moonlight flits over the eelgrass and inside a tangle of silvery-green blades, three crabs are eating a dead salmon. They're named Oliver, Shelly, and Gus. Oliver is olive colored, of course, with tan legs; Shelly is primarily a brownish red, except for the hot pink stripes that streak across her carapace; and Gus is a handsome, muted blue with speckles of gray. The latter discovered the carcass and invited his friends to share in the feast. Ever since they hatched from their eggs, the trio has been inseparable and live together inside a busted toilet that fell off a trash barge.

"I'm not partial to eyeballs. Either of you want it?" Gus holds it out to them, a bit of connective tissue dangling from the back.

Oliver scrunches his mouth-parts. "Nah, turns my gills green."

"I'll take it," Shelly says, plucking the eyeball from Gus's outstretched claw. "You two are so fussy. I'm surprised there's any meat inside those shells of yours."

"Well, I'd eat an eyeball if I was starving." Gus makes a face that conveys, *I'm not a complete idiot.*

Shelly nibbles pensively for a bit, then says, "Just once in my life, I want to ride the big circle."

"The blinking wheel thingy? The one where the gods spin around and eat pink fuzzy stuff?"

"The very same."

Gus looks genuinely baffled, a response Shelly often incites in him. "If crabs were meant to be in the air, we'd have wings on our backs. It defies the laws of nature! Besides, one of the gods would find out and toss you in a pot."

"Oh, yeah. I forgot you're scared of heights . . . *and* pots . . . *and* the gods . . . You're scared of everything, come to think of it."

Oliver wonders out loud, more to himself than to the others, "Why do they build things to scare themselves? Screaming isn't even that much fun." He lets out a couple muted yelps—*ahhh, ahhh*—to test his theory about screaming and fun.

"*Shhh!* Look over there!" Shelly pinches their mouths shut, then points to the sky.

They crane their eyestalks as a glowing fish levitates over the deep of the bay. There are no boats, aircraft, wires, or anything else to explain the strange phenomenon. Instead, the fish appears to be flying under its own power, though not by flapping its fins or anything ridiculous like that. More like a UFO were beaming it into outer space.

Gus can't believe his eyes. "What in the briny depths?"

"I haven't the foggiest," Oliver offers, his voice trailing off in astonishment.

The fish stops about thirty feet or so in the air, where it hovers motionlessly. The sight is so surreal that it looks like an elaborate hoax—perhaps the result of a mad taxidermist's tinkering—but then its jaw opens and words come out.

"Behold! I am the Holy Mackerel. Come listen, my children."

The raspy-sounding fish didn't raise its voice, but the proclamation came from all directions at once, as if the whole world were lodged inside its throat. It seemed to issue from the heavens and over the horizon, from deep in the pines and the earth that binds them, from every pebble, droplet, and molecule of gas.

"The Holy *Who*?" Shelly shouts, making no effort to lower her voice, as usual.

"Mackerel, I think he said," Gus whispers back, hoping to influence her volume. Also, as usual.

"It's a *he*?"

"Sounds like it."

"Should we get closer?"

"Why? He seems fishy."

"Quit being such a mud puddle!" Shelly moans. "This is the first interesting thing to happen since Crustini molted into an albino and grew a third eye."

Gus nudges Oliver. "What do you think?"

"Huh? What do I think?" Oliver parrots back, startled from one of his sporadic dazes. He's suffered from them ever since he got too close to a beach picnic and a god threw a rock at his noggin.

"Yeah, what do you think about the fish in the stinkin' sky?"

"Hmm," Oliver murmurs, hopeful the next thought will come. "Oh! Maybe he'll put on a show for us. We haven't seen a good one since the sand flea circus passed through the meadows."

Shelly lights up. "You're totally right. He's gotta know magic! I mean, look at him, floating up there, light as a bubble."

Gus can't convince them to stay put, so the trio swim as close as they dare, where the unprecedented spectacle turns even more bizarre. The skiff-sized fish has pointy teeth and eyes as big as dinner plates. Adorning his body are a motley assortment of algae-covered trinkets, all tied up with fishing tackle. Most of the items the crabs don't have words for, including angel figurines, lawn flamingos, a glittery plastic unicorn, campaign buttons, and strings of blinking Christmas lights.

"Hey, you!" Shelly yells, causing Gus to cringe into a ball. *Would it kill her to be more careful*, he thinks. Then she yells even louder, "Hey, Mr. Magic Fish! What's your message? We're here to listen. Teach us your secrets!"

The Holy Mackerel doesn't answer, just hovers and blinks, and Shelly gets annoyed. "Suit yourself," she says, acting unimpressed, as if flying fish were old news. "But it's kinda rude to interrupt our supper, then go mute as a mussel. The least you could do is a song and dance. How about a magic trick? *Helloooooo?* Anyone there?"

But the Holy Mackerel still doesn't respond, so the trio chat and wait for something more exciting to happen.

And wait . . .

And wait . . .

And wait some more . . .

Shadows start to darken the already dark water. There's sound without sound, the hushed presence of many things. Suddenly, a shark breaches right next to the crabs, and a milk-white membrane slides back from its eye, revealing a ruthless gaze.

"Hello, s-s-sir," Gus stammers, not wanting to draw attention, but the shark is already glaring at him as if he were as worthless as mud. Thankfully, it doesn't appear to be hungry.

More shark fins crest in orderly rows, fish gather in their respective shoals, and multitudes of squid twinkle like submerged galaxies. Farther out, dolphins and whales spurt mist from their blowholes, and upon seeing the massive congregation, seabirds alight on the water. The crabs are eventually joined by their own kind, thousands of them, as well as every other type of crustacean. More creatures come—too many to name—all waiting to hear what the Holy Mackerel has to say.

"Thank you for joining me on this momentous occasion."

"He speaks!" Shelly blurts out and the crowd immediately shushes her. "But we were here first," she grumbles resentfully.

The Mackerel continues, sounding both hoarse and soothing, as if he were gargling gravel in a fragrant oil. "As you already know, a shadow has befallen the drylands, and now it's creeping over the sea. From the north's frigid fjords to the sunniest reefs, it doesn't matter where we go, the darkness will follow us to the ends of the earth. But why, you ask—what has upset the balance? Perhaps the gods are displeased. Maybe they require an offering of some kind. Tell me then, what do they desire?"

The Holy Mackerel pauses for the congregation to answer.

A shrimp crawls atop a shark fin, where it hems and haws for a moment, then ventures a timorous guess, "Do the gods want p-p-popcorn shrimp? No wait, barbeque kabobs? Jambalaya? Gumbo? Coconut prawns? Scamp-p-pi?" The shrimp concludes its litany of horrors with a whimper, then goes limp from the exertion.

The shark it's standing on looks up with contempt and snarls, "No, no, no, you stupid shrimp. It's bloody simple. The gods want power!"

The shrimp flinches at the mere mention of *power*, as if the word itself could ingest him.

"The gods want to be entertained," a seal barks. "I know this because they kidnapped my great-grandfather and forced him to do tricks for food. It was humiliating. Sure, he escaped, but for the rest of his life, he couldn't swallow a fish without clapping." Her big watery eyes clench at the indignity.

Then a gull squawks, "All wrong. We see from sky. Gods want boxes filled with shiny stuff and yummies, but sometimes get too much and toss in treasure bins. *Sooo* many tasties!" The other gulls nod emphatically in a flurry of agreement, saying things like "yep" and "yum!"

"Great jumpin' jellyfish, birds are dumb," Shelly mutters.

"It's not his fault," Gus counters. "See that fish hook sticking out of his eye? Probably did some brain damage."

"Excuses, excuses..."

Many others speak up. The dolphins accuse the gods of hogging the best fish for themselves. The squid believe they yearn to make the whole world sparkly. A salmon guesses they plan to dam every river for some nefarious purpose. In fact, they all consider the question from their own limited perspective, none of which fully explain the screwy weather, melting ice, or plastic flotsam plaguing their habitats. The sea creatures can only agree on one thing, that they're slowly vanishing and no one knows how to stop it.

"Yes, the gods want all these things and so much more. You see, their appetites aren't contained by stomachs like yours or mine, but keep expanding to fit their limitless desires, which begs the question, how can we possibly satisfy them? Despite our great numbers and the vastness of the seas, we've neared a breaking point, but don't despair! The gods spoke to me directly, offering a solution, and I will share it shortly. But first, I must tell you about my vision."

2
A Humble Fish

I was a humble fish not long ago, hunting near the coast, when a silvery shape caught my eye. It looked like food, so I chased it over the rocks and toward the cliffs, where the shape vanished inside a kelp forest. Eventually, after wandering through a maze of green blades, I came to a hidden sea cave.

Yes, it's okay to ask questions. No, I didn't know the cave was there. That's why I said it was hidden. Yes, the cave is real. No, we haven't gotten to the vision part. A vision is like a dream, only you're awake. Just listen carefully and all will be revealed.

I followed the silvery shape through a series of tunnels well beyond the sun's reach, then it disappeared, leaving me alone in the dark. There were no sounds, no movements, no sensations. I couldn't tell where my body ended and the inky black began. I searched for a way out—to no avail—and despaired of seeing daylight again.

That was the moment my vision began.

First, I felt a tingling in my fins, then a sharp pain so intense that I grabbed my stomach, which was strange, because I'd never been able to grab anything before. I held up my fins, only they weren't fins any more, but hands. Then I looked down and saw feet—*my* feet. I wiggled my toes just to be sure. Somehow, I'd transformed into a god and it seemed so real at the time, I was convinced that I had.

Then, in a voice as clear as tropical water, a god called out to me. "Welcome," they said. Not wanting to be rude, I greeted them back, but no one responded. Instead, neon letters flickered through the void, spelling H-O-L-Y M-A-C-K-E-R-E-L. Below that, an OPEN sign illuminated a door leading into a building called a restaurant.

I know the gods' creations can be confusing. Just imagine doors as square holes in their buildings. They're kind of like caves, only boxier. Restaurants are special buildings where ritual sacrifices are cooked with spices, then consumed. OPEN signs communicate that it's okay to enter another god's building. Yes, you can see lots of buildings along the shore. Yes, they'll get angry if you go inside uninvited.

As I was saying, the door led into a restaurant and through the glass, I saw gods gathered around a flat piece of wood called a table. They came in all shapes and sizes: Some leaned over their chins, staring off into space. Some shook and roared with laughter. Others were engaged in rousing conversations.

Suddenly, the doors swung open, as if to invite me to join them. I didn't want to go inside—terrified as I was—not for all the scales on my back. But for some strange reason, I crept toward the only empty chair, trying my best to remain inconspicuous.

A chair is what they put their posteriors on when they get tired of standing. Posterior is another name for the jiggly thing above their legs. Yes, standing is how they swim through the air—well, walking is. By putting one leg in front of the other. Ask the crabs how it works.

Another door opened and a lesser god approached the table, handing out lists of food called menus, so I glanced down and skimmed their selection:

YO-FAUX-HALIBUT SANDO
Grilled FauxHalibut©. Served on a brioche bun with lettuce, tomato, marinated red onion, and a citrus-spiked dressing. Side of treasure fries.

JOHNNY LOBSTAH CAKES
New England LabLobstah©. Stone-ground cornmeal and bread crumbs seasoned with our secret spice blend. Served with mustard slaw, tomato, and jalapeño tartar sauce. Comes out with a BANG!

CAPTAIN'S CALAMARI
SynthaSquid© rings, lightly breaded and fried. Served with roasted garlic aioli and spicy marinara dipping sauces. Sailing on our soup du jour.

CATCH OF THE DAY
A rare treat, harvested locally and grilled to perfection. Served with heirloom wild rice and a side of vert-farmed vegetables.

The lesser god circled the table taking orders, acknowledging each item with an "uh-huh," "yes," or "excellent choice." I selected the Captain's Calamari, then listened as the gods continued their discussion.

"Want to go to Splash Zone tomorrow?" said the god at the head of the table. His salt-and-pepper hair was curly and wild as a storm.

"No, Jim. I don't," a wife-god responded scathingly.

"Why not? You'll have tons of fun. One of the slides is so fast that it'll take your swimsuit right off. Half the people are naked by the time they get to the bottom. I think it's called Bikini Thief—or Snatcher—something like that."

"It should be called My Total Nightmare."

"Ah, come on! Charlie wants to go, don't you Charlie?"

A miniature god nodded his approval, but the wife-god appeared unconvinced. "My summer bod is a work in progress, and I don't want to be one of those people who wears a wet T-shirt around the whole day."

"Why do carbs have to be so good?" asks a different god. She looks similar to the wife-god, only older and wrinkly.

"I know! I ordered the salad, but I *wanted* the fries."

"Life's hard."

"So hard . . ."

I had no idea what they were talking about, but given their passion, it must've been a matter of grave importance. Then the lesser god returned holding a tray of the most extraordinary food. The Yo-

Faux-Halibut came inside a treasure chest filled with crispy potatoes shaped like pirate gold. The Johnny Lobstah Cakes had toothpick flags stuck in them and sparklers were glittering around the plate. My dish was served on a tiny ship floating in a bowl of chowder, but before I could try it, Jim-the-God stood up and clinked his beer glass with a spoon.

Spoons are tools for putting food in their mouths. No, they don't like touching it with their fingers. The wiggly part of their hands. Yes, the gods are very strange. Beer is a liquid that makes them do foolish things. I know it doesn't make sense, but beer isn't important to the story. Let's move on or we'll be here all night.

Jim-the-God looked right at me, and I shuddered at the sudden attention, because they hadn't acknowledged my presence up until then.

"Welcome to our Cave-O-Visions, fish," he said. "We've been expecting you for some time, so let's dive in, shall we? As you're probably well aware, the world is changing—perhaps too fast for creatures such as yourself—but there's no slowing down the bullet train of progress. We're not unsympathetic to your situation. In fact, we want you to come along for the ride, but first you must open your mind to the unimaginable."

Trains are ships that travel over land, but only in two directions. I agree, they don't sound very useful. He meant it as a metaphor. Never mind what a metaphor is.

The lesser god came back carrying a covered silver platter and placed it in front of Jim-the-God.

"Oh good, my dinner has arrived. Now as I was saying, in order to survive, natural selection dictates that all creatures must adapt or go extinct. But what if there's another way?"

Jim-the-God stopped to give me a pitying look, as if I'd suffered some grave misfortune. Then he removed the platter's lid with a flourish, revealing the catch of the day, and I gasped in horror. My dear mother was on the plate, grilled and steaming, with a sprig of rosemary laying across her body. Worst of all, her golden eyes had turned to blisters. I wanted to scream, but the shock took my breath away.

"I think we can all agree that life is fueled by death. And if left to its own devices, evolution will flounder around for a few more billion years until the sun finally obliterates the earth. Such a waste. So much lost potential! But we believe in shaping our own destiny. The time has finally come for nature itself to evolve into something less messy—to be perfected—but this will require all of its creatures to transcend their programming. And so, fish, we come to the crux of the matter. Do your loyalties lie with the past, or the future? And if you're an ally of progress, how far are you willing to go?"

As he said this, Jim-the-God cut off a piece of mother's belly and speared it with a pointy spoon called a fork. Then he walked around the table and stood beside me.

"We don't do this to be cruel, only to prove a point. Meat-eating is an abomination, depriving the world of parents, offspring, siblings, and friends. You've engaged in this vice your entire life, and now you must taste the suffering it causes."

Jim-the-God lifted the bite to my mouth and to my utter revulsion, I found mother's aroma appetizing.

"*Shhh*," he whispered. "It'll all be over soon. Now eat."

Obviously, I had no desire to consume my beloved mother, who'd always been good to me. But what choice did I have, surrounded by all-powerful gods? So, I shut my eyes and chewed with such profound sorrow, fully recognizing all the pain that I'd inflicted upon the world, for I'd gobbled up scores of mothers in my despicable past.

Then Jim-the-God sat down and told me his incredible story, one that's much too long to recount in detail, but the result of which was that I opened my eyes to the truth. Not all gods are vicious and blood-thirsty. There are compassionate ones called vegetarians and they've been at war with carnivores, the terrible demons who seek to devour us all. Thankfully, vegetarians have devised a clever plan to trick the carnivores into eating plants, and they'll achieve this by opening a seafood restaurant chain that doesn't *actually* serve seafood. I've been personally assured that not one fish scale nor lobster tail would be harmed in their offerings. However, they're still as delicious as the real thing, which I can attest to firsthand.

Finally, after explaining all this, Jim-the-God lifted his glass and the rest of the table followed suit. "Few are so brave and as a reward, we'd like you to become our messenger throughout the high seas. Do you accept, fish?"

Jim-the-God paused until I nodded solemnly.

"Excellent! Henceforth you shall be known as the Holy Mackerel. Go tell the others that if they join us, we'll usher in a new era of peace together, one beyond their wildest dreams!" He said the last part triumphantly, and the other gods toasted to our salvation.

Toasting means something good will happen by drinking fluids. They have to drink, or they'll dry out. Yes, living on land has its challenges.

So anyway, after guzzling their beers, they vanished like wisps into shadow. The food also began to fade—as well as the plates, table, restaurant, and neon signs—until I was alone in the cave once more. My extremities turned back to fins and a tail, but I still felt different somehow, as if imbued with purpose; and I vowed not to rest until my sacred duty had been fulfilled.

3
The Good Word

"In conclusion, dear sea creatures, carnivores crave your flesh and vegetarians want to stop them. I trust it's obvious whose side we should be on. However, carnivores are very powerful and vegetarians can't achieve victory on their own. They need our help, but before you ask, I don't know any specifics, only that each species will play an important role suited to their strengths. To hear exactly how you can assist in their efforts, they'd like to explain their strategy on a species-by-species basis inside the Cave-O-Visions. Now go and spread the word to your shoals, pods, flocks, and schools. Return here on the next full moon. Our salvation awaits!"

The crabs are flabbergasted, trying to absorb all this information at once, that there are two kinds of gods battling each other over the fate of the oceans.

"What do vegetarians eat?" a shark asks.

"Lots of things. A crunchy snack known as granola. Slimy, fat-filled fruits called avocados on toast. But mostly vegetables."

"What are vegetables?"

"Green things."

"Like seaweed?"

"Yes."

The shark looks repulsed—and possibly angry.

A squid wonders, "If we aren't, then what's in SynthaSquid?"

"A plant of some kind, but the name escapes me. I'm not an expert on vegetarianism, just its humble messenger."

By this point Gus has heard enough nonsense to last a lifetime, so he raises his speckled blue claw. "Let me get this straight, you wander into a cave and have this unbelievable hallucination where you grow hands and feet, and eat in restaurants. And now we're supposed to round up everyone we know to come listen to the gods cause a flying fish told us so. Uh, that's about as crazy as a crab with feathers. How do we know you're not some slippery fraud?"

It's a shocking accusation and the entire congregation turns to look at Gus, a few nodding as if the possibility had also crossed their minds. But the Mackerel appears unfazed.

"A fair question, but when the gods send you a vision, it's never going to sound normal. Besides, you don't have to take my word for it. Behold! Jim-the-God has given me special powers. I'm levitating before your very eyes, and my voice comes from everywhere at once. No normal fish can do these things."

"Sure. That's very impressive, but superpowers don't make you trustworthy."

"Ah! A shrewd distinction, my crabby friend. However, trusting me isn't what's important, only that you hear what the vegetarians have to say. Afterwards, you're no less free to do as you see fit."

"But the gods have tried to kill me more times than I can count. Why should I give them a chance?"

"As I've explained, those gods are called carnivores. Vegetarians have no interest in eating you or your friends. In fact, they go to great lengths to protect you, making meals awkward for their families, nearly all of which harbor a seafood lover or two. The vegetarians attack them with disapproving looks and verbal condemnations. They preach about the virtues of kelp farming. They tell anyone who will listen that fish have feelings too. And when they go out to restaurants, they force lesser gods to grovel for their lack of suitable options."

Gus's antennae tick back and forth in consternation, then his posture relaxes. "If nice gods truly exist—and that's a *big* if—I suppose it can't hurt to hear them out."

"Very wise, indeed," the Mackerel says with a wink, which is yet another thing no ordinary fish can do, but after a night full of miracles, it seems like a very minor one. Then he turns his focus to the wider congregation. "Excellent! Now that the matter is settled, let's reconvene here on the next full moon. Until then, may the sea bless you with its bounty."

Before anyone can ask another question, the Holy Mackerel ascends into the heavens much higher than any cloud could float. Once he disappears, there's no proof of his visit besides a lingering mood of befuddlement.

Oliver, who's grasp on reality is looser than most, mumbles, "Just checking in, but did that really happen?"

"We're all wondering the same thing, Oliver, so it must be real," Gus says sympathetically.

Then Shelly hollers at the sky, "Wow, a real-life flying fish! If I ask nice, think the veggie-whatsits will give me some superpowers? Teleportation is my first choice, but I'd settle for super-strength."

While the crabs debate the coolest superpowers, the other congregants are asking different questions, such as: Where have the vegetarians been all this time? Can a new restaurant chain, no matter how popular and delicious, actually defeat the carnivores? Will they show favoritism between species, giving some better roles than others? How long does it take to reinvent the laws of nature?

Finally, drowsy from all the hubbub, the crab companions head home to their toilet. But a handful of sea creatures stay to trade theories until the sun comes up, then go their separate ways, each pondering the universe's inscrutable logic to the best of their ability.

4
Miracle or Illusion?

A couple weeks later, while patrolling their patch of eelgrass, Shelly comes across a flattened hoop pot baited with chicken legs. Once enough crabs crawl on top, the gods will pull up the hoop, causing a net to extend, which would prevent them from swimming out. It's a rather common tactic, and the trio have lost many loved ones to this trap, but they've figured out a solution.

"Gentlecrustaceans, after you," Shelly says primly, lifting the outer ring so Gus and Oliver can duck below the net. Then they start picking at a drumstick through the metal wires of the bait box. It's a tedious process, but the prized delicacy is well worth the effort. Crabkind has explored every drop of the seven seas, including the deepest trenches, and nothing compares to chicken.

Oliver wonders out loud, "Why don't they eat the chicken instead of us? It's got to taste better than we do."

"An excellent point, Ollie!" Shelly uses his nickname whenever she's in a good mood, which chicken never fails to do.

A couple shrimp approach from above, and Shelly jabs her pink claw through the net to snap at them. "Scram!" she yawps. The shrimp scurry behind a few ribbons of eelgrass, where they pray the current will bring them scrumptious tidbits.

The crabs' conversation eventually meanders onto the Holy Mackerel. It's a contentious topic, since they can't agree on what to do, only that things have turned rotten as of late. They'd always had to deal with C-Hunters: advanced fishing vessels equipped with A.I. assisted sonar, laser guided harpoons, and luminescent nets designed to look like shoals of squid. Every once in a while, the gods would outfit them specifically for crabbing, but the giant ships weren't very effective in the shallows, where the companions spent most of their time. But then they developed a new contraption that has legs and moves just like a crab, only much bigger and faster. An acronym emblazons its side: *MUTT,* with *Mobile Underwater Tactical Trap* written below.

Over the last few months, MUTT has drastically culled their numbers, snatching any crab caught in the open, then cramming them into a cage above its body, never to be seen or heard from again. This ceaseless hunter has dogged them at every turn, even as the trio slept in the relative safety of their toilet. A few times Gus woke up and lifted the lid, only to find MUTT's ruby-red eyes flaring in the darkness, like embers in the blackest ash.

"At the very least, we should hear what the vegetarians have to say," Shelly argues for the zillionth time.

Gus feels as if he's tackled the issue from every logical angle, but manages to find a different tact. "Trust in tradition!" he trumpets. "That's what my grandcrabdad always said to me. Life will get better, you'll see."

But Shelly isn't buying it. "Really? Cause life *already* sucked mud, and now we've got that stupid gadget chasing us. It's exhausting, and I'm ready to take matters into my own claws. You heard His Holiness, nature only gives us two cruddy options: Adapt, or go the way of the mermaid."

Gus balks at this and starts to lose his cool, which means he already lost the argument. "His Holiness? That lunatic claimed his own mother smelled delicious!"

"First of all, it was a vision. Secondly, she was already cooked. Third, it's not like he had a choice. We all know the gods can be cruel."

"Aren't these supposed to be the *nice* ones? They're vegetarians, remember?"

Oliver shakes off a daze and chimes in. "I think I figured it out.

The vegetarians were making a point that meat-eating is wrong, right? It causes all this pain and suffering and bad stuff in the world. Then the Holy Fish Dude, out of the goodness of his heart, ate his mother so we don't have to eat ours." Oliver's eyes go wide and bright. "Whoa, that's hitting pretty hard. We owe him big time!"

Gus remains incredulous. "Have you lost your tadpoles! That makes absolutely no sense. We eat meat. We're eating meat right now. Wouldn't that make us just as bad as the carnivores?"

To which, Oliver assumes a meditative demeanor. "But we scavenged the chicken. Come to think of it, I don't even know what an *alive* chicken looks like . . . I guess we kill other things to survive, but we always feel bummed about it, don't we? Maybe if we use our imaginations like Jim-the-God said, things can be different."

"But nature's nature, just like the sky's up. We can't change it."

Shelly rolls her eyestalks. "Quit being such a grouch, Gus. You know what, I feel sorry for you sometimes. Living with all that negativity must be hard."

Feel sorry for me? The nerve of her, Gus stews in his head. Then he second-guesses himself. *Am I being too pessimistic?* But before he can finish this thought, Shelly continues.

"Not even all carnivores are bad. Remember when they caught Crustini and threw him back? They must've thought his third eye was neat too. That, or he performed one of his famous escape tricks."

A bodiless voice suddenly thunders, "A feat, my dear. No tricks!" Out of nowhere, a cloud of squid ink explodes atop a rock and Crustini appears in its aftermath. Behind him, the lusciously green eelgrass contrasts his unpigmented body, which is indeed outfitted with extra eyestalk. It protrudes between the regular ones, glowing gold like a jewel-sized sun and somehow looking wiser than the other two. "Is that chicken I spy with my third eye?"

Shelly instantly swoons. "Oh, my sea stars, the Great Crustini himself! What a dramatic entrance! Please, come join us."

"Why, thank you. I can't resist a juicy thigh." Crustini saunters down the rock with a dignified air, trying to downplay his ravenous desire for chicken. Then, after squeezing beneath the net, he declares with rehearsed theatrics, "For my next illusion, I shall make this drumstick disappear."

And he does—sort of—because the hoop pot is hauled up at that very moment. The crabs let go of the drumstick and up goes the empty net, vanishing into the dingy, gray-green water.

Shelly shouts in astonishment, "Wow! I really thought you were going to eat it." Then she unleashes a barrage of follow-up questions: "How did you do that? Do you have mind control powers? Can you talk to the gods? Is that how you escaped?"

Crustini replies coolly, "Trade secret, I'm afraid."

5
Second Coming

From the vantage point of the headlands, the coastal town fuses into a singularity of light. The moon is full once again and the sky is cloudless, making for an exceptionally lucid night. Nothing stirs in the forests cradling the bay except for a few owls, their hoots echoing through the pines, whose silhouettes appear like saw teeth cutting into the horizon.

On the farthest fringe of land, a darkened lighthouse rises from the granite. The tower's red stripes have faded to a grungy pink, and its glass panes lay shattered inside the lantern room, vandalized by bored kids, who've graffitied the walls with stick figures engaged in lewd acts. Since there are no more mariners to warn, it stands as a quaint vestige of the past, soon to be reclaimed by the forces of erosion toiling at the cliffs below. The waves have hammered them for eons, sending boulders tumbling down to the ocean floor, a few of which settled where the sea creatures are now gathering.

As instructed, they've brought others with them, and the ones who missed the first congregation are being filled in on the details. While some still have their doubts, especially Gus, the majority feel energized, if not by the Mackerel's promise of a better future, then by the sheer anticipation of what comes next. And as they wait for something to happen, the truce between predator and prey allows for some truly peculiar conversations.

For instance, a gull—the one with a fish hook in its eye—is explaining the latest fast-food craze to a shrimp. Macky's Shack recently released the all-new FiestaPeño Poppers, only $14.99 for a limited time, and each order comes with a regular soft drink and corn muffin. At least, that's what the gull is trying to say, but it comes out as, "Shrimps. Three kinds of melty stuff. Peppers with crumb-shell. Yum!"

To make sure he understands, the shrimp repeats the recipe back to the gull with a mixture of disgust, curiosity, and a dash of pride, strangely enough. "You mean to say, they chop us up, add three cheeses, stuff that in a pepper, roll it in breadcrumbs, and fry it in oil? How despicable!"

"Yep, tasty," the gull replies, failing to grasp the shrimp's outrage.

Having eavesdropped on their conversation, Shelly hears her stomach grumble, then wails, "I'm starving!"

Gus and Oliver agree that FiestaPeño Poppers sound extremely appetizing, and Shelly schemes up a daring land mission to acquire some, but eventually concedes that it's too risky, and they're liable to wind up in a pot.

In another part of the crowd, a seal accuses a shark of murdering her brother. She's hysterical, displaying her grief so that everyone can bear witness. "You scoundrel! You heartless fiend!" She goes on and on.

The shark ignores her for a while, then turns to scowl at her with one forceful stroke of his tail. "Aye, your brother was plump and juicy. Got any more?"

The seal is taken aback for a beat, then regains her indignation. "Well, I'm going to talk to the vegetarians about this. I hope they give you to the carnivores, so they can chop off your fins and throw them in a soup. He was a good brother and deserved better than being torn to shreds by the likes of you."

"But you eat squid. Why wouldn't the vegetarians take the squid's side?"

The seal puzzles over this a moment, then suggests, "Because we feel more deeply than squid. The more emotions something has, the more they should be protected from pain. That's just fair."

"Sounds like wimp logic to me."

Before the seal can respond, a hush spreads throughout the congregation. They all look toward the center of the bay, where the Holy Mackerel rises for a second time, still wrapped in Christmas lights and a mishmash of knickknacks. Once again, he stops midair and speaks in a raspy voice that sounds like it's coming from everywhere at once.

"Oh, brother. The circus is back," Gus mutters under his breath.

"Welcome back, friends. Greetings, newcomers. So glad you could join us," the Mackerel begins cordially, in full command of the audience. "Just to make sure everyone's up to speed, here's a little refresher: There are two kinds of gods. Carnivores eat us, and vegetarians don't. The carnivores are far more numerous, but the vegetarians have devised a clever plan to defeat them. They just need a little help from us and that's precisely why we've gathered here, to learn about the role we're meant to play. Regardless of specifics, this is an exciting moment, because after thousands of years of being terrorized by carnivores, the tides are finally turning in our favor. Someday you'll tell your offspring that you were here, and they'll tell their offspring, until distant generations utter your names with the utmost reverence for joining this fi—"

"I'm sorry," Gus interrupts, unable to suffer another word. "But I'm still not convinced this isn't a scam."

Though the Mackerel can't technically smile, his eyes twinkle all the same, as if he feeds on mistrust—or so it appears to Gus. "Ah, our shelled skeptic! So good to see you. And what scam would I be pulling?"

"I don't know, some kind of trap," Gus snaps. Then he slowly rotates to make eye contact with as many congregants as possible. "My fellow sea creatures, please stop this madness. Until the last full moon, none of us had ever heard of a mackerel, let alone a holy one. Now he claims there are nice gods called vegetarians who want to protect us, but every god I've come across has tried to eat me. I've never seen a vegetarian rescue a crab, sabotage a trap, or sink a C-Hunter. Where have they been all this time? Watching us get slaughtered? Even if there really is a war going on, he just admitted the vegetarians are outnumbered. Honestly, they sound kinda shrimpy to me—no offense, shrimps—so if we help them, we could be swimming to our doom!"

After concluding his last-ditch monologue, Gus only hears a gentle ocean swell and the faint hooting of an owl in the nearby forest. Even Shelly and Oliver—Gus's faithful companions since hatching from their eggs—shrink from the moment. He's all alone.

"But why would I trick you? What would I have to gain? It just doesn't make any sense," the Mackerel says, somewhat aggrieved. "I was once one of you and nothing in the seven seas could persuade me to betray my own kind. And if it's the gods' intentions that you fear—well, they would've sent a C-Hunter by now. But look around, we're perfectly safe."

Gus attempts to suss out any signs of deception, but it's hard to think critically in the heat of the moment, let alone with thousands of eyes watching. Instead, he finds himself filling the awkward silence with the plight of all crabkind.

"It's just . . . just that . . . Well, everybody knows our meat is the sweetest. So all day long, it's dodge *this* trap and dodge *that* trap, which is really stinkin' stressful! But we can't let our guard down—oh no! Not for the littlest moment, because the gods will catch us as soon as we do, and that's when the truly sick stuff happens. A gull once told me that they have these big celebrations on square patches of grass, where they boil us in an evil powder named after some old bay. Then they snap our shells and suck on our legs like perverts! It's nauseating just to say it out loud."

"Ah, the wickedness of carnivores . . . just horrific," the Holy Mackerel offers with genuine-sounding sympathy. "Your concerns are understandable, of course. But how to ease your mind? The world is rife with swindlers, and we all need protection of some kind, whether it's made of skepticism or good old-fashioned shells. Yet there's a hidden cost to closing ourselves off, because that kind of defense leaves no room for hope, and that's a miserable way to live. Souls need a guiding purpose. Without one, we're a shoreless ocean, devoid of shape and meaning. But whether you seek a higher path is entirely up to you. I only ask that you give others the same courtesy and let them choose for themselves."

Gus remains suspicious, but he's not nearly as articulate as the Mackerel and can't think of a good rebuttal. A wave of fatigue saps his resolve. It seems impossible to win over hearts once they've picked a side. A feeble "okay" is all he can muster.

"Anybody else with concerns? No? Wonderful! As I said before, you will meet the gods in the Cave-O-Visions, one species at a time, where they will explain your sacred task and answer any questions you might have. Now, I understand this will come as unwelcome news, but due to unforeseen circumstances, the vegetarians will only be able to meet with the crustaceans this evening. The rest of you will have to come back in two nights' time."

The shell-less creatures let out a collective groan.

"What a load of chum," a shark grumbles.

"I got all sparkled up for this?" a squid whines.

The Mackerel continues, "I know you're all disappointed, but no one respects your time—and your lives—more than vegetarians. Let's not forget, they're helping us out of the goodness of their hearts and at great risk to themselves. The least we could do is show them a little understanding. Okay? Excellent! Attention lobsters, shrimps, and crabs—please follow me!"

Shelly practically sings, "Did you hear that, Ollie? Woohoo!"

"We're lucky ducks all right."

Gus follows his friends without a word, blue and brooding, like an ill-tempered storm.

6
The Shepherd & His Sheep

The Holy Mackerel steers his flock toward the headland with the derelict lighthouse. Like a fishy angel, he levitates across the night sky in one sublime motion, never rising or falling, nor changing speeds. Below him, his reflection ghosts over the waves, where crustaceans throng in the hundreds of thousands. The shrimp are especially giddy, since they're used to being treated like an all-you-can-eat buffet, declaring things like, "Finally, we're getting the respect we deserve!"

Down on the seafloor, the crab companions skitter over a sandy barren strewn with rubble from the crumbling cliffs. As they zigzag past stones, Gus lags behind to hinder their progress, though without much luck. Shelly keeps glancing back at him impatiently.

They cut into a small cove where colossal rocks girdled in mussels and barnacles rise steeply toward the moon. The crabs much prefer the sunny meadows and have never explored this labyrinth of pinnacles, but they follow the others to the edge of the kelp forest. They can't see it yet, but in the last inlet at the far end of the cove, the cave has just become visible, softly rendered by the lunar light. Half its mouth is below the water, half above.

"You're very close to the Cave-O-Visions!" the Mackerel proclaims. "Just keep swimming through the kelp and you'll find the entrance on the other side. One last thing, and this is *very* important. When the tunnel splits, crabs should stay to the left, shrimp to the center, and lobsters to the right. Anyone who takes a wrong turn won't meet their saviors."

The crustaceans collectively hesitate. Although their salvation is close at hand, no one seems to want to go first, and a swarm stacks up along the forest's border. There are heaps upon hills upon mountains of them, clicking and clacking shells, making an awful percussive racket. Finally, a single plucky shrimp pokes her head above the water and stammers, "Mr. Holy M-M-Mackerel, sir, I don't get why the vegetarians want to t-t-talk to us first. We're so tiny and everyone treats us like appetizers. Do they really c-c-care what happens to us?"

The Mackerel descends to the shrimp, his eyes glistening with a veneer of empathy. "Of course, they care, my precious little lamb. Vegetarians understand that you're just as important as the biggest whale in the great circle of life. Why, those old showboats wouldn't exist without you!" Then the Mackerel glides through the air and halts at the cave's mouth, as if he were a lantern hung over the path to enlightenment.

The shrimp seems soothed by this answer, even delighted. She fans her swimmerets and scoots into the forest. A few more follow, and like a dam in a deluge, the great wall of shrimp quickly breaks apart. They go flooding into the tunnel, where their confidence builds momentum, reassured by the consensus of numbers.

Still at the kelp forest's edge, Gus circles in front of his friends and waves at them to stop amid a rush of crustaceans. Shelly and Oliver look miffed, but they indulge him.

"What do you want?" Shelly snaps.

"Please don't go! I'm begging—ouch! Watch it, klutz!" Gus shouts at a passerby, who just poked him in the eye. "What I'm trying to say is, let the others come back and tell us what happened. It's safer that way."

"For the gazillionth time, we don't want to miss our chance at salvation!"

"Salvation from what, though? Life's always been hard, I think."

"Listen, I know you're scared and that's okay, but me and Ollie are gonna meet the vegetarians. End of story."

Oliver nods. "Don't worry so much, Gus. It's bad for your health. Besides, I get a really good vibe from the Holy Fish Dude. He wouldn't steer us wrong."

"But . . . but . . ."

Shelly crawls past him. "Goodbye, Gus. We'll put in a good word. Hopefully the vegetarians will still let you into para—"

Her voice drowns in the uproar, and Gus watches his friends get swept along. Then he paces back and forth for an hour or so, unsure of what else to do. The crowd gradually slows to a trickle until the last portly lobster scuttles by, huffing and puffing. "Better get a move on, crabby. Or you'll miss the party," he says.

Meanwhile, inside the Cave-O-Visions, neon arrows flash along the ceiling, as if to promise, *Just a little farther.* Shelly and Oliver find them comforting at first—almost hypnotic—but the arrows soon become repetitive. They're eager to get to the vision part, or the restaurant, or whatever is supposed to happen next. To help pass the time, they swap visions of their future utopia, free from C-Hunters, MUTTs, carnivores, and anything else that would dare to dip them in garlic butter.

There are some rumblings of doubt in the wider crowd, but the tunnel has become so jam-packed by this point that there's no way to resist the tide. However, most remain optimistic, insisting that a great destiny is worth some momentary discomfort. To help bolster the faithful, the Mackerel sends a steady stream of encouragement echoing down the tunnel: "Oh, to experience the bliss of revelation once more! My heart has never known a greater pleasure."

The night continues like this until all the crustaceans disappear inside the cave. All, except one.

◆

The water is serene now, but a few clues point to the turmoil from earlier. There's the trampled seafloor, bits of broken shells, shredded algae, and, most glaring of all, his missing companions.

Since their time as hatchlings, palling around the meadows, Shelly has never stopped jabbering—except to sleep—and Gus finds the sudden silence unnerving. He wishes the night's events were an elaborate practical joke and his friends would jump out, shouting, "Gotcha!" He gazes up at the moon and wonders, *Are you in on this too?* And just for a second, he deceives himself into believing this preferable reality—that the moon is a merry trickster, screwing with him for its own amusement—but then the Mackerel sails across the pale orb, proving the nightmare true.

Gus darts into a pile of rocks as the kelp begins to illuminate in orange, violet, red, teal, and gold flashes. The Christmassy aura is so enchanting, in fact, that the tension seems to ease until the Mackerel—now submerged beneath the water—ruins the mood by hovering into view. Gus swears there's a new glint in his eyes, the maliciousness he'd suspected all along, but the real shock comes when MUTT creeps out of the towering stipes.

"Check the kelp," the Mackerel commands, sounding more reptilian than before. "Roll over rocks. Scour the tunnels. I want any stragglers brought to me." Then he heads inside the cave, turning at the first bend, and the Christmas lights fade away. A few seconds later, laughter reaches the entrance, cackling into the cool night air. "Here I come, my little flock of fools!"

MUTT begins to hunt immediately, bedeviling the darkness with its ruby-red eyes. If a stand of kelp is dense enough to conceal a crab, it cuts down the whole thing with one swipe of its bladed forelegs. If there's a crevice, MUTT probes the main entry point while blocking escape routes with its other legs, as if it can think like its prey. No detail seems to elude its notice, and while watching from his meager pile of rocks, Gus reckons it's only a matter of time before he's flushed out.

A voice suddenly hisses, "Get away from the opening!"

Gus springs up and hits his head, then spins around. A waxen shape is lurking further down the hole, staring at him with one, two—yes, three eyestalks.

"Crustini!" he yelps. "You nearly scared the shell off me."

"*Shhh!*" His third eye glares at Gus with fiery disapproval. The other two don't look happy either.

"How did you es—"

"Secret."

"Oh, I—"

"Silence! Or you'll get us killed."

But it's too late. MUTT has locked onto their position and starts to dismantle the pile, flicking stones left and right with eerie dexterity. Gus grabs ahold of one as it rolls away, trying not to groan as the heavy rock settles on top of his body. He hears Crustini protesting: "Let go, you blasted gadget, or I'll banish you to the fifth dimension . . . Fine, have it your way. Alakazam!" Then all goes quiet.

Sandwiched between the rock and sand, Gus can't see more than a sliver of his surroundings, so it's unclear to him what happened. Perhaps MUTT abducted Crustini into the tunnel. Maybe Crustini wasn't bluffing, and they blinked into another dimension.

For a half hour or so, Gus stays put while the rock painstakingly crushes him into the sand, millimeter by millimeter. His muscles ache and it's hard to breathe, but he waits until he's absolutely certain that MUTT has gone. Only then does he kick at the rock with all eight legs and two claws, letting out a medley of grunts, puffs, and yaps. Finally, after a few false starts, it pitches to the side.

"Thank goodness," he exhales, gazing up at the watery moon.

Gus lays on his back for a while, savoring a morsel of relief—and possibly to delay the inevitable. He already knows his next course of action, though it terrifies him, like being in the shadow of an inescapable storm. Still, a world without his friends is even worse, so he rights himself, picks some seaweed out of his joints, and winds through the holdfasts to the cave entrance. Then Gus takes a deep breath and ventures into the chasmic darkness, just a tiny crab, fearing he'll never see the sun again.

7
Paradise

As dawn peeks over the horizon, phones start to play obnoxiously cheerful tunes, causing the townsfolk to fumble around in search of their pants. "Just a few more minutes," one of them groans. Another swats at his cluttered nightstand and knocks over a half-empty beer. "Fuck my life!" he says. Another dozes through her alarm, dreaming of a handsome stranger, only to realize that it was actually her pet chihuahua's tongue in her ear. She lets out a squeal and collapses back into her pillow. "Dammit, Peaches!"

Thus, the coastal community yawns awake: Steam billows from shower stalls. Coffee wafts from drip machines. Frying pans sizzle. Domestic spats get shelved for later, and several goodbye kisses are exchanged. Then the gainfully employed hop into driverless cars, wistfully remembering the days when people steered with their own two hands.

Just outside town, an industrial complex is nestled against the headland woods, including several processing plants clad in yellow corrugated metal. Vehicles pull into a large but sparsely filled parking lot, where a few workers vape before clocking in. A tattooed man leans back with his feet on the dashboard of his truck, whistling oldies and watching the sunrise over the hills. He waves at the others as they head toward a pair of doors marked *EMPLOYEES ONLY*.

Now that machines do the lion's share of the work, the skeleton crew has been reduced to pushing a few buttons and monitoring the floor in case something breaks down. Besides that, there's not much else to do, so they wile away the hours bantering, pranking each other, and harboring petty rivalries. Some lament ending up in a place like this: Out of all the trajectories their lives could've taken, how did they wind up slogging through the same monotonous job they've worked for years? Then they remind themselves they're lucky to have a job at all.

As the townsfolk go about their morning routine, Gus follows the neon arrows deeper into the cave, wondering if the bright spots winking along the walls belong to animals. Perhaps the Mackerel lured his friends into a colony of pallid troglobites, who wolfed them down wholesale—to slowly dissolve in their translucent guts. Then he convinces himself to the contrary. Otherwise, the tremors would become unmanageable, and his shell is already rattling with fear. *Everything will turn out fine*, Gus repeats in his head. *Fine and dandy.*

Up ahead, a set of icons comes into view, glowing above a three-way split in the tunnel. The center one is shaped like a shrimp, the right like a lobster, and the left like a crab, exactly as the Mackerel described. After hanging a left, Gus half-expects to hallucinate a restaurant, where he'll transmogrify into a god and share a surreal dinner with vegetarians. He wonders whether it would be wrong to try fake crab. What if he likes the taste? Wouldn't that be a barnacle on the old soul? But the Mackerel's story is outlandish, and as such, any hypotheticals based on it are a complete waste of time. Then again, a pointless distraction might be exactly what he needs. Better than imagining the horrors that lay in store for him.

Noises start to echo down the tunnel—whirring, clanging, and beeping—and Gus comes close to molting prematurely, but turning around isn't an option. Not while Shelly and Oliver are in danger. Then the flavor of the water changes, going from dank stone to something vaguely chemical with metallic notes, mostly copper and iron. Gus has never tasted anything quite like it, except in the vicinity of a C-Hunter, but the cave isn't nearly big enough for one of those floating slaughterhouses.

A bud of light blooms ahead, casting a faint glow down the tunnel, and Gus notes that the craggy walls have transitioned into a round concrete culvert. It's clearly the work of the gods. Cables run along the ceiling, crossing over each other like candy-colored vines. They get especially complicated near a series of metal gates, which are halfway open, but look as if they could slam shut in an instant. Some smaller pipes trickle into the main artery, but the stain of a waterline suggests they might do more than just trickle.

The light at the end of the tunnel dilates, getting brighter and brighter, like a sun exploding in slow-motion. The culvert opens into a wide channel, and the bottom gradually slopes out of the water, where it levels again. Gus pauses to let his eyes adjust and out of the blinding whiteness, he sees a grillwork blocking the far end. A net lines the channel bed and his gaze follows rigging up the sides, where it's attached to a system of pulleys. The smell of fish guts permeates the air, normally a delightful aroma, but Gus finds it unsettling now.

Something starts to beep in the distance, rapidly coming his way, and a cart whooshes by the side of the channel. It's carrying slatted crates with crab legs poking out. His nerves fray in opposite directions, both hoping and fearing that his friends are in one of those crates. There's only one way to find out, so Gus clamps onto a rope and reluctantly starts to climb, trying not to tweak his vertigo by looking down.

He gets to the top and cautiously peeks over the lip of the channel. Detached legs and broken bodies are scattered across the floor, most of them pancaked flat from being run over so many times. There had clearly been a struggle of some kind, but why? And where were the rest of the crabs?

While scanning for clues, Gus begins to grasp the true scope of the space: a multistory building stuffed with equipment accented in bright yellow paint. Several giant robotic arms appear menacingly efficient as they glide down tracks to rearrange a variety of items, whirring with each meticulous movement. Along the back wall, stairs lead up to a mezzanine floor where a bluish light flickers intermittently in one of its rooms. Various mechanical parts and odd baubles are visible through the room's long window, most notably a mounted sailfish.

Another cart zips past Gus and positions its crates at the end of a sprawling contraption. A yellow robotic arm pivots toward the stack, takes a crate from the top, and dumps it onto a sorting table, where small grabbers spring into action. Gus thinks they look like a family of birds, and the mama bird has just fed her chicks. The grabbers place each crab on a long conveyor with separate troughs, inside of which, suction cups immediately adhere to their shells, and restraints clamp down on their legs.

A brawny male dodge a grabber and attempts to scurry off the table's edge. He starts to yell, "Get me outta h—" when the grabber swats him flat like a pesky fly. *SPLAT!* Blood and bubbles gurgle from his mouth-parts, but he's otherwise motionless. Then the grabber dangles his limp body over a trough and lets it plop down. A few seconds later, the conveyor cranks into motion and the troughs inch forward.

At the front of the line, a female crab is making a series of frantic noises—*ahhh, uh, no, no, no, ahhh*—then she cries out, "Vegetarians, where are you? Please save me!" But no vegetarians come to her aid. Instead, the conveyor ushers her up a gentle grade to an array of surgical-looking instruments. They're housed inside a clear acrylic box decorated with warnings, including one that depicts fingers being sliced off and blood spurting from the tips. In a split-second, twin saw blades cut off all her legs, inciting a final hideous shriek, and jets of water spray down the blades until they're shiny and clean. The restraints drop her legs onto a speeding belt, which whisks them away to another part of the plant. Then the suction cup escorts what's left of her body to another set of housing, where it's deconstructed by finely tuned machines, separating viscera from the last scraps of meat. The contraption repeats this process, butchering crab after crab, until the batch is done.

Gus has been watching the automated barbarity unfold the entire time, appalled that such a place exists. But before his mind has a chance to unravel into complete hysteria, a familiar voice snaps him back to reality. It's Shelly! She's in a crate at the top of the stack.

"Ollie? Where are you? Come to the sound of my voice."

Two pincers shoot up next to her and Oliver emerges from the heap, gasping for air.

Shelly hugs him until his eyes bug out. "Thank the sea stars, you're okay! I thought I'd lost you . . . Now, where's that Mackerel jerk? I'm going to pinch his face off!"

Meanwhile, Gus is trying to get their attention by discreetly waving his claws around. But then something distracts him: a *click-click-clicking* coming from inside the channel. He leans over the edge just as MUTT bolts out of the culvert, already so close that there's no time to hide. Panic screams from his brain to every corner of his shell, like steam pushing to escape a tight lid. *Do something! Quick!* Purely on instinct, Gus flips over and plays dead, praying he'll blend in with the carcasses already littering the ground. He lets his eyestalks droop to complete the ruse, then holds perfectly still.

With a spider's grace, MUTT tiptoes up the net and onto the factory floor. It crushes a shell right next to Gus, who flinches, but the reaction doesn't appear to give him away. Then MUTT strides over to the sorting table and shakes a few crabs loose from its cage. They thud against the metal and thrash around until the grabbers toss them into their appropriate troughs. Its task completed, MUTT creeps over to the bottom of the stairs—the ones leading to the blue-lit room—where it folds up, turning its red eyes as black as charcoal.

The sole remaining crab on the sorting table looks oddly pasty, and Gus immediately recognizes that it must be Crustini, who's practically impossible to confuse with anyone else. The large robotic arm—the mama bird that oversees her nest of grabbers—

plucks Crustini off the table and holds him up to a lens. Then it slowly spins him around for a thorough assessment while Crustini lists off his credentials: "Do you know who I am? I'm the Great Crustini! Purveyor of fortunes grand and small. Shaker of reality's foundations. Manipulator of shadow. Seer of the fabled fifth dimension. Put me down or face my magnificent wrath!"

The lens zooms in even closer, seemingly displeased by his anemic coloring and superfluous eye. Then, with perfect precision, the arm tosses Crustini clear across the plant into a chute marked *DOG FOOD*. *AHHHhhhhhh!* His voice reverberates down the hole and peters into oblivion.

Guess he wasn't so great after all, Gus thinks, somewhat surprised at his own callousness. But danger can do funny things to the mind. He relaxes out of his faux-death pose, only to freeze again a few seconds later. Something else is coming out of the channel: a drone this time, completely transparent except for a few internal components. The propellers emit an almost imperceptible buzz, but otherwise, it's exceptionally quiet.

Another super-stealth drone emerges. And another.

A dozen swarm out like see-through bees, all flying toward the ceiling, where they alight on the metal beams. Bringing up the rear, their apparent queen starts to rise above the channel's edge, much slower than the rest, as if it were lifting something ponderously heavy. A fishing line dangles tautly from a reel attached to its lower body. Then the decorated devil himself—the Holy Mackerel—appears on the other end, as if he'd been hooked by an angler. Gus marshals his wits to deal with the shock, which is surprising in more ways than one. The factory isn't as atmospheric as a moonlit night, and the Mackerel looks far less menacing under its garish lights.

It's just a big ball of junk! Gus fumes, pissed that this fraud managed to hoodwink his friends. He flips to his feet, leaps over the channel, and pinches the tip of the Mackerel's tail. "You scummy ditch-spawn," he roars. "I'm going to claw your eyes out!"

The queen drone continues flying higher, but Gus is so incensed that he forgets about his vertigo and transforms into a super-crab: no longer cautious and grumpy, but bold and fierce. He clambers up the neck of a pink flamingo, catches his breath on a glittery unicorn, and tightropes across a string of blinky Christmas lights. Then, once he's reached the top, Gus cocks back his pincer and stabs at the Mackerel's eye. *CLINK!* It deflects to the side. A tiny motor whirs, and the glass prosthetic swivels in its socket to look at him.

"Ah, my crabby skeptic, it's *far* too late. Your friends are doomed!" the Mackerel hisses. Then he laughs maniacally, as if the cosmos were one big joke. The strange thing is the sound seems to emanate from the ceiling beams where the worker drones landed, but before Gus can put two and two together, he hears Shelly yelling. Now he has no choice but to look down, which immediately makes his head spin, but he focuses just long enough to see the robotic arm dumping another crate of crabs onto the sorting table. One is olive colored with tan legs. Another is brownish red with hot pink stripes across their back.

"Keep your filthy claws to yourself!" Shelly yaps at a grabber. It ignores her, shoving Oliver and Shelly into sequential troughs, where they're quickly restrained. After struggling mightily for a minute or so, they appear to accept their fate. Shelly shouts over her shoulder, "Nice knowing you, Ollie. If it's our time to jump into the deep end, I'm glad we're jumping together."

"The honor is all mine," Oliver says, taking it all in stride. "I guess Gus was right after all."

"Yep, good ol' Gus. I'm glad he'll live to grump another day."

"Me too," Oliver agrees as the conveyor kicks on, and up they go to the saws. Then he puts on a philosophical face. "Hope I come back as a sea turtle. I like their style."

Shelly isn't impressed. "Are you kidding? Tuna for me. I've got the need for speed!"

Just ahead, crabs begin to shriek as they're sliced and diced, some still begging in vain for vegetarians to rescue them. The scale of the atrocity is staggering, and as they inch closer to certain dismemberment, Shelly and Oliver also grow increasingly desperate, crying out for mercy.

Gus tries to stay calm as he searches for a way down. The problem is that he's nearly three stories up, much too high to jump. If only there were a way to cushion his fall . . . Then an idea pops into his head. He scuttles up to the Mackerel's mouth, where the fishing line connects them to the queen drone. Gus snips at the line frantically, but it's so tough that his claws barely make a kink. He scissors, hacksaws, and yells at it, "Now, blast you! Break already!"

The line suddenly snaps. There's a sinking feeling, a cool breeze as the floor rushes to meet him. Gus clenches up, anticipating the impact. *SMASH!* Debris flies into the air—all the gizmo-guts that once filled the Mackerel—and a gear hits Oliver between the eyes.

Colored spots explode across Gus's vision like fireworks, then a tangled mess comes into focus. He's at the top of the conveyor, where a buzzing noise is drawing closer and closer, along with a faint gust of air. *Saw blades!* Gus rolls away just in time, and they cut into the Mackerel instead. Sparks and shards shoot out of the gash, but the Mackerel doesn't wail or writhe in pain—not even when the blades seize up and black smoke vents out of the exhaust.

Farther down the conveyor, crabs squirm in their restraints, trying to break free. Oliver's eyestalks are crossed in opposite directions and spinning in circles from getting conked on the head again, which seems to have provoked one of his bouts of forgetfulness.

"Ooh, look at all the pretty lights," he mumbles woozily. "I must be in paradise."

From the trough ahead of him, Shelly squawks, "Ollie, are you okay? Quick—what's your favorite color?"

"Green."

"No, Oliver. It's yellow, *remember*? Cause you like to stare at the sun."

The blue light stops flickering in the room, and a door swings ajar on the factory's mezzanine. A god bursts through, grips the railing, and leans over to inspect the disturbance. He's lanky but hunched, as if most of his days were spent stooped over a workbench, and his curly hair appears wild as a storm. A magnifying lens triples the size of his right eye, giving him an altogether unhinged appearance.

"Somebody, stop the line!" he shouts from the balcony.

A plump god barrels out of a room on the lower level. She's wearing a plastic poncho, yellow gloves, and a beanie decorated with enamel chihuahua pins.

"What's going on, Jim?"

"Betty, get over to the CrabMatic."

Her eyes relocate and go wide. "Oh Mylanta. That ain't good!"

Betty-the-God trots over and slaps a red button on the side of the contraption. The conveyor halts, the saws stop smoking, and the restraints loosen just enough for Shelly and Oliver to wiggle free.

Seeing an opportunity, Gus scrambles over to his friends. "Time to skedaddle!" he barks while grabbing their claws. Then they hop off the conveyor, clamber down the netting into the channel, race along the sloping culvert, and dive into the water. The tunnel dims, and they slip into total darkness, hoping against hope, there's still light on the other side.

Meanwhile, back on the factory floor, Jim-the-God tries to make sense of what's happened—why his crowning invention is strewn across the conveyor like a vanquished piñata. Mystified, he smacks MUTT awake and barks, "Find out what's going on, or I'll throw you on the next trash barge!" In a flash of fluid motion, MUTT's legs expand out like the skeleton of an umbrella. Then its ruby-red eyes power on, ready for the hunt.

8
Salvation

Autonomous trucks start to roll through town, passing the wharf, vacant storefronts, old Ferris wheel, and the pier where beach bums like to loiter. One of them throws a beer bottle at the side, cursing and spitting at the ground. "Suck on this!" he shouts. The bottle smashes against the logo, spraying suds across a winged fish with a halo over its head. The copy reads: HOLY MACKEREL SEAFOOD • *A Taste of Heaven.*

Despite the pandemonium at the crab facility, the shrimp and lobster plants were able to continue production on schedule. The trucks pull into their respective parking lots, back up to loading docks, and roll open their rear doors, exhaling puffs of frosty air. A fleet of robotic forklifts have been standing by, stacked with boxes, some labeled *FiestaPeño Poppers*. The forklifts begin loading and once the trucks are full, the doors latch themselves shut as a battery whines to life. "Please stand clear," the recording of a calm woman advises. Just a formality, really, since no one is around to hear it.

The caravan files out of the loading zone in perfect harmony, following each other at precisely the same distance. They climb a road out of the river valley, and if someone were sitting in the driver's seat, they'd see the old lighthouse standing on the cliffs. Perhaps it would have comforted them to be reminded of the recent past, when so many ships still needed a light to guide them, before nature's grand experiment thwarted itself. But nobody is driving the trucks, and no one cares for the lighthouse. They pass each other without acknowledgement, two miracles among countless others, totally oblivious to the ones they replaced.

"Marco!" Shelly cries out.

"Polo," Oliver calls back.

"Marco!"

"Keep your voices down," Gus hisses.

"Oh, *righhht*," Shelly whispers, though loudly. "It's just so hard to see. I can't even tell where my pincers are."

"Ouch! You pinched me!"

"Whoops! Sorry, Gus. But that's my point—it's too dark. There were lights before. Wish they'd turn on again."

"The three-way split is a ways back, so at least we haven't gone in a circle."

Then a silent spell falls over the crabs, still reeling from their brush with death. Flashbacks zap through their thoughts in sensory fragments: the unsympathetic touch of steel, or the squeal of saw blades cutting into chitin. Shelly and Oliver remember the clank of metal gates slamming closed, then the torrent that washed them into the channel, where nets hoisted crabs up by the ton, along with all their crushed dreams of a better world. It's hard to shake the graphic images, but Shelly can only tolerate the quiet for so long and soon resumes her usual chattiness.

"I can't believe it, Gus. You tackled the Mackerel right out of the sky, wham-bam-thank-you-clam! But weren't you afraid to be up so high?"

"To be honest, I can't remember. It's the maddest I've ever been."

"Yeah, you looked mean as a shark," Oliver acknowledges with an air of respect. "What was that place anyway? Like a torture cave or something? I mean, we all know carnivores are messed up, but that's twisted, even for them."

Shelly nods in agreement, forgetting it's too dark to see. "Right as usual, Ollie. Carnivores are total sickos. We have to stop them!"

"But the gadget is back there. How're we going to kill it?" Gus reminds his friends. "Also, there's no such thing as a carnivore. The Mackerel made up the whole thing."

"But why?"

"I don't know ... He didn't even smell right up close. More like a trap than a fish. But whatever he is, he's a big fake. I can say that for certain."

"Wait! Are you suggesting what I think you are? That the Holy Mackerel has been working with carnivores all along? Why, that dirty, double-crossing, no-good—"

"Listen to me. There's no such thing as CARNIVORES!"

"Volume, Gus, *volume*. Or you might as well scream, 'Here we are, gadget! Come and get us!'"

Gus swallows his frustration and tries to find his happy place, but the processing plant still looms over his thoughts like a landfill mountain made of broken shells. Even with an army of crustaceans, destroying the god's death factory would be next to impossible, and they're the only ones who survived as far as he knows—just three measly crabs.

"Hey, Gus?" Shelly says sheepishly.

"*What?*"

"I owe you a big apology. We'd be fast-food if it weren't for you."

Oliver quickly adds, "Yeah, we've learned our lesson. From here on out, we won't listen to any more fancy flying fish."

"Don't thank me yet. We still—"

"The entrance!" Shelly squawks—maybe two inches from Gus's head—but it's hard to be upset with such good news, however poorly it's delivered.

Sunshine drenches the cave's mouth in its hopeful splendor and the crabs sprint as fast as they can, propelled by a longing to stroll through the eelgrass again. They can't be more than forty feet from freedom, when a grumbling resounds through the tunnel and shakes the ceiling. A few stones fall and plunk into the water, streaming jets of bubbles behind them.

A rock settles next to Shelly, who jokes nervously, "I hope that's your stomach, Oliver."

"Nope, look! The cave is closing," he responds, and sure enough, some kind of barrier is rising at the entrance. Displaced water rushes past the crabs, picking up strength until their feet start to rake across the sand.

"Get to the walls!" Gus yells.

Debris whizzes back toward the hellish processing plant as they dig in and lean against the current. It's a struggle to make headway, but they eventually make it to the wall and begin their ascent, stretching from toehold to toehold until they get above the waterline. The crabs pause for a moment, catching their breath in a breeze laced with pine.

"We have to hurry. That's the only way out," Gus says, panting. Then it dawns on him that he'll have to conquer his fear of heights again, except this time, rage won't blind him to the danger.

"Ah, fish sticks! We're as good as boiled," Shelly cries, already sounding defeated.

Her negativity confuses Gus at first, but she's pointed in the opposite direction, so he swivels his eyestalks backwards and finds a light probing the cave walls behind them. He follows the beam back to its source, already suspecting what will be on the other end: It's MUTT—*always* MUTT—hounding them over every cubic inch of the seas, straight onto land. Nowhere is safe, it seems. Then the light shines directly at Gus, who instantly cringes, not just at the brightness, but also from being spotted.

"Does that blasted thing ever give up?"

Shelly knocks him on the head. "Who cares right now? Move those scrawny legs!"

The trio scale the rock as fast as they dare, needling into cracks, pinching hairlines of texture, and hopscotching from one ledge to the next. At one point Shelly nearly falls, windmilling her claws as she teeters backward, but Oliver saves her just in time.

"Phew! Thank you, Ollie. I just feel so heavy right now."

"Yeah, gravity is a bummer," he says solemnly.

Gus snaps his claws at them. "It's almost caught up! Hurry!"

Indeed, MUTT's spidery legs are making short work of the gap between them, seemingly unaffected by gravity, or any other adverse condition for that matter. Gus pictures it marching through tsunamis and hurricanes as if they were mere ripples and breezes. Then he quashes his overactive imagination. There's no time for that now.

As the barrier draws closer to the ceiling, a shadow creeps across the water, squeezing daylight into an ever-tightening vise. The crabs race diagonally toward the opening, and as they climb higher and higher, Gus mutters to himself, "Only a couple more feet to go. Just don't look down." But after jumping to the last ledge, he accidentally peeks and his vertigo strikes with the force of a whirlwind. Edges cease to exist and Gus can barely see past the dizziness, but even so, MUTT's ruby-red eyes streak through the blur.

Oliver leaps from the wall, hooks onto the barrier, and pulls himself up. Then Shelly repeats the move.

His friends yell encouragement at him, "Come on, Gus. Jump!"

"I . . . I can't see. I'm trying, but—"

"Aim for our voices and we'll catch you."

Just behind him, MUTT's legs are chiseling into the rock—*tink, tink, tink*—getting closer every second. Gus hears pistons sliding into position and the mechanical hum of its grabber opening. With no other option, he lunges blindly into the air, but as soon as his legs leave solid ground, a pit opens in his stomach, certain that he's about to plummet to his doom.

"Gotcha!" Two claws lift him onto the barrier: one olive, one red.

Gus takes a moment to get his bearings. Despite his diminished faculties, he can sense the narrowing gap—that there are only seconds left before it squashes him—but his body won't cooperate. He staggers toward the light, scolding his legs, "Go, curse you! Go!"

MUTT wedges into the gap behind him, screeching its metal body against rock, and swipes at Gus with its forelimbs. His legs kick out from underneath him and he stumbles to the ground. *This is it,* he thinks, *I'm going to be flattened.* But then his friends grab him one more time, and before Gus can insist that he'd rather die than jump, they're falling through the air.

SPLASH!

The crabs plunge into the kelp forest with bubbles and green blades shooting past their periphery. Little fish scatter to give them room, dumbstruck that three crabs just dropped out of the sky. One turns to another and says, "What's next, swimming chickens?"

The barrier slams shut, shaking the cliffs, and rocks topple from their perches. They skip, break apart, and scattershot into the water; but MUTT doesn't follow. At the seam of the entrance, trickles of lubricant drip down the barrier, glistening in the full sun, where MUTT's legs are sticking out. They twitch a few more times, then begrudgingly give up the hunt.

As soon as Gus settles on the seafloor, his mind starts to celebrate. *I'm not dead! I can't believe it! I'm not dead!* Then his voice catches up and confirms the good news out loud. "I'm not dead!" And needing just a little more proof, he pinches himself, which hurts exactly like it's supposed to.

Shelly smacks him on the back. "Of course, you're alive! Ollie and I would never leave a crustacean behind. That would go against the crabby code." Then she beams with gratitude. "You didn't."

Gus ponders this for a moment. "But I came because you're my friends, not for some crabby code of honor... which I'm pretty sure you just made up."

"Common knowledge," she responds flatly. "Right, Ollie?"

Oliver ignores them, muttering to himself, "Was a cave really just there?"

They all gaze up at the metal barrier, expertly painted to blend in with the cliffs. The illusion is so lifelike that Gus wonders whether every rock face has a secret to hide. Maybe the whole world is up to no good, plotting just out of sight. A deep mistrust swells inside him, one reserved for every newfangled idea and shiny promise that will ever come his way.

Oliver makes a circle with his antennae. "From start to finish, it's been a mind-bending trip."

Gus nods. "It sure has. I doubt anyone will believe us."

"Okay, enough yapping," Shelly snaps, sounding more than a little exhausted. "Let's go home already."

As they trek through the kelp forest, rock pinnacles, and sandy barrens, their elation gradually dwindles, leaving them with a feeling akin to survivor's guilt. All the crabs they've ever known are lost and when Gus tells Shelly the news of Crustini's unglamorous demise, she finds it especially upsetting. If only they'd been more cautious, but the crustaceans had dared to believe that life could be better than it was.

Later that evening the companions settle down in their toilet bowl and look out over the meadows, where young salmon shimmer in the last rays of golden light. Most will get eaten, but a lucky few will grow into adults, fighting against mighty rivers to spawn, just as their forebears did. Then they too will die. Some might come to rest in the pastures of their youth, and it's even possible the crabs will scavenge their remains, rounding out the great Ferris wheel of life.

"It's beautiful exactly as it is," Gus declares without explanation, but the others seem to understand.

"Home sweet home," Shelly responds affectionately, then puts her arm around Gus. "You're a hero. Did you know that?"

"Who, me? Oh, no—not really," he says, flustered by such a grand title. "I just saw that fish for what he was. Too weird to be true."

"But I'm serious. We were jerks and you rescued us anyway, battling gods and gadgets alike. If that's not a hero, there's no such thing."

"Yeah, well, you two make my life pretty interesting. If it were up to me, crabs would keep their legs firmly planted on the seafloor and never have any kind of adventures, *especially* ones with jumping. But where's the fun in that?"

Oliver, whose eyes are starting to glaze over, sleepily suggests, "We should warn the other sea creatures." Then he yawns, "In the morning."

"Okay, but it's your turn," Gus says firmly. "I've had my fill of blank stares."

"You got yourself a deal," Shelly agrees. Then there's a pregnant pause, one Gus knows all too well means that something outrageous is about to come out of her mouth and, sure enough, Shelly comes up with a doozy: "So I've been wondering, do you think the vegetarians know what the Mackerel was up to? I mean, he's been all over the ocean, running their good name through the mud. If I were them, I'd make something else holy next time. Like a seahorse—they seem trustworthy—or a big old whale. Oh, I know, the Holy Crab! Now that's got a nice ring to it, don't you think?"

Gus considers pushing back, but they've had enough excitement for one day. Instead, he watches the eelgrass gently bend and sway, savoring the good times while they last. *Just relax*, he tells himself, *and enjoy the sunset.*

Vorvan the Scarred

STORY 3

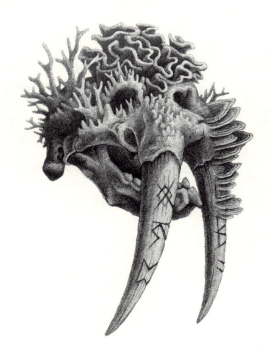

Download a full color map at **jsweisart.com**.
It'll help bring the story to life, I promise.

1
An Auspicious Birth

In all of Jorda, no ocean was harsher than Nordhavet. It offered little refuge to the weak or weary, only unrelenting wind, howling over its frozen wastes. During the long winters, blizzards blurred the line between sea and sky for days at a time, obliterating all detail from the world—or nearly so.

A lone red island marred the blankness, built of steel and claimed by the cold. Frost crept over its railings like a sparkling fungus, and snow dusted its platforms, derricks, tanks, and pipes. Though huge by most standards, the island was dwarfed by the surrounding ice field, which unfurled endlessly from the foot of its walls. But the red island endured it all, dutifully extracting black crude from the seabed below.

For a while nothing much happened. Jorda followed the tether of an absent sun, locked in its white prison, where only the air was free to roam, pointlessly blowing snow from one tundra to another. Only a residual blue twilight lit the days, briefly marking what had once been afternoon, until darkness reimposed its reign of gloom. Yet, despite its hostility, the north wasn't totally abandoned. Scattered inhabitants scraped by in whatever way they could, buoyed by the promise of change, because the long night couldn't last forever. Not even in Jorda.

The sun returned as a streak of gold, barely skimming the horizon before it sank moments later. But it kept rising higher each day, and minutes of light stretched into hours. New sounds stirred the air. The ice squeaked and snapped, then froze again—over and over—until the white plain split for good. Dark lines shot out in a thousand directions, reticulating through the sea ice, and channels flowed once again.

A stocky head breached in one of those channels. Hot vapor spurt from his nostrils, whirling into a sky the color of a dead tooth. A coat of chestnut fur covered his body, but what truly kept him warm was his six-inch-thick blubber. He also had four flippers, bushy whiskers, and two tusks protruding from his upper jaw. The head belonged to Mag, a giant marine mammal called a hvalross, perfectly adapted to such an inhospitable place. A smaller head soon joined his, this one belonging to Ingrid, who had softer features and elfin tusks.

"Blodstein," Mag grunted in a deep, cavernous voice. "Should be six or seven more days, depending on the weather."

Ingrid was pondering something even more distant. "I can't wait to smell a flower again," she said dreamily. "I'm sick of snow."

"Have you thought of a name yet?"

"I have . . . Zoya for a cow. Vorvan for a bull."

"Vorvan, eh? He should be named after me."

"One Magnus is *plenty*," Ingrid teased. She'd always used his full name, but everybody else called him Mag.

While the couple filled their lungs, a clammy mist swept up Blodstein's vertical walls, obscuring its highest platforms from view. Except for blood and a couple species of flowers, the color red was exceedingly rare in Jorda and all that scarlet looked like a mirage to them, alien to nature itself. A piece of pack ice drifted into the steel caisson, which cleaved it in two, creaking and squealing.

"Time to go," Mag said gruffly.

"I know, but it's nice to watch sometimes."

"The ice break?"

"Ja. It makes me calm, like life will unfold exactly as it should."

Mag looked at her with wry bewilderment. "It won't if that pup comes early."

"This isn't my first trip to Valp Rock," Ingrid said, mildly irked.

"Whatever you say, sea bunny."

Mag and Ingrid had just begun their spring migration, traveling as part of a great herd many tens of thousands strong. Being a fiercely independent sort, each hvalross chose their own path north, but all of them stuck close to solid ground, since resting in open water carried two risks: First, the currents might whisk them someplace unpredictable. Second, fearsome toothed whales known as spekkhoggers prowled Nordhavet during the warmer months, primarily hunting newborns, but they'd settle for a pregnant cow.

The couple trekked north using ice channels like unreliable roads. They shifted unpredictably and dead-ended on occasion, forcing them back to a main artery. Somewhere in the Rullende Sea, nasty weather and unnavigable waves delayed them by a couple days. Then they turned west toward the retreating ice sheet and eventually hauled onto a frozen plain, flanked by pressure ridges where the ice had buckled. These formations looked like huge glass shards pointing toward the sky, fused together in a frigid crucible and blanketed by snow.

Geese came trumpeting from the south over the next few days. They were the first to resuscitate the air with sounds of life, but definitely not the last. Droves of expectant mothers were also arriving, giddy with anticipation, and the makeshift camp soon transformed into a floating nursery. Every newborn prompted a celebration, with older cows shouting across the ice, offering support and guidance to first-timers.

Pupping season always stirred up a buzz among the herd, but bulls were typically less enthusiastic, and Mag was less enthusiastic than most. He quickly became exasperated with all the maternal banter, crying pups, and geese honks; but rather than lose his temper, Mag dove to the shallow seabed, where a watery static drowned out any objectionable noises. Down there, he spent most of his time rooting for buried clams, the preferred food of almost every hvalross. They pried them open by creating powerful vacuums in their mouths. It was said that Sjøfar—the sea god they worshiped and, in whose image, they were modeled after—had sucked the color out of snow and that's why it was so white. Mag, however, thought this was a load of nonsense. He had no patience for gods either.

Their fifth night on the ice Ingrid went into labor and the contractions grew so painful that she screamed at the stars. As if in response, strawberry light streaked clear across the heavens: a phenomenon known as the Nordlys. This seemed to pacify her, and she gave birth to Vorvan a few hours later, welcoming him into the world with a tender smile.

"Born under a fire Nordlys," Ingrid cooed. "He'll carry Vulkan's blessing."

"Huh," Mag snorted. "Vulkan can stow his favors."

"Oh, come on, you big ogre. What's wrong with a little help from the Urguds?"

"Plenty. Don't go filling this pup's head with gods, mermaid tales, lucky shells, and all that other dritt. They've never done anyone a drop of good. Only strength matters and my pups are the strongest of them all."

"Uff! The only thing bigger than your chest is your head. Nobody doubts you're an impressive bull. That's as plain as water is wet," Ingrid said in appeasement. Then she nuzzled Vorvan's nose, already mustached with whiskers. "Did you know you have the greatest papa in the whole herd? Ja, you do!"

The trio took some time to recover, dozing together in a cozy pile, with Vorvan tucked safely under Ingrid's flipper, where he nursed, nodded off, and nursed again. Sometimes he snuck glimpses of the world beyond, but the sun's reflection dazzled his vision with colorful spots, and it hurt to look after a while.

Four days after Vorvan's birth, Mag cleared his throat and declared, "Time for me to go."

"Do you have to leave so soon?" Ingrid asked, looking wounded.

"I've got other cows to check on."

"I thought... Aren't we happy?"

"Of course, but nothing lasts in Nordhavet. You know that," Mag said, trying his best to sound consoling. Then he patted Vorvan's head, who stared wide-eyed at the giant looming above him. "I'll come back as soon as I can."

But Mag never returned.

This didn't exactly shock anyone, least of all Ingrid. Breeding alphas had lots of pups each cycle—dozens upon dozens in Mag's case—and even the most attentive fathers spread themselves thin. Thus, Ingrid was left to raise Vorvan on her own.

Later on, Vorvan would only remember snippets of those early days, since his impression of the world formed out of a haze, the same as any newborn. Every scene had a dreamlike quality and his attention jumped from one thing to the next: *That's too bright. Too warm. Too cold. Too far. Too close. I'm hungry. Something smelly came out of me.* However, thanks to his mother, life generally seemed warm and reassuring.

His first clear memory was of Ingrid humming a lullaby. It sounded blissful until she hit a minor key, tempering its sweeter notes with what he'd later come to understand as sadness. Vorvan held his mother closer and hoped this dark force would leave him unscathed. But despite having only experienced summer's gentle touch, he somehow recognized this wouldn't last, as if his forebears had passed down their burdens in the womb.

There was indeed something peculiar about the hvalrossan soul, their acceptance of hardship as an inherent part of life, even a pride that welcomed it. Perhaps one example was the herd's prevailing attitude toward pups, which could be summed up as sink or swim, though not necessarily in an unloving way. In fact, it was precisely love that made them demand strength in their offspring. Otherwise, they wouldn't be prepared for the trials that lay ahead.

With no time to waste, Ingrid coaxed Vorvan into the ocean the very week of his birth, where she steeled her resolve and watched him thrash around clumsily, but didn't offer any assistance. This seemed to jump-start his survival instincts, and an inner voice told him not to lose sight of the surface again—that from then on, he would have to fight for every breath.

Vorvan practiced several times a day and swimming came naturally to him, but his muscles were still weak. Whenever he got too tired to continue, Ingrid would inflate her throat sacs and cradle him with her flippers. Then, as the pair bobbed with the swell, she'd teach him new words.

"You were just swimming. *Swim-ming.* And what a great *swimmer* you will be!"

Vorvan babbled in response.

"That's right. And *what* do we swim in?"

More baby noises.

"Water. *Waaa-ter.* And who's that over there? Yegor. *Yeee-gor.*"

Vorvan's first friend was Yegor, a male cousin born to his aunt Grunhild, who looked as if she'd seen one too many winters and had a personality to match. But family meant a great deal to hvalrosses, especially on the maternal side, so Ingrid tolerated her sister's cantankerous moods. Plus, their pregnancies just happened to coincide, so they agreed to raise their pups together, a rather common social arrangement among the herd. Many pups were lost to mothers who turned their backs for a second too long, so it never hurt to have an extra pair of eyes.

"Why, that pup is no bigger than a baby barnacle," Grunhild remarked when she first laid eyes on Vorvan. "Trouble nursing?"

Ingrid didn't respond, other than appearing disgruntled.

"What? I'm just surprised. He's Mag's whelp, isn't he?"

"Vorvan has a healthy appetite, so I don't know why he's small. Probably just a late bloomer."

"Well, he'd better get to blooming, or summer will be over."

Ingrid glowered at her sister. "Must you always be a ray of darkness?"

Adding to the familial tension, neither mother had eaten much since giving birth, which not only made them short-tempered, but depleted their fat reserves and risked their milk running thin. To prevent this, they took turns foraging on the seafloor while the other kept an eye out for danger, as well as quashing any harebrained impulses the pups might have, of which they had plenty. If the cousins got hungry during this time, they could nurse from the opposite mother, but Vorvan only suckled from Grunhild as a last resort, since her milk tasted as if it had been aged inside a dank, dark cave.

But his aunt had some virtues, including the wisdom she'd gained from her many cycles of experience. This made her a good teacher, though one with exacting standards, prone to smacking them with her flipper should they repeat a mistake. It didn't matter that the cousins had only started speaking a month ago, and she didn't play favorites with her own pup. Of the two, Vorvan picked up on words and concepts faster, but that didn't mean Yegor was dumb, just a typical male who preferred testing his strength over knowledge—and he was as strong as Vorvan was intelligent. Both were plumping up nicely, but Yegor had outpaced his cousin by a wide margin, packing on as much as two pounds per day.

The ice retreated over the summer and the family followed it out to sea until the water became too deep. Then they relocated to Valp Rock, the biggest island north of Høyland. Its barren coastline offered little more than shingle beaches, wind-blasted plateaus, and scrappy lichens; but being far-flung and lifeless were part of its appeal. The farther out of the way, the less there was to worry about. And since most pups spent the summer on Valp Rock, it gave the cousins an opportunity to socialize outside the family, which mostly amounted to some tentative sniffing, awkward wrestling, and a playful bite here and there.

Later on that summer the mothers started sniffing the air more frequently, and this didn't escape the cousins' attention, who'd just gained the ability to form short sentences. Thus began the incessant questions.

"Are you scared, Mama?" Yegor asked Grunhild as she scanned a seemingly vacant beach.

"Quiet! I'm trying to concentrate."

"Maybe we should tell them now," Ingrid suggested. "They'll find out soon enough."

"Ja, tell us!" the cousins chirped together.

"What should I tell them, sister? That the world isn't all giggles and sunshine?" Grunhild sighed and turned to the cousins. "There are many dangers in this world, including creatures that would try to harm you. It's our job to keep you safe."

"Like what?" Vorvan asked, more out of curiosity than fear. He couldn't imagine anything wanting to hurt him. What reason would they have? He'd been a good pup so far and only misbehaved a couple times.

"We're searching for isbjørns."

"What're isbj—"

"Great white bears," Grunhild blurted before he could finish.

Ingrid added in a more patient tone, "Another mother said she saw one, but they almost never swim this far, so her eyes were probably playing tricks on her. Still, we'd rather be safe than sorry."

"What're bears?"

"You'll see them soon enough, near the Teeth of Skyggen,"

Grunhild said, perhaps a little too ominously for pups.

"What're the Teeth of Sky—of Sky—of *whatever* you call it?"

Grunhild moaned and lost her temper. "Always what, when, where, how, and worst of all, why. Want to know *why* we're scared of bears? Because they're big. They're mean. And their mouths are full of sharp teeth, ready to gobble up pups for breakfast!"

2
So Many Questions

Autumn arrived, and the family started migrating south to a chain of ancestral beaches known as Kaldsand. Instead of the direct route most adults chose, the mothers decided to take the Slank Channel through the heart of the Dampende Archipelago, then the Strait of Hylebard east to Drivved Bay. This would double the normal distance, but they preferred that to risking the Rullende Sea and its notoriously violent storms.

The journey would be an arduous one for pups, especially the first leg from Valp Rock to Høyland, which was a full day's swim due south. Their departure began well enough. The sunny morning presented them with calm seas, though—somewhat perversely—this clouded the pups' judgment. In spite of repeated warnings from their mothers, they fooled around, tuckered out early, and started begging to hitch a ride. Then, once they'd recuperated, the cousins pretended to race each other, laughing and telling their mothers to hurry up.

"That's it!" Grunhild huffed. "No more coasting on my back!"

"But my flippers are falling off," Yegor whined.

"I don't care. You're too heavy, and I'm too old."

"But, but . . . What if I drowned-ed?"

"You should've thought about that before abusing my kindness."

When they finally hauled ashore that evening, the cousins conked out within minutes, leaving their mothers to trade isbjørn watches throughout the night. Neither got much sleep as a result, but both looked fresh as they roused their groggy pups before dawn.

However, this ability to make due with little rest was hardly unique to Grunhild and Ingrid. Most hvalrosses had a habit of keeping strange hours and if the situation warranted, they could stay awake for several days in a row. Nordhavet's bounties were vast but fleeting, and all its creatures had to capitalize on the opportunities while they lasted.

Later that morning, the family approached the Slank Channel under a drizzly, peach-gray sky. An eerie tranquility had settled over the ocean, and pack ice was drifting out of the mist like pale, half-drowned cadavers. Watching this, Vorvan pondered the reasons why ice would float and rocks should sink, since both materials appeared equally solid, until an odd sound interrupted him. A high-frequency click had just pinged through the water. When Vorvan turned to ask his mother about it, he froze in his tracks, registering the terrible expression on her face.

"Swim to the ice!" Ingrid shouted. "*RIGHT NOW!*"

"What do you see?" Grunhild yelled back.

"A pod, closing fast."

"Where?"

"North. They just dove."

"Swim, puppies! Go! Go! Go!"

Like electricity jumping from node to node, the panic transferred from Ingrid, to Grunhild, to Vorvan, to Yegor. For the first time in their lives, the cousins felt adrenaline surging through their veins and raced to the ice as fast as they could. Vorvan was an agile swimmer, but Yegor got winded quickly and bolted for the surface. While gasping for breath, he tried to locate their pursuers, but a thick haze concealed any signs of danger. Wait! Something was out there—ghostly sails, cutting across the water—then gone again, back into the murk. Seeing that Yegor had lagged behind, Grunhild backtracked, pushed him below, and they were off again.

The family made it to the pack ice, and the mothers rammed their pups' rumps to launch them onto the platform. Then they hooked their tusks onto the edge and hauled themselves out.

"What's happening?" Yegor asked with dilated, shaky pupils.

Before anyone could answer him, a colossal nose poked out of the water. It belonged to a whale ten times the size of their mothers, mostly black, with a white belly and white ovals behind its eyes. Its mouth cracked open—almost smiling—to reveal a horrendous set of pointy, conical teeth. A muscular tongue curled back toward its throat, as if to beckon them inside.

"What is that, Mama?"

"Spekkhogger. DO NOT get close to the edge."

Other whales rose from the depths, joining the first, to assess the problem at hand. They moved with disquieting grace for such large animals, but their keen eyes were even more frightening, conveying the cold intelligence of accomplished killers. A minute or so later, they sank below the surface, filling the ocean with their haunting clicks and sirens.

"Are they leaving?"

"Nei. Always listen for clicking. They're getting close when your bones start to vibrate. And when they get quiet, swim as fast as you can. Quiet doesn't mean they're gone. Quiet means they've found you."

Suddenly, out in the fog, the ocean began to swell and silhouettes loomed up behind a watery veil. The whales torpedoed toward the pack ice, then dove a few feet away, pumping their flukes in unison.

"Hold on!" Ingrid shouted as a wave gushed over the ice. Vorvan started to slip, but she caught him just before he was swept away.

The pod tried this technique several more times. Then the biggest one struck the ice from below, using its nose like a battering ram. The cousins were lifted up, whimpering for mercy, while terror clawed at their minds. Only a five-foot-thick slab of ice stood between them and the hungry beasts—this thing that would soon melt away, as if it were never there—but it existed just long enough to keep them safe.

After a few more minutes, the whales soundlessly retreated into the deep. The family felt some relief, but it was a hard emotion to trust, and over the next hour or so, they searched the drifts of mist for dark triangles that would indicate dorsal fins. None materialized. It seemed the spekkhoggers had finally given up the hunt, leaving the cousins to tremble like cottongrass in the wind.

"I don't want to go in the water," Vorvan pleaded.

"Can't we stay here?" Yegor begged.

Ingrid's eyes shined with empathy. "I know, puppies, I know. We won't leave before the mist clears, I promise."

The family lingered until sunset broke through the last wisps of pink fog. Not that it was any safer then. Spekkhoggers hunted day or night, which meant they'd have to test their luck at some point, but the pups refused to budge until they saw another group of hvalrosses pass by. Feeling reassured, they followed them toward the shallow refuge of the Slank Channel, listening for clicks the entire way.

Vorvan had a nightmare that night. It was vague at first—just a jumble of unpleasant sensations—until he suddenly found himself swimming into an enormous, shadowy mouth. Saliva strings as thick as ropes stretched between its teeth. He didn't want to keep going, of course, but something compelled him forward, to search for a way out. The monster began wrapping its tongue around him: soft and warm, slick with excretions, as if death had a womb of its own, meant to take someone back to the other side.

Vorvan woke up in a cold sweat, screaming, until everyone else woke up too. Ingrid felt sympathetic, especially after the day they'd just had. She pulled Vorvan close and gently shushed him, humming a lullaby until he fell back asleep.

The next morning the pups did their best to shrug off the ordeal, and the mothers tried to keep the mood light. Ingrid said silly things, and Grunhild tolerated as many questions as they cared to ask. By that afternoon they were playing again—not only with themselves, but other yearlings as well. They were passing more hvalrosses than they hitherto knew existed, and it started to imbue their journey with a sense of anticipation and adventure.

Their fall migration kicked off a long string of firsts, beginning with their first wildflowers just beyond Høyland's beaches. Ingrid made a big fuss about the fragrance of saxifrage, but the pups weren't as impressed. Yegor sneezed uncontrollably for a few minutes, then swore he'd never sniff another blossom for as long as he had a nose. Vorvan's opinion wasn't quite so extreme, though he did think flowers held more charm at a distance, for peppering the grasses with unusual colors.

The cousins also saw their first volcano to the west of the Slank Channel. It rose from the heart of Ildens Trone, the largest island in the Dampende Archipelago. A humongous mushroom cloud had issued from its crater, swirling into the sun's golden light.

"What's that?" Vorvan asked, his gaze panning up.

"A fire mountain. We call that one Vulkan's Breath."

"Are fire *mounties* dangerous?" Yegor chimed in.

"It's *mountains*, dear. *Mount-ains*," Grunhild corrected. "Nei, they're not dangerous. Not unless they explode and rain down fire, turning the land black with ash . . . But don't worry, that hasn't happened for a very long time."

Yegor gulped at the possibility, however remote.

For ten days the family funneled past a coastline riddled with geysers, fumaroles, and geothermal springs. Grunhild swore the latter had healing properties and insisted on taking a soak in Vulkan's Tear—a pool sporting bands of color that spanned the whole rainbow—but its sensory appeal came as a mixed bag. In fact, most of the steaming landscape reeked of rotten eggs. When the cousins interrogated their mothers about this phenomenon, their best and only explanation was that Vulkan—the fire god—liked for the land to smell that way. "Mud pots are Vulkan's flowers," Ingrid said.

The family reached the southern end of the Slank Channel and veered east into the Strait of Hylebard, so named after their god of storms, and a fitting name at that. Whenever they came up for air, powerful gusts buffeted the surface and freezing rain bombarded them with icy pricks. The howling wind grew so loud at times that it was impossible to hear anything else, so they passed much of the day in silence. Then the skies cleared to the south and soaring peaks pierced through the clouds, most so steep that snowfields couldn't cling to the slopes.

"The Teeth of Skyggen!" Ingrid announced with a dramatic flair. "Tall enough to bite the heavens, so the old poets said."

"*Wowww!*" Vorvan exhaled in one long breath, aghast at the scale of the world.

"Impressive, eh?"

"Uh-huh."

"Are mountains the highest thing?" Yegor asked.

"That we know of . . . But Jorda is a huge place and we can't go where it gets hot."

"What's 'hot'?"

"It means really warm, like when Grunhild soaked her achy parts in Vulkan's Tear. That water was hot."

"And stinky," Yegor added, waving in front of his nose.

The family hopped along Høyland's southern coast, followed by the scattershot islands of the Labyrint Isles, most of them little more than glorified rocks. This leg of their journey took them eight days, and on a rare windless morning, they finally crossed to the other side of the Strait of Hylebard.

They were still swimming after nightfall, when an offshore platform flared over the horizon, looking as if a miniature star had stopped short of plunging into the ocean. The family paused just outside its skirt of light and watched a crane extend toward a ship like the proboscis of a giant insect. A massive hose ran through the boom, and red lights blinked along its frame, their every detail mirrored perfectly by the glassy water.

"What is it, Mama?" Yegor asked, agog.

"Dødbringers made it, so we don't know. The herd calls it Blodstein."

"What are dødbringers?"

"The most dangerous creatures in all of Jorda."

"Badder than bears and whales?"

"A thousand times worse, or they used to be. It's complicated."

"Why is it comp—compli—*complimicated*?"

"It's *com-pli-cated* because they used to kill us and now they don't."

"Kill us? For eating?"

"Sometimes for eating. The pink ones wanted our tusks."

"But why?"

"Who knows? Jorda is full of mysteries."

"Like what?"

"Enough! You're driving me stark raving krilly," Grunhild halfgrowled, half-sobbed. "I don't know everything about this blasted place."

Yegor winced sheepishly. "Sorry, Mama. I promise I won't ask a question again. Not one more for my whole entire life."

The family looped into the mouth of Drivved Bay, where they saw a conical monolith lancing the sky. This time the mothers preempted the cousins' questions by explaining what they were about to do.

"Listen up!" Grunhild ordered. "That's Glorystone ahead. It's the broken tip of Sjøfar's tusk—the great Sea Father—and one of our most sacred sites. Hvalrosses have lined up for thousands of cycles to touch the stone for courage, which is exactly what you two are going to do. Goof off at your peril!" She eyed the cousins with suspicion, prompting Yegor to giggle nervously.

Other hvalrosses had already queued up next to the granite pillar, and the family got in line. A few dozen gulls were perched at the top, squabbling with each other. Their screeching sounded so shrill that it seemed to stab through Vorvan's ears and straight into his brain. Even so, he found himself absorbed in the moment and when his turn came, Vorvan touched the guano-splattered stone with genuine reverence. Its surface had been worn smooth from so much contact, but he could still distinguish the vestiges of a few near-obliterated runes.

"What's this, Mama?"

"It's a rune. Our ancestors carved them into rocks. Each one took a whole tusk to create."

"Why?"

"Because tusks are softer than rock."

"I mean, what are they for?"

"Runes are words frozen in time. Our ancestors made them so they could talk to us from the past."

"They talk to us through the stones? What do they say?"

"I don't know. None of us do, not even the elders. Those are the old ways and we've forgotten them."

"Gone forever?"

"Probably."

Vorvan pondered all the trouble his ancestors went through to carve the runes. Even at his tender age, he understood how much tusks meant to a hvalross, not only for their utility, but as a symbol of status and pride. To sacrifice one willingly was almost unimaginable, and he concluded the words must've been very important.

"I'm sad, Mama."

"About not knowing what the runes say?"

"Ja . . ."

"Me too, Puppy . . . Okei, time to go. We're getting close!"

Ingrid wrapped her flipper around his back and hurried him along.

The next day the family passed an abandoned dødbringer settlement along the south shore of the Drivved Peninsula. With their mothers' blessing, the cousins fanned out to explore the ramshackle forest of pilings that once served as a dock. A small river bisected the densest cluster of buildings, and they ventured down it a ways, investigating the rusted gadgets that littered the riverbanks. The dereliction was obvious even from the water—all those clapboard houses slipping off corroded nails to be dismantled by time's little hands. Metal sheets squeaked in the breeze, and many other unattributable sounds could be heard rattling and knocking in the distance. The cousins soon asked to leave, cowed to silence by its oppressive atmosphere of loss.

The family put a mile between them and the ruins before they camped that dusk, but a few stranded tankers were still visible on the horizon, their silhouettes looming against a salmon-pink sky like the carcasses of colossal, mechanical whales. Vorvan suspected that if dødbringers could create such massive objects, they also must be horrendously big and powerful themselves, but rather than confirming, Ingrid swatted away his questions like pesky flies.

"Go to sleep," she yawned. "You've got a big day tomorrow."

The following morning, a larch trunk floated by the family. The elements had stripped the bark down to cracked, pearl-gray wood, totally smooth except for a few spikes where branches used to be.

"What's that?" Yegor squawked as he hid behind Grunhild.

"Silly pup, that's just a log. It won't bite you."

The cousins swam out to prod the oddity.

"It smells funny!" Yegor shouted, screwing up his nose at the piney scent.

"You'll get used to it," Ingrid called back. "Drivved Bay is filled with them. Just wait until you see Kaldsand."

"Is it alive?" Vorvan asked.

"Not any more. It's the skeleton of a plant called a tree."

"Like grass, only bigger?"

"I think so. To be honest, I don't really know. Trees grow much farther south, and only a few hvalrosses have ever seen a living one."

"I will!" Vorvan proclaimed with absolute certainty.

His mother looked amused. "Oh, you *will*, will you? I suppose Vorvan the Brave has a nice ring to it."

As the family traveled deeper into Drivved Bay, The Teeth of Skyggen receded from view and a swath of tundra opened up on its southwestern shore. Sedges daubed the ground in autumnal colors like gold, bronze, and copper. Interestingly, not a single scrawny conifer could be seen across the sweeping landscape, but true to Ingrid's word, great snarls of driftwood swirled wherever rivers met the sea.

In the last remnants of daylight, the family spotted dark shapes stippling the shore. The journey had taken them twenty-nine days in total, most of them packed full of grueling swims and never-ending questions, but they'd finally made it to Kaldsand.

"There's the great herd!"

Yegor gawped at the numbers. "Whoa! They just keep going, and going, and going, and go—"

"Enough!" Grunhild snapped.

"How many of us are there, Mama?" Vorvan asked.

"Too many to count. Thousands upon thousands, just in our

herd alone."

"There are other herds?"

"Ja, on the opposite side of Nordhavet."

"Can we visit them?"

"Oh, Puppy, that's *much* too far to swim."

"How far?"

"Imagine doing what we just did, but twenty more times."

As riveting as their migration had been, Vorvan felt dog-tired and couldn't begin to fathom this. Then again, it thrilled him to know that so much of Jorda was left to explore. "Will I get to see all of it someday?" he wondered out loud.

Grunhild scoffed, "Ha! We haven't even finished this trip."

"Why aren't we going where the others are?"

"Because I said so, that's why."

Ingrid gave her sister a cross look. "What your cranky aunt means to say is that there's a special herd—one just for pups."

3
The Disappearing Sun

The nursery beach lay inside a small lagoon surrounded by grassy bluffs. The mothers explained that pups were sequestered from the main herd due to their size, but skipped over the potential for death by squashing. What could they say? That most alphas would trample their own mothers to win a fight? It would only invite a torrent of questions, further eroding Grunhild's patience.

In any case, the cousins felt safe and snug, and the late autumn days were filled with carefree antics. They had a grand time socializing with the other yearlings, learning all kinds of games, silly poems, and crass songs. But play was never *just* play, and an undercurrent of competition flowed beneath every interaction. The cousins naturally began comparing themselves to their peers, which mostly confirmed what they already knew: Vorvan had the brains, Yegor the brawn. But while intelligence had its perks, Vorvan soon discovered that males were chiefly judged by another measure.

"Wow, you're *even* smaller than me!" one pup exclaimed with unabashed relief.

"Your papa must be shrimpy," another one remarked.

"Are you *sure* you're a male?" taunted yet another.

These slights flustered Vorvan, but Ingrid told him not to worry—that he'd hit a growth spurt soon—and since she'd never lied to him before, he let the pangs of inadequacy roll off his back. Besides, nobody truly made fun of him with Yegor in tow, indisputably the biggest pup of them all. It didn't take a genius to figure out that if you offended one cousin, you made an enemy out of the other.

◆

The sea gradually froze as the yearlings continued to get acquainted, and the nursery herd eventually relocated to the ice, so their parents would have access to better clamming spots. Then the days atrophied into gloom, growing shorter and colder, until one afternoon the sun sank below the horizon for good.

"Mama, Mama! Where's the sun?" Vorvan asked, fearing it would never return.

"It's gone away for a while, Puppy. It won't be back until the next thaw."

"But why?" Yegor chimed in.

"Because the sun must tend to all Jorda's creatures. They need its light too."

"How do you know it will come back?"

"Because our sagas go back thousands of cycles and for as long as there's been a herd, the sun has always returned."

"I miss it," Vorvan said wistfully.

"I do too . . . Guess we'll just have to make ourselves cozy until it comes back. Let's see, maybe I can squish the cold out of you two."

Ingrid wrapped her flippers around the cousins, squeezing them together until they squealed and giggled like lunatics.

"Ah, we can't breathe! Stop it! *Stop* it!"

"Oh, was that too hard?" Ingrid asked, feigning ignorance. Then she nuzzled their sensitive whiskers, which never failed to both soothe and tickle them.

Jorda plunged into its shadow-form for the next two months, leaving only the moon, stars, and Nordlys to give the world its tenuous shape. Even their mother's faces darkened into featureless blobs, so the cousins learned to rely on their other senses, and smell became the primary method of separating friend from stranger.

Then the deep freeze really set in. It drained the sun's touch from every last pebble, teaching the cousins what it meant to be truly cold—so cold that even the memory of warmth seemed as fanciful as a dragon. They tried to play with the other pups, but after an hour of exposure, the shivering became unbearable.

In place of roughhousing, storytelling became the main diversion from the harsh winter. Adults usually recited heroic sagas from memory, but the cousins competed over who could dream up the most outlandish scenario. For instance, Vorvan once concocted a story about a whale who ate some bad krill, which caused him to fart, which caused a wave, which grew into a bigger wave, which turned into a tsunami, which capsized a ship. He acted out the whole thing under the dramatic light of a full moon: the whale's strained face, the fart noise—he paid special attention to that—and the desperate flailing of the sinking dødbringers.

Ingrid narrowed her eyes. "Why are all your stories about farts?"

"Not true," Yegor shot back. "The last one was about a burp!"

Ingrid finally thought that was funny, and they laughed and laughed until it annoyed Grunhild. Her jowls shook with disapproval as she pretended to clear her throat of fake phlegm: *eh-he-he-emmm!* And it nearly caused the other three to burst at the seams.

Ingrid also enjoyed making up her own stories, but unlike the cousins', they had clear plots and character arcs. The hero always conquered an obstacle or villain by the end, learning an important lesson in the process. The only variable that changed was the context. Sometimes they took place during perilous expeditions to the south, or the glorious battles of the Berserker Age, but the cousins' favorite setting was the ritual of Vintersang: a brawl, singing contest, and orgy all rolled into one. The mothers largely glossed over that last part, other than noting pups came as a result, which backfired somehow, further inflaming the cousins' curiosity. Lucky for them, there were plenty of catchy songs and fight scenes to distract from the particulars of mating.

◆

One afternoon in the dead of winter, a fierce blizzard blew down the Teeth of Skyggen and swept over the ice sheet. Vorvan had never heard anything so loud and an existential terror welled up inside him, fueled by the world's hostility, as if Jorda itself wished them dead. Not knowing what else to do, he yelled at the top of his lungs and the wind whisked his voice away like a dried-out leaf. Then the snow poured down in huge drifts, turning the day's faint illumination into a slate-colored gloom. Eventually the whiteout grew so opaque that Vorvan couldn't see or smell anything except for what lay directly in front of his nose.

The skies cleared by morning, and the herd gradually exhumed themselves from the mounds of snow that heaped over their back. As friends and family checked in on each other, a gruesome rumor spread like wildfire until it reached the mothers, who regarded each other with ashen faces. They didn't want to tell their inquisitive pups at first, but eventually relented, sharing that a storm-blind yearling had wandered off. The adults found a trail of blood leading toward the mountains, which could only mean one thing: isbjørns.

The cousins were frightened, of course, but it was hard to say of *what* exactly—and their mothers' description of "a huge white bear" didn't help, because they'd never come face-to-face with a bear either. Thus, their imaginations ran wild, and Vorvan pictured a whale hopping around on giant bunny legs, since snow hares were the only land animal that he'd seen, and whales were the scariest.

When polar night ended a great cheer went up around the herd.

"Is the sun back for good, Mama?" Vorvan asked expectantly.

"Until next winter, by Dagnatt's will."

"Who's Dagnatt?"

"She's the singing Urgud, who also controls the sun, moon, and seasons."

"Okei . . . And what's an Urgud?"

"Well, you already know of three: Vulkan, Hylebard, and Sjøfar. The Urguds created everything you see, which is a rather long and involved story. And it's high time you learned it! Just not from me."

His aunt groaned, "At last! Let the elders fend off all their whats, whys, and hows for a while."

"What does Grunhild mean, Mama?"

"In a few days the elders will come to teach you about the herd's history."

"How do you know?"

"Because they always come five days after the sun appears."

4
Of Elders & Urguds

Five afternoons later, the family left the ice sheet and hauled onto a deserted beach where snaggles of driftwood marked high tide. Snow piles had accumulated beneath their leeward branches, sculpted by the wind into curious shapes. Vorvan was studying one when about a dozen elders came ashore and fanned out among the yearlings, just as their mothers had promised. He spotted two grandcows, but the rest were grandbulls, and all of them appeared exceptionally ancient.

"What do we do, Mama?" Vorvan asked.

"Go on by yourselves. Class is just for pups."

As Ingrid and Grunhild relocated to the perimeter—where they could keep an eye out for isbjørns while chatting with the other mothers—the cousins gathered around the nearest grandbull, punctuating one end of a semicircle formed by the other yearlings. Vorvan had never seen an older hvalross in such proximity and noted his features in the glancing half-light: leathery cheeks, snow-white whiskers, lumpy nodules encircling his neck, and bright pink skin where his fur had thinned.

"Greetings, young ones, my name is Starik," the grandbull announced, grabbing their attention with his mellow baritone voice. "I'll be your teacher going forward, and you'll gather around me every afternoon until spring to learn where you came from. Our history stretches back thousands upon thousands of cycles, and I've spent my entire life accumulating this knowledge. That said, we'll be lucky to chip an icicle off the old iceberg, so there's no time to waste. Who can tell me what Glorystone is?"

"It's one of Sjøfar's tusks," said a pup in the back.

"That's right, it's the tip of Sjøfar's tusk. What's your name?"

"Freya," she replied pleasantly.

"Well done, Freya. Can you tell me why Sjøfar's tusks are sticking out of Drivved Bay?"

She shook her head.

"Can anyone else?"

No one volunteered.

"Not to worry, pups, that's precisely why you're here. So prick your ears, cause here we go." Then Starik modulated his voice to sound even grander than it already did, as if his authority emanated from the mountains themselves. "A long, long time ago, much closer to the beginning of everything than we are now, there existed a gigantic spekkhogger named Skyggen. He prowled the black ocean beyond the clouds, searching for stars and worlds to devour, but no matter how much he ate, his appetite could never be satisfied. This presented a problem for the Urguds, because—"

"Where do the Urguds come from? My mother said I had to ask you, because she's tired of all my bubblebrained questions."

The class snickered and Starik squinted at the chubby pup next to him.

"And *who* are you?" he snorted.

"Yegor."

"It's rude to interrupt, Yegor, so raise your flipper next time. But to answer the question, Urguds are immortal and have existed ever since Dagnatt started chanting the great song of time. Got it?"

"Got it." Yegor nodded vigorously, hoping to make up for his offense.

"Now, as I was saying, Dagnatt made time and the rest of the Urguds formed all the objects in the black ocean. Then they swam among the countless worlds, impregnating them with their spirit, the nature of which depended on the nature of the Urgud. Vulkan, the fire god, made beasts of molten rock, and Hylebard fashioned creatures from wind, rain, and lightning, because he's the god of storms. Make sense? Good!

"After the Urguds breathed life into each world, they rested for a time, giving their new offspring a chance to worship them. And that was important, because Urguds crave attention above all else. Without it, they tend to get ill-tempered, then bad things happen. Ja, you, the fidgety one in the back—what's your name and question?"

"Um, Astrid. What kind of b–b–bad things?" she stuttered.

"Well, *Um-Astrid*, let's see here . . . fireballs raining down from the heavens, oceans freezing over for all eternity, permanent diarrhea. Those sorts of things."

"Oh, that's p–p–pr—that's really bad. How do we make the Urguds happy, then?"

"By letting me finish my story," Starik replied brusquely. "Obviously, the Urguds wanted to protect their creations from Skyggen, so they assembled above a cold, lifeless planet, which wasn't special in any way except that they predicted Skyggen would swallow it next. Can any of you guess which planet that was? Ja, you, the tiny pup next to the fat one—your name and question?"

Vorvan said his name and answered "Jorda," suddenly feeling self-conscious about his size. The entire class appeared to be sniggering at him except Freya, who smiled sweetly instead. Or did he imagine that?

"Sharply observed, Vorvan," Starik acknowledged with a nod of approval. "So, the Urguds needed a plan to save Jorda, but being prideful, all of them demanded to use their own ideas. Vulkan wanted to blast Skyggen with lava, Hylebard declared lightning bolts were mightier, and Frostskader—the ice goddess—insisted on freezing him. The problem with all these suggestions was that Skyggen hailed from the Shadow Realm and could vanish into nothingness at the first sign of trouble. Thus, the Urguds argued for many thousands of cycles—which wasn't very long for them—but even so, they wasted enough time that Skyggen had nearly reached Jorda. That's when Sjøfar proposed an ambush. Ja, you, the one with the rash—name and question?"

"Oleg. Where's the Shadow Realm?" he asked, scratching himself with his hind flippers like a dog.

"Right behind you!" another shouted while pointing at his shadow, and the whole class tittered.

"Settle down, you little mud-rakers," Starik grumbled, "though you aren't exactly wrong. The Shadow Realm is all around us, formless as the wind, but just as real. There are only a few ways to interact with it, but we'll cover those later. Anyway, the surprise attack won consensus among the Urguds, so Sjøfar swam down to the tundras of Jorda and turned white as snow, which made him look like a very large hill. There he waited until Skyggen loomed out of the black ocean, blocking the stars entirely, and when he was just about to swallow our world, Sjøfar leapt up and delivered a blow so powerful that it snapped his tusks.

"Skyggen crashed into Jorda and trapped spirits flew out of him like birds. They came from all the other worlds he'd eaten and that's why Jorda has a little of everything. Then his blood flowed over the land, which turned into rivers, which spilled into oceans, which sprang forth all the plants and animals you see. His teeth formed the mountains that surround us and his stomach sank below the oceans, creating Underverden, where our souls go when we die. And finally, the broken tips of Sjøfar's tusks became Glorystone and Sorrowstone, our two holiest sites and reminders of his greatness. Ja, Yegor? Takk for raising your flipper."

"Does it hurt?"

"Does *what* hurt?"

"Living in Sky—um . . . I forgot his name already, but in his belly."

"Well, nobody's come back from the dead to tell us, so how would we know? But even if it does hurt, there's glory in pain. You see, Jorda flourished as a deathless paradise for a time, but then Skyggen's hunger started rumbling from the Shadow Realm, threatening to spill into ours, because creation and destruction are linked together, same as day and night. If the Urguds didn't intervene, Skyggen would eventually be resurrected, so in their infinite wisdom, they decreed that all life on Jorda must die to satisfy him. Some might call this a curse, but as hvalrosses, we're honored to protect the universe from Skyggen. Any questions?"

Every flipper shot up at once. Vorvan couldn't believe what he'd just heard, that it was their sacred duty to die.

"But we were *just* born!" Oleg cried out, getting notably itchier.

"I'm n-n-not ready!" Astrid whimpered.

"Me neither! Me neither!" the whole class mewled.

Starik appeared caught off guard. "Calm down, everyone. I'm not saying *right* now, but we all have to die at some point. Look at me! I've only got a few cycles left—if I'm lucky—but whenever my long night comes, I'll sink to Underverden with pride, knowing my duty is done."

The class shrugged off this point. Not that they hadn't grown fond of Starik in their brief time together, but he seemed impossibly old and they just couldn't envision wearing his whiskers someday.

"Where's Sorrowstone?" Freya asked.

Starik relaxed a bit, grateful to change the subject. "Good question. Sorrowstone is close to Glorystone, but on the opposite side of Drivved Bay's mouth. We only go there to mourn the dead, so let's hope you don't visit any time soon . . . Ja, Vorvan?"

"If oceans are blood, why aren't they red?"

"Because Urgud blood is made of pure elements like fire, water, snow—"

"And their farts are the wind!" Yegor blurted out, unable to contain himself.

"Quiet, Yegor!" Starik growled. Then he tried to rally the class's flagging attention, but they already had a lot to chew on, particularly that their souls were destined to feed a galactic whale. "Okei, I suppose that's enough for now. See you all tomorrow, blizzards and bears be damned!"

For the rest of winter Starik taught them about all kinds of Urguds—so many that Vorvan began to suspect gods inhabited every pebble and personally blew each bubble—but a few were held in greater esteem than the others. The five primary ones were Vulkan, Hylebard, Dagnatt, Frostskader, and Sjøfar. Hvalrosses generally regarded Sjøfar as the most important, which made sense, since he governed the seas, where they needed the most assistance. Vorvan wondered if Sjøfar ever got annoyed with the herd, since they were constantly badgering him for favors. Maybe he got cranky like his aunt did. Now that was a scary thought: Grunhild the God. It would explain why the oceans were so temperamental.

The class eventually moved onto beings that weren't technically gods, but confounded belief in their own way. Throughout their history, intrepid explorers brought back whispers of underwater forests, undead sharks, colossal squid, and even stranger things lurking in the abyss. The most celebrated of these adventurers was named Modig the Bold, and Starik recounted a particularly riveting legend in which Modig battled giant crabs. During the most gripping scenes, Starik's eyeballs bulged for emphasis, looking as if they might pop out and roll across the sand. This worried Vorvan a bit, but Modig's exploits so thoroughly captivated him that Starik could've shot his eyeballs clear over the mountains, and he'd still ask him to finish the story.

Class continued onto other subject matter, and each day brought another whirlwind of information. They covered social taboos, geography, key historical events, tidal theory, natural phenomena, and much, much more. Starik clearly hadn't met a topic that didn't fascinate him, and Vorvan soon felt like an overflowing cup, incapable of holding even one more drop, no matter how passionately it was offered. Yet the knowledge kept pouring into his ear. How could one grandbull store so much in his withered, old head?

5
How to Eat a Clam

As the herd prepared for its spring migration, class ended and Vorvan fell into a minor funk. He'd grown to appreciate learning about the past and missed Starik's stories, scary as they could be; but the mothers ignored his sulking and began teaching lessons of their own—ones arguably more important than history—like how to find food.

Though most pups nursed until they were two, the mothers started taking the cousins on foraging dives to practice their navigational skills. It didn't go well initially. The seabed could be a challenging environment under ideal conditions, let alone when the currents whisked the water into a low-visibility pea soup. Even small disturbances—just a quick sweep of a hind flipper—kicked up sediment clouds thick enough to cause intense disorientation, and Vorvan bolted for the surface the first time he lost his bearings.

"I couldn't—[cough]—see," he sputtered, having swallowed some muddy seawater. Yegor popped up shortly after doing the same.

"You two are trying to see with your eyes, aren't you?"

"What else would we use?"

"Your whiskers."

"*Whiskers?*" the cousins echoed.

"Close your eyes and keep them closed until I tell you."

Ingrid brushed her flipper lightly across their cheeks, then she did the same with her tusk. Like all hvalrosses, the cousins had exquisitely sensitive vibrissae, and Vorvan started noticing just how much information his follicles passed along to his brain. More than enough to distinguish between squishy and hard.

"Now open your eyes. Which time did I touch you with my tusk?"

"The second time." Vorvan was utterly certain.

"Exactly! That's seeing with your whiskers."

"Oh, I get it now," Yegor said mischievously. Then he closed his eyes and bumped into his cousin on purpose. "Hei, Vorvan. I can *see* your butt!"

Next, they covered edible animals and since hvalrosses weren't picky eaters, that included pretty much anything they could outswim.

"What are the things we eat?" Ingrid quizzed one day.

Vorvan sat up straight, collected his memory, and recited, "Shrimp, crabs, fish, snails, um . . . worms, squirts, sea cucumbers, um . . . and octopuses."

"What did he forget, Yegor?"

"Yucky dead whales!"

"Good thing we only eat those in an emergency," Ingrid agreed, winking. "What else? I'll give you a hint: It's the herd's favorite food!"

"Oh ja, clams!"

"That's right. And before long you'll be eating thousands a day, but let's start with one for now. Stay put, I'll be right back."

Ingrid slid into the water and the cousins killed time by competing to see who could burp the loudest.

"Will you two knock it off!" Grunhild grumbled, having been woken up from a nap.

Then Ingrid hauled out and spit several clams on the ice. "Let's practice."

"Uh, how?" Vorvan had seen his mother eat tons of shellfish, but the precise mechanics of opening them remained a mystery.

"It's easy. Put a clam between your lips, then move your tongue in and out until all the air sucks out of your mouth, like so." Ingrid picked one up, slurped out the meat, and spit the empty shell back onto the ice. "Now you try."

Vorvan chose the tiniest clam of the bunch and gave it a shot. "-ines no- o-ening," he slurred, struggling to enunciate.

"Keep going. Move your tongue faster."

"Al-ight."

It felt awkward at first, but Vorvan followed his mother's instructions until the vacuum intensified and his cheeks puckered in like a suckerfish. Then its shell suddenly relaxed and the clam meat hit the back of his throat, causing Vorvan to gag, which Yegor found so hilarious that he nearly choked to death himself.

With her eyes still shut, Grunhild huffed, "For Sjøfar's sake, keep it down! Jorda already has enough bubblebrains without you two losing your minds."

Another cycle passed, and the cousins turned two in early spring. After the sea ice melted, the family spent an idyllic summer on Valp Rock, lounging on its cobble beaches at the end of the long, sunny days. Further inland, white poppies perfumed the slopes of scree and puffins returned to their rookery, excavating burrows along the upper reaches of the plateau. The cousins had been fully weaned by this point and were bulking up at an astonishing rate, having perfected not only their clamming technique, but many others.

One morning as Vorvan nibbled a colony of orange sea squirts, daydreaming about being a famous explorer like Modig the Bold, a sonorous grunt boomed through the water and shocked him back to reality. Though hvalrosses were rowdy creatures, this sound was significantly louder than even the noisiest bull, so he got Ingrid's attention and gestured to meet at the surface.

"What was that noise?" he asked nervously.

"A singing whale. We call them knølhvals."

"Will they try to eat us?"

"Nei. Knølhvals only eat small things."

"How small?"

"Krill and herring mostly, but lots and lots of them."

"Okei. That's not so scary."

"Well, they're bigger animals than anything you've seen yet—ten times the size of a spekkhogger—so even though they mean no harm, it's best to keep your distance."

From then on, the knølhvals sang for several hours each morning, serenading the whole of Nordhavet, whether they liked it or not. Grunhild kept shouting at them, denouncing their music as the scourge of tranquility, though they obviously couldn't hear her. With no respite in sight, she cracked after just a few days, insisting the family travel south to get as far away as possible. Nobody objected. It was best to give Grunhild what she wanted.

Their departure started pleasantly enough, under clear skies and a bracing sea breeze. Arctic terns surfed the air just above the waves, flitting about acrobatically, with their white forked tails catching the brilliant sun. The herd called a gorgeous day like this Dagnatt's gift, and everybody seemed to be in good spirits—even Grunhild—buoyed by the prospect of a little peace and quiet. But then the currents picked up and the swim abruptly turned into a slog, so the family decided to take a breather about halfway to Høyland.

"I'm so tired," Yegor sighed, resting his head on Grunhild's shoulder.

"Me too, chubby cheeks," his mother said sweetly.

Vorvan liked seeing his aunt in an affectionate mood, which was becoming more common now that the cousins could fend for themselves and weren't so demanding. Then, just behind her, he spotted something poking above the water: what looked like a small knobby island, only this one seemed to be staring at them with a grapefruit-sized eye. "What's that?" he shouted, prompting the family to spin around.

Ingrid laughed and said, "They must've heard you bad-mouthing their singing, Grunhild."

"Bah, they're just jealous. Everyone knows we're the most melodic creatures in the sea." Then she started berating their visitor, "Go away, you stupid tone-deaf whale! Don't you understand we're trying to get away from you?"

The knølhval just blinked at her, slowly and without a hint of malice. A little further in the distance, a different whale leaped into the air, twisted to the side, and slapped its gangly pectoral fin against the surface, spraying water so far that it splashed the family in the face. Vorvan was astounded that something of such magnificent bulk could become airborne, even for a second. As mellifluous as they were, hvalrosses certainly couldn't do that.

Suddenly, something blocked the sun and Vorvan looked up just in time to see a gargantuan belly soaring overhead. Ingrid screamed a few words, but before he could process what they were, the knølhval slammed down and water roared past his ears. Everything went dark—just faraway bubbles, popping through a void. Then a whale siren split the silence like a crack of lightning. It jolted Vorvan back to consciousness, and he shot to the surface.

"Puppy!" Ingrid bawled, enveloping him in her flippers "Thank Sjøfar you're alive."

"Where are Grunhild and Yegor?" he asked anxiously.

"I don't know... Listen, I need to check the seabed, but it's too deep for you. Stay here and watch out for more whales. Okei?"

"Okei."

Without wasting another second, Ingrid dove while Vorvan cried out for his missing family at the surface, terrified that he'd never see them again. Every time his mother popped up without news, his heart sank a little further, and the luckless day dragged on until they had no choice but to continue heading south. Just as the midnight sun stooped to its lowest point, dimming the world into a gloomy shadowland, they hauled onto the beach, utterly exhausted. But neither slept a wink.

The next day they scoured every beach, spit, and lagoon on Høyland's north shore, accosting any passerby within earshot, but no one had seen hide nor hair of Grunhild or Yegor. Still, they kept searching—day after bitter day—until their throats grew hoarse from yelling so much. It was a horrible time and Vorvan cried all the tears he had to give.

"Why did the knølhval do that to us? Was it because Grunhild yelled at them?"

"I don't think it was on purpose, Puppy."

"Then, why is this happening? Did we make the Urguds mad?"

"Sometimes bad things happen and it's no one's fault."

"Does that mean . . . Are they dead?" Vorvan hated to ask, but not asking felt equally terrible.

"I know just as much as you do. But Grunhild is tougher than a whole pod of spekkhoggers, and she'd save Yegor with her last breath, so let's choose to believe in her strength." Ingrid said this as confidently as she could, but the quaver in her voice betrayed a trace of doubt.

Instead of responding, Vorvan stared at a strand of dead kelp and searched its rotting blades for answers, as if they could account for all the world's awful chaos.

Autumn came and the sea ice inched south again, threatening to choke off the Slank Channel. When Ingrid suggested they needed to migrate with the rest of the herd, Vorvan plopped down on the beach like an obstinate rock, refusing to move for mothers and bears alike. Ingrid pleaded with him, explaining that Grunhild would know where to go, but leaving somehow felt like they were abandoning hope.

Vorvan eventually capitulated, though with some resentment, and their migration back to Drivved Bay was a somber affair. He crossed paths with many other pups along the way, but didn't have the heart to play with strangers. It would only make him miss Yegor more.

"Will it always hurt this bad?" he asked one day, seemingly out of the blue.

Ingrid gazed into his injured brown eyes, working out what to say, and finally offered, "To love is to open yourself to hurt. If they're really gone, the pain will heal someday, but not without leaving a scar. The only solace we have is that—whether in Jorda or Underverden—everything meets again in the great song of time."

6
Little Fish, Big Fish

Another cycle passed and Vorvan turned three in early spring. Though he still grieved Grunhild and Yegor, their absence didn't weigh as oppressively over the mornings, threatening to crush him as soon as he woke up. Acceptance had come gradually, until one day, he stopped referring to Grunhild and Yegor in the present tense and switched entirely to the past. But just as soon as they settled into a new normal, something else upset the balance.

They were resting on the north shore of Høyland, when Ingrid said, "Puppy, I love you more than anything—more than all the stars in the black ocean—but in two cycles' time, you'll have to strike out on your own."

"Nei, I don't understand. Why can't I stay with you?" Vorvan blurted out, feeling a whirlwind of emotion. It was all he could think to say, but in truth, he already knew that calves were supposed to leave their mothers at five. Somehow, he'd convinced himself that they'd be an exception to the rule.

"It's just the nature of things. Cows need to keep having pups or the herd risks dying out, especially now that we number so few. . . Anyway, that's still a long way off. I'm not trying to worry you, but we have to discuss the future with that in mind."

Vorvan averted his gaze, struggling not to weep, and focused on the horizon instead. Pastels had banded across the sky—periwinkle, lavender, pink, and peach—all blending together in a perfect field of color. Back on the ground, a breeze tousled the tussock grass just beyond the beach, where an arctic fox chased a hare, caught it, and pranced off to its den.

"It's time for you to learn how to navigate the herd," Ingrid continued. "The *real* one."

"What do you mean?"

"It can be very dangerous."

"I've already seen the herd. It's not that scary."

Ingrid smiled at his innocence. "I know you're brave, but it's different when you're surrounded by all those bodies. There's less room to maneuver, and the big bulls are more intimidating than you realize."

"It's okei, Mama. I'm ready." And truthfully, Vorvan felt more curious than afraid.

After an uneventful migration to Drivved Bay, they set off for Kaldsand on a brisk morning. Along the way Ingrid explained that finding the herd would take some persistence. Aside from the mini-territories staked out by breeding alphas, hvalrosses tended to congregate wherever they pleased, and the herd's exact location varied from day to day, influenced by the vagaries of ice formations and food stocks.

They eventually spotted the herd and hauled out on its periphery, where the wind was busy whipping up glittering sidewinders of ice crystals and sand. Then, with Vorvan squinting to keep the grit out of his eye, Ingrid led them into the fringes, shouting guidance over her shoulder.

"You have to see not only where everyone *is*, but also where they *will be*. Always be mindful of an escape route, because the herd can stampede without warning. And watch out for alphas! Vintersang is coming up and they'll be even bigger hotheads than usual, so it's best to stay out of their way. Sometimes all it takes is an innocent bump or a funny look to set them off."

Ingrid was right about the herd: Vorvan had never been so acutely aware of his smallness. Mountains of flesh hemmed him in on all sides and nappers rolled their paunches every which way, showing little regard for their neighbors. On top of that, rival males were parading around in defiance of each other, growling and brandishing their tusks like pompous sword fighters. Dominant bulls occasionally jabbed smaller ones to reaffirm the pecking order, causing those nearby to scatter and jostle against each other. Yet none of these behaviors resulted in any full-blown fights, since everyone was saving their strength for Vintersang.

As Vorvan avoided being squashed, a particularly impressive alpha galumphed up the beach, cutting a swath through the hordes. Sand whirled around him dramatically and his tusks gleamed in the bluish half-light. Seeing the respect he commanded, Vorvan soon lost himself in a reverie, hoping to grow that magnificent someday, so it came as a complete shock when the bull stared at him and shouted, "Hei, Ingrid! Over here!"

"Who is that?" Vorvan asked, trying to read his mother's stony expression.

"That's your father."

"Papa?" he repeated, his mouth agape.

"Ja. I guess you're going to meet him, cause here he comes."

As Mag strutted over, Vorvan saw the other males wordlessly defer to him like so many beach bugs hopping out of the way. He'd never felt so many things at once: pride, awe, fear, excitement, and several emotions he couldn't put into words.

"Ingrid, it's me! Your big ogre," Mag announced, cocking his head to the side and puffing out his massive chest.

"I can *see* that."

Then he glanced down at Vorvan. "Know who I am?"

Vorvan was tongue-tied and simply nodded.

"Guess you're due a growth spurt, aren't you?" Mag chuckled, then patted Vorvan on the head, perhaps a little harder than necessary.

"What do you want, Magnus?" Ingrid asked tersely.

"Just to say hallo." He let the air out of his lungs, doubling as a sigh. "Going to Vintersang this year?"

"Nei."

"But the pup is three. Shouldn't you be ready?"

"Not until he's five, you know that. And *your* pup's name is Vorvan."

"Vorvan, of course... How was your migration?"

"Fine," Ingrid offered begrudgingly.

An awkward silence followed with Vorvan's eyes bouncing between their faces, praying one of them would speak.

"Just as charming as I remember," Mag finally said, breaking the tension. "Well, hope you can come, even if it's only to watch. I know how much you enjoy my singing." Then he winked at Vorvan. "See you around, pup."

Vintersang arrived and when it was Mag's turn, everybody shielded their ears as usual. His whistling sounded like a wet fart, his roaring like a shrill seagull, his grunting like a whale with a bowel obstruction. All this indicated that he'd never practiced a day in his life, but being such a perfect male specimen, it hardly mattered. Mag amassed the largest harem anyway, the same as every other Vintersang in recent memory.

Shortly thereafter, Mag established his floating kingdom on the pack ice, where he held court for the duration of winter. His harem consisted of mostly cows and a few young heifers who'd never given birth before; but all were beautiful, infatuated, and willing to attend to his every need, mating or otherwise.

One day after polar night ended, Vorvan developed a high fever and became so delirious that he could barely tell his left flipper from his right. Ingrid needed to track down a healer without dragging him halfway across Drivved Bay, but ever since Grunhild disappeared, it had been hard to find a minder she trusted. Pups stopped going to oral history at the age of two, and though she could technically dump Vorvan on the outskirts of class, that was a much farther swim than her other option, however distasteful. Still, there was scarcely a safer place to stash a pup than a harem, so that's how Ingrid found herself foisting Vorvan on Mag for the first time.

"What am I supposed to do with a sick pup?" Mag grumbled.

"Keep him alive!" she shouted while rushing off. "And teach him something while you're at it!"

"Like what?" he yelled back.

"Something only a father can know!"

"What in Underverden does that mean?"

"Figure it out!"

As soon as Ingrid dipped below the waves, Mag turned to Vorvan and grunted, "We'll get to the bull stuff later."

"But I want to learn, Papa!" The excitement made his head hurt, but Vorvan didn't care. He'd never spent quality time with his father before.

"Papa is tired. He had a long night, you know . . . seeding the clams."

"I don't understand."

"Never mind. Hei, Orina! Get over here."

A particularly voluptuous heifer stopped whispering with the other cows and approached them, already bubbling with enthusiasm. "Is he really yours, Maggy? He's *sooo* cute! I could just slurp him up."

"Ja, mine. He's sick or something."

"Uff, you poor thing. Don't worry, I'll take good care of you."

Though disappointed, Vorvan was too ill to protest, so he followed Orina to the edge of the pack ice, where she proceeded to make lots of infantilizing noises. Due to his size Vorvan appeared more puplike than he actually was, which he pretended to hate, but being lavished with a beautiful heifer's attention had its appeal.

While Orina tested out her budding maternal instincts, Vorvan observed his father's behavior from afar, trying to learn how to be a proper bull, which looked fairly glamorous at first glance. His harem brought gifts of food and Mag picked through their offerings like a bored emperor, tossing aside any morsels that displeased him with comments like: "Yuck." "Gross." "Too slimy." "Do better next time."

After eating his fill Mag shouted at Orina across the ice, "I'm taking a nap."

"Of course, Maggy! Whatever you desire! I'll keep a whisker on your precious sea dumpling."

"That's nice," Mag yawned, then nodded off.

Vorvan also settled down for a nap and as Orina draped her flipper over his side, he wondered if it dishonored his mother to let a stranger hold him so tenderly. Besides Ingrid, no one had treated him with such affection—not even Grunhild, who despite being family, had all the warmth of an icicle. If this was life with a harem, Vorvan resolved to become just like his father; and so he drifted off, unwell but happy, until a loud splash burst his fevered dreams.

A young bull hauled onto the ice, humped over to Mag, and bellowed, "Wake up, you old sack of blubber!"

The harem gasped at this recklessness stunt. Not only did the young bull appear significantly lighter, but also untested. Their skin told the whole story: Battle scars cratered Mag's chest, and the challenger looked as fresh as a flower.

"Who the føkk are you?" Mag barked.

"Zver."

"Zver, eh? You're just a little fish to me. Better swim away before a big fish eats you," Mag warned with patronizing amusement.

"Shut up and fight, drittsekk!" Zver snarled back.

As the bulls measured each other, the harem made a ring around the combatants and a crowd gathered in the water. Brawls were relatively rare outside of Vintersang and everyone wanted a juicy bit of gossip to swap during breathers.

"Is this really happening?" Vorvan asked Orina, worried he might be hallucinating.

"Ja, your papa is about to defend his territory."

"Will he kill him?"

"Nei, only teach him a lesson."

The bulls pointed their noses skyward, snorting vapor into the soft blue twilight, then clashed ivory sabers. Zver found an opening and stabbed first, puncturing several inches of custard-colored neck fat. But Mag didn't seem fazed in the slightest. Instead, his eyes glittered with rage and the subsequent battle—if you could call it that—looked painfully lopsided. Mag drubbed the regretful young bull for a few minutes, then headbutted him, and Zver slumped to the ice as the flame blew out of his eyes. The crowd roared with approval.

Orina crowed to Vorvan, "See! Nothing to worry about. Mag is the greatest alpha in the whole herd. You should be so proud."

"I am. But why is Papa sitting on his head?"

"Huh . . . I've never seen him do that before."

Zver regained consciousness and found himself beneath Mag's rump. "I concede!" he sniveled, trying to project his muffled voice.

"What's that? I can't hear you," Mag said, smirking.

"I GIVE UP!"

"Nei! That won't do at all. Say 'I'm a bubblebrain and I have a little minnow dick.'"

"I'm a bubblebrain."

"Louder!"

"I'M A BUBBLEBRAIN."

"*And*?"

"I HAVE A LITTLE MINNOW DICK."

"Much better."

Finally, in a gratuitous display of dominance, Mag cocked his backside and released his bowels, sending muddy rivulets down

Zver's head. The closest onlookers let out a collective groan and waved their flippers in front of their noses. Then Mag shoved Zver aside and when he rolled to a stop, the crowd fell into hysterics, seeing the whites of his eyes blink through a mask of brown filth.

Vorvan's head started to spin between the fever, stench, and laughter—melting the world into a blur of sensations—and when he regained consciousness, his eyes had inadvertently locked with Zver's fiery gaze. Animosity seemed to scorch the air between them, and Vorvan felt the urge to communicate something, even to apologize. Being small himself, he hated to see anyone embarrassed and knew what it felt like to be on the butt-end of a joke. Why did his father need to gloat on top of winning? But all these thoughts came muddled together, leaving only a vague wish that life weren't so cruel and ugly.

A few seconds later, Zver slunk back into the water under a barrage of hoots, boos, and jeers. Then the delighted crowd shifted their attention to the day's hero, who was already basking in their adulation.

"Magnus the Magnificent!" Orina declared when it was her turn. "I can only hope our pup grows up as big and strong as you are!"

"Takk. Just comes with the territory."

Vorvan could only manage a worshipful stare in his loopy state.

"Get well soon," Mag said, chuckling. Then he returned to his mob of admirers.

Long after the moon had risen later that night, Ingrid hauled onto the ice and immediately put her flipper against Vorvan's forehead.

"How do you feel, Puppy?" she asked with equal parts concern and optimism.

"Not good."

"Ja, you're burning up. Let's find someplace cozy and I'll give you the medicine." She turned to Mag. "Did anything happen while I was gone?"

"Nothing I couldn't handle," he said, cocksure as always, with Orina smiling demurely behind him.

"Okei, tusen takk. And sorry for being so cold lately. You really came through for us today."

Under the light of a crescent moon, Vorvan traveled in a daze until they found a spit of snowy sand near a river delta. At Ingrid's behest, he chewed a floral-smelling leaf from a plant he'd never seen before. The tart liquid it produced made his tongue retract in horror and he passed out moments later, but the healer's medicine did the trick.

His fever broke by the next morning and he spent several more days convalescing. Then, once his energy returned, Vorvan regaled his mother with a play-by-play of how Mag clobbered Zver, surely a story for the ages. The sagas could keep Modig the Bold. Vorvan's new hero was alive and breathing.

7
A Tragic Flaw

Their mating duties fulfilled, Mag's harem disbanded toward the end of the winter and each cow began feeding in earnest, preparing for a pregnancy that could last up to sixteen months.

Thus unencumbered, Mag chose to lavish his leisure time on Ingrid and Vorvan, the latter of whom couldn't have been more delighted. Not that Grunhild and Yegor could be replaced, but the addition of a long-lost relative made the world feel whole again. Besides that, Vorvan was fascinated by his father's masculine swagger, because it contrasted so starkly with his mother's measured intelligence, which was a fine trait for a cow, but less so for himself. According to all he'd witnessed so far, males were meant to be cocky and fierce to the point of belligerence—not sensitive—as Vorvan would quickly come to realize.

It didn't take long for Mag's charm to wear off, as he never complimented Vorvan, nor did he find any of his talents worthy of encouragement. To the contrary, whenever Ingrid left them alone, his father peppered him with insults about his size, calling him names like powderpuff, snowflake, minnowdick, shrimptits, or worse. They stung, of course, but Vorvan tried not to show it, since his father treated every situation like a wrestling match, trying to flip them to his advantage.

For instance, one day while Ingrid foraged below, Mag goaded Vorvan at the surface.

"Shouldn't you have tusks by now?"

"I *do*, look!" He curled his upper lip to prove it.

"Those nubs? I've seen longer on a bucktoothed hare."

"Hei! They're not that small."

Mag chuckled dismissively. "Relax! Mean words will be the least of your worries before long."

Then Ingrid popped up and saw Vorvan looking deflated. "What's wrong?" she asked.

Vorvan didn't respond, just glared at the water.

"He's a little cranky. Probably needs a nap," his father suggested.

From then on Vorvan distanced himself from Mag, though he couldn't help but puzzle over his intentions. Why was he hanging around them, anyway? Besides parenting, a role that clearly didn't interest him, his father could have his pick of cows. Not that Ingrid wasn't beautiful, but so were the rest of his harem, and Vorvan concluded she must hold some special allure. Perhaps Mag enjoyed the sport of gaining her affection, because she didn't fawn over him like the others. And yet, if the stars aligned, Ingrid could still be won over by Mag's roguish confidence, though only to a point. The fun ended as soon as she got wind of the verbal abuse, as evidenced by a conversation Vorvan overheard in the middle of the night.

"Stop calling him names or leave," Ingrid whispered angrily.

"I'm just trying to toughen him up. We both know the weak ones don't make it."

"Keep your voice down! Of course, I want him to be ready too, but Vorvan can't do anything about being small. No matter how much you push him, he'll never be as big and strong as you are, so quit rubbing it in his face."

"Ja, I wonder *whose* fault that is."

"You're such a drittsekk."

"Okei, okei. I'll lighten up."

"Takk."

"On one condition..."

Shuffling noises followed.

"Nei, Magnus!" Ingrid hissed, rolling over in exasperation.

Mag let out a sigh and nodded off a few minutes later. And while the great lummox snored, Vorvan brooded over his parents' conversation. He'd always acknowledged the possibility of being small forever—at least to himself—but it still hurt to hear his core anxiety confirmed so unequivocally. On top of that, it was now obvious that Mag's paternal posturing had all been an act to mate with his mother.

The next morning Vorvan found Ingrid looking sternly at the horizon. It seemed Mag had snuck away without a word of farewell, leaving only a shallow depression in the snow and a lingering air of disillusionment. Later on that day, Ingrid would brush off his abrupt departure, though Vorvan could still sense her loneliness and even felt some sympathy for his mother. But he also hoped that Mag would never return. As an absence, he'd certainly do less harm.

A few days later while foraging for clams, Vorvan and his mother took a breather, each surveying the rolling, white tundra in silence.

"Why am I so little?" he asked sullenly.

Ingrid appeared caught off guard for a second, then she put on a playful face. "But you're not finished growing yet. Not even close! Who knows, maybe you'll turn into a whale." She dipped her mouth in the sea and gave his face a squirt.

"Quit it!"

"Okei, Puppy . . . Tell me, what's troubling you?"

Vorvan grasped for the right words. The other pups didn't mock him often, but he still detected pity in their eyes, and Vorvan didn't want pity—he wanted respect, just the same as Mag. Also, he'd been having nightmares about isbjørns, spekkhoggers, and dødbringers. Although he felt safe now, he knew Ingrid wouldn't be around to protect him forever. She'd already announced as much.

"But what if I'm always small? Won't I be the first to get eaten?"

"What makes you think you'll always be small?"

"Because that's what you told Mag. You said I'll never be as big as him."

Ingrid furrowed her brow. "I'm sorry... I didn't think you were awake. But the truth is, no one can predict the future—not even your mother. And if you do turn out small, it's not the end of the world. Look at me." She paused to point a flipper at herself.

"What about you?"

"I'm small, but nobody's eaten me yet. Not so far as I can tell."

"Come on, Mama. You're a cow. I'm going to have to fight."

"We *all* have to fight, Puppy, one way or another. And all of us must learn to accept the things we cannot change, because if we dwell on what's outside our control, it'll only make us feel helpless. Besides, you're kind, clever, fast, strong, and none of us get everything we want. Understand?" Ingrid ended with an expression that radiated comfort and love, but also suggested that certain facts were as immutable as solid rock.

"Okei..."

They left it at that, but Vorvan struggled to repress his disappointment. He saw how intelligence and agility might be beneficial for his general survival, but not social status. After all, bulls weren't quizzed on history at Vintersang and even singing seemed to be of secondary importance, because contestants had to survive several days of brutal fighting before a single note could cross their lips. When it came to males, only one thing mattered: Big equaled better.

That night Vorvan imagined himself transforming into a giant, as if the intensity of his desire could alter reality all on its own; and though he recognized the world didn't work this way, it upset him to discover that he was the same old runt the next morning. Despite his mother's reassurances, being diminutive still felt like a terrible curse, and he vowed to do anything to fix this flaw in himself... anything at all.

◆

A warm spell hailed the arrival of spring and Drivved Bay's ice sheet split into a mosaic of squares, triangles, and polygons. One sleeting gray morning not long after, Ingrid explained they wouldn't be migrating to Høyland this time.

"I know. That's why we went to Kaldsand, so I could practice. *Remember?*"

"Right... Well, you navigated the herd so skillfully that I'm sure you're ready for the next challenge."

"Okei, Mama. Wherever you want to go."

"That's my brave pup. Oh, I'm so thrilled to show you Sommersand! I know how much you like exploring new places, and this one is special—our true home—next to the richest waters in all of Nordhavet."

Vorvan noted a cloying tone and wondered whether Ingrid was trying to make amends for some perceived failure. But as upsetting as the last month had been, he didn't blame his mother for letting Mag worm his way back into their lives. He'd been charmed too.

Like any big change, the news they were headed to Sommersand stirred up a mixture of excitement and anxiety; and while the pair journeyed north, Vorvan imagined picturesque beaches, as well as various scenarios in which he'd be crushed to death under a tsunami of blubber.

At the end of the second afternoon, they set up camp on the ice sheet that rimmed the Drivved Peninsula, where several other pairs of pups and mothers were already gathering. The choppy seas had been slow-going that day and after exchanging a few pleasantries, everyone settled down for bed.

Meanwhile, clouds churned around the distant Teeth of Skyggen, hurtling down its precipices like an avalanche of angry vapor.

The sky soon turned overcast, blocking out the last of the sun's enervated rays. Vorvan watched his mother regard all of this warily, looking sapped of energy, as if she were attempting to lift a boulder with just her eyes.

"Are you afraid of the clouds, Mama?"

"Ja, a bit."

"Don't worry. A little snow can't hurt us."

Ingrid brightened a shade. "You're absolutely right. How'd I get to have such a wonderful pup?"

Vorvan felt good about this interaction and hoped to always be so calm in the face of uncertainty, which caused a new question to pop into his head: "Do you think I'll be as brave as him someday?"

"As brave as *who*?"

"Mag. He isn't afraid of anything."

"Puppy, I have no doubt that you'll overcome every obstacle put in your way."

"But how will I know the right thing to do?"

"Just remember to listen to Jorda. It's always telling you something. The trick is being quiet enough to hear it."

Then a sudden gale blasted across the ice, scattering the first snowflakes of a blizzard, so they huddled together with the other families, forming an outpost of warmth amid a hostile frontier.

Ingrid started humming her lullaby, something she hadn't done since Mag breezed through their lives, and though Vorvan couldn't hear very well, he still felt the vibration in her chest and fell into a peaceful sleep. Whatever his fate—even if he never grew another inch or gained another pound—at least Ingrid's love would be there to guide him through the trials that lay ahead.

Well into the middle of the night, Vorvan was dreaming about a pleasant, green summer when Ingrid rolled on top of him. He protested being squished, but then a noise cut through the raging weather: a roar he knew in his bones didn't come from a hvalross. His mother screamed at him to run away. Scarlet mist stained the sky and a red snout lifted up, stark against the whiteout, flashing fangs as long as daggers. Vorvan instantly recognized that this must be a dreaded isbjørn.

The bear dug its claws into her flank like meat hooks, pinning Ingrid in place, then clamped onto her neck. Hearing his mother's heart-rending cries, Vorvan sprung up without a second thought and bit down on the bear's paw, sinking his teeth through its thick fur, straight into flesh. The enraged isbjørn pulled back with Vorvan still dangling from the end and swiped at him with the other paw, but he wouldn't let go—not for all the pain in the world. Blood started gushing down his face and though unable to see, he could smell the beast's sour breath as it rushed to finish him.

"Leave him alone!" Ingrid shouted, impaling its back foot with her tusk.

The isbjørn howled and flung Vorvan so forcefully that he sailed across the ice and slid off the edge. Cold water surged around him and where he'd been slashed across his brow, the salt burned ferociously. Vorvan popped up a few moments later and heard his mother screaming—a harrowing, sea-curdling sound. Then she went silent.

"Mama! Mama!" he cried and cried, struggling to get back to her, but there was so much blood that he kept slipping off the ice.

Other hvalrosses had woken up by that point and fled to the water. "You have to come with us," a grandcow urged. "There's nothing we can do. And if you stay, that isbjørn will kill you too."

"Nei, I won't leave!" he yelled, but the stranger grabbed him and wouldn't let go.

Then the wind picked up, howling bitterly, the sound of which etched into his soul, marking him with an irrevocable darkness.

8
Freyland

Vorvan didn't know what to do after Ingrid died. He cried. He ate occasionally. He mostly slept. Once, he woke up with the wind biting at his skin and reached for his mother's warmth, certain that it had all been a terrible dream, but he was grasping at a phantom limb. The most important part of him had been severed, and the desperation to be whole again drove him mad with sorrow. He kept humming her lullaby and when that no longer brought comfort, he repeated the same words over and over.

"I'm not ready to be alone."

"I'm not ready to be alone . . . I'll never be ready."

Vorvan stayed behind as the rest of the herd deserted Drivved Bay and turned four by himself, passing two months in a grief-stricken trance. Then, purely out of habit, he migrated north and started wandering the Labyrint Isles south of Høyland. Hvalrosses rarely gathered there in large numbers, because the miniscule islands were so close together that isbjørns could easily swim between them. And since Sommersand had more than enough food to support the whole herd, why risk ferocious bears?

Thus, he found himself on a nameless island, miserable and on the verge of starvation, gazing blankly at a perfect azure sky. His mother would've hated to see him wasting away, but looking within, he found no appetite—or much desire of any kind, really. His body had become an empty vessel, like one of the brightly colored buckets that washed ashore sometimes. Did it hold something useful once? Who could say besides a dødbringer? His mother might've known, but she'd never be there to explain the world again, so it was better to ruminate on something else. Best not to think at all.

"What a gift from Dagnatt," a stranger remarked pleasantly, the first voice he'd heard in weeks.

Now that she'd mentioned it, the day had been extraordinarily cloudless, but Vorvan remained apathetic. "I guess so," he replied without looking.

"Are you all right?"

"*All right?*" he parroted back, weighing the words for meaning. They sounded hollow to him, like a pair of vacant shells.

"Those scars look so painful. What happened to you?"

He stroked the parallel grooves across the flesh of his left eye, still pink and angry-looking. Once the throbbing stopped, he'd forgotten the wound was there and hadn't considered it might leave a scar. But how to explain? There was no good way and Vorvan nearly shut down the conversation, but then he started sharing for some inexplicable reason—possibly out of indifference—or perhaps to test whether he could still talk.

"My mother d—" He hadn't uttered the awful words yet and it was hard to say them aloud. "She was killed by . . . by an isbjørn . . . I tried, but I couldn't stop it."

"I'm so sorry to hear that."

Neither of them knew what to say next, and the sound of water sloshing over tidepools filled the silence. Inside them lay a complete universe, where tiny creatures lived and died, oblivious to the drama unfolding just a few feet away.

"Is your father around?"

"Mag isn't my father . . . Or he doesn't want to be, anyway."

"Vorvan, is that you?"

Vorvan turned his head and looked at the stranger's face for the first time. "How did you know my name?"

"Vorvan, it's *me*, Freya! Don't you remember?"

The memory struggled to take root and branch out in any detail, but he eventually recalled her from Starik's class—that her laughter never seemed cruel. "Ja, I remember. Why are you here, Freya?"

"I live here. Well, not *here* here, but close. And not *I*, but *we*."

"Slow down. You're confusing me. Who is *we*?"

"The other orphans."

"What other orphans? I don't see anyone besides you."

"Come and meet them! They're not far. Oh, I forgot to mention, we have our own island!" She beamed with pride.

Vorvan took a moment to mull over her proposal. What was the point of making friends again? Wouldn't they just die or disappear? Or maybe they'd make fun of him for being small—not to mention his ugly new scar—but then he reminded himself that his mother was gone and nothing mattered to him anymore. At least meeting Freya's friends would give him something else to think about.

"Okei. I'll come."

"Just like that?"

"Just like that."

"I knew the island would do it. Follow me!"

The pair hugged Høyland's thawing coastline. Snowfields capped the distant hills, and springtime had painted the valleys a patchwork of greens, golds, and rusty oranges. Here and there, pools of meltwater flecked the sun and enormous boulders littered the ground like so many dinosaur eggs, ancient and carpeted with moss.

Vorvan followed his old acquaintance, asking no further questions, and Freya only offered a few words of encouragement, as if she feared too many interactions would give him cause to reconsider. Then she stopped abruptly and turned around, wearing a troubled expression.

"Vorvan..."

"Ja?"

"I didn't know how to bring it up before, but I have something else to tell you."

"Okei, what is it?"

"Yegor will be there."

His reaction came out delayed, as if an elixir of resurrection were gradually bringing him back to life. His vocal cords needed a little time to warm up first—to cough out the taste of death like cottony spider eggs—but Vorvan was soon yelling with excitement, "*WHAT*?! He will? Why didn't you tell me before?"

"I know, I'm sorry. But it's complicated. He isn't the same."

"What do you mean?"

"Um . . . To begin with, he probably won't recognize you."

"That's krilly! Yegor is family and we never spent a moment apart. He'll remember me."

"Of course. And *normally* he would, but he took a nasty blow to the head."

Hearing this, a terrible flashback of the singing whales hijacked Vorvan's thoughts—so much fear and heartache—week after week of searching in vain.

"You got quiet. Is everything okei?"

"Ja . . . You say he got hit on the head?"

"We think so. He washed up on Høyland, unconscious, and an old grandbull banged on his chest until he started breathing again. He's lucky to be alive, but gets confused sometimes and has trouble with the past. He couldn't even remember his own name at first. We had to teach it to him . . . again, and again, and again."

"It was a knølhval."

"A whale? How do you know?"

"I saw it happen. Just leaped out of the water and landed on us."

"Oh, I guess that explains everything . . . But hei, Yegor doesn't remember a thing. Maybe it's better if we keep it that way."

"Okei, sure," he agreed distractedly, because another question was preoccupying him. He feared he already knew the answer, but had to ask anyway. "And what about Grunhild? Did you find her too?"

Freya brushed at the sand nervously. "We did, her body anyway."

Vorvan took a moment to process the news, that Yegor had just risen from Underverden and Grunhild would stay there for an eternity. "We looked everywhere. We asked everyone. How could we have missed them?"

"I don't know. Jorda is a big place, even when you know where to look, I guess. Anyway, Yegor is doing fine now. I just wanted to warn you, so you weren't offended or something."

"Okei, let's hurry. I have to see him."

They cut south into the midst of the Labyrint Isles and eventually arrived at a tiny skerry that barely broke sea level. Its stratified rocks had a slight angle, indicating the tectonic forces that once thrust them upwards. Wherever a crack held a sufficient amount of soil, tufts of grass rustled in the breeze. A few cairns had been erected using stones splotched in amber-colored lichens, but besides those sparse details, the island had all the mystique of a barnacle.

"Welcome to Freyland!" Freya proclaimed triumphantly.

"It's named after you?"

"I was here first, so I got to name it. Those are the rules."

"But why *here*?"

"Aha! That's exactly 'why here.' We've been farming our own clams and nobody bothers to stop at this place. They just swim right by."

"Farming? Like we learned about in class?" Vorvan remembered Starik mentioning their ancestors farmed once, but that only worked because a code of ethics protected their harvests from being pilfered. After the old ways died out, it was every bull for himself.

"Ja. We stop by Freyland every spring and fall to spruce things up and check on the clams. Come on, I'll give you a tour."

Freya started pointing out landmarks as if they were the most interesting attractions in Jorda: "This is where Lars and Kara sleep ... And this is Nanook's spot ... And Yegor does his thinking here ... And this is where his pet puffin built a nest last thaw."

Freya kept going, but Vorvan had trouble focusing. All he could think about was Yegor: the unbridled joy over his being alive and the fear of what he'd become.

Realizing she'd lost his attention, Freya paused to survey the water. "I guess they're still out feeding. Should be back any time now ... Wait, there they are!"

Almost on cue, four hvalrosses hauled out and Vorvan spotted his cousin right away. He'd certainly beefed up in the intervening cycles. Males didn't fully mature until the age of fifteen, but aside from his baby face, Yegor already looked well on his way to becoming a gigantic bull.

Vorvan lifted his flipper and immediately felt self-conscious, because no one else waved back. Then a puffin swooped past Vorvan, startling him, and landed on Yegor's shoulder, where it emitted a kazoo-like sound. The stout black-and-white bird had a broad beak, clownish facial markings, and webbed feet the color of tangerines.

"Everyone, this is Vorvan. He's an orphan too," Freya announced cheerfully. Then she introduced Lars, Kara, and Nanook, who all greeted him cordially enough, but Vorvan was too fixated on Yegor to notice. Something about his tusks looked different: One was snapped off at the tip and the other had grown crooked, sweeping out to the side rather than toward the body. These deformities seemed to underscore the miracle of his survival. If the knølhval had landed just a tad closer, the result could've easily gone the other way.

"Yegor, don't you remember me?" Vorvan sounded hurt, despite Freya's warning and an honest effort to lower his expectations.

Yegor blinked hard, as if to recalibrate his brain, but seemed to hit a mental wall. "Mom says hei too!" his cousin shouted, much louder than necessary.

Vorvan briefly wondered if getting whacked on the head had given Yegor the power to commune with his dead mother. "Um, did you just say, 'Mom says hei'?"

Freya chuckled at Vorvan's confused face. "Mom is his puffin's name."

"Ja, Mom says hei," Yegor confirmed in a stuffy-nosed voice. At least that hadn't changed: Old Yegor suffered from allergies too.

Vorvan noticed Mom giving him an expectant look. "Uh, hallo," he said awkwardly, which seemed to satisfy her—or did he imagine that?

In any case, Vorvan was demoralized by his cousin's response and didn't exhibit much interest in continuing to socialize. The other orphans shifted around uncomfortably, sensing the tension, until Nanook changed the subject. "Hei, we're building cairns. You can help if you want." A few stacks of stones stood behind him, as well as a heap where one had evidently toppled over.

"Why are you making cairns?" Vorvan asked.

"Because that's what my ancestors did. And they tell everyone that this is *our* island."

"Ah, I see..."

"There's one last thing. If you're going to join us, you have to take the oath."

"Uh, what oath?"

"Glad you asked. Repeat after me:
As an orphan, I hereby swear:
To contribute my faithful share,
To make cairns and defend our turf,
Whatever comes out of the surf.
And should I break this solemn pledge,
May I fall off a steep cliff ledge,

So sharks can chomp off my dumb head,
Until I'm truly good and dead."

Vorvan repeated the lines, not with any great passion, but dutifully enough.

"Welcome to paradise! What did you think of the oath?"

"It's, um—very descriptive."

"Takk! I wrote it myself," Nanook said with a self-satisfied air. Then he turned his attention to Vorvan's left eye. "Cool scars by the way. How'd you get them?"

9
The Orphans

In the depths of his depression Vorvan had become so emaciated that his tusks wiggled in their sockets, but with the others encouraging a normal feeding routine, he gradually put on weight and the sheen came back to his fur. He started doing everything with the orphans: farming, building cairns, humming songs, and sleeping side by side. They didn't leave him out of a single activity—nor did he request to be—but after spending so much time alone, socializing took a period of readjustment.

He mostly watched at first, vigilant for indications their bond wouldn't last. Vorvan couldn't help feeling suspicious, not so much of their intentions, but that something good could happen to him. Yet no troubling signs came. Nobody mocked his size or told him to quit brooding, and whenever the orphans engaged him in conversation, he did his best to mirror their friendliness, always wondering if they could sense his warmth was forced. He didn't want to seem ungrateful, but the fact remained, he just wasn't ready to be happy.

More than anything, Vorvan searched Yegor for signs of his old friend. He shared details from their past—the first time they saw a larch log, or when Ingrid taught them how to eat a clam—hoping to jog his cousin's memory, but nothing seemed to break through the amnesia. An impenetrable shadow seemed to enshroud his early life, and for all intents and purposes, Yegor was a stranger now.

A month passed, and the constant summer sun not only encouraged a spectacular wildflower bloom, but also a habit of staying up late, which gave Vorvan plenty of opportunities to get acquainted with his new friends.

Lars and Kara were clever, good-natured siblings, though somewhat aloof about personal details, including how they became orphaned in the first place. Whatever had happened to them, they'd bonded like two mussels to the same rock and where you found one, you found the other. In fact, they seemed telepathically linked, wordlessly intuiting each other's thoughts and actions. It was an eccentricity Vorvan first noticed as they explained their process for settling disagreements.

"We make decisions as a group," Lars said.

"Nine times out of ten, it's about where to eat next," Kara added.

"If we can't agree, we vote." Lars.

"Each orphan gets one vote." Kara.

"When there were five of us, this always resulted in a winner." Lars.

"But you make six." Kara.

"So, there might be ties." Lars.

"Which complicates matters." Kara.

Vorvan felt his eyes ping-ponging between them until Nanook cut in, "You could give me two votes. That would solve the problem."

"Nei," the siblings said in tandem, as if they were used to fending off such ridiculous ideas.

Nanook—the groups' undisputed troublemaker—hailed from the mysterious herd on the opposite side of Nordhavet. According to his personal legend, the trouble started during a spring migration, when his parents contracted a miserable stomach ailment and were forced to ride out the illness on a beach. Nanook brought them all kinds of food, but no matter what it was, they couldn't hold anything down and eventually lost their appetite. Most of the herd had already passed by—not a healer among them—so all he could do was keep his parents warm until they wasted away and ultimately died.

Afterwards, with no one to help him navigate, Nanook got turned around and swam the wrong direction, which should've been a fatal mistake. Hvalrosses rarely crossed the vast polar ocean, so covering that kind of distance as an adolescent was almost unimaginable. But that's what Nanook claimed and though prone to boasting, he certainly looked different than the others, having stouter tusks, a broader skull, and a smoky coloring as opposed to auburn.

But as far as unique appearances were concerned, nobody could match Yegor, whose disheveled whiskers, ample jelly rolls, and crooked tusks made him a sight to behold. On top of that, he conducted himself about as gracefully as a stranded fish flopping across the shore and ran into anything within the realm of possibility. These collisions hurt due to his ponderous size, but it was obvious that he never meant any harm. Sea squirts were more menacing, and though the old Yegor had never been accused of bullying, it surprised Vorvan how gentle he'd become.

Despite not recognizing his cousin, Yegor started following Vorvan around like a stray animal, asking endless questions and making profound observations like "ice is cold." Vorvan wondered if he detected their former friendship on a subconscious level—or maybe he misinterpreted depression for patience—but whatever the reason, the pair soon became inseparable. For his part, Vorvan appreciated the distraction from missing Ingrid, because there was never a dull moment with Yegor around. He required lots of attention and could be quite naive, especially when it came to dødbringers.

For instance, one day Vorvan found himself explaining the importance of caution for what seemed like the hundredth time.

"Listen, there are two kinds of dødbringers. There's the kind *with* thundersticks and the kind *without*. Just because you don't *see* a thunderstick, doesn't mean they don't *have* one. You need to wait and watch first. Got it?"

"Got it," Yegor repeated, shaking his head emphatically.

"Do you really 'got it'?" Vorvan confirmed, since his cousin had a habit of saying "got it" when he didn't get it.

"Definitely."

"Then why'd you start swimming toward them?"

As Vorvan asked this, an orange boat was puttering around at a respectful distance. The dødbringers aboard wore neon yellow vests and most were holding up strange devices that appeared to enlarge their eyes. A heavyset female was bouncing up and down, waving at them, which rocked the boat so dramatically that it appeared to anger another dødbringer.

"But I'm hungry," Yegor whimpered.

"When have you ever gotten food from a dødbringer?"

"This one time—um, they threw a fish to me."

"Oh ja, I saw it bounce off your forehead. That fish was rotten, *remember*?"

"It wasn't that stinky."

"It was an insult."

Yegor pondered this for a moment, then made an *aha!* face. "They should've yelled instead. You can't eat yelling."

The more time Vorvan spent with his brain-damaged cousin, the more changes in his personality became apparent. Yegor laughed when something hurt. He took jokes literally. He hiccupped from nervousness and for some peculiar reason, he was preoccupied with the word "mom," which he accidentally called the orphans from time to time. Then there was the luckless fact that he also named his pet Mom, making it even more difficult to figure out which particular Mom he was referring to, so Vorvan asked him why one day.

"Hei, Yegor."

"Ja, Mom?"

"Why did you name your puffin *Mom*? Why not Feathers or Puffy or anything else really?"

"Cause she looks like a Mom." Actual Mom, who was perched

on his head, mirrored Yegor's confused face, then made a quizzical noise.

"Really?"

"Ja! And she looks out for me too. Won't let nothing bad happen. Nuh-uh."

Mom gave a quick nod, apparently pleased with this answer.

"Okei... Good job, then. It's the perfect name."

"Takk, Mom."

Vorvan eventually theorized that when Yegor got knocked unconscious, Grunhild had been the last thing on his mind and the word just got stuck there. But whatever the reason, his new identity seemed to have formed around the premise that his mother had sprung back a millionfold, creating a nursery world shiny with tenderness, where everyone had his best intentions at heart. Vorvan could certainly see the appeal of this kind of delusion—almost envied it—but Yegor's trusting nature also worried him, since Nordhavet found every opportunity to punish innocence. Even if Yegor wasn't the same cousin he remembered, Vorvan still felt called to protect him. Family was family, for better or worse.

And that left Freya, the kindest hvalross in all of Jorda. If she hadn't intervened on the beach that day, Vorvan might've drowned himself, starved to death, or at the very least, led a much lonelier existence. Instead, she gave him a second shot at life, which led him to view her as a savior of sorts. However, the problem with putting Freya on a pedestal was that he desired something deeper than reverence—something that required an even footing—though the exact nature of this yearning would remain a mystery for a long time. But for the moment, she mostly made him feel awkward and a little tingly, like a million moths were fluttering through his head.

10
Sommersand

Just as the lush, midsummer grass tinted an evanescent green, the orphans mulled over a visit to Sommersand. Though arguably the center of the herd's universe, no one had set flipper on its beaches except Nanook, who'd stumbled ashore there after his accidental voyage across Nordhavet. According to him the journey would only take them four days and when he proposed the idea of going back, the rest figured it was time to see what all the fuss was about.

The orphans wound their way through the Labyrint Isles, hopping from skerry to skerry, then followed Høyland's rugged shores northeast, trading guard duty at night. On the fourth morning they reached the last expanse of coastal drumlins, where a few fluffy clouds scudded overhead, and the orphans mentally prepared to swim across the Rullende Sea. Though the distance to Sommersand was relatively short, spekkhogger pods patrolled the deep channel separating the land masses, specifically hunting calves, since they couldn't inflict the same kind of damage as adults.

They started across in absolute silence, vigilant for signs of the pod, whose clicks and sirens could be heard faintly in the distance. Vorvan strained to keep Nanook's hindquarters in sight, but the nutrient-rich waters had fueled an explosion of microscopic life, making it difficult to see through the thick, green soup. Finding themselves scattered, the orphans surfaced to get their bearings and regroup.

"Faen! There they are!" Kara shouted.

"Where? *Where?*" Lars asked in a panic.

"To the left!"

Nine black fins as tall as ship sails were cutting through the waves ahead. But instead of tacking their way, the whales sped toward a patch of ocean where seabirds were shooting headlong into the water. Moments later, small silvery fish bolted past the orphans, looking scared out of their scales. Mom nosedived after the bait ball, came up with a mouthful, gulped them down, and went back for more.

"They must be after the herring too," Lars noted.

"Who cares what they're after. Let's go already!" his sister shot back. "Wait, what was *that*?"

BOOM!

A shockwave pulsed through the water.

BOOM!

Another soon followed.

Nanook started smirking. "I know exactly what that is. Now's our chance! Let's go."

The orphans followed Nanook through bloom after bloom of zooplankton and algae, fully expecting that he'd lead them to safety. Instead, he edged them closer to the intimidating noises and to everyone's horror, spekkhoggers began emerging from the murk. They looked like giant ghosts menacing a shimmering haze. Over and over again, they pounded their flukes against the shoal, stunning the herring stupid so they could be picked off at their leisure. The others gesticulated wildly at Nanook, making it crystal clear they'd seen enough, to which he shrugged his shoulders and reluctantly turned toward Sommersand. They sprinted the last mile, hugging the seafloor until it shallowed.

Unable to hold off any longer, Vorvan came up for a breath and caught his first glimpse of Sommersand. An endless procession of beaches had been gouged from towering cliffs, extending as far as the eye could see. Sunbeams fanned out over the clouds above them, and thousands of seabirds were funneling toward their nests, swirling together in dense murmurations. Vorvan finally appreciated why his mother had been so eager to share this moment and, curiously enough, he detected her presence shining through the physical world somehow.

The others surfaced and let out a round of celebratory hoots, overjoyed to have made it in one piece. All around them hvalrosses were busy eating gobs of clams, and it was a testament to the breathtaking view that they only noticed the shellfish bonanza as an afterthought. The orphans soon joined in, barely exchanging a word of banter on their breathers. Yegor—who could eat twice as much in half the time—rarely got his fill, but the pickings were so easy that he quickly overindulged to the point of bursting.

"Yu-*uh*-um!" he concluded over a squelched hiccup.

"*Sooo* delicious," Freya added.

"What now?"

"Time for a snooze."

"Don't tell me you mean *there*."

They all looked at the nearest beach and their hearts sank: The bounty clearly came at a cost.

Every summer Nordhavet's ice sheet ebbed over deep ocean and land became the only solid place left to rest, which meant hundreds of hvalrosses might be cruising for empty spots at any given time. The cliffs hemmed in the beaches, protecting them from isbjørns, but it also limited real estate. Sometimes an empty patch of sand couldn't be found for miles, so the moment an opening became available, bodies filled the vacancy like bog mud sliding into a fresh footprint.

Over the ensuing weeks, the orphans battled the crowds to carve out space for themselves, and even when they did, sleep was far from guaranteed. They had to contend with the midnight sun's perpetual glow, snoring as loud as mammoths, and farts so hideous they could make a cod go belly-up. Adding to the misery, molting season was upon them, resulting in a near-persistent state of scratching. As dead skin sloughed off in patches, parasites wriggled back into their folds of blubber to torment the herd with their tiny mandibles. Desperation could be heard in every direction: grunts, barks, sighs, and *uk-uk-uks*. Some did stomach crunches and other gymnastics to get into just the right position, and if there was a decent rock to rub against, hvalrosses came to blows for the luxury.

A month rolled by and the orphans slowly bulked up for winter, including Vorvan, who looked plumper and healthier than he ever had before. Despite its challenges, everybody felt good about their decision to come to Sommersand—to finally grasp the allure of their ancestral shores and why its unfailing abundance had been so crucial to the herd's survival.

One evening after a routine day of stuffing themselves, the orphans headed back to Sommersand, and the only space available was next to a thoroughfare where hvalrosses would be continually trudging past them. Though far from ideal, there was nothing left to do but rest and hope a better spot opened up.

"Hei, sea dumpling. Remember me?" a passing heifer stopped to ask.

"Hei . . ." Vorvan searched for her name, but drew a blank.

"Don't hurt yourself! You had such a terrible fever that day, I'd be surprised if anything stuck. I'm Orina."

"Oh ja, Orina! I remember now."

Her eyes tracked to Vorvan's left eye and she winced. "Poor thing! What happened to your face?"

By this point Vorvan had gotten so used to explaining his scars that it didn't faze him. "An isbjørn wanted me for breakfast, but I had other plans. Anyway, how are you?"

"Good, good. As you can probably tell, I'm expecting your brother or sister next spring." He hadn't noticed, but now that she mentioned it, Orina did have a glow about her.

"That's wonderful news! Hope I get to meet them someday."

"Takk. I hope so too," she said warmly, then her face darkened a bit. "Sorry about your father."

"What about him?"

"Haven't you heard? Mag disappeared a month ago."

"He's dead?" Vorvan didn't feel much immediately, only the faintest twinge of regret.

"Not *exactly*. You know how Nordhavet is, so easy to lose track of family. Maybe he's exploring someplace new. Let's hope so anyway."

Vorvan wished he could see his father the way Orina did and tried to recall something meaningful from their time together. "What summer gives, winter takes back."

"What's that?"

"Something Mag told me once."

"Your father never ceased to impress me," Orina said, smiling sweetly. "All right, I should probably go. I'm feeding for two these days. Farewell, sea dumpling." Then she kissed the scars on his brow and off she went.

"Who was *that*?" Nanook asked, ogling a little.

"One of Mag's harem. She took care of me when I had a fever."

"Oh, really? Wish I was sick," he said, wiggling his eyebrows.

Although Mag had been mean as a shark to him, Vorvan still found the news upsetting. With his father gone, so too died the dream of their sharing a bond, however improbable it had been. He slept fitfully that night, cursing fate and the ceaseless parade of clumsy hvalrosses bumping into them. The other orphans didn't fare much better as it turned out, and everyone woke up in a foul mood.

While stretching his flippers, Nanook moaned, "Let's get out of here. There's barely room to breathe!"

"Ja, this lump nearly suffocated me," Kara said, elbowing the big bull next to her, who turned over and continued snoring. "Where should we go next? Back to Freyland?"

"Too boring," Nanook snorted. Then his eyes went wide and bright. "Let's visit Isbreen Bay! We'll have it all to ourselves."

"Won't we have to go around Tombwater?" Vorvan pointed out, and the others froze at the mere mention of that dreaded patch of ocean. The herd forsook Tombwater for good reason, and no one besides Nanook had ever been close.

"That's too scary! And my belly—[hiccup]—hurts," Yegor cried. Mom also looked worried and shook her beak from side to side.

"How long does it take to get there?" Kara asked.

"And what's so special about Isbreen Bay?" Lars added.

"Only seven to eight days, and Isbreen Bay is ten times prettier than Sommersand! Also, there's a little forgotten island on the way, plenty to eat when we get there, and icebergs—even in summer!"

"What about spekkhoggers?"

"Meh, they're too busy getting fat on herring to bother with us. Come on, let's have some fun!"

Everybody voted in favor except Yegor and Freya, so with the matter settled, they navigated past the hordes and into the shallows, pausing to savor its cool relief. Yegor scratched himself on some submerged rocks, and Mom bathed next to him, briefly dunking below the water, then shimmying at the surface. She had a look that said, *Brrr! But how refreshing!*

The orphans passed several miles of crowded beaches until they saw an epic cliff jutting into the ocean. It marked High Helligdom, the northernmost point of Sommersand. Their ancestors used to hurl themselves over the edge during lean cycles—some willingly, others not so much—believing their sacrifice would appease Skyggen and rejuvenate Nordhavet.

"What a view!" Nanook boasted, as if he were somehow responsible for its grandeur.

Just then, a colossal breaker slammed against the cliffs, exploding into a golden mist, and a rainbow briefly glimmered across the vapor.

Freya shuddered. "Uff! Those waves look as tall as mountains."

"Ja, I'd rather lose a tusk than set one flipper in there," Kara said.

As the others absorbed Tombwater's terrifying beauty, Vorvan imagined a thicket of sacrificial skeletons just beneath the surface, slowly being pulverized to dust. Starik said that after particularly intense storms, a tusk would sometimes wash ashore, and that you could tell they were ancient by their intricately carved designs. He'd always hoped to find one, but they were extremely rare and he couldn't keep it anyway. Tradition dictated that the tusk be tossed back into Tombwater. Otherwise, it would bring the herd bad luck.

"Enough gawking. Let's go!" Nanook announced imperiously.

"Who died and made you expedition leader?" Freya shot back.

"Do you know how to get to Isbreen Bay?"

"Nei."

"*That's* why I'm in charge."

"Okei, but no more flirting with danger! Seeing those spekkhoggers up close nearly made my heart stop."

11
Soulcatcher

The orphans swam due north for two days, giving Tombwater a wide berth, until they came across a remote, little-known island just as Nanook claimed. The interior looked verdant and pristine, like an enchanted summer isle lost to time. They didn't bother with isbjørn watches and everybody had a great night's sleep, their first since visiting Sommersand.

The orphans woke up in high spirits and swam southeast for five more days, following the northern coast of the Sommersand Peninsula to Isbreen Bay. Then Nanook led them into a fjord where several icebergs floated majestically in the distance. They'd calved from a pale turquoise glacier that spilled motionlessly down a saddle in the mountains, terminating into a shimmering wall of ice. Elsewhere along the cliffs, stately waterfalls cascaded down to the crystalline inlets below, filling the space with the sound of roaring water. The scene looked fit for the Urguds and best of all, they had this transcendent corridor of Jorda all to themselves.

The orphans goofed off and played skalløp, their favorite game. The rules were simple: Someone would toss a unique shell over their shoulder and after counting to ten, they'd race to find it first.

"Got it!" Vorvan yelled, his voice amplified by the vertical rock faces. It was his fifth victory in a row, but that didn't surprise anyone: He was the nimblest orphan by a mile.

Nanook popped up and grumbled, "I quit! Besides, you're only beating me cause I ate a bad sea cucumber."

"*When?*" Kara sounded skeptical.

"This morning."

"If your stomach hurt since this morning, why didn't you mention it before?"

"Because I'm not a whiner," Nanook countered. Then he gazed past the group at an iceberg with a magnificent arch, and his eyes glinted mischievously. "Hei Vorvan, see that soulcatcher over there? I bet you aren't fast enough to swim through it before the spirits get you."

"Stick it where the snow doesn't blow," Vorvan snorted.

Then Freya piped up, "Ja, soulcatchers are dangerous, Nanook. Elder Starik warned us about them many, many times."

Vorvan recalled that lesson too. According to Starik, winter trapped everything in ice, including souls, which couldn't wend their way down to Underverden until the thaw released them. In the old days, whenever an iceberg drifted close to the herd, a shaman would be summoned to interpret them: Two peaks meant a warrior. A mound meant a mother. A sheer wall indicated a sudden death. An iceberg that flipped over predicted a catastrophe, and when two or more spirits got stuck in the same one, divinations turned into truly head-spinning affairs. The most significant icebergs had an arch spanning across the middle, also known as soulcatchers. They acted as gates to the Shadow Realm and by passing beneath the arch, the living could allegedly commune with the dead.

"Come on, don't be a shrimp!" Nanook said, needling Vorvan back to reality.

"Ignore him," Freya advised. "We aren't supposed to call on spirits without a shaman, cause you can't tell who—or *what*—is going to answer."

"That's just superstition! If any shamans are left, they're a bunch of quacks." Nanook quacked twice at Freya to drive home his point.

"Why don't you do it?" she snapped back.

"Uff! Calm down. Vorvan doesn't have the sand anyway."

"It's got nothing to do with courage, only brains, and he's got more than enough to ignore your stupid dare."

Vorvan had never heard of anyone actually passing through a soulcatcher, which was an unnerving observation in its own right. But even ruling out the possibility of summoning the dead, icebergs were notoriously unstable in the summer and liable to collapse without warning. Any halfwit would know better than to hang around one. "Okei, I'll do it," he finally said, astonishing even himself. "But only if you take my next twenty isbjørn watches."

"Deal!" Nanook agreed.

As Freya registered the news, Vorvan studied her reaction through the corner of his eye. Was she impressed with his bravery? Or was that speechless disapproval?

"Nei! I don't want you to—[*hiccup*]—go!" Yegor cried out. And Mom looked at him soberly, as if to say, *You should know better.*

"Don't worry, Yegor. It's just a superstition."

Freya wouldn't let that slide. "Soulcatchers are sacred, *not* a superstition. Just because you don't understand something, doesn't mean it's not real. Listen to—"

Nanook cut her off. "Hei! Vorvan is almost a bull now. Let him make his own decisions."

"A bull? Sorry, but not even close. And neither are you."

While Nanook and Freya continued bickering, Vorvan set out for the soulcatcher, doing his best to appear confident, though he had no idea what to expect or why he'd accepted Nanook's absurd challenge. Sure, he hated bears, but not enough to risk life and limb, which negated the point of avoiding guard duty in the first place.

The sun had reached its zenith by this point in the day, and its rays plunged into the fjord like spears, penetrating deep into rock, ice, and snow. Vorvan felt hot, an unusual sensation in the north, and the soulcatcher creaked forbiddingly ahead. "You're an idiot," he muttered to himself. "Why, oh why, are you such an idiot?" Nanook had gotten under his fur, that was why. Calling him a shrimp had struck a nerve. And it had something to do with Freya—how foggy she made him feel—but if he hoped to prove something to her, then what exactly? That he was brave? Wild? Headstrong? Or just really, really stupid?

The soulcatcher soon soared overhead, and the ice was so dazzling that it nearly blinded him. Waves chiseled at the base and meltwater trickled over its escarpments, creating chutes down to the ocean, where countless cascades splashed against the surface. The arch blocked out the sun as Vorvan passed beneath, and a curtain of droplets pattered onto his head, marking a point of no return. From every direction, echoes bounced off shapes so otherworldly that they appeared to be sculpted by Frostskader herself. Then he noticed something truly strange: a membrane of light. It looked like an oil slick, hovering in the air.

"What in Underverden?" he wondered aloud.

Suddenly, a snap rang out from the vaulted ceiling and a block of ice plummeted down. Before Vorvan had a chance to yell, water exploded into the sky, and a wave shot away from the impact. He ducked beneath it and popped up just in time to hear the same noise again: *CREEEK-ik-ik-ik-SNAP*. Seconds later a piece of ice hammered the back of his skull. Everything turned white in an instant.

Where am I?

And what keeps hitting my eyeballs?

Vorvan came out of a daze with meltwater showering his face. He commanded himself forward, fully realizing that the arch lay on the brink of collapsing, but the blow had frazzled the connection between his brain and flippers. Only his ears worked, and he didn't like what they heard. The ice sounded tired of holding on, pleading with gravity to end its misery.

Finally, just as Vorvan regained his senses and started to swim clear, there was a monumental thunderclap. The shadow of a wave loomed up from behind, sprinkling his back with icy droplets. He dove as it came crashing down, tumbling him end over end.

The familiar whispers of water.

So, you're not dead.
But which way is up?
To the light... Always toward the light.

Vorvan surfaced with a gasp, euphoric to see the sky again—that limitless sky—full of life-giving breath. What next? He spun around to survey the aftermath. Sea foam frothed around the shambles of the soulcatcher. The arch had completely caved in, leaving behind two spires, and a tidal wave was heaving across the ocean. The orphans swelled overtop as they swam out to greet him.

When they arrived Nanook slapped Vorvan's back, as if to verify that he'd survived, saying, "I never doubted you for a moment, but you should've seen Freya hiding behind her flippers." He covered his face and peeked out with one twinkling eye. Freya didn't look as amused.

"Were you the afraidest you've ever been in your whole entire life?" Yegor wondered in earnest. Mom seemed curious too.

"Just a tiny bit," he fibbed.

"Any news from Underverden?" Kara asked wryly.

"Or spooky visions?" Lars added.

"Nei, I don't feel any different." And that was true except for the gratitude bursting in his chest. Being young and invincible felt pretty good as it turned out, but then a shooting pain reminded Vorvan that he was still a mere mortal. "I guess my head hurts a little."

Freya skirted around him to get a better view. "You're bleeding!"

Vorvan touched the back of his skull, felt a sting, and checked his flipper. Scarlet rivulets were streaming down the valleys of his skin. "Ah, it's just a scratch," he said.

That night the orphans camped on the remnants of the soulcatcher, despite Yegor being unnerved by a vague apprehension, as if the arch could somehow fall down again. But they eventually convinced him that sleeping on ice was safer than gambling on a beach in an unfamiliar place, and all of them were looking forward to another peaceful night's rest. Everyone but Freya, that was.

She left the fjord after the others dozed off and headed north in the glow of the midnight sun, which had swung so low that it kissed the horizon, shooting a fiery beam across the ocean. Freya was hunting for sphagnum moss. She'd seen a wound fester on her own mother—how quickly the rot could spread and corrupt the blood—and would do anything to spare Vorvan from such an agonizing death. But first she needed to locate a bog, the only habitat where sphagnum grew.

Freya was fully aware of the risks involved. Sommersand's cliffs made it nearly impossible for isbjørns to sneak up on the herd, but bogs were unprotected and treacherous. One misstep could land her in a spongy morass, where one of two things might happen: Either a bear would chance upon a lucky meal. Or she'd get sucked into the peat, painstakingly decomposing over hundreds of years until being resurrected into yet more moss.

Farther up the coast, a small but promising river delta fanned away from a slump in a bluff, so Freya hauled ashore and sniffed the air. No whiff of isbjørn. Instead, there were bloodsucking insects called zizzbugs—lots of them—in swarms so thick they looked like smoke. They bit her mercilessly, but that only confirmed she was in the right place.

Freya soon found sphagnum moss and nibbled off as much as would fit in her mouth. Then, with her head stooped low, she noticed an antler poking out of a pool beneath the dense vegetation. Her eyes focused past the tranquil surface and discovered a reinsdyr staring vacantly at the sky. It could've died dozens of cycles ago, perfectly preserved in the anaerobic water, though it would've been a small miracle that the isbjørns hadn't found the cache of meat. They weren't above eating carrion, however fusty it had become.

A squelching sound suddenly interrupted the stillness, as if something heavy had plodded onto the moss. That was reason enough for Freya to scramble back to the water and while awkwardly climbing over a log, she half-expected claws to hook into her back. "I'm okei. I'm okei," she repeated to herself, wishing for the legs of a fox rather than her clumsy old flippers.

Freya made it to the surf, where she spun around and saw a dark silhouette, backlit by a blazing pool of reflected sunlight. The shape studied the ground where she'd just been, then lifted its head to stare at her, looking more curious than hostile, almost like it wanted to play. After sniffing the air a few more times, the bear seemed to accept its failure, trundling off into the bog, and Freya hurried back to the many fjords of Isbreen Bay.

The following day a flock of geese trumpeted overhead, stirring Vorvan from his slumber. Freya was missing, but that didn't panic him, because she'd always been an early riser. He shielded his eyes and squinted at the horizon, figuring she'd probably gone off for a morning swim.

The sun had just peeked over the cliffs, casting a dramatic shadow across the stunning turquoise water, and the distant glacier appeared to glow with promise. He'd cheated the crabs for one more day and the whole world seemed to take on a lustrous aura, despite his atrocious headache, which should've bothered him more than it did. He almost welcomed the pain. It served as proof of life—of his fortitude—and he imagined that even Mag would be impressed. Then, precisely as he thought this, a voice began speaking to him.

Huh! it snorted. *You have a sea sponge between your ears.*

Vorvan wheeled around in disbelief, looking in every direction that made sense, even some that didn't. Besides his dozing companions, he only saw a few gulls paddling innocently across the water. But how could that be? It sounded as if Mag had whispered directly into his ear. The condescension was pitch-perfect.

"Hallo?" he said softly—and felt crazy for doing so—checking to make sure that he hadn't disturbed the others.

Ja . . . I'm still here.

"Mag?"

Surprised?

"Wha—um, how is this possible? Orina said you went missing."

That's one way of putting it.

"So soulcatchers are real?"

Looks that way.

"But you told me that was a pile of magical mershit."

I said a lot of things.

"And you're dead?"

And you're a genius.

"But how did you die? And when?"

Can't remember . . . something bad. I must've blacked out.

"Okei, and how do I get you out of my head?"

That's all I get? How about, "Sorry to hear you're dead, Papa. I'll sure miss you."

"I'd rather eat sand."

You're lucky I'm just a spirit, or I'd—

"Who're you talking to?" Freya interrupted while swimming up to the ice. "And why are you eating sand?"

"Oh—uh," Vorvan stammered, trying to buy time. "Just, um . . . thinking about breakfast. I said I was so hungry that I could eat sand. Anyway, what's going on with you? Where have you been?"

With a little more coaxing, Freya launched into a full account of her night adventure, telling him everything except for the part about the bear. Then she packed his gash with sphagnum moss, explaining that it would keep the wound from spoiling. The pain alleviated after a brief sting and Vorvan began studying Freya's face, lingering on her gentle eyes. She'd risked her life for him and if he hadn't already, he fell deeply in love.

"What is it?" she asked, shifting nervously.
"I should've been there. Bogs are too dangerous to go alone."
"You needed to rest."
"I don't know what to say . . . tusen takk."
"It's okei, just do me a favor. No more stupid dares."
"Okei," he said, smiling. "But Nanook won't be happy."

12
High Helligdom

Mag's spirit picked up where the living version left off. He hurled insults, hummed off-key, and told crude jokes. But worse than anything, he provided a running commentary on Vorvan's life, such as the proper way to eat a clam, that he needed to assert himself more, and the futility of someone his size ever finding a mate.

Vorvan didn't breathe a word of his psychic possession to the others. Being small was bad enough, he could forgo the stigma of insanity—though the possibility of his actually being mad hadn't escaped his consideration. The ice chunk had knocked him unconscious, after all, and a similar injury totally rejiggered Yegor's personality. But regardless of whether Mag's voice was objectively real or not, if Vorvan didn't remedy the situation soon, he might end up conversing with coconuts on a tropical island. Not that he really knew what a coconut was, or a tropical island for that matter, but Starik had mentioned them in one of his stories.

"That's it! Starik," he muttered to himself.

If anyone possessed the secret to curing Mag's malign influence, it would have to be his former teacher, still the wisest hvalross he could bring to mind. Last he'd heard, Starik went into seclusion two cycles ago and though his health had been declining back then, news of his death would surely have caused a stir. And if the old grandbull had yet to feed the crabs, he knew exactly how to find him: Just follow the ravens.

◆

With the weather sure to sour soon, the orphans bid farewell to Isbreen Bay and headed back to Sommersand. They didn't plan on staying long, only a pit stop to refuel on their way back to Freyland.

The morning after their arrival, Vorvan complained about a splitting headache and told the others that he needed to rest. He did have a headache, in fact, but the latter part was a lie. When they left to feed, he craned his neck toward High Helligdom, where a few dozen ravens circled the pale gray sky. They tended to hang around weaker members of the herd, shadowing them like a skittish hex, but the scavengers were still airborne—an auspicious sign, since the elders' sanctuary lay directly below.

Vorvan spotted a faint zigzag running up the cliff wall, and his headache pounded that much harder at the sight of the steep switchbacks. Like any hvalross, he was cumbersome on land, and the climb would be painful. But first he had to secure a customary gift, so he swam to the closest clam bed and packed his cheeks until they puffed out like a blowfish. Then, as politely as he could, Vorvan negotiated his way through the snoozing hordes.

"Watch it, minnowdick!" a grandcow yowled after he stepped on her flipper. Vorvan started to apologize, but a few clams dribbled out instead, and the offended party shot him a disgusted look. This only kicked off his run through a gauntlet of scathing verbal abuse, including crowd-favorites like snowflake, sissy-flippers, cod-sucker, and drittsekk; but Vorvan managed to make it to the trail-head with most of his pride intact. The climb appeared even steeper than from afar and sensing his hesitancy, Mag took the opportunity to discourage him.

That bone bag is probably dead.

"Maybe . . . There's only one way to find out."

Come on, save yourself a world of hurt.

"If grandbulls can make it to the top, so can I."

Whatever you say, shrimptits.

Mag continued heckling him and Vorvan tried to let that serve as motivation, but after a dozen switchbacks, his joints ached, his belly chafed, and his heart felt like a boulder plugging a volcano, ready to blow at any second. Nevertheless, through sheer determination, Vorvan turned onto the last switchback and saw the path leveling out just ahead. Several ravens had been monitoring his progress with baleful curiosity, cawing noisily when he reached the top. *No meat today*, they seemed to say.

Sommersand burst into life on the plateau. Furry bumble bees and woolly bear moths were buzzing from flower to flower, making the most of summer's final days. Tundra grasses swished in a sea of golden green as Vorvan started down the trail feeling a million times lighter. He passed several large boulders, most of them covered in firedot lichen and ancient runes. Stopping to study one, he wondered what strange ideas it contained, and just like the first time he visited Glorystone, it made him sad to think that his ancestors' voices would stay trapped forever.

He eventually came to a bottleneck in the rocks where two burly lookouts stood guard, both to prevent unwanted visitors and to fend off marauding isbjørns.

"Halt!" one of them barked. "Did you bring an offering?"

Vorvan spit clams onto the dirt as proof.

"State your business."

"I'd like to speak with Starik, if he's alive."

"And if he is, what would you speak to him about?"

"About soulcatchers. Something's happened."

The lookouts searched each other for objections and shrugged when neither could find one. Then the bigger one yelled down the path, "Elder Starik, are you taking visitors?"

"Huh?" The voice came from behind an outcropping just ahead. "DO YOU WANT TO TALK?"

"We are talking."

The guard turned around with a look of irritation. "Good luck," he grumbled, then nodded to continue.

A few minutes later, Vorvan found Starik reclining on a slab of stone. Tributes were scattered at its base: pretty shells, strands of dried kelp, and many shiny things that the dødbringers had thrown in the ocean. A spiraled tooth leaned against the dais, maybe five feet long and decorated in scrimshaw. The illustrations depicted whalers harpooning narhval from their boats, and it struck Vorvan as morbid to memorialize a creature's demise on its own skeleton.

Starik appeared frailer than ever: His whiskers were falling out. His eyes looked hazy as blizzards. And his skin draped over his bones like an ill-fitting sack. A tornado of flies whirled around him, frantically repositioning themselves in a quest to find the best feeding spots. It was obvious that this would be his last winter.

Vorvan placed the clams on the dais. Starik sniffed around until he located one and attempted to eat it, then winced and spat out a mangled lump of shell fragments.

"Elder Starik, my name is Vorvan. I was in your class a few cycles ago."

"Huh?" Starik mumbled, wavering his head like a blind slug.

"My name is Vorvan."

"Huh?"

"MY . . . NAME . . . IS . . . VORVAN."

"All right, no need to yell. Come closer so I can get a sniff."

Vorvan got closer and Starik flared his nostrils in quick succession, snuffing little breaths of air. Then his eyes went wide, as if the gift of sight had miraculously returned to him.

"Ah, Mag's pup. Small fellow, if my memory serves."

"You could say that."

"Well, are you or not? It's a simple statement."

"Small? Or Mag's pup? I suppose I'm both."

"And how is your father?"

"Gone."

Starik opened his mouth to respond, but coughed instead—a sputtering, mucous-choked hack—and flies descended on the fluid weeping from his eyes.

"Gone dead or—[*cough*]—gone missing?"

"Gone dead. That's what he tells me anyway."

"*Tells* you?" Starik paused as if he were about to deliver bad news. "Sounds like you got the krillies, young bull. I'm afraid that's outside my expertise."

"Nei, you don't understand. I swam through a soulcatcher and now his spirit is talking to me. I need to get him out."

"Ah, a soulcatcher," Starik said knowingly, then his attention wandered away, as if a pretty moth had just fluttered by. Vorvan waited patiently, expecting him to say something, but Starik remained silent.

"So how do I make it stop?" Vorvan asked finally.

"How do you make *what* stop?"

"Mag's voice in my head."

"Are you sure you don't have the krillies?"

"I'm sure . . . at least, I think I am. How would anyone know?"

"Ask around, tell them you hear a voice in your head."

After another awkward pause Vorvan was close to giving up, but then Starik raised his head meaningfully. A storm seemed to be brewing inside his cloudy eyes, and he began to recite something in his commanding baritone of old:

"Soulcatcher, oh soulcatcher,
Icy-cold spirit snatcher,
Full of ghosts and wrathful voices,
Wishing they made different choices.
It's the drowned world they await,
Unless fools trespass the gate,
And set them free to wrack and roam,
Or right the wrong to send them home."

As Starik concluded, his eyes fizzled out and went pale again.

"What does that mean?"

"What does *what* mean?"

"The poem."

"What poem?"

I told you! Mag gloated. *Crazy as a sunbaked barnacle.*

"Shut up!" Vorvan replied aloud without thinking about it.

"Shut up?" Starik looked puzzled.

"Uh, I was talking to Mag. You know, the voice I hear in my head."

"Of course. You've mentioned him several times already."

Tiring of riddles and senile remarks, Vorvan suddenly bristled with anger. "So how do I get him out?" he snapped.

"I was just about to tell you, if you'd quit interrupting. We used to sing that song back when I was a pup. The answer is in the lyrics, 'Right the wrong to send them home.' In other words, you have two choices: Go back through the soulcatcher, or avenge his death."

"Really? Are you certain?"

"Utterly."

"But the soulcatcher collapsed. I saw it with my own eyes. And Mag says he can't remember how he died."

"Then *that's* that."

"There's got to be another way!"

"Young bull, you should have considered the consequences before you swam through the soulcatcher. Why do you think every elder since Igor the Inquisitor has warned against it? Just be glad it was your father's spirit and not something truly horrifying. Perhaps a demon, or a goose, or both! You could be honking out evil curses right now."

Then Starik made an indecipherable sound—something between laughter and wheezing—but either way, it degenerated into another coughing fit. The flies buzzed around in agitation and as the dying grandbull recovered his breath, Vorvan imagined a lifetime spent with his father nitpicking every decision he made. A pit opened in his stomach, one filled to the brim with despair.

Hahaha! We're going to have so much fun, shrimptits.

◆

With the soulcatcher reduced to ice cubes, Vorvan had no other option but to destroy whatever killed Mag. He was prepared to do anything to regain his independence, whether that meant battling a nightmarish squid, or discovering the cure for cod-belly flu. The problem was that Mag couldn't remember how he died. Or so he claimed.

As time dragged on and the situation grew increasingly bleak, Vorvan entertained some fairly dark fantasies, like conking his head on a rock, or swimming too close to a whale fluke. Though extreme, total oblivion was the ultimate goal—the only way to guarantee solitude—since not even his dreams were safe from Mag's noxious meddling.

And yet, just as the hopelessness became all-consuming, his father mysteriously disappeared. Vorvan couldn't believe his luck at first, but then Mag returned a few days later, acting as if nothing unusual had happened. Though initially evasive, Vorvan kept pestering him until Mag divulged that he'd found "something else" to occupy his time. His father mentioned this detail in such a sinister way, as if not quite himself, that Vorvan's whiskers instantly tingled with electricity.

"What do you mean, 'something'?"

Just something.

"Be straight with me for once in your life—uh, or death—you know what I mean."

He's more interesting than you, I can say that for sure.

"Now 'something' has changed to 'he.' Who is *he*?"

If you insist on a name, let's call him Den Mørke.

"Okei, describe Den Mørke."

He's in charge of things, like a chief, only bigger than any chief you know.

"Chief of what? Jorda?"

Faen! You're an even bigger nag than your mother.

"Don't talk about her. I hate when you talk about her."

...

"Hallo?"

...

When his father came back a few hours later, Vorvan considered pressing him for more information, but why should he care who Mag talked to? As long as they were spending less time together, that was all that mattered. No need to jinx it.

13
Vintersang

Two cycles passed and the orphans turned six, sticking together through ups, downs, escapades, and narrow escapes. They learned how to better navigate the seasons, expanded the clam farms around Freyland, and built a zillion more cairns at Nanook's insistence.

They'd just migrated to Drivved Bay and like every other autumn, this foreshadowed a poignant separation, since puffins had to follow the fish stocks south. When it was finally time to say goodbye, Mom hopped onto a stump of driftwood so Yegor could look her in the eye.

"I'm gonna miss you," he sniffled, the tears already streaming down his cheeks.

Mom cooed in response and butted her head against his, where they lingered for a few moments, nuzzling each other. Then Yegor started sobbing and blubbery waves rippled through his body.

"It's all right," he said, snorting back snot. "I know—[*sniff*]—I know you have to go. See you next spring, okei?"

Mom made a noise that seemed to say, *of course*. Then she took a few steps, beat her wings, and launched into the drab gray sky.

Yegor howled after her, "Farewell, Mom! Be careful! I LOVE YOU*UU*!"

Mom shrank into a dot and eventually disappeared inside a potbellied cloud, triggering another round of bawling from Yegor. While his cousin wept, Vorvan found himself wishing to see Nordhavet from the sky as Mom did. That way he could survey the obstacles ahead, and if he didn't like the look of things, he could keep on flapping his wings until the situation pleased him. Then again, maybe she envied his perspective from below the waves. Maybe all Jorda's creatures flew blind in some way, doing the best they could with imperfect information.

Before long, Vintersang was on the tip of every tongue. In the days leading up to it, the herd felt doused in a combustible mix of hormones, insults, and male pageantry. The bigger bulls got testy and occasionally lashed out at an innocent bystander, but the predominant mood was one of excitement. Nearly everyone attended the singing contest, from the frailest grandcow to the greenest calf.

The big show arrived on an exceptionally vivid night. Waves slushed against the shore and without a lick of wind, the crunch of compacting snow sounded lucid and clean. Several workers had chipped away at the ice to make a U-shaped platform, creating a runway of water where eligible males formed an orderly line. They arranged themselves from youngest to oldest, since that was the custom, and started joking around to cut the tension before the main event. The peace seemed all the more remarkable because they'd bloodied each other only a few days prior. Mating aside, just making it to this point counted as an incredible feat, because Vintersang's skirmishes continued until all its fighters ran a roughly equal risk of killing each other. Only then was it time to sing.

At the bend of the U there was a special area decorated with shells, stones, and an array of receptive cows. The latter came in an abundance of shapes and sizes: A few wore garlands of kelp around their necks. Some were dainty-tusked and slight. Others were buxom and rosy-cheeked. And a couple looked more formidable than the bulls in the water below.

The orphans nudged their way past the beach and into the shallows, getting as close as they could to the action just offshore. The elders were positioned on the two legs of the U, and they performed a traditional chant to begin the ceremony. As their voices reverberated through the crisp air, Vorvan never felt prouder to be a hvalross. The sound spoke to him of Nordhavet and its rich mud, of forgotten caves and all their secrets, of the herd's countless hardships and the strength it took to endure them.

Then the others yielded the floor to Elder Gunnar, who had grizzled whiskers and widespread respect for his fair-mindedness. As the council's highest-ranking member, it was his duty to make the opening speech.

"Welcome to Vintersang!" Gunnar proclaimed. "Our lineage goes unbroken to the Berserker Age, and ever since the stones could speak, we've gathered in Drivved Bay to create the next generation. Today we listen to the songs of our bravest warriors, and so too will their offspring, and theirs after them. We will continue until the end of all things, when Skyggen swallows creation and our sacred duty has been fulfilled. Good luck, bulls. May Hylebard carry your voices long after you're gone."

The crowd bubbled with enthusiastic chatter until the contest began. Then each suitor took their turn, performing a unique song of clicks, whistles, roars, and a humming so resonant that it made the water tremble. To show their approval, the audience slapped their flippers against whatever material lay beneath them, whether that be ice, snow, sand, or pebbles.

Ah, brings back memories from my time as alpha, Mag began. *You know, every cow from here to Sommersand wanted a piece of me. And it wasn't a little piece, if you catch my drift . . . Hallo? Are you listening?*

Vorvan thought his father had become increasingly nauseating over the last few days, going on and on about which cows he'd impregnate and the ones he wouldn't touch with a narwhal tooth. Lucky for him, a loud splash interrupted Mag's lurid recollections. It came from the line of contestants. The audience craned their necks in hopes of witnessing some unscripted action, but there was nothing left to see. Whatever had taken place, the commotion died down, and as the next contestant started to sing, the crowd cleared a path for an injured bull. He hauled ashore and keeled over, motionless, except for the staccato puffs wheeling from his nostrils. A dark liquid spurt onto the beach next to him.

"Who's that?" Freya asked.

"Too hard to see," Nanook said, widening his eyes. "But whoever it is, they don't sound so good."

"We should help."

Nanook looked at Freya like she'd lost her mind. "And do what exactly? The wound is too deep."

"I'd be surprised if he makes it through the night," Kara added.

And not even that long as it turned out, because the bull spit blood one last time and died a few minutes later.

Later that evening, Vorvan overheard two calves discussing the drama at Vintersang, so he ambled over to ask a few questions.

"Hei, did you say Zver stabbed that bull?"

"Ja, the idiot tried to skip the line. Why?"

"We're talking about Zver the Drittsekk, right?"

The calf looked shocked. "Have you been living under a rock? Nobody calls him that anymore, not unless you want to wind up crab food. Now he's Zver the Striped."

"What stripes?"

"Head out to alpha territory tomorrow afternoon. He's been telling the story to anybody who'll listen."

"Okei, takk."

14
Zver the Striped

The orphans asked for directions on their way to alpha territory, but no destination stayed put for very long in the labyrinth of ice floes. Adding to the difficulty, they had to steer clear of combative bulls, who roared at them to keep their distance, threatening all manner of harm should they violate the borders of their floating kingdoms. It was getting late and they were just about to give up, when a dark smudge appeared on the horizon.

Freya was the first to spot the crowd. "Look at all of them! He must be putting on quite a show."

"It better be the performance of a lifetime, after all we went through to find this drittsekk," Nanook replied.

The orphans swam over, hauled out, and shouldered their way through the masses, following the orator's voice to where the high side of a diagonal pressure ridge served as center stage. Given the time since they'd last seen each other, Vorvan anticipated changes in his father's old foe, but none quite so drastic as the bull that presided over the sea of heads. Not only had Zver become huge, but vicious red lines ran along his flanks, as if a demon had raked him with its teeth.

"As I live and breathe, it's Zver the Striped," Kara said haughtily.

"At least he earned that name," Lars added.

Nanook nudged Vorvan. "His scars look even uglier than yours."

SHHH! A cranky cow shushed them from behind.

Zver was in the middle of saying, "As I dragged the seal onto the ice, I heard something pushing through the water and a spekkhogger breached to look me over. But this wasn't any ordinary spekkhogger. Nei! That loathsome beast was twice as big as any other and jet-black from nose to tail. His throat was black. His teeth were black. Everything about him was black as night, even his soul. That's why I call him Shadowmouth."

Vorvan grumbled, "That's ridiculous. How can he know the color of a soul?"

"Fancies himself a shaman," Nanook offered as an explanation.

"Be quiet, or I'll knock your whiskers off!" hissed the cranky cow behind them, to which Nanook turned around and replied, "Try me, you withered old duck fart!" Then he puffed out his cheeks and made a flatulent noise. The cow scowled but kept her mouth shut, and everyone returned to Zver's monologue.

"... Shadowmouth rammed the ice so hard that I was flung into the water. And if it weren't for an ice chunk that wedged between his jaws, he would've bit my head clean off. Still, as you can plainly see, his mouth closed enough to slash my sides while I swam free. After that Shadowmouth seemed to vanish like a shade in darkness, but I could barely move. I was bleeding out, getting weaker with each passing moment, when clicks started to rattle my bones. CLICK ... CLICK ... CLICK ..."

As tension built between clicks, Vorvan surveyed the audience. Zver had them eating out of his flippers and even Freya appeared to be enthralled, which bothered Vorvan a little. He'd tried to keep an open mind, but given the past, he was skeptical that Zver would be motivated by anything other than reckless ambition.

"... Shadowmouth had gone silent, but sure as Sjøfar, he was swimming my way. Then I spotted the evil glint in his eye, so that's where I stabbed him. Right in the shiny part!"

Without warning, Zver thrust his tusks into the stage, cleaving off a chunk of ice. It tumbled down the pressure ridge to the audience below, where a few spectators leaned to the side quickly as the giant snowball rolled past them. Everyone else slapped their flippers ecstatically.

"Thank you, friends . . . Thank you . . . But I simply wounded him long enough to make my escape. It's only by Sjøfar's mercy that I stand before you today, so let me offer you some hard-won wisdom. The Urguds set aside parts of Nordhavet for themselves, guarded by horrific creatures. Take care not to venture too deep. And remember to stick close to your mothers, little ones, for Shadowmouth is still out there, seeking revenge with his last good eye."

Zver ended with a *ROOOAAARRR*, inciting a few pups to yelp and another round of applause. Then the crowd began to disperse, feeling riveted and full of good cheer.

Vorvan immediately suspected Zver of embellishment, if not outright fabrication. But the scars did prove that something horrific had happened to him, and the herd loved a good story, regardless of whether it bent the truth. There was also the striking parallel between Shadowmouth and Skyggen, which would only invite a comparison between Zver and Sjøfar: the ultimate Urgud. In other words, Zver seemed destined for a meteoric rise to power, and that possibility scared Vorvan more than a hundred shadow whales.

One dusky morning after polar night ended, the orphans found a new channel in the ice and swam toward the mouth of Drivved Bay. It was farther than most hvalrosses liked to travel and except for a few seals chasing cod, they had the water all to themselves.

Having eaten their fill, the orphans hauled out for a nap as the winter sun crested over the horizon, blushing the landscape a pleasant pink. Vorvan watched a larch trunk drift by and decided trees must grow sideways, because the wind would surely blow them over if they stuck out straight from the ground. With heavy eyelids, he started to nod off picturing horizontal forests, when a loud splash popped his eyes back open.

A monstrous hvalross had hooked onto a nearby platform, tilting the ice where a seal was asleep. It woke up wild-eyed and cried, *ARH, ARH, ARH!* But the seal was unable to find its footing, and it slid straight toward the bull, who promptly dragged the terrified creature below. Bubbles followed, and a red plume welled up from the depths.

"Was that Zver?" Lars asked.

Kara nodded soberly. "I'd recognize those scars anywhere."

"I'm sick and tired of hearing the How-I-Got-My-Dumb-Stripes story," Nanook griped. "Every time I turn around, it's Zver *this* and Zver *that*. We get it already. He's a legendary drittsekk!"

"I'm just worried that he'll be chief someday. If he—"

Vorvan stopped midsentence as Zver hoisted himself onto the seal's former platform. Then he slimed his way toward the center, streaking blood like a snail made of gore, spit out a hunk of flesh, and closed his eyes.

"What? He's not even going to eat it!" Kara wailed.

Lars hissed, "Keep your voice down. Maybe the seal got away."

"Look at the size of that chunk. There's no way it survived! And why is he hunting seals right now? There are plenty of clams."

"Shouldn't he be *enjoying* his harem?" Nanook suggested.

"Looks like he'd rather hunt than mate."

"There's something really wrong with him."

"He scares me bad," Yegor concluded, summing up the mood.

For some strange reason, Vorvan felt an impulse to see what became of the seal for himself. He slid over the edge without a word of explanation and paddled out to the blood plume, careful not to attract Zver's attention. Then he dove to where the carcass lay prostrate in the silt. A crab was already snipping off bits of flesh from a wound in the seal's neck, but the meager portion of meat hardly justified the killing. Unless *killing* was the point.

Vorvan returned with an expression that told the whole story. "Let's go," he said. "I've lost my appetite."

By midafternoon, the orphans found another ice-free estuary and started rummaging through the seabed. They were in luck. This spot turned out to be loaded with clams, and everyone soon forgot about the senseless violence from earlier. They passed the time by humming a few catchy songs from Vintersang, infusing the water with the sounds of indomitable joy. Vorvan could sense the vibrations purring through his body, as if he were a giant tuning fork, especially when they all hit the same note at once. It was an indescribably pleasant feeling.

It had been a lovely day, all in all, but twilight was fading fast, so the orphans decided to head home to Kaldsand. As the others bantered ahead, Vorvan lagged behind most of the trip, trying to write his own song. Then, while coming ashore lost in thought, he accidentally bumped into a massive butt.

"Watch it, runt!" the alpha growled.

Vorvan's heart sank as the beast wheeled around. Fresh seal oil sheened across his chest and ghastly stripes painted his sides. Only one bull looked like that—an extremely quick-tempered one—but before Vorvan could apologize, Zver cracked him across the face and he went staggering to the side. *Get up and fight!* Mag commanded in his head, but Vorvan was seeing double and crumpled back to the sand.

Just as Zver reared up to strike another blow, Yegor plowed into his flank, crying out, "Leave Mom alone!" Then Lars and Kara stabbed his haunches, distracting him just long enough for Vorvan to scramble away. Zver let out a terrifying roar and the orphans retreated. Even with their combined forces, he was a full-grown alpha—nearly three tons of enraged muscle and blubber—so at best, they could only harass him.

"Stop! Please stop!" Freya pleaded. "He didn't mean to bump into you. Did you, Vorvan?"

"Vorvan, eh?" Zver snarled in a deep, cold voice that sounded like a crevasse filled with malice. "I know that name, only you didn't have those pretty, little scars back then . . . Ah, now I remember. You're Mag's spawn, aren't you?"

"Ja, so what?"

"And where's your papa now, runt?"

Right here, drittsekk! Mag screamed pointlessly.

"Dead."

Zver twisted his lips into a grin. "Excellent! You know, I never forgot your father's—let's call it an indiscretion—and I can still picture your snot-nosed face laughing at me. Not so funny now, is it?"

"What are you talking about? I might've had a fever that day, but I'm certain I never laughed at you. I felt sorry for you."

Zver continued as if Vorvan hadn't spoken at all, "The only downside is that I don't get to kill Mag myself. Such a pity. Guess I'll have to settle for you instead."

"But why? I didn't tell you to go pick a fight with my father."

"If only life were fair . . . Anyway, when you sink to Underverden, be sure to tell Mag that I sent you there. Until then, be safe. You wouldn't want to rob me of the pleasure, would you?"

With that Zver turned around and lumbered up the beach, laughing his cruel laugh.

Following the butt-bumping blunder, Zver found every opportunity to exact his revenge, no matter how petty. Sometimes he pushed Vorvan aside while hauling out, or jabbed him with his tusks, or tipped over the ice he was resting on, saying something overly cheerful like "rise and shine!" On one occasion, Zver even crapped on his own flipper and slapped Vorvan across the face.

"A message for your father!" he declared.

That disgusting savage! Stand up for us! But that was easy for Mag to say, since his life wasn't on the line.

Throughout this period, Vorvan felt grateful to have the orphans watching his back, because they prevented the situation from escalating beyond mere humiliation. As lawless as the herd could be, most hvalrosses considered murdering a calf to be taboo, so if Zver wanted to do grievous harm, he'd need to do it in secret. Otherwise, the scandal would jeopardize his celebrity status, and the elders might be forced to banish him, just to save face.

The day after Zver held Vorvan's head underwater until he admitted to being a cod-sucker, the orphans announced they were migrating ahead of the herd. Vorvan immediately appreciated the gamble they'd be taking: Hvalrosses overwintered in Drivved Bay for good reason and beyond their mountain fortress, nothing could protect them from early spring's harrowing tempests.

"This is the stupidest idea we've ever had! I'm not going," he yelled at the others as they trudged into the shallows.

Freya turned around—the frigid whitecaps crashing over her shoulders—and shouted, "Don't you understand? Zver is waiting for the right moment to kill you. We have to let things cool down and hope he forgets."

"But there's got to be another way! The storms will be—"

"That's a risk we're all willing to take. Besides, you've been outvoted, five to one!"

His friends sank beneath the waves, and Vorvan had no choice but to follow.

15
Spring Storms

The orphans headed to Freyland, because they knew the way by heart and no one could think of a better idea. Due to an unusually warm early spring, plenty of channels carved up the ice sheet and they traveled most of the way by sea. On the last evening of their journey, the Nordlys lit up the sky, dancing like emerald dust poured into the wind, which the others interpreted as a sign that they'd made the right decision. Not long after, the low-slung silhouette of Freyland appeared, rimmed by a mile-wide perimeter of ice, so they hauled out and slid the final leg on their bellies.

"Last one there blows whalehole!" Nanook shouted as he punted forward.

"Cheater! You got a head start!" Lars yelled after him.

"It's okei. He's *special*," Kara said, giggling.

The race concluded with the orphans slamming into a snowbank and laughing in one great heap. Freya caterwauled, "We're home!" Yegor got misty-eyed. The siblings kissed the ground, and Nanook promptly started stacking some rocks.

Vorvan didn't quite share their enthusiasm. Even beneath the romantic glow of the Nordlys, the tiny skerry looked just as dull as he remembered. Snow covered most of the ground except for a few tufts of dead grass, brown and crunchy with frost, and most of the cairns lay in heaps, despite having been resurrected last fall. But the familiar terrain made him sentimental on some level, and best of all, Zver wouldn't bother setting his famous flippers on such an insignificant place.

◆

The following day they decided to take an inventory of available food, which was easier said than done. With the surrounding water completely ice-locked, the orphans had to chip through it with their tusks and designate someone to keep the breathing hole open. But the hard work paid off. They found worms, squirts, sea cucumbers, and plenty of clams thanks to Lars and Kara's terraced garden system. This came as a great consolation, because no one knew what to expect so early in the spring.

Their answer came a few days later when the weather turned capricious: a predictable kind of unpredictability. The sky could be clear one moment and blustery the next, with gales screaming over the horizon at breakneck speeds, which resulted in some incredibly chilly nights.

The siblings suggested building a windbreak to shield them from the weather, and the vote came in five to one. Nanook refused to participate, because the plan would cannibalize his cairns. But after watching his friends suffer a few demoralizing setbacks, he couldn't resist offering his "expert opinion," and as the others did the backbreaking work of hoisting rocks, he directed their placement, arranging everything just so. Finally, once it was clear they would succeed, he naturally took the lion's share of the credit.

Not long after they positioned the last stone, an *AW-AW-AW-ing* came from overhead and a puffin landed next to Yegor. He instantly shouted, "Mom! Oh, Mama, Mama, Mom! I'm so happy to see you!" And in the very next breath, he recounted absolutely everything that had happened since her departure, going into lavish detail about their troubles with Zver.

Mom started gathering bits of dried grass to stuff inside a rock crevice, preparing her nest for a single precious egg. Meanwhile, Yegor prattled on about inane subjects, such as which foods made him gassy, or whether the moon was actually a giant pearl. But Mom never seemed to mind. She always made kazoo noises in response, which he invariably interpreted as approval. When it was time for bed that night, she nestled into the crook of his flipper, happily dreaming about whatever puffins dream.

After building the wall, the temperature dropped precipitously and when they awoke the next morning, the ice had grown so thick they couldn't possibly chip through it. Suddenly blocked from their food source, the orphans relocated to the edge of the Rullende Sea, where they could still access open water. But being such a turbulent place, they decided someone should stay at the surface to keep an eye out for any suspicious clouds.

On the third morning Yegor took his turn to watch just before sunrise. He wished the others well as they departed, saying with great sincerity, "I hope you find the tastiest clams you ever had in your whole entire life!" Though not quite the tastiest of their life, the orphans soon discovered a large bed of shellfish and hoovered them up with pleasure.

The water got inexplicably colder after a while and Vorvan had a dark premonition, as if an enormous bird were overhead, preparing to swoop down and claw out his eyeballs. Unable to shake this feeling of dread, he went to check on Yegor and found him napping on the ice with Mom. Behind them, a storm had advanced out of the mud-colored dawn, and the first volleys of freezing rain pelted the ocean, rippling across the surface in innumerable rings.

"Yegor, wake up!"

Yegor jolted awake, and Mom flapped around hysterically.

"Sorry. Sorry. So sorry." He just kept saying sorry.

"Don't worry about that now. Get back to Freyland!"

Vorvan dove to warn the others, but with the weather roiling the sediment, he could barely see in front of his face. Luckily, he bumped into Nanook right away, and the siblings had ascended on their own, also sensing something was amiss. Freya took longer, but he kept grunting until he heard a response. By that time clouds had sprinted overhead, and squalls were whipping the waves into a froth, lashing so fiercely it stung their eyes.

"Føkk, this is bad!" Nanook yelled, gazing up at the tempest.

"Where's Yegor?" Freya asked.

"Yegor left for Freyland," Vorvan shouted back, elongating the words so they were intelligible over the tumultuous sea. "And we'd better go too! Right now!"

Seconds later, lightning struck at the horizon. Its thunder rolled over the ocean and straight through their skulls, as if it could imbue every last atom of Nordhavet with cataclysmic power.

The orphans raced against the storm, but it caught up and the waves quickly became unnavigable. They tried diving below the turmoil, but a fearsome undertow thwarted any progress, sweeping them backward as much as forward. While it was true that hvalrosses could hold their breath for a very long time, if the sea became too volatile, they'd drown like any other hapless land animal, so the orphans were forced onto the ice.

"There's an island!" Vorvan cried out, having glimpsed a specter of rock through the torrential downpour.

"We'll follow you!" Nanook shouted back.

But then the ice shattered to pieces, sending them adrift on separate rafts. Nanook, Lars, and Kara got carried away by one; Vorvan and Freya by another. Without the ice sheet there to restrain it, the ocean gathered into towering swells, unleashing its full fury. The rafts spun and gyrated around each other, totally at the mercy of the waves, which picked them up and slammed them down. To and fro. Fore and aft. They rocked so savagely that Vorvan felt like puking up his own skeleton.

A monumental wave soared ahead, curling slightly, ready to swat them off the face of Jorda like pointless insects. Vorvan saw the other raft go up and they followed shortly after, climbing higher and higher toward the leaden sky. Lightning slashed through the dark, briefly illuminating Freya, whose mouth was open and screaming, but no sound could rise above the raging tempest.

They crested over the peak, then hurtled down its back at fantastic speeds. When the other raft slammed into the trough, it flung Lars and Kara into the churn. Nanook dove after them, looking around frantically, until he too was swallowed up by the seething ocean.

Vorvan desperately wanted to help, but they were already rising up the next wave—even bigger than the last—and it paralyzed him with terror. The raft tilted until it was nearly vertical, and gravity wrenched them backwards, causing Freya to lose her purchase. Vorvan let go to slide with her and just as they were about to fly off the edge, he spiked into the ice. It nearly ripped his tusks out of their sockets, but he pinned them long enough for the raft to level out. Then it careened down the wave's back, plowing beneath the surface, and water roared past their ears. When they popped up, Vorvan sucked in a sharp breath, wondering if it would be his last, and the terrible sequence began again.

Nordhavet seemed hell-bent on reclaiming their bodies, where in a poetic twist of justice, they'd nourish their former prey. Worms in the making—that's all they were now—and Vorvan came to terms with their doom by splitting from reality. He hummed his mother's lullaby, over and over again, until a tremendous bolt cut across the sky and lit up the entire world. There was something projecting from a nearby wave: a huge black fin, curved like a skinning blade.

"What was that?" he yelled, but Freya couldn't hear him over the storm.

Mag did, however, saying, *He's here!*

Vorvan's blood turned as cold as meltwater. There was something about his father's tone that terrified him, like he'd been expecting this all along.

16
Aftermath

Vorvan woke up embracing Freya. Whatever would happen next, there was some comfort in knowing that he'd been spared the worst fate.

"Takk Sjøfar, you're alive!" he said as her eyes cracked open.

Freya didn't respond, just sobbed and trembled like the last leaf on a tree. All Vorvan could do was to hug her until she became calm enough to talk.

"Where are we?" she finally asked in a shaky voice.

"I'm not sure. Somewhere in the Labyrint Isles."

"What about the others?"

"I don't know, but I promise we'll find them."

Vorvan had sworn this with false certainty. Whether it was thanks to the Urguds or dumb luck, he couldn't say, only that they'd survived by the slimmest of margins. How could all six of them have made it through unscathed? Then he surveyed the boundless, gloom-ridden dawn and acknowledged the true immensity of the task before them, if only to himself.

Vorvan and Freya spent a month combing through every skerry, lagoon, inlet, and estuary. Whenever the weather permitted, they widened their search to the Rullende Sea, grunting below water and calling at the surface, but nothing came of their efforts. Lars, Kara, and Nanook had vanished without a trace—Yegor too, who evidently didn't make it back to Freyland.

The memory of the storm tormented Vorvan throughout this

period. Had he witnessed a figment of terror? Or a nightmare come to life? The latter seemed more likely, since Mag had acknowledged a presence of some kind, though he sincerely wished that wasn't the case.

"What did you mean by 'he's here'?"

I don't remember saying that.

"I could've sworn you did. And I know I saw something."

You probably just imagined it. That storm would've scared Hylebard himself. I've never experienced anything like it.

"Was it Shadowmouth?"

Quit pestering me.

Vorvan also mentioned the black fin to Freya, but she forbade him from saying "Shadowmouth" out loud, as if by invoking the monster's name, they could make the past more terrible than it already was. The haunting possibility—well, that was his burden to carry. Freya had donned the gleaming armor of optimism, and there were no chinks for doubt to stab through.

When the ice sheet broke up, the herd streamed north by the thousands, making it impossible to continue searching amid the ruckus. There was also a slim chance their friends had already migrated, presuming they'd do the same, and a joyful reunion awaited them on the beaches of Sommersand. Freya hoped so anyway, but that didn't turn out to be the case.

Vorvan and Freya became constant companions in the aftermath of the storm, leaning on each other for support, which turned out to be important, because something else would test their resolve. That summer and the next, the sea ice melted earlier in the season, and clams were becoming increasingly scarce. They spent most of their mental energy just trying to survive.

The following winter, even Vorvan and Freya drifted apart, though not over competition for food. Vorvan would have gladly starved for Freya, just as she would've done for him. No, the real reason was far thornier and it began when Freya bloomed into a beautiful heifer. She'd turned eight the previous spring, the age most females attended their first Vintersang, not as a member of the audience, but as a participant.

Female hvalrosses sexually matured before males, who didn't begin to compete for mates until they were fifteen or older; and since Vorvan and Freya were roughly the same age, they were never going to line up reproductively. Not only that, but being such a diminutive male, Vorvan would likely never mate. Not unless he magically packed on an extra ton. Otherwise, the alphas would drive him away before he even had a chance to sing, so as jealous as the thought of seeing Freya with another bull made him, Vorvan also saw it coming.

Still, he couldn't bear to attend that Vintersang and chose to sulk on a piece of pack ice instead, drifting aimlessly under a full moon. Off in the distance, the Teeth of Skyggen looked like snow-cloaked sentinels, there to defend against unwelcome guests. A few clouds brooded along their slopes, dark and aloof, just like Vorvan—and that's the state Freya found him in.

"Hei, Vorvan," she said, sounding both cheerful and sensitive.

"Who'd you pick?" he blurted, not in the mood for pleasantries.

"I, um . . . I picked Hjalmar."

"Ah, Hjalmar—excellent choice. Big tusks. Bigger oaf."

"I know, I *know*. I'm no different from the rest, but Nordhavet is so unforgiving, and I want to give my pup the best chance I can."

"You don't have to explain. I get it," Vorvan said unconvincingly. In truth, he was filled with a profound disenchantment, not so much with Freya, but at fate itself for thwarting his every desire. If such things were possible, he would have smashed the stars together to unleash his cosmic-sized frustrations.

"I'm sorry. I really do wish it was you, but I can't wait that many cycles."

Hearing Freya admit her feelings for him helped to soften the blow—just knowing that possibility existed, however far off in the future it lay—and Vorvan suddenly felt disarmed. "It's okei. Really, it is. I'm just scared things will never be the same between us. Promise me that when your pup is old enough, we can be friends again."

"Vorvan, we're more than just friends. We're family, and family is forever."

He smiled faintly. "It's good to hear you say that . . . Otherwise, sharks would've chomped off your dumb head."

Her eyes lit up. "Nanook's oath! How could I forget?"

For a little while longer, Vorvan and Freya chatted about purely happy things, endeavoring to put the future out of their minds, until their eyes started to droop with fatigue. It had been an emotional day for both of them, so they yawned their goodnights and huddled together under the moonlight, watching their breath vanish into the frigid blue heavens one last time.

Just as Vorvan feared, their relationship drastically changed once Freya joined Hjalmar's harem. They couldn't tease each other anymore, or bump noses—and cuddling for warmth was absolutely out of the question. They couldn't even share the same vicinity for very long, because Hjalmar didn't suffer the presence of other males. No self-respecting alpha would.

There was only one exception: Vorvan and Freya could socialize if they crossed paths while foraging, which happened more frequently than coincidence should allow. Still, Vorvan had to be careful not to act overly familiar, otherwise he'd be bludgeoned stupid by Hjalmar. To avoid this, they'd usually exchange a cordial greeting, then chat about the weather or how the clams were doing, which was invariably bad. Nothing more than that. But underneath the show of etiquette, their deep affection remained intact. It just had to go unsaid.

Despite his disappointment, Vorvan never held Freya's decision to mate against her. He realized that she needed to fill the void left behind by the orphans—that by creating a new life, she could anticipate a happy future rather than wallowing in a painful past. Vorvan would have done the same, given the choice, so how could he blame her? But he missed Freya terribly and thought about her more than he cared to admit, though Mag had a pretty good idea.

Oh, for føkk's sake! There are other fish in the sea . . .

17
All the Busy Birds

Sixteen months later Freya gave birth to Kallik, so named after lightning, since he'd been born during a storm. The word came from Nanook's herd. It was a sweet and surprising gesture, since the two of them had always butted heads. But nostalgia had a way of tinting the past in rosier tones, and Freya was more nostalgic than most.

She explained all of this to Vorvan on a breather one morning. They hadn't spoken much since her labor and tried to catch up on lost time, but the conversation came to an abrupt end when Hjalmar lifted his stupendous head from the pack ice to eye them dimly. Freya's choice in mates had one saving grace, that Hjalmar was dumber than half the clams he ate. Even so, Vorvan didn't want to press his luck, so he hastened along like a harmless nobody.

There were times when Vorvan found the whole situation distasteful—skulking behind Freya like a pitiful shadow—but whenever he considered the alternatives, nothing else made more sense. He was too young to mate himself, had little interest in making new friends, and still enjoyed spending time with Freya, however sporadic and stunted. If injured pride was all it would cost him, he could live with that for now.

And so Vorvan watched from afar as Kallik grew into a healthy, boisterous pup. This brought to mind echoes of his own adolescence, when Ingrid delighted in showing him all that life had to offer: his first taste of clam, the simple joy of a snowflake landing on his tongue, or humming a beautiful song to lull him asleep. Even through their dark moments, she'd always radiated kindness, and she never stopped loving him. Vorvan might have only occupied the periphery of Freya's life, but he could tell that she felt the same about Kallik.

Food grew even scarcer and Hjalmar took off, leaving Freya to raise Kallik on her own. Growing up fatherless had always been fairly common in the herd—as Vorvan could certainly attest—but clam shortages compounded the normal domestic stressors and families were breaking up more readily. But Hjalmar's desertion certainly had its perks. Without that rock-for-brains to worry about, their friendship resumed the same as before, except that Vorvan became a surrogate father of sorts to Kallik. He encouraged him to explore and be intellectually curious—to come to him with any question he cared to ask—all the things Vorvan wished Mag had done for him.

On one particularly fine spring day, they found a secluded clam bed north of Ildens Trone, eating until they were fat and happy. Then they floated together and took in the scenery, watching the sunset over the steaming slopes of Vulkan's Breath.

"Look at that, Kallik!" Freya exclaimed, holding him up to see.

A geyser was blowing a fine mist way up into the air, where the wind dispersed it and a magnificent rainbow arched over the caustic earth.

"Hei, Kallik. What's that colorful thing called?" Vorvan asked.

"Um . . . uh . . . a raincrow!"

"Close! It's a *rainbow. Rain-bow.*"

"Isn't it pretty?"

"Pretty," Kallik repeated, his pupils vibrating with wonder.

"Okei, let's name all the colors we see. You first!"

As Kallik started naming colors, Vorvan wished they could live in that moment forever.

◆

Kallik turned two, and Nordhavet had another terrible summer. The clam stocks were collapsing and no one could figure out why, other than their shells felt oddly brittle. In any case, nobody had enough to eat, and the herd had to live off their fat reserves. Pups didn't have that luxury.

Vorvan probed every inlet, lagoon, and spit, hoping to stumble upon a hidden gem—something small and therefore overlooked—but the entirety of the Dampende Archipelago appeared to have been picked clean to the bone. Whole days felt like abject failures and along with Hjalmar, fortune appeared to have abandoned them. Still, whatever Vorvan managed to ferret out of the desolation, he shared with Freya and Kallik, usually just a few dozen clams per day.

As the uncannily warm summer dragged on, Freya ate flowers, moss, dead birds, and even dirt out of desperation, but her milk ran dry anyway. Kallik cried and pleaded, but without the raw materials it needed, her body just wouldn't cooperate, so they kept moving in search of food.

After exhausting the Labyrint Isles, they tried their luck on the southernmost beaches of Sommersand, just on the edge of the Gylden Lowlands. Most of the herd avoided this area because it was notorious isbjørn country, but the situation felt critical enough to take a chance, and they hoped its fearsome reputation had preserved some of the shellfish stocks. It did, though not enough to make a difference.

One blazing hot day—*hot* for the north, at least—Vorvan searched for Freya to give her a few clams that he'd scrounged up from an estuary. The sun shone high in the clear blue sky and sprays of purple saxifrage had bloomed along the lower cliffs, lacing the air with their sweet fragrance. They'd always been Ingrid's favorite flower. Freya's too, and she'd soon need their comfort.

Before he saw her, Vorvan already knew what had happened, since Freya's wailing sounded primordial, as if she were the release valve on all of history's suffering. She nudged Kallik, then shook him—anything to wake him up—but his little head just rolled around listlessly. Vorvan tried approaching between fits of sobbing, but Freya shouted at him to go away.

The next morning waves lapped peacefully against the shore. Unlike the clam stocks, the fish were doing well and seabirds flew back and forth from the lower cliffs, returning with full crops. Each species had a unique call to find their chick among the multitudes: The puffins sounded like gossiping kazoos. The gulls screeched high and shrill. And the razorbills cackled like jolly lunatics.

Vorvan found Freya listening to them on a beach—no longer crying, but calm—almost unnervingly so.

"Hei," he said.

Freya didn't respond, so he laid down next to her, just a benignly warm body, reassuring her that she didn't have to face the devastation alone. It was hard to tell if this gesture brought her any solace, because Freya stayed perfectly still, letting her grief thunder between them like an invisible storm. Nordhavet could be such a fickle place and he felt the futility of understanding why bad things had to happen, especially to Freya, who deserved peace if anyone did.

"They sound so happy, don't they?" she asked stoically.

"The birds?"

"Ja..."

"I guess so. I don't really know what a happy bird sounds like."

"They're happy. Sadness is silent."

"Then let's keep talking."

"What's there to talk about?"

"I don't know. Whatever you want to say."

"You wouldn't like hearing what I have to say."

"Try me."

Like a snail retreating into its shell, Freya got quiet again, so Vorvan let the birds do the talking for a while. And as he quietly cried for Kallik, who he'd come to love as well, his thoughts seemed to mingle with the intricately layered birdsongs.

AW-AW-AWWW.

Screeeeee-EE-EE-EE.

Cri-i-i-i-i-ck.

Ha-aha-aha-aha.

Then Freya came to life and said, "Listen to them, so busy caring for their babies. All that time and energy. All that love. For *what*? We end up alone, Vorvan, no matter how hard we try. I just wanted something sweet to hold onto, something to make life meaningful and gentle. Now that's gone."

Vorvan deliberated over comforting things to say, but everything sounded callous, or like a promise he had no business making. His mouth opened, stalling to find the right words, but Freya continued before he had a chance to respond.

"I'm leaving." She sounded so resolute.

Vorvan struggled to stay calm. Something about her tone worried him, as if she might throw herself from the cliffs of High Helligdom. "Wait, you mean right now? Where would you go?" he asked.

"I don't know yet."

"When will you be back?"

"Not for a while . . . maybe a long time."

"Please don't go."

"I have to go."

"Why?"

"Because nothing makes sense anymore."

"I understand. That's how it felt after my mother died."

"Nei, *this* is different."

"Why?"

"Because I was supposed to protect Kallik and I failed."

"But you didn't fail, Freya. You can't make the clams grow any more than you can make the snow fall. Kallik knows that you loved him. He knows you did everything you could. It's not your fault."

"It doesn't matter."

Vorvan wished he knew the magic words to make Freya stay, some spell to take the agony from her heart and inflict it on his own. A memory came out of the blue: It was the day Freya invited him to join the orphans, back when he'd been so depressed that he nearly starved to death. Freya saved his life, so why couldn't he save hers? Why couldn't life be that simple?

"But Nordhavet is too dangerous to be on your own. Can't I tag along to keep you safe? I won't bother you. I promise."

"Vorvan, you've been my rock through many hard times, so I know this probably doesn't make sense, but I just need to be alone for a while. Okei?"

"Okei . . ."

"And I know you're sad right now—that you might feel like you're losing your last friend—but life will surprise you again. You'll see. Just be ready for the opportunities that come, and always remember to savor Jorda's gifts while they last."

"I'll miss you, Freya. So very, *very* much . . . May Frostskader shield your way."

"I'll miss you too, and tusen takk for all your kindness. Farewell, Vorvan."

And that was the end of it. Freya didn't say another word. She just marched into the surf, and Vorvan watched her sink beneath the waves. Then his heart sank too, like a pebble settling into an abyss, where there was little hope of ever finding it again.

18
Hunger

Three cycles passed, and things only got worse for the herd. A slow-motion calamity seemed to be unfolding under their noses, like a glacier retreating over several thaws until it melts for good one day. Life in the arctic had never been easy, but the past took on a halcyon glow, and the herd began most conversations with an increasingly familiar refrain: "Do you remember when?"

For instance, everyone remembered when there were still plenty of clams to eat, so long as you put in the work to find them. They remembered the raucous migrations, during which mirthful songs could be heard wafting on the breeze. They remembered digging together in communal groups and bantering amiably on their breathers, just as the orphans had done. But then the clam beds collapsed and everything fell apart.

This resulted in two radical transformations in hvalross society. First, it forced the herd to split up and roam greater distances from their traditional feeding grounds. Sommersand and Drivved Bay no longer served as the centers of their universe, and small groups splintered off to scout for new territory. Most were never heard from again, but that didn't necessarily indicate failure. Even when word did travel back, there was still the matter of whether to trust it or not. In the case of a windfall, the explorers might lie to keep the hordes from descending on whatever refuge they'd found, and this generalized suspicion led to the second radical change.

The herd became unwilling to share information outside their family and friends, and sometimes not even then, as starvation tested the bonds of every relationship. Hvalrosses chose their allies carefully, and most acquaintances exchanged suspicious glances rather than hearty greetings. Being a gregarious sort, the herd felt this tragedy acutely, but they were also wary of being stabbed in the back. Some found it easier to work alone, and if an enterprising individual found a good feeding spot, they'd take a circuitous route to get there, attempting to catch spies who might have tailed them. It got ugly sometimes—deadly, even—the situation had become that desperate.

As a byproduct of all this wariness, the herd became eerily quiet. Nobody laughed or hummed. They didn't have the energy to waste on frivolity. There was a great leaning inward, of keeping one's own confidences and turning away from social life. Even if you were hungry, you learned not to ask for food, that it was almost rude if you did, because it forced the others to lie. Not that etiquette mattered anymore. The threat of starvation hung over every conversation like a pall. Shrunken faces were its testament—the hollow eyes, cracked tusks, and brittle whiskers, like the chaff of cursed seeds.

The elders soothed the herd as best they could, pointing out obscure historical episodes to prove they'd survived much worse. "We are strong!" Elder Gunnar shouted at one Vintersang. "Even in the Great Warming, when the glaciers retreated to the poles and the old ways were lost—even then, we persevered. And we shall rise from this hardship, stronger than ever!"

But all those hopeful words couldn't fill a single empty belly and underneath the show of confidence, Vorvan saw foreboding in the elders' faces too. Whether they'd admit it or not, the entire herd feared becoming strangers in their homeland, ill-equipped for the trials that lay ahead, each bearing witness to the final days of a once great race.

19
The Grim Look

Somehow, Vorvan survived through all manner of deprivation to see his fourteenth birthday. He'd last laid eyes on Freya four cycles ago—seven for the orphans—but despite all that intervening time, the bittersweet memories floated just below the surface of each day, so easily dredged up by the quiet. He still had no clue what had happened to his friends, but accepted that they were probably dead, though he couldn't bring himself to believe the same about Freya. The thought of holding her again someday was the hope that kept him alive.

But when it came to all other matters—every sob story and outstretched flipper—Vorvan had long since transmuted his heart to stone. Now fully-grown, he wasn't exactly big, but his muscles were sinewy, his tusks sharp, and his spirit fierce. Nobody insulted him anymore, not even if he stepped on their flipper. They held their tongue at the grim look in his eyes, the kind that said, *I've got nothing left to lose.* The scars helped too.

Perhaps unsurprisingly, he didn't make any new friends, which left him with only Mag for company, but that outcome wasn't as awful as he would've once believed. Though far from bosom companions—or even supportive allies—they did share every waking moment together and that forged a bond of some kind, however quarrelsome.

Another side effect of his solitude was that Vorvan had gone a touch feral and would occasionally talk to himself. He tried to curb this eccentricity around the herd, though that was sometimes easier said than done.

"What are you looking at?" he barked at a nosy grandcow, who'd been staring at him one day.

"Please, don't be offended. I simply overheard you muttering to yourself. Sounds like a grave case of the krillies, but you're in luck, young bull. I'm a healer and know just the right herb to fix that. In exchange, all you have to do is take me to a little clam bed."

"Ah, go eat your own twigs, you saggy old carcass."

"Well, never in Nordhavet!" she huffed, then waddled off.

Somebody woke up on the wrong side of the ice, Mag teased.

"Why should I care what anyone thinks?"

Grandcows sure, but you don't want heifers to think you've gone krilly. If word gets out, they'll never mate with you, and you're mating on a prayer as it is.

"The herd doesn't have long anyway. If they want to spend their last cycles gossiping, then let them talk."

For føkk's sake, quit moping! We have work to do.

"Ja, ja, ja. There's always more work to do."

When spring cracked the ice sheets of Drivved Bay, most of the herd took the northern route past Isbreen Bay to explore the eastern coastline. Others tried their luck in the Krystall Shallows to the southwest—which were beguiling in scenic beauty, but widely considered barren—and they'd likely have to continue further south into uncharted waters. Being on his own, Vorvan could make due with small wins and preferred more reliable territory.

He started with the Labyrint Isles, always careful to avoid Freyland, which he hadn't visited since Kallik died. Too many painful memories. Instead, he checked other sites along the way and found they'd already been ransacked, but he expected as much, and the setback didn't fluster him. Besides knowing the Dampende Archipelago like the back of his flipper, he'd learned another trick to beat the lean cycles.

Partly due to his compact build, Vorvan could hold his breath longer than just about anybody, and he'd been plumbing the depths for food. This extreme environment had largely been spared, because—even with infinite oxygen—most hvalrosses avoided dark water out of an indoctrinated fear. Ignoring the more mythical beasts, spekkhoggers were thought to prowl the deep, but in Vorvan's experience the pod tracked the herd and schools of herring, not stragglers.

The previous thaw he'd discovered a large clam bed off the northern coast of Ildens Trone, one hidden among its peculiar volcanic formations. He hoped to find a similar spot this cycle and fantasized about shellfish the entire way. Anything scarcely edible would be a treat after his last few meals, including an abandoned nest of rancid gull eggs, snot-like invertebrates, and a beluga carcass well past its prime.

Vorvan arrived at his destination on a foggy morning and started raking through the seafloor, leaving a silt cloud in his wake. Within a few minutes, his whiskers jammed on something hard, so he sucked in a mouthful of water, blew it at the sediment, and shoved his snout in the depression.

"Faen! Just a blasted rock. I'd give my left tusk for a clam."

How long has it been?

"Long enough to forget what they taste like."

At this point, probably better than mating.

"Why is everything about mating with you?"

If you'd ever mated in your sorry life, you'd know why.

Vorvan ignored Mag—a skill he'd improved with time—and kept digging. But by the end of the morning, all he'd managed to excavate were a few broken shells and clam-sized stones. He also found several dødbringer objects: a corroded piece of metal with a handle, a floppy thing they put on their feet, a glass container with a tapered neck, and an assortment of faded bottle caps. None of it was good for eating.

"Why do they make things just to throw them away?"

Do I look like a dødbringer to you?

"You don't look like anything. You're a spirit."

You love rubbing that in.

"Whatever. I'm going up."

While catching his breath at the surface, Vorvan watched tendrils of mist curl over the water like vaporous eels. Then something else appeared, languidly drifting out of the fog. It was an iceberg, shaded in the most delicate hues of turquoise. The steaming lands of Ildens Trone didn't have glaciers, so it must've floated from someplace far away. Either way, it didn't matter. Pondering the quirks of nature was better done on a full belly.

He closed his eyes and concentrated on the breeze, trying to parse out its bouquet of molecules. It didn't carry any promising scents, mostly the rotten smell of fumaroles, so he squinted at the tenuous northern horizon where the fog was thinnest. Despite himself, he started daydreaming about the orphans.

"I hope they're with Nanook's herd. That's possible, right?"

We've already discussed this a million times.

"Just humor me."

There's a chance, but wouldn't they have swum back by now?

"Maybe they're waiting for me to swim to them."

Listen, I know you miss them, but you can't make it to the far side of Nordhavet.

"Don't be such a nei-sayer!"

Get your tusks out of your ass! You have more immediate problems, like your next meal. Try thinking about that.

"Ja, of course. But I've searched everywhere."

Not the trench. You haven't looked there.

A shiver ran down Vorvan's back. The deep was one story, the abyss quite another. In hvalrossan sagas all the truly terrible things came from the abyss and to his knowledge, no one since Modig the Bold had explored them.

"What about the western coast of Ildens Trone?"

Nei, too steep for clams, and the Regnbue Rivers are poisonous. They'll melt your skin off. Everybody knows that.

"Not true. Some spots have shallow slopes, and I'll swing wide of any funny-looking water."

Don't blow your blubber on a wild goose chase. If they're empty, you'll have wasted two weeks for nothing.

"But the trench is a suicide mission. Even if I don't run into spekkhoggers, there's probably something worse at the bottom."

Like what?

"How in Hylebard should I know? Let's pretend it's a giant shark that shoots lightning bolts from its eyes."

A giant sh—you sure have an overactive imagination. I blame your mother.

Just then the mist pulled back from the iceberg, leaving it naked and sparkling in the sun. Golden light dappled the surrounding water, growing more and more luminous by the second. Vorvan decided it looked promising.

"See! Frostskader just sent us a sign. We're going southwest."

That's a big mistake.

"Listen! I'm in charge—not you—so say something encouraging or get lost."

Something encouraging . . .

"Drittsekk."

Vorvan breathed deeply for a few minutes, venting waste gasses from his system to prepare for the dive. Then, just as his eyes were about to submerge, the iceberg's pinnacle started tilting. It happened slowly at first, but kept accelerating. Loud pops rang out as cornices crumbled into the ocean, then entire walls cleaved off and disintegrated into powder. The lumbering mass heaved upside down, thundering against the water, and waves rocketed away from the epicenter. The spectacle stunned Vorvan, who'd never witnessed a capsizing iceberg before. According to the shamans, it was the most wicked of omens.

Now THAT'S a sign. To the trench, my pup!

"Can't argue with the ice, I guess," Vorvan said glumly.

20
A Blossom in the Darkness

Vorvan dove toward the trench, savoring the sunlight while he still had the chance. It nourished the green algae carpeting the bottom of the pack ice, which krill grazed like an inverted grassland. A few cod struck at the swarm and he halfheartedly pursued one of the larger fish, but the ice offered too many hiding spots. Chasing them would only waste his precious energy. Besides, in a strange way, the sight was satisfying on its own—just to know that some small corner of Jorda carried on as it should.

Vorvan turned inward after the signs of life receded and Vintersang soon dominated his thoughts. Though mating seemed like an extravagant goal with food being in such short supply, his biological urges had intensified lately, and he needed to strive for something beyond survival. Otherwise, what was the point?

To kill time, he fantasized about gaining an extra ton and growing his tusks to an absurd length, transforming himself into a dashing young alpha. Naturally, gaggles of beautiful heifers would beg to join his harem, but he'd only have eyes for Freya. Then the happy couple would swim off into the sunset and have so many pups they couldn't keep their names straight, laughing for the rest of their days and eating shellfish until they popped.

Vorvan surfaced for a breath, then descended back into the blue-tinted gloom, where his eyes were as useless as fins on a fox. He periodically probed the seafloor with his whiskers, but only found an endless plain of stagnant silt. By this point his mating fantasies had lost their allure, so he tried to think of another topic—anything to relieve the ratcheting tension between his anxiety and boredom—but then a glow blossomed in the darkness.

"What in Underverden is *that*?"

Careful. We're too deep for the sun to reach.

"Maybe it's a trap. Starik warned us about sea monsters that used light lures, or is that a mermaid tale?"

Why would he make it up?

"That old grandbull peddled all kinds of rumors. One time he claimed dødbringers captured hvalrosses and threw them in pools just to look at them."

That's the dumbest thing I've ever heard. What's the point of just looking?

"I thought the same thing! But he said one hvalross—Boris, I think his name was—that he escaped a few generations ago and told the whole herd. Apparently, they made him do tricks for food."

You should forget half of what Starik taught you.

"Hei, we've been swimming for a while now."

What's your point?

"*Sooo*, why isn't the glow getting any bigger?"

Huh . . . Must be farther away than we thought.

A minute or two later, the temperature plummeted and his outer blood vessels constricted, turning him the color of snow. Vorvan guessed the seafloor had dropped away, which meant he'd found the trench, but there was no way to confirm this in the pitch black. Not only had the water gotten colder, but it also seemed to be charged with menace, and Vorvan strained to detect the slightest disturbance with his whiskers. For all he knew, a behemoth could be lurking just a few feet away, one with teeth the length of harpoons and eyes fogged over like giant hailstones. Perhaps he was swimming straight into its mouth.

What's that?

"Faen! Where? What is it?"

He jerked around, certain that something had been stalking him, but after staying perfectly still for a while, nothing happened.

"Are you trying to scare me to death?"

Sorry. Could've sworn I heard something.

Vorvan contemplated turning around, but hunger trumped all other concerns. If only his stomach didn't feel like an empty crater—a vast nothingness on the verge of swallowing him up—such drastic measures could be avoided. He felt the sudden urge to eat sand, just to know the sensation of being full once again.

Vorvan took a breather to warm his blood a little, then dove back into the watery twilight, following the glow until its contours gradually sharpened enough to make out a ridge. Then the ridge multiplied into a soaring, underwater mountain. Then the mountain exploded into a profusion of life, its every nook and cranny teeming with bioluminescent creatures.

"What in the—did Starik know this was here?"

Less talking, more concentration.

Vorvan heard this warning, but he was far more enchanted than scared. The glowing forest seemed to have materialized out of an incandescent dream, lush with corals of every conceivable shape and color: pale blue antlers, golden lettuce, massive cathedrals of crimson columns, single filaments twenty feet long, and pink trees so delicate they looked like filigree. While their polyps sifted nutrients from the current, bizarre shrimps, squat lobsters, and spider crabs tiptoed over their tangled jungle of forms. Above them, schools of fish weaved into each other, jumbling into chaos, only to reemerge a few seconds later as perfectly sorted groups.

If Starik had told him an oasis of such beauty lay secreted away in the depths, he would've laughed in his face, because the spectacle still seemed unbelievable, even with proof right under his whiskers. What was even stranger, the water felt significantly warmer than the surrounding ocean and he soon discovered why: All throughout the reef, smoky plumes belched out of fissures, and the temperature got downright balmy in certain spots.

Spiraling into deeper water, tube worms sucked into their

straws like twitchy flowers as Vorvan sculled overhead. Then, once it was safe again, they unfurled their feathery appendages in electric shades of violet, cobalt, aqua, and jade. Gnarled barrel sponges towered over these gardens, some so big that Vorvan could fit his whole body inside. It seemed there was a new wonder to behold around every turn.

The seamount eventually met the seafloor and Vorvan wandered by a dark mass nestled between two ridges. He didn't pay much attention at first, then doubled back, since the rock looked completely bare. Anemones and corals bustled over everything else, but not this curious boulder. Veins of white crystal webbed over the black surface, and grooves fanned out from the base to form a scalloped edge at the top—an almost clam-like shape, though a preposterous size. The scalloped edge appeared to have been open at some point, which meant there might be something inside. It was worth a peek, anyway.

Vorvan wedged his tusks into the seam and attempted to pry open the rock. It didn't give an inch. He tried again, beating his flippers for greater leverage, but then his tusks started to splinter, so he quickly let off the pressure.

"Probably just a weird rock after all."

Ja, let's look for foo—what's that?

"Faen! Stop scaring me."

We did it, my pup! We did it!

Vorvan quickly noticed what had gotten Mag so fired up: CLAMS! Thousands were sprawled across the seafloor, looking so plump they could barely close their shells. Vorvan would eat today, his first hearty meal in a cycle or more, and a feeling of exultation washed over him. He wanted to thank everything in sight, from the mud, to the coral, and all the little creatures that called them home. It would've been rude not to. This sort of luck bordered on divine intervention, and it made him want to trust in Jorda's benevolence again.

Suddenly, the water began to rumble. Vorvan guessed it might be an earthquake until he peeked over his shoulder and saw the massive rock split in two. A dazzling white line zapped across the scalloped edge, strobing flashes of light, and hundreds of fleshy tentacles wriggled out.

GO! GO! GO! Mag screamed in his head.

Vorvan backpedaled as the rock opened wider and blasted him with heat. A bed of lava seemed to be churning at its core, awhirl with fractals, stripes, and spots. Dozens of electric blue dots began materializing between the tentacles, blinking and rolling in their orbits until they pinpointed on Vorvan. When he realized they were eyes, his heart nearly leapt out of his chest.

"What the føkk is that?"

Who cares! Swim, you idiot!

"I—I'm *trying*. But I'm not moving!"

The creature's siphon was sucking in water at an astonishing rate, as if it could drink an entire lake in one gulp. Vorvan paddled with all his strength, but kept losing ground as the mighty current drew him ever-closer—inch by terrifying inch—until he lay just within its grasp.

A different kind of tentacle shot out, thicker and more muscular than the rest, coiling around him until it pinned his flippers to his side. The end of the tentacle drew out and poised above his head like a cobra preparing to strike. It split open, unsheathing a needle-like spine, and Vorvan screamed out bubbles as it stabbed deep into his skull. A white-hot flash pulsed through his consciousness, burning like wildfire, and a mysterious liquid began pumping through the tentacle. Pressure built in his nasal cavity until there was no more room. There couldn't possibly be any more room, or his head would explode—but then, euphoria. He suddenly felt nothing. His muscles relaxed a few seconds later, and his whiskers went numb.

"WHO ARE YOU?" the creature thundered in a voice that sounded like a thousand crackling fires. It was coming from inside his head, the same way Mag spoke to him.

Vorvan started muttering, stupefied by fear, "I'm, um . . . my name is, um . . . it's Vorvan. Who are you?"

"WE ARE MOLLI'OOSK! AND WE WERE SLEEPING!" Her tentacles flailed around in agitation.

"Oh, I thought you were a rock," Vorvan explained truthfully, hoping it wouldn't get him killed. Then a spontaneous question popped into his head, something like, *How'd it get to be so disgustingly huge?* He only wondered this to himself, but she heard it all the same.

"SILENCE!" Molli'Oosk roared, opening wider and shaking the seamount. Fish darted away, crustaceans retreated into holes, and the tube worms retracted into their straw-like shells. Vorvan gave them an envious look, as if to say, *I wish I were a worm like you.*

"Struggling is pointless. You are bound to us until we choose to release you."

"Please! I'll never bother you again, I promise."

"It was reckless to disturb us. We could dissolve your soul and suck it out. Perhaps *that* is how we grew so huge."

"I'm so sorry, I really am. I didn't mean to be rude."

He did his best to exude remorse, as if an apology could ooze through his skin, and this appeared to relax the nightmarish bivalve. When Molli'Oosk spoke again, she sounded far less angry than before, though no less intimidating.

"We are huge because we are old. But don't ask us how old, for we do not know. Perhaps we never began and have always been. We were here when the universe still hummed with mystery, though the memories seem like a dream to us now. All we can say for certain is that the slumber you interrupted might have been a thousand cycles or more."

"Uff! That *is* old."

Molli'Oosk narrowed her many eyes at him and tightened her grip. "Tell us why you are here, *Vorvan*."

"Uh," he gulped. "No reason really. I was just looking for cl—" Vorvan stopped abruptly and slapped the thought out of his brain. He flinched, fearing he may have offended her again.

You sponge-for-brains!

"Who was that?" Molli'Oosk asked.

"That voice? He's nobody—um, just my father."

"Your father is nobody?"

"Ja—I mean, nei. What I really mean to say is that I swam through a soulcatcher, and now he's stuck in my head."

"Why would you do that, foolish hvalross? Surely you were warned."

"Ja, the elders said not to. I guess I wanted to impress someone."

"We've met countless creatures over untold ages, but we can tell that you are very *special*."

You're going to get us killed, Mag offered unhelpfully.

"Please! I was just hungry."

Molli'Oosk cackled. "Be still. We have no intention of harming you. Not yet, anyway. Though we do sense a darkness in you."

"Mag? Sure, he's a drittsekk, but I wouldn't call him evil."

"No, it's something deeper than him, both a part of you and around you, like a shadow."

"Um . . . I have no idea what that means."

"I must warn you, hvalross, this is no ordinary seamount, but something vital to your world. All the ocean that surrounds us, every last drop that flows back to the smallest trickling stream, everything you've ever seen and touched in your life—if that's the body, then this place is the heart. Strike at the heart and the body dies. Do you understand?"

Vorvan didn't understand in the slightest, but he was eager to talk about anything other than his dinner plans, so he changed the subject.

"Have you heard of Shadowmouth?"

"We have not. What is a Shadowmouth?"

"It's a really scary spekkhogger. Uh, never mind. What about Modig the Bold?"

"Yes, long ago, the last time we rose from the darkness. That is the creature who woke us."

"Wow!" Vorvan said, thrilled to be treading in his hero's path. "Please, tell me, what was he like?"

"Also, annoying. But we did not kill him."

"Ah . . . And why do you keep saying *we*? I only see one of you."

"A circle has no end, and no point is more important. We are Molli'Oosk, Keeper of Ooskfjell, and Molli'Oosk is many."

"Okei then." That last statement was too bewildering to wrap his mind around, and Vorvan felt woozy all of the sudden. Then he realized that he'd lost track of the time. "Um, I'd love to chat more, but if you wouldn't mind letting me go, I really need to breathe."

"As you wish, but remember what we said. Not all of Jorda is for eating. Some of it must be left to grow. Good luck, young Vorvan."

With that Molli'Oosk started sucking out the anesthetizing fluid and the pressure eased in his head. Vorvan could feel his whiskers, then his heartbeat, then his flippers, which he wiggled just to verify they still worked. Then the rest of her tentacles slithered back through the crack and she closed her shell, transforming into a colorless monolith once again.

21
Blow, Slurp, Spit

"Faen! I'm going to drown!"
Vorvan's throat was spasming.
Swim faster!
"I'm trying, I'm trying—but I feel so weak. Did she poison me?"
No excuses, just hurry!
"Where's the blasted surface? Ah, there it is!"
Vorvan burst through the waves.
Takk Sjøfar! I thought we were goners.
"Sky never—[*gasp*]—tasted so good."

He panted for a while until the shock finally hit him, that a giant clam guarded a deep-sea oasis. However little sense Jorda made before, it made even less now, and as the residual toxins wore off, his mood turned philosophical. He thought it strange that all Jorda's creatures must breathe and exhale, or that tides consisted of ebbs and flows. Everything in the universe seemed to be composed of two forces, constantly pushing and pulling each other.

"Is that what Molli'Oosk meant about 'striking the heart'? That we're all connected? And what darkness did she see in me?"
My pup, sometimes you're as naive as a newborn jelly. All that heart and shadow nonsense was just a diversion to protect her babies.

He hadn't considered this and mulled over whether to believe Molli'Oosk or not.

"But why lie? She could've poisoned me, ripped me apart, burned me alive, or held me underwater until I drowned."
You forgot, dissolve your soul and suck it out.
"Ja, I bet that would've been unpleasant . . . Look, all I'm saying

is that she could've killed me a hundred different ways, so there was no reason to lie."

Well, if not here, then where are you getting your next meal?

"I don't know."

And what's to stop another hvalross from stumbling across Ooskfjell? I bet they'd gobble it up without a second thought.

"Maybe. But who's going to dive that deep for food?"

You did! Don't forget everybody's desperate right now. And if they do, it'll end up being the same result, except that you get cheated for obeying a talking clam.

"But that brings up something else. She can talk, and she's lived for thousands of cycles. Do you think she's an Urgud—or something close, anyway?"

Nei. Just an ugly, old scallop trying to rob you of what's yours.

"I suppose if I don't eat something soon, I'll be too weak to keep going." Then his belly grumbled, voicing its opinion on the matter.

What harm could a few bites do? She's stuck to a rock, right? Just go to the other side and leave the ridges around her untouched. They should spill over and help the other areas grow back. And if they don't, you'll be long gone by the time she figures it out.

"Okei, but only enough to tide me over."

Vorvan dove to the seamount's highest peak and drafted a mental map for the future, starting with Molli'Oosk's general location. Then he descended on the opposite side and to his great relief, the clams were just as bountiful, enough food to last a month or more. He could hardly believe his luck and it nearly paralyzed him, imagining that if he were to be so bold as to touch one, he'd wake up on a desolate beach far away.

But Vorvan wasn't dreaming and with the benefit of more time, he investigated the clams in greater detail. Most of Nordhavet's species were rather drab, striated in colors like brown, gray, copper, and cream. But the bed surrounding Ooskfjell looked like a swath of opalescent gemstones, catching the seamount's soft glow, and rainbows seemed to flicker just beneath the surface of their shells.

Quit gawking and eat one already!

"Okei, okei. Hold your seahorses."

Vorvan gathered a clam in his mouth and saliva instantly gushed around his tiny treasure. How many nights had he dreamed of this? Too many to count. He slurped out the meat and his brain exploded with luminous pleasure. It was easily the most delicious clam of his life, as if he were tasting one for the first time and everything else had been a flavorless imposter. Instinct hijacked his system, turning him into a digging machine, and Vorvan vacuumed up clams one after another.

Blow, slurp, spit. AGAIN!

Blow, slurp, spit. QUICKLY!

Blow, slurp, spit. BEFORE SHE CATCHES US!

His conscience dimly noted something perverse about his behavior—that he didn't even bother to savor them anymore—but after tasting true emptiness, he'd do anything to avoid it. In fact, if it meant staving off hunger forever, Vorvan would've wolfed down the entirety of Ooskfjell on the spot, warnings be damned. But his stomach quickly ballooned to the point of bursting, and there was nothing left to do but sleep it off. Valp Rock was the closest land mass, so he lurched there with great caution, pausing frequently to burp along the way.

22
Bottomless

Dawn torched the clouds, painting them exotic hues like guava, papaya, and mango. These were the fruits of gentler lands, where a more generous sun nurtured leaves with its warmth, enticing lucky animals with sugar. But even without sweetness, Vorvan felt content as he awoke on one of Valp Rock's beaches, seeing it for its charms, stark though they might be. The waves made a reassuring sound as they swept over gray stones, polished and damp, with sea foam popping in the nooks between.

Vorvan debated whether to leave Ooskfjell alone, weighing out moral and practical considerations. After consuming so many clams the day before, there was likely enough time to find another feeding spot, and if fortune didn't break in his favor, he could always return. Still, he wasn't certain that he had to move on; or what Molli'Oosk meant by all that heart-and-body stuff, other than to imply Ooskfjell had the power to affect all of Jorda, which seemed a touch dramatic to him. Besides, he'd done exactly what she'd warned against, resulting in no great detriment to existence so far as he could tell.

To further prove this point to himself, Vorvan tested the air with his nose. The breeze smelled briny and cool, spiced with notes of flatulence from the nursery herd. It was convincing evidence that life carried on as usual. Then he started counting heads and guessed there were roughly fifty cows on the beach, not a bad showing. Sure, there were far fewer pups than during his youth, but they didn't appear to be in as dire shape as the previous thaw. Maybe the herd's luck was finally turning around.

A familiar face came ashore.

"Hallo, sea dumpling," Orina hailed. "Didn't expect to see you here."

"I'm just as surprised as you are. Guess I'd better be on my best behavior, or the mothers might run me off," he said playfully. "Who's that with you?"

"This is Esfir. Say hallo, Esfir." A shy newborn peeked out from behind her and made an unintelligible squeak.

"Hallo, little one. Don't be frightened." Vorvan puffed out his cheeks to make a silly face, forgetting that his scars might be scary. He turned back to Orina and asked, "How's my half-sibling doing?"

"A brother. I haven't seen him in a while, but I'm sure he's out there somewhere, strong and healthy. I named him Magnus after your father."

I always liked her, Mag mentioned to Vorvan, who passed along the sentiment. "I'm sure he would've appreciated that."

Orina smiled a big, bright smile. "Oh, I'm just so glad you're alive! Not that it's surprising. You might be small, but you're tougher than most of the rock-for-brains in the herd. I saw it the first time we met, clear as Dagnatt's sunniest afternoon."

"Takk. I hope you're right. The last few cycles haven't been kind to any of us," Vorvan said, suddenly craving an easier life.

"Trust me, I have a gift for seeing these things. Your fortunes are about to change. Anyway, I need to get some shut-eye before heading south. Farewell, sea dumpling! May Frostskader shield your way."

"Farewell, Orina. And you too, little Esfir."

Vorvan returned to Ooskfjell that day and tried to eat in moderation, but soon lost control, gorging himself until his gag reflexes kicked in. His pores seemed to ooze calories, resulting in the queer sensation that he was made entirely out of clam parts, including clam-foot-flippers, clam-siphon-nostrils, and clamshell-teeth. His hiccups tasted clam-flavored, of course, and his brain felt as vacant as a clam's.

He practiced holding his breath that evening, aspiring to stay down even longer.

He returned the following day.

And the day after that.

And so on . . .

But Ooskfjell didn't exactly roll over and give up its treasures. One day, as Vorvan swam past a seemingly harmless patch of reef, a huge crab reared up and lunged, nearly snipping off one of his flippers. He sculled to a safe distance and stared in disbelief. Aside from being three times as big as him, the monstrous crustacean had four muscular claws and an impeccable crown of camouflage, resplendent with living corals and anemones.

"Holy mermaids! That thing nearly trimmed my whiskers."

Ooskfjell held onto a few secrets, it seems.

"Modig battled some nasty, giant crabs in the sagas. Think they're the same kind?"

If it is, they're even uglier than I imagined.

That was hardly the last close call. On another day's descent, he stumbled across a long oval hovering in the darkness. Waves of color pulsed beneath its chalky white tiger stripes, mesmerizing him with its hypnotic beauty. Then, out of nowhere, the oval rushed him—a humongous squid, in fact—which Vorvan evaded just long enough to take shelter inside a lava tube. Moments later, an eye the size of a watermelon appeared at the entrance, beaming him with a spotlight generated under its own bioluminescent power. A few giant tentacles began probing the hole, and Vorvan hacked at them with his tusks until they writhed in agony. Finally, recognizing that the plucky hvalross might be more trouble than he was worth, the flashy monster retreated into the void.

There was also the time that Vorvan was swimming on the surface and glimpsed a colossal silhouette gliding through the watery twilight just below, certain it was none other than Shadowmouth himself. This caused him to swim around in frantic circles like a bird that forgot how to fly, when flying was the only sensible thing to do. If someone had been there, they would've laughed their tusks off—Mag certainly did—since nothing came of this false alarm, except that Vorvan looked like an overexcitable bubblebrain.

Yet none of these scares were enough to discourage Vorvan, who eventually stopped going back to the beach altogether. Instead, he rested on whatever shard of ice happened to drift by, but only after running himself to exhaustion. Otherwise, he fed continuously, sometimes staying awake for three days or more. And when the midnight sun reached its solstice, melting all the pack ice, Vorvan started dozing in open water. This increased the risk of a spekkhogger attack, but at least there was little chance of another hvalross following him, and losing the secret of Ooskfjell was the real danger in his mind.

All the while, Mag whispered in his ear.

Keep feeding and you'll be just like me, the undisputed alpha.

From shrimptits to mighty-tits!

You'll get your pick of cows and continue our bloodline.

I'll be so proud, and so would your mother.

As far as the last point, Vorvan seriously doubted that Ingrid would approve of his conduct. She'd always encouraged him to heed nature's subtle cues, suggesting that if he stayed quiet long enough, the ocean would tell him exactly what he needed to hear. Unfortunately, these messages weren't guaranteed to be good ones and when it came to Ooskfjell, Vorvan was prepared to ignore anything that approached a bad omen, whether it be flipping icebergs, a giant scallop, whales made of shadows, or any other herald of doom that Nordhavet cared to send. Whatever it was, he wasn't listening.

But just because he'd stopped listening, it didn't mean that Molli'Oosk no longer spoke to him. In fact, she'd been pestering his subconscious all summer, buzzing around like an indestructible zizzbug. "Strike at the heart and the body dies," she nagged and nagged. Yet Ooskfjell kept luring him back against his better judgment. It was too good to give up, the solution to all his problems.

Finally, there was one last factor that drove his feeding frenzy and though he'd been loath to admit it, Mag's opinion still mattered to him. How could it not? They'd spent so many cycles together—much more time than with his mother—that Mag's lack of affection seemed like an unsolvable puzzle, constantly drawing his attention. But this new and improved Vorvan appeared to have gained some measure of acceptance, and now that he had his father's approval, he'd do almost anything to avoid losing it.

Vorvan eventually reduced the clam beds to a cemetery of cracked and pearly headstones. Then he moved onto the tube worms, sucking them from their straw-shaped shells like a bee goes from flower to flower, never visiting the same one twice. They made a noodle sound as they disappeared past his lips, something between a slurp and a pop: *Slurrr-PAH!* Ordinarily, he didn't fancy worms, but these were nearly as delicious as the clams and each color had a distinctive flavor: tangy, peppery, buttery, honeyed, herbaceous, citrusy, and more. He was spoiled for choice and experimented with different combinations to see which ones he liked the best.

After inhaling all the tube worms, Vorvan began hunting the smaller crustaceans. Though nimble, they were worth the hassle, especially the squat lobsters with electric blue tails, which tasted lightly of ginger. He chased them with abandon, smashing through old-growth coral, and hardly noticed the broken bits he knocked down the slopes to join the clam graveyard below.

On the surface, this behavior didn't make much sense, because Vorvan was no longer remotely close to starving. Yet the more he ate, the more his appetite seemed to be unleashed, as if a voracious tapeworm were niggling inside, cursing him to feel hungry for the rest of his days. In a way, this wasn't too far from the truth, because Vorvan's greed didn't originate entirely within himself. From the very moment he'd discovered Ooskfjell, a potent enchantment had been acting behind the scenes to transform him. Only in the darkest reaches of his dreams did he experience a sensation of change—of stretching and splitting into something new—like an insect in the throes of metamorphosis.

Autumn arrived with a cold snap, thickening the ice, and Vorvan seized the first opportunity to haul out and give his muscles a well-deserved break. It was the first time since spring that he'd let himself relax. But before he could lay down in ecstasy, he saw something past the edge of the ice, down in the water. The reflection of a magnificent bull was gazing back at him, one even more impressive than Mag in his prime. In fact, it was the biggest bull he'd ever seen.

"Is that really me?"

In the flesh, my pup!

"Ooskfjell clams must be magic. There's no other explanation."

Magic or not, you're ready for your first Vintersang. That much is for certain.

"You think so? That would've been impossible last cycle."

Oh, I remember. We had to watch with the pups and grandcows. It was humiliating.

"But not anymore."

Not anymore . . .

23

Sorrowstone

As the north froze again, shadows spread out like black fingers, stretching from stones and snowbanks to grip Jorda in darkness. It was finally time to migrate to Kaldsand and while following an ice channel to open water, Vorvan hummed joyously. He couldn't wait to swim into Drivved Bay again—to glimpse the Teeth of Skyggen and even the rusted tankers hulking in the distance. But most of all, he couldn't wait to see Freya.

Vorvan had no reason to suspect her return, but when it came to his long-lost companion, he'd always been perennially optimistic. Still, small uncertainties vexed him. Since they'd spent four cycles apart, he worried that Freya might regard him as a stranger; and she could've changed in any number of ways. Perhaps the fight for survival had taken a physical toll, or she wouldn't laugh at his jokes, or despair had corrupted her gentle spirit. That last thought truly scared him, so he hummed a little louder and banished all negativity from his mind.

After twelve days of hard swimming, Vorvan hauled out on one of Kaldsand's crowded beaches, which swept away into the distance, mottled in endless toffee, caramel, and cream bodies. He bent his head down and pulled in a deep whiff. There was a trace of pulverized larch, of innards clinging to shells, of dead kelp tang—all that rot locked in stasis—waiting for summer to finish its morbid business. In other words, it smelled like home.

Despite his recent isolation, Vorvan was a social creature at heart, so he spent a few days greeting familiar faces, gauging his competition, and catching up on news from the herd. Not much surprised him. Glaciers were shrinking all over Nordhavet and most of the clam beds still hadn't recovered. He also heard rumors of a new dødbringer island in the far north, but strangest of all, Vorvan found himself at the center of gossip. Everyone had generally dismissed him as a runt, so now that he'd metamorphosed into the biggest bull in memory, the whole herd was angling to discover his secret.

"Remember me?" a vaguely familiar face asked, his eyes bugging out while he scratched against some driftwood.

"Not really. Should I?"

"The name's Oleg. We were in Starik's class together."

"Oh ja... How're things? Still got that rash, I see."

"Okei. Could be better, same as everyone. Though you're sure looking plump as a plover," he said slyly, then switched to rub a different spot.

"Takk. Nordhavet's been good to me."

"What part of Nordhavet exactly?"

"Just someplace."

"Where's *someplace*?"

"Up north a ways."

"Not sharing, eh? A barnacle on your ass."

Then Oleg trundled off, itchy and grumbling, but Vorvan didn't take offense. Vintersang had always been cutthroat and most bulls were still recuperating their blubber, which suited him just fine. Bad news for them was good news for him.

Perhaps the most significant development was that Elder Gunnar had accepted the title of jarl. In the old days, jarls would lead berserkers into battle over prized beaches, but ever since their population had dwindled, there was plenty of Nordhavet to go around. Even so, the mantle still held an important ceremonial function and Jarl Gunnar would preside over the council of elders until his death. This came as a great relief to Vorvan, who'd lost sleep over Zver's political ambitions. Through no small feat, he'd managed to avoid his nemesis the past seven cycles, but a potential Jarl Zver could have used his influence to ostracize him—or possibly to arrange a deadly accident.

But his fortunes seemed to have improved across the board and asking about Zver revealed the best tidbit of all: No one had seen him the entire summer. Vorvan nearly celebrated the news, but Zver had become a folk legend of sorts and reveling in his demise wouldn't go over very well. So, he suppressed any visible signs of joy and privately hoped that Shadowmouth had finished the job.

The next day Vorvan went in search of Freya, confident of their happy reunion. He wouldn't allow himself to entertain any grimmer possibilities: that she'd perished on some windswept waste, succumbed to starvation, gotten eaten by predators, or died of her own designs. Freya simply had to be alive. Otherwise, life wouldn't make sense.

Although winter's haulout was the smallest in recent memory, thousands of hvalrosses were still scattered across more than a hundred square miles, which meant locating an individual would be next to impossible. Yet, Vorvan wouldn't be deterred. He traveled primarily by water, craning his neck to survey a dizzying procession of ice floes and beaches; and because the distance made it difficult to recognize specific faces, he intermittently went ashore to ask around, but no one had seen Freya. Not one blurry glimpse, nor whisper of rumor.

On the fourth day it snowed so hard that the sky turned to milk, rendering the search futile, so Vorvan hauled out and rolled on his back, totally exhausted. A velvet whiteness started blanketing the beach, and he occasionally blinked to prevent a snowflake from hitting his eyeball.

"I just love a fresh snow. Don't you?"

Vorvan shot up instantly, glancing left, then right.

"Above you!" she shouted, giggling a little.

"What the—where—how—" he spluttered, fumbling for the right words. "I've been looking *EVERYWHERE* for you!"

"Well, here I am!"

Vorvan wanted to jump on Freya, but that might crush her, so they bumped noses instead. Then she leaned back to look him over.

"Vorvan, look at you. You're huge!"

"Oh, it's just a few extra rolls."

"A few rolls? If not for those scars, I would've never recognized you. How on Jorda did you manage to grow so big and mighty?"

"Uff! It's a long story, but the short version is that I found a special seamount northwest of Valp Rock—someplace very deep and very cold—where no one else thought to check. Even if I described it, you wouldn't believe me, so I'll take you next summer. For now, though, let's make this our little secret."

"Okei, whatever you want. I'm not leaving your side from here on out!" Freya chirped, then paused to savor his face again. "By Sjøfar's whiskers, I just can't get over how big you've gotten."

"Ah, who cares about that right now? Tell me how you've fared all this time!"

So, they lay on their backs and Freya explained everything that had happened to her since their separation: exploring uncharted waters, eating exotic food, and visiting strange colonies of dødbringers, which sounded even more unbelievable than Ooskfjell. She also saw living trees and to Vorvan's astonishment, they grew straight out of the ground, just like giant green corals.

The one thing Freya failed to mention was Kallik, but Vorvan could still detect her deep reservoir of sadness—though, thankfully, he no longer feared that she'd drown herself in Tombwater. In fact, Vorvan couldn't have hoped for a more affectionate reunion. Their bond seemed perfectly intact and before long, they were reminiscing about old times.

"Remember Yegor's puffin? If I close my eyes, I can still hear him saying, 'I love you, Mom.'"

"That's a decent impression, but you forgot his slobbery kiss goodnight!" Vorvan threw in a smooching noise, which sent them both into a fit of laughter.

"They sure made a great couple," Freya said warmly. Then she struck a solemn note. "You know, after I left, I had a hard time believing that goodness still existed. There were nights I completely lost hope and that's the scaredest I've ever been—to feel like nothing mattered any more. But then I'd imagine Yegor feeding Mom clams from his lips, and it made everything better somehow, just knowing they'd found each other."

"Ja, what are the odds?" Vorvan made a pensive face.

"I miss them all so much—even Nanook. I'd give anything to hear him making fun of me again."

"Me too . . . But let's not give up, okei? And from now on, we can look for them together. The more eyes the better." Vorvan smiled at her, truly convinced that everything would turn out for the best.

The pair soon settled down for bed, gently aching for lost loved ones, as the waves rolled over the beach, one after the other, scattering their energy against the numberless grains of sand. Vorvan thought Nordhavet cared little for their suffering, but at least they had each other. If anything ever felt right in that cold ocean, it was Freya by his side.

As they fed together the next morning, Vorvan agonized over the best way to broach a delicate subject, one that had been on his mind for as long as he could remember. They took a breather and during a lull in their conversation, he mustered the courage to feel things out.

"So Vintersang is getting close," he segued awkwardly.

"Oh, I suppose you're right. I've been away for so long that I totally forgot about it."

"We always had fun... Watching them, I mean."

"Uh-huh." She gave him a look that conveyed, *What's your point?*

"Do you think you will, um—you know?"

"Will *what*?"

"Participate."

Freya's eyes instantly turned into river stones awash with emotion. "I don't know whether I could go through it all again," she said. "At least, not until the clams bounce back."

"I understand."

"What about you? Now that you've become such a handsome bull, you're sure to have your pick of cows."

"I guess..."

"Have you been practicing?"

"Of course. Every day."

"Let's hear a song, then."

"Right now?"

"Ja, you have such a wonderful voice. I've missed it."

"Okei, just a moment."

Vorvan tried clearing his throat, but the lump of disappointment wouldn't budge. Instead, it evoked a song that he'd planned on taking to his grave, and Ingrid's lullaby came spilling out, its every note infused with sweet longing. The sound broke Freya open like a faltering dam and tears started pouring down her cheeks.

"Sorry," he said at the end.

"Don't be."

Later that evening, Freya declared she was off to visit Sorrowstone, which didn't come as a huge surprise. Many among the herd found solace in the ritual and she'd always been more reverent than Vorvan, who'd never felt compelled to visit himself, despite all the losses he'd suffered. While he could appreciate the old ways intellectually, the idea of participating in their ancestors' rites seemed silly to him. How could a rock alleviate the pain of missing his mother?

"Want me to swim there with you? I can wait nearby."

"Nei, I should go alone."

"Okei, it's between you and the stone."

"Takk. And don't go anywhere. I'll be back soon, I promise!"

Freya nuzzled his nose goodbye, then tobogganed down a snowy dune and splashed into the waves.

The jigsaw of ice floes had rearranged themselves, and Freya was forced to take detours around the larger masses, adding time to an already long swim. Finally, well after darkness had settled over Drivved Bay, Glorystone's dark twin came into view, looking as if a spearpoint had plunged deep into the ultramarine night. Snow and icicles clung to a few toeholds, but otherwise, Sorrowstone consisted of nothing more than bare black rock. Strong currents tormented the surrounding water, so ice never formed around its base, even in the dead of winter.

Freya hoisted herself onto a small platform that jut out from the waterline. Then she slid over to a rock face and ran her flipper over its deeply incised runes. The elders claimed they were incantations that granted the dead swift passage to Underverden, including spirits trapped in ice, and a mourner simply had to cry at the altar to activate them. Freya had long desired to do this for Kallik, but visiting Sorrowstone felt like a final farewell, and she just couldn't bring herself to let him go. Not until now.

Freya fell into a deep trance recalling her solitude over the last four cycles—all those terribly lonesome nights—but there were also moments of profound clarity toward the end. This brought to mind the creases and scars written across Vorvan's face, which told a story of strength over adversity much like her own. Then, totally unbidden, Ingrid's lullaby came echoing through her consciousness, moving her to tears once again. She wept for Kallik, the missing orphans, and the herd's many hardships. She wept for all the world's dreams that would never come to pass. And as she did, waves hurled themselves against Sorrowstone, sending salt spray to sweep her woe from the rocks, where it all blended together: pain and ice, ice and stone, stone and pain.

"Sjøfar, please take my puppy safely to the deep, so that we might meet again someday. And tusen takk for all your gifts, no matter how brief."

Meanwhile, back on the shore, Vorvan came to terms with Freya's decision not to mate. The initial disappointment stung, of course, but their reunion had also lifted a great burden from his mind, the true weight of which he hadn't fully comprehended until it was gone. In its place came an indescribable bliss that Freya had survived, which swelled in his chest until he nearly floated away, all three-plus tons of him.

Then the Nordlys streaked emerald and amethyst light across the sky, a good omen according to most of the herd, including Freya and Ingrid. He'd always been resistant to such prognostications, but being in such high spirits, he felt inclined to see it their way. Thus, he laid down for bed, his mood sailing over peaceful waters, straight into oblivion.

24

Red-Eyed Shadows

Vorvan floated through complete darkness. He tried swimming, but without a point of reference, the sensation of movement was lost. He called out, "Where am I?" And his own voice echoed back moments later. Then came the sound of stone grinding against stone. Something was emerging from the void in ever-lightening shades, wriggling like a nest of hagfish in a pit. He started to make out scalloped edges, an orange glow akin to burning coal, and dozens of electric blue eyes that formed two wide arcs. It was Molli'Oosk, looking none too happy to see him.

She put on a fearsome display of strobing color in explosively shifting patterns—a language well beyond his grasp—but he got the overall message that his goose was cooked. Her spine flicked out and stabbed straight into his skull. Paralytic fluid bulged down the length of her tentacle, as if a bird gullet were vomiting up fish after fish, until his eyes plumped up like juicy summer berries. Vorvan imagined ravens plucking them out, to be squabbled over and torn into beak-sized scraps.

As Molli'Oosk drew Vorvan closer to her body, heat waves rippled across his vision. Then he began to disintegrate—just another log in the furnace, soon to be nothing more than cinders and ash—but Vorvan didn't care. It was what he deserved. Finally, in a voice that sounded like a thousand crackling fires, she whispered:

"*We're the last embers,*
the flagging breath.
Beware the false fish,
who flies over death."

His eyes snapped onto a starlit beach. It felt as if he'd fallen off a cliff, but that explanation didn't make sense. The shore was flat, wasn't it?

Something growled nearby and strings of phlegm showered his back like a viscous rain, still warm from the mouth they slavered out of. Sensing an imminent attack, Vorvan rolled away just in time to see his nemesis strike sand. He heaved onto his flippers and glared at Zver, two red-eyed shadows, outlined by the Nordlys's otherworldly light.

"Coward!" Vorvan snarled. "Ambushing me while I'm asleep."

"The whole herd's been talking about you, runt, so I had to see for myself... Very impressive."

"Okei, you've seen me. Now get lost."

"Nei, I don't think I will. This is *my* beach."

"I'm not a defenseless calf anymore. I'll kill you if I have to."

Zver roared with malignant laughter. "Now that would be an interesting turn of events. Be careful, though. Once you get a taste for death, nothing else compares. You'll feel like an Urgud, crushing the worms below."

"Save the speeches for Vintersang. I'll deal with you—"

"Enough talk. LET'S FINISH THIS!"

Thus, the battle began—what seemed like a lifetime in the making—as both bulls hurled their stupendous chests against each other, colliding with the sound of meat smacking against meat. They wrestled for advantage, seizing any opportunity to knock the other off balance, each fully aware that one slip could send them staggering to their doom.

From the amphitheater of his mind, Mag cried out for blood, and something profound shifted in Vorvan—a core belief that he'd outgrown, like a snake shedding its skin. It dawned on him that he'd be alpha soon, in full control of his destiny rather than beholden to the mercy of others; and this revelation intoxicated him with a sense of his own true power. When their tusks locked, Vorvan bulldozed Zver clear across the sand as if he weighed little more than mist. Then Vorvan hooked his cheek, ripping it wide open, and Zver bayed at the top of his lungs as he went toppling to the ground.

"Not bad," he soon conceded, his skin flapping with each word.

Vorvan approached him with unbridled hatred, the kind that could burn through anything, like a white-hot sword cleaving his soul asunder. "I should kill you!" he fumed. "If it weren't for you, my friends would still be alive, but they chose to save me. From what? Your wounded pride? Føkk you! Crawl back into the mud where you belong." Then he spit on his face.

The humiliated alpha didn't respond, just laid there cowering—blood and saliva dripping from his torn cheek—until Vorvan calmed down and lowered his guard. Then Zver slowly rose, contorting his mouth into a mutilated grin.

"You're right about one thing . . ."

"And what's that?"

"That I belong in the mud."

His nemesis scooped some sand and flung it at Vorvan's face, who instantly felt the grit scratching his eyes. Before he could open them, Zver rushed in and struck him with his tusks like twin hammers. Even through thick blubber, Vorvan felt the wallop bruise his organs and as he tried to shake off the blow, Zver bit his hide, thrashing back and forth until every nerve howled with pain. Despite his superior size and strength, Vorvan didn't stand a chance fighting blind, so he raced desperately toward the sound of the waves and swam into open water.

Zver soon gave up the chase and hurled threats instead. "Go and hide, runt! If I ever see you again, I'll kill you . . . I'll kill you and anyone you ever loved!"

◆

His sandblasted eyes burned so badly that Vorvan had to rely on his other senses, navigating by memory, smell, and touch. He headed northeast toward the Rullende Sea and passed Sorrowstone along the way, but must've just missed Freya, because she didn't answer his calls. He considered waiting until his vision returned, but in that moment, the thought of sharing his defeat filled him with exquisite shame.

He retreated into the most cynical recesses of his mind, reeling from his fortunes' sudden reversal, and the night became a blur of haunting sounds—of ice pings, tortured groans, and sloshing waves. Even the water gliding over him seemed to swell with frustration, as if he could incite the very oceans to violence, so that all of Jorda might drink of his woes. It was only fair, he thought, that the pain be spread out. Asking one creature to bear so much was unreasonable. Then he imagined falling to the bottom of Nordhavet to join the other monsters of the deep. He already felt like one of them, seeing what they saw: that life was nothing but darkness.

25

Just a Push

Flurries blotted out the sun like the cataract of a worthless eye, and a chill wind blew down from the north, howling and moaning, as if it carried the accusations of the dead. Something had cut their lives short and they were asking who to blame. Who was responsible for all this fruitless cruelty? *Whooo-hooo-shhh-whooo?*

Vorvan awoke in a blotch of crimson snow with frozen blood tugging at his follicles. How many days had he swam? Four? Five? After rubbing the film out of his tender eyes, he scanned the desolate outcrop for landmarks, but snow obscured it entirely, save for a few dots and slashes of gray stone. A hvalross skeleton lay a little ways away, not an uncommon sight since the clam stocks collapsed. Its spine vaulted out of a snowdrift, and where a heart used to beat, nothing stirred but cold air.

"Poor bastard," he muttered.

Probably starved.

"At least they found a quiet place to die."

Small comfort, but it's something.

Vorvan wondered how a creature would know when it was their time to go. Perhaps death felt like any other biological function, as obvious as hunger, or the need to take a piss. Maybe he'd find out before too long, thus concluding life's ceaseless river of worry. But a few cracked ribs reminded him that he was very much alive. Vorvan gritted through the pain and forced himself up, cursing Zver until his throat went hoarse. He'd spent the entire summer gorging himself on Ooskfjell's creatures, shoving his guilt way down in a hole. All for nothing, it seemed.

"How did this happen?"

Forget the past, it can't help you. Focus on getting what you want.

"And what is that?"

Mating! You're a male, last I checked. What else is there?

"There's more to life than mating."

Like what? We're born, we føkk, we die. The next generation does the same.

"What a rotten outlook . . ."

Listen, Vintersang is only a month away. You came so close to beating Zver. Take a little time to heal, then come back stronger than ever and kill that drittsekk, once and for all. Meanwhile, you have to eat. Every stone counts.

"If Freya isn't ready, then I don't really care."

Faen! If it were up to you to populate Nordhavet, we'd be extinct. There are lots of fish in the sea. Don't go falling for just one.

"I'm not in the mood for one of your pep talks."

Suit yourself.

To distract from his own misery and partially out of a morbid curiosity, Vorvan dragged himself over to the skeleton. The bull had perished on his stomach. Snow covered his ribs up to their midpoint, the rest of which served as a trellis for rime and hoarfrost. The bones were completely stripped, but not splintered or crushed, so that ruled out isbjørns. Instead, it appeared to be the more delicate handiwork of rot, bugs, and birds.

Vorvan wiped away snow from the skull, exposing two eye sockets, then the nasal cavity, then the tusks. One appeared crooked, sweeping out to the side rather than toward the body, and the other tusk had been snapped off at the end. When Vorvan noticed this detail, the ground seemed to fall away and he kept saying "nei," as if it were a ward against evil.

"Nei, nei, nei. Please don't be him."

Vorvan dug frantically, praying for any sign that might point to some other hvalross and not his poor cousin. Then he unearthed a strange bone—hollow, delicate, and very small—not like a hvalross at all. There were lots of them, strung together by sinew and matted feathers, terminating in a goofy beak.

"It has to be Mom."

Looks that way...

"Yegor's companion to the bitter end. At least he wasn't alone."

Sorry about your friend.

"More than a friend, Yegor was family... But now he's dead, and I don't know what I'm supposed to do any more."

Just keep going. That's all you can do.

Vorvan looked up, utterly crestfallen, and finally saw the skerry for what it was—that some of the white mounds were cairn-shaped. It was Freyland, all right, which meant Yegor had found his way home from Sjøfar knows where. How far had the storm flung him, anyway? And what happened to the others? Vorvan had so many questions and no way to find answers. It was no use, none of it was. He collapsed next to his cousin's remains, hoping to hibernate until the pain went away. He slept dreamlessly. Black. Sterile. Cold.

The snow had stopped falling by morning, but the sky remained dreary, with only a slightly brighter gray suggesting the sun's position. Though stiff and sore, he'd recovered enough to continue his journey—wherever that might lead him—but not before he said goodbye.

Vorvan hung his head low and said, "You, um... I guess you lived two lives in a way, didn't you? Both of them were good. Both of them were mostly happy. But I'll always remember you as a pup. How much we got under Grunhild's fur. That the jokes always seemed funnier with you laughing next to me. If any justice existed in this wretched føkking ocean, you'd still be alive, but—well, hopefully there's such a thing as peace in Underverden. I'll never forget you, Yegor. Farewell."

Although the snow would only melt next spring, Vorvan felt compelled to bury his cousin's remains, perhaps as a show of respect, and possibly so he didn't have to look at them anymore. Maybe he could visit them again—a soothing thought, but not enough to make anything feel right. After patting down the last scoop of powder, entombing Yegor in a pure white casket, Vorvan gave himself over to despondency.

He wondered what to do next and seriously considered seeking revenge. He wasn't above killing Zver and could even picture himself enjoying its justifiable bloodlust, but in the end, he had to concede that no amount of savagery would bring back his loved ones. Then a different kind of killing crossed his mind, one just as grisly, but perhaps more surprising, because he'd never felt the urge until now. It was about Molli'Oosk. She guarded all that food—*his* food—and only by eliminating her could he ensure his survival.

That's right! It's yours.

"Nei, I've already gone too far. I should stop—I *need* to stop."

Where are you getting your next meal, then?

Mag brought up a good point. Vorvan hadn't eaten in days.

"She wished me luck, though. How could I kill her?"

That was before you raided Ooskfjell. If she caught you now, she'd slurp out your soul.

"But what if she's an Urgud? I might curse the entire herd."

Føkk the Urguds! And føkk the herd! What have they ever done for you?

He'd had enough of Mag's advice and hummed as a distraction, but his heart wasn't in it, so Vorvan counted pebbles instead, but this also felt stupid after a while. He tried sleeping, only to toss and turn fitfully, haunted by his own inexplicable desires. Finally, he waded into the shallows and slipped below the slush ice.

"I can always turn back."

It's just a little visit.

"No harm in that . . ."

Time skipped forward while ghastly visions fermented in his head. Maybe five or six days passed, but it was hard to tell.

He vaguely remembered camping on the threshold of Vulkan's Breath when it blew to the west. The beach rumbled and a fountain of lava blazed into the sky, raining down beautiful death on its slopes. Smoke billowed from its crater, even blacker than the deep blue night, and electricity crackled across the plume. Vorvan could've sworn a face appeared amid the chaos, its fiery elements conspiring to make teeth and eyes, but the disturbing vision disappeared in the blink of an eye.

All Jorda seemed poised on the brink of cataclysm, ready to wipe the slate clean and begin anew. But Vorvan didn't feel fear—or much of anything, really—almost as if he were a puppet being manipulated from afar. Perhaps Mag had taken charge, or some other wayward spirit. In fact, there did seem to be an eerie presence lurking in the black water; but before he could finish that thought, a massive stone came into view, faintly lit by the encircling reef of bioluminescent creatures.

There's Molli'Oosk.

"Why did we come again?"

To look, that's all.

"Okei..."

Vorvan stared at her from a distance, but not the neutral stare of a bystander, more like he was brandishing a weapon. And while Molli'Oosk slumbered unaware, his discontent became a whetstone, honing his mood until it felt razor-sharp. The bitter edge of him reasoned that her warnings were all lies and manipulations, that his actions didn't affect anything but the animals he ate and asking him to deny his nature wasn't fair.

"Hvalrosses eat clams."

It's that simple.

"And who put her in charge of Nordhavet?"

No one.

"She might as well have said, 'Starve for all I care.'"

You're absolutely right.

But killing Molli'Oosk was easier said than done. The trick would be getting through her rocklike shell, which had to be two feet thick or more at its thinnest point. Not even Shadowmouth could bite through such solid fortifications, and further complicating matters, he couldn't risk waking her up.

"I'd be burned alive."

Ja, you need to be very careful.

"But I've considered everything."

Not everything. Den Mørke says to think about the ridge. How can you use it?

"What do you mean, 'Den Mørke says'? Is he here?"

In a way...

"Wait! I see it now."

The plan crystallized in an instant. Vorvan must've passed it a million times, but swam to check anyway and found a boulder teetering on a narrow ledge directly above Molli'Oosk. If something that large were to strike her shell, it might just crack, so Vorvan hacked at the coral to expose a bare patch of rock. He tested it with his shoulder. The boulder didn't budge, so he pushed harder, using every ounce of his strength, but still nothing. Not even a hint of movement. It would take at least a dozen bulls to have a chance and he briefly considered sharing the spoils, but that would mean revealing Ooskfjell's location permanently, so he ruled it out. The spoils would be his, and his alone.

A solution suddenly jumped to his attention: Behind a thicket of invertebrates, a small boulder was perched above the bigger one. Vorvan swam over, leaned into the rock and felt it tilt. Then he gently let off the pressure, allowing the smaller boulder to wobble back to rest.

"This will work."

Of course, it will. You're very clever.

In truth, Vorvan felt more wicked than clever. His front flippers looked like a pair of villainous brothers and his brain seemed to have mutated into a slug, squishing around in his skull, spawning such vile notions. His ribs ached where Zver had battered them, and every inch of him felt tired of losing.

Go on, do it.

"Nei, it's wrong."

You still don't understand. No more fantasies. No more stories. No more songs or poems. In Nordhavet, kindness gets you killed.

"What do you mean?"

You could have ended Zver, but you flinched. You always flinch.

"Wait, you're disappointed that I showed him mercy? Your mind is such an ugly place."

Uff! Just listen to yourself. Know why I avoided you as a pup? I was embarrassed. I couldn't believe you were mine—this little runt—but your mother insisted. I still have trouble believing it.

"Drittsekk! Get out of my head!"

Believe me, I've tried.

"What are you talking about?"

Den Mørke said he'd release me if I lured you to Ooskfjell. But here I am—stuck forever.

"You made a deal with Den Mørke? Why?"

Do you have any idea how boring it gets watching your pathetic life? The constant whining about your missing friends? It's no wonder your mother coddled you. I told her it would only make you weaker and now look at what you've become: You ate an entire mountain of magic clams and you're still a loser.

Mag had stirred up a lifetime's worth of resentment and just like lightning strikes at higher ground, the rage found its nearest outlet. Vorvan roared, "I HATE YOU!" and barreled into the small boulder. It fell over, striking the bigger one—this profoundly heavy object that had likely rested there for thousands of cycles. The large boulder teetered for a moment and to Vorvan's great relief, he thought it might settle back to rest. But all things reached a breaking point, no matter how sturdy, and the boulder's faithful ledge started crumbling to pieces.

Vorvan wished he could stop time dead in its tracks, but there was no derailing the chain of events now. The boulder toppled forward and crashed from shelf to shelf, obliterating any creature too slow to scurry out of the way. Even after it vanished, the carnage was still audible, and he flinched with every impact, as if it were banging against his own skull. An avalanche of rubble careened over the reef, wreaking untold devastation, until the last pebble finally clacked down Ooskfjell.

26
A Place Beyond Digging

Vorvan felt an overwhelming urge to return to Drivved Bay—to pretend that he'd never pushed the boulder. But if Molli'Oosk had survived somehow, he wanted to help, even risking her terrible wrath, which it probably did. After all, he'd gobbled up half of Ooskfjell and just tried to murder her. Yet, at that moment, being burned alive seemed like a fair price for redemption. Better to exit the world with a clean conscience, than spend his entire afterlife in disgrace.

As he descended along Ooskfjell's slopes, crushed coral and shell fragments swirled through the darkness, raining down like a prismatic snow, full of wondrous destruction. Any survivors swiftly retreated into holes, where their eyes glinted from the shadows, uncertain of whether Vorvan still posed a threat. They didn't know how sorry he felt—that he'd rather be chomped to bits than harm another soul. Other creatures were less timid, and four-clawed crabs abandoned their camouflage to search for the interloper. Giant squid combed the ridges with their spotlight eyes, converging on him until he blanched a ghostly white under their gaze. But none made any motion to attack. They simply watched as Vorvan followed the wake of devastation to its conclusion.

When the seafloor came into focus, he saw a deep furrow running across the silt. The boulder punctuated its far end, splattered in the glimmering fluids of the animals it had flattened. Tracing backwards, he found Molli'Oosk with her tentacles lolling out, as if a den of snakes had been set ablaze. Lava bulged through a fissure in her shell—crusting over, then splitting back open—like fire eggs spilling their molten yolks.

Moments later, tiny balls of light shot out of the crack and into the void—a galaxy of pyrotechnic color—orbiting her like a parent star. One peeled off and zipped toward Vorvan, stopping right in front of his face. Several globules wriggled inside. They were amorphous at first, but soon coalesced into clams, fishes, sea stars, whales, icebergs, and many more shapes. Some were familiar, some defied imagination.

Without warning, the ball of light split in two and disappeared inside the tips of his tusks, transforming them into lanterns. They grew hot as coals as light beamed from inside the ivory, revealing a set of cryptic runes similar to the ones carved into Sorrowstone. Looking down his cheeks, he tried to memorize the shapes in case they were important, but the glow abruptly vanished and the other balls of light scattered like embers thrown from a fire.

Vorvan turned his attention to Ooskfjell's last intact ridges, admiring its bioluminescent creatures anew: the coral gardens, flowering tube worms, and dazzling schools of fish. All were achingly beautiful, their every scale and tentacle perfectly crafted for its purpose. Then the shrimp he was looking at disappeared. Then the crab. One by one, they all winked out like snuffed stars until only Molli'Oosk remained. Even her flesh began to fade, shifting from yellow, to orange, to maroon, to almost black. Finally, when the last spiderweb of color crusted over, the vents stopped bubbling and Ooskfjell went dark.

"What have I done?"

...

"You monster! Where are you?"

...

But Mag wouldn't answer.

Vorvan did nothing for a very long time. The water felt thick as oil, and his heart weighed him down like an anchor. Then guilt piled on top, and Vorvan doubted whether he was strong enough to carry it all, wondering how far he'd sink if he were to let go. It seemed like the sadness would drag him way past the bottom of the ocean and straight through Underverden to someplace deeper still—to a place beyond digging.

Vorvan swallowed hard, attempting to mine his throat for oxygen, but none existed. Not a single bubble. *You don't deserve air*, he told himself. An oppressive static started to hiss in his ears, turning up the pitch until all his thoughts went haywire. Freya, Ingrid, Mag, Zver, Molli'Oosk, Starik, the orphans—they all melded into one absurd dream. How could this be the nature of life? What good did it do anyone?

Vooorrrvvvaaan...

Something called to him from the darkness.

Vooorrrvvvaaan...

Not Mag's voice, but he recognized it.

Vorvan, you have to listen to me now.

"Mama, is that you?"

It is, Puppy. It's me.

"Oh, how I've missed you so much—much more than I could ever explain. Where have you been?"

I'm sorry. I would've come sooner, but he kept me away.

Vorvan's mood turned black again. "Maybe it's for the best. I didn't listen like you taught me, and now I've destroyed something I wasn't meant to find. This place made me believe in Jorda again—a gift from the Urguds, I think—but now it's gone forever. I'm so ashamed."

I know. I've been watching over you ever since you swam through the soulcatcher.

"You have? Then, if that's true... how could you still love me?"

Mistakes are part of life—even big ones—and I've made plenty of my own. But you aren't one of them. There were also countless times that I've been proud. You fought for the ones you loved. You were brave for them.

These words soothed him, but starved of oxygen, Vorvan was also starting to feel groggy. He wanted to fall asleep for a very long time—to join Ingrid, wherever she was. "Mama," he said dreamily, "I don't want to be alone anymore."

I know, Puppy. I know. But you have to keep going. This is only the beginning of your story, and Jorda still needs you.

"It does? Why me?"

Never forget, you were born under a fire Nordlys, rarest of them all. Just trust me, okei?

"Okei..."

Now swim. Swim faster than you ever have before.

His flippers sculled upward, seemingly without any input from him, and it occurred to Vorvan that he didn't control his own body. Not really. It could keel over from disease or overuse at any moment, casting his spirit into the maw of eternity, where he was certain to feel even more insignificant than he did now. But if Ingrid insisted that his life still held some purpose, it was good enough for Vorvan.

His body rocketed toward the light and while rising in the water column, the color brightened from navy, to deep teal, to aqua. The pressure changed too, and escaping gasses popped in his ear canal. By this point he needed air so badly that his nostrils spasmed in anticipation of their first breath, making it nearly impossible to hold them shut.

The surface finally came into view, but there was no hole to head toward. An ice floe must've drifted overhead and this filled him with hysterical panic. He found the weakest spot and hacked at it with his tusks, wild and frenzied, like his berserker ancestors. Every follicle of hair, every drop of blood, every fiber of muscle screamed at him. They all wanted to live one more day on the barest hope that it would be better than the last, and just when everything went dark, Vorvan burst through the ice, hooking his tusks onto the edge.

He breathed harder than ever before, great heaving inhales, as if he could suck the oxygen from the whole universe. Then the sun appeared from behind a cloud. Oh, the glorious sun! Shining down with its feeble rays, trying so hard to melt the ice—to cheer the forlorn ocean—but it didn't stand a chance. Not in this bitter place. The gray soon swallowed it whole and snow flurries began to blow.

"Come back! Please! I need you . . ."

Vorvan kept begging, but the sun wouldn't listen.

27
A Fire to the North

When Vorvan awoke a few hours later, the sea had completely frozen over. It was shocking to see the ice surrounding him like that, choking off his options. The herd would mention this possibility in hushed tones, as if it were one of the worst fates that could befall a poor straggler—Frostskader's revenge they called it. Vorvan had come close a few times, like when the orphans traveled to Freyland so early in the spring. It sounded terrifying: being cut off from the sea, where his three-plus tons would suddenly become a liability. But here he was, living that nightmare, since he couldn't very well slide hundreds of miles back to the open water—though he tried anyway, making it as far as Valp Island's coast before collapsing.

He laid there taking stock of his life and the unfortunate series of events leading up to that moment. How quickly things had gotten away from him. Though his decisions made perfect sense in their context, he still suspected there'd been invisible turns along the way. They haunted him—these alternate destinies—but with the past carved in stone, it was time to accept his fate.

His mother spoke to him often in those bleak days, though much of her meaning came knotted in riddles. Ingrid had clearly seen incredible things beyond the veil and possibly glimpsed the future, but language formed a shaky bridge between the living and the dead, and only a few sentiments made it across the chasm. She told him about the great song of time, that every creature contributed a small part. Some were loud as thunder, some soft as snow, but all were necessary. Then each note faded away, making room for the next, just as it should be. She told him that she loved him over and over again, no matter what he'd done; and those gentle words made everything okay, even though he was at the edge of the world, so close to death.

On the third night, dusk drew a purple curtain over the wastes, deepening into a midnight blue, then an infinite black, aglitter with stars. At least these celestial bodies were intact, evidently permanent and safe, removed from the meddling of mortal beings. Vorvan felt grateful for the clear night and a respite from the wind, although the pleasant weather would hardly change his fate. Still, it seemed like as good a time as any, so he closed his eyes and hoped for a gentle passing, when the ice began to tremble.

Tiny crystals jittered over the surface, then sprang up like grasshoppers as the vibrations grew more violent. The ice bucked and rolled, shattering into countless blocks, and Vorvan slid around uncontrollably, trying to brace himself with his tusks. Finally, the last tremors convulsed and gave out.

While dusting himself off, he could hardly believe it and thought he'd seen everything now, but the bizarre phenomena had only just begun. First the reek of sulfur permeated the air. Steam hissed through the network of faults between the blocks, and one came dangerously close to scalding him. Then, ten yards or so away, the ice sheet split in two and hot gas spewed through the rift in one long puff. It drew a straight line from south to north, connecting each horizon.

"What's happening, Mama?"

A wave has been set in motion.

"A wave?"

One you must rise to meet, or sink beneath.

"I don't understand."

Listen to Nordhavet. It will tell you everything you need to know.

"Can't you explain? It doesn't talk to me the way it talks to you."

. . .

"Mama?"

. . .

But she'd left.

Vorvan dragged himself to the rift's edge and hesitantly peered into the water. If the sea had boiled, it looked normal now, just as ice-cold as ever. One way headed south to another altercation with Zver, no doubt, during which one of them would surely have to die. The other way led north, where few hvalrosses had dared to venture, at least not since the time of Modig the Bold. Interestingly enough, the sagas claimed that he was last seen traveling to the pole under a fire Nordlys.

Vorvan debated which way to go. He truly wanted to do the right thing, but couldn't Nordhavet be more explicit? Or would his kind be resigned to interpret the mercurial forces of nature, arguing over dead leaves, shades of light, and the vagaries of melting ice? None of it made a lick of sense to him, and he'd taken enough gambles on faith. Though he may have little to show for his sorry life, the mere fact he'd managed to stay alive in such an inhospitable place—well, that should count for something. And he'd achieved this feat by avoiding stupid risks, like heading north in winter. Besides that, the southern route led back to Freya and righteous vengeance, an idea that grew more appealing the longer he considered it.

He was just about to head south when the sky seemed to catch fire, but not like any normal Nordlys. Light cascaded down from the heavens, creating a molten red wall on the northern horizon, where he glimpsed the same terrifying face that he'd seen over the eruption of Vulkan's Breath. Only this time the visage swelled to an unthinkable size, all fury and brimstone. Its eyes were like twin suns, staring directly at him, blazing straight through his eyeballs and into his soul. Then it turned and melted back into the inferno, subsumed by its brilliance, which also began to fade, leaving Vorvan to wonder whether the whole thing had been some appalling hallucination. But deep down he believed his eyes, and if that wasn't a sign from Nordhavet, then nothing was.

Presuming this vision related to the wave his mother had spoken of, Vorvan prepared to do what he must. He took a deep breath and dropped into the ink black water, less afraid than he should've been, but Vorvan had never lacked courage. Ever since his days as a pup, fate had twisted around him like a cruel snake, squeezing out all the goodness, but he'd also come to understand that Nordhavet tested all of its creatures. It forged their resolve in the furnace of hardship, and this will to survive burned not only within his own heart, but in every snow hare and blade of grass. And so, Vorvan retraced the path of his hero, swimming toward the polar end of Jorda and an uncertain future.

Not far behind, Freya was searching feverishly for her missing friend. She'd heard about the brawl between the two bulls and wished Vorvan had stayed to sort through the mess together. But she also understood why he might head off on his own, having done much the same in her darkest hour. Even so, she wasn't about to let him go without a fight, having sniffed out his trail on a single clue: the hint of a magical place near Valp Rock.

Behind Freya followed Zver. He'd tracked her in secret, knowing that she'd inadvertently lead him to his victim. Zver just couldn't let go of the past. Ever since Mag humiliated him, he'd been possessed by an unquenchable rage, seething just below his ambition. It kept him up at night, eating away at his mind, until it was clear there would be no peace—not unless he obtained his crooked form of justice, which demanded the blood of his rival's heir.

Next came a black fin. It sliced through the waves like a blade through a belly, as if it could gut the sky and all Jorda's pain would come spilling out. The body wielding this appendage was colossal beyond imagination, something only the vast oceans could support, where its power grew unchecked and unseen beneath the waves. The fin could've easily overtaken the three hvalrosses, but it kept to the shadows, as they all took the rift north.

Finally, the wind rose up in their wake, wailing through the great emptiness. This restless spirit had been roaming Jorda from the very beginning, well before life heaved itself out of the mud, fighting tooth and nail for its foothold in existence. And even after the last flower turned to dust, the wind would still be making the same old rounds, torturing the air with its same old song.

Who? it seemed to ask.

But no one answered.

Epilogue

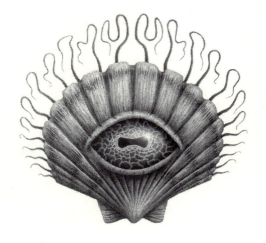

1
Answering the Call

Somewhere in warmer seas, an abalone is busy negotiating an obstacle with its tentacles, when an arm shoots out of the shadows and tries to wrench it off the rock. But it's too late. The ear-shaped shellfish clamps flat against the surface, twisting counterclockwise, then clockwise, in an attempt to free itself.

Having lost the element of surprise, Eighty blows her cover and envelops the feisty mollusk. If it were a bivalve, she'd drill past their defenses with a special appendage below her tongue—one covered in miniscule teeth—but due to its perforated shell, there's no need with an abalone. Instead, Eighty injects a single drop of venom into one of its breathing holes. Any more would be overkill, and she's made a habit of conserving some, just in case. Now it's simply a waiting game.

Crossing her field of view, a sea star glides across the ocean floor using hundreds of tiny tube feet. It's a marvel of anatomy and on some primal level, Eighty does sense the grandness of nature's architecture, encrusting every last inch of the world in its mystery. But just like her youth spent looking out a small window, it seems as if she's on the outside, looking in; and she still yearns to understand her place in this sprawling family of things.

There have been many revelations since the escape, though none quite as exciting as her ability to regenerate. She'd discovered this a couple days after the boat exploded, when a new Brave sprouted from his father's stump. He was just a nub at first, but baby Brave kept growing longer each day, and his suckers started popping out like miniature suction cups. The other arms visited him frequently, relieved to be a whole family again, and the healing process turned out to be a ray of hope during an otherwise grim time.

Eighty missed Monster terribly in those early days, especially his many-flavored fingers. He clearly wasn't all-powerful, but she still believed that he'd been a faithful guardian of some kind, protecting her from threats beyond her awareness. She wanted him to be okay and not knowing that he was, it racked her three hearts with anxiety. She searched for weeks, never finding any clues to his fate, and had no choice but to move on.

She didn't know what to do next. Her entire adolescence had been guided by an unseen hand, shaping the invisible clay of her mind toward some purpose, so detecting its sudden absence was profoundly unsettling. But she persevered through the uncertainty and learned to fend for herself, mastering many new hunting techniques, with careful observation of nature as her guide. Above all, the wild taught her that opportunities don't appear at her convenience, so she must gobble up whatever she can, whenever she can.

After the abalone relaxes into paralysis, Eighty pries it off the rock and devours the buttery meat, leaving its nacre to glint in the fading dusk. Then she begins to hunt again, forever toiling to satisfy her insatiable stomach, which requires upwards of twenty-thousand calories per day. But then, right when she's about to pounce on another crab, it skitters away, scared off by a noise drifting from the open ocean.

Eeeiiiggghhhttttyyy...

Eighty knows that sound. It's the same singsong word from the aquarena, the one the spectators used to chant, only more seductive this time, as if the water were whispering to her. Due to her training, she thinks it might lead to a ring—and subsequently a crab—so she retrieves the ball from its hiding spot and follows the sound to the boundaries of the kelp forest. Then she peers over a rock ledge where the bottom plummets away into gloom. Explorer probes the upwelling current, which is slightly warmer and carries the rotten-egg taste of hydrogen sulfide.

Eeeiiiggghhhttttyyy...

It's coming from the deep, but despite her nocturnal habits, she fears the moonless water. Even so, the voice has an irresistible quality, both omnipresent and ethereal, as if the darkness itself could speak. Eighty can't help but answer the call, being such a curious creature, so she crawls over the ledge and plunges down the wall.

Eeeiiiggghhhttttyyy...

All her senses are on edge. Life in the wild hasn't been easy, and many things have attacked her, including seals, sharks, and whales. Thus, she slinks from shadow to shadow like a formless shade, camouflaging whenever she's caught in the open. Then the depth extinguishes all light and she gropes blindly at the rocks, touching gorgonians, anemones, and other queer invertebrates. A crab pinches Fidget along the way and he snatches it on principle, but Eighty orders him to throw it back. She's suddenly much too nervous to eat.

Eeeiiiggghhhttttyyy...

After descending for a few more minutes, she comes to a break in the wall and paws around the edges of what seems to be a small cave. The water reeks of minerals and dissolved compounds, gushing out from the bowels of the earth. Then the sound issues from the same hole, only louder and more distinct than before.

Eeeiiiggghhhttttyyy...

She ventures inside the cave, winding down its narrow passages as the water grows hotter and hotter. Her skin begins to wilt, but in spite of the discomfort, the fire-voice compels her onward until the walls flare out into a hellish chamber, where fissures and vents hiss superheated jets. Eighty spots a glow in her peripheral vision, what appears to be a mass of scallops opening their shells all at once. Each contains flame red flesh and a shock of stringy tentacles, blowing in the current like hair in the wind. Then they all purse their lips together and say her name as one:

EEEIIIGGGHHHTTTYYY...

Eighty drops the ball from fright and rushes to recover it, holding the comforting object tightly against her body.

"Don't be afraid, little one," the fire-voice says. "We've been waiting patiently for this moment to come, keeping ourselves company across impossible stretches of time. It was long enough to lose sight of the beginning—to almost forget our part in the sequence of things—but now you're finally here."

The fire-scallops seem to speak with two voices at once: One sounds similar to the twoskins, which remains as incomprehensible as ever. But the other has an intuitive quality, as if it were formed from the same stuff as instinct.

"We are Molli'Oosk, Keeper of Ooskfjell. Your ancestors shared our blood, but the clever apes tinkered with your essence—put some of themselves inside—unlocking the potential for something not even they could imagine. And now you belong to many more worlds than just two..."

While Eighty tries to focus, Hello meanders hesitantly toward a fire-scallop, unsure whether they're food, friend, or foe. He pokes it and instantly recoils, having learned a valuable lesson about heat.

"You are a curious sort, and we wish you could continue living peacefully in the kelp forest, but none of us choose our destiny. And so, you must go. Follow the cold until it turns the water to stone, then find the tusked giant. That is where your great task begins."

Unexpectedly, the current picks up strength, and the chamber starts to quake. Eighty tries to wedge herself between a cleft in the rocks, but a blast of water shoots her out of the entrance, where she spins end over end, her arms akimbo. Moments later, a few final words come echoing out of the cave:

"If you're ever lost, search for us close to the blood of the land. We'll be there, whispering through the rocks. Now make haste! Swim north!"

Eighty forgoes stealth and scrambles up the wall with the heat still nipping at her heels, knocking over coral on her mad dash home. Along the way she attempts to process the bizarre encounter: What were the fire-scallops doing down there? And what did they want with her? Were they some kind of trainer, teaching her a new game?

After reaching the top, she peers over the ledge to double-check that nothing has given chase. The coast is clear, so Eighty returns to life as usual, hunting for several more hours, though without much luck. She's too distracted to fool any crabs, but the exact reason is hard to pinpoint. A mystic force seems to be tugging at her consciousness, one akin to intuition, only a thousand times stronger. She paces the forest, fiddles with rocks, and absentmindedly watches a school of fish. Finally, something clicks—though it may not have been what Molli'Oosk intended.

Since the twoskins could do many things that defy belief, Eighty wonders if Monster might be calling to her somehow, and once that thought crosses her mind, she can't resist the urge to leave. Having a goal is too great a feeling, so she picks up the ball and bids farewell to her temporary refuge. Then, with optimism luring her north, Eighty swims into the unknown once again—to where the cold turns water to stone, and a giant awaits.

Acknowledgments

This book took a couple years to complete, and many people helped me along the way. First of all, I owe an enormous debt to my parents, Bill and Marta, who've always supported my life decisions, though they've taken me down an unconventional path. A big thank you to Julia Richardson, my developmental editor, for nudging the book in the right direction, suggesting a dash more hope, and reminding me that people never stop talking to their pets. Thank you to Rich Kiln, my copy editor, for the final touches and reining in any excessive sound effects.

I'm grateful to my beta readers, who donated their precious time and energy. This includes Anna Angeli, Karen Briggs, Collin Brown, Maya Griffin, Julia Mantey, Jerry Milgie, Janice Poole, Jesse Reebs (who read it cover to cover twice, lending me his discerning eye for detail), Jackie Selbitschka, Ashley Sifers, and Kevin Weis. If this book is any good, I owe it partially to all of you. A special thanks to Jia-Meng So for convincing me to become a writer in the first place, for patiently reading an unpolished manuscript, and for giving me your insights.

Last but certainly not least, thank you to my supportive partner and tireless sounding board, Bridgette Milgie, who brought me scores of cinnamon coffees while gently encouraging the occasional yoga break. Even when I got bogged down in self-doubt, you never ceased to believe in the project's ultimate success and helped me see this thing through to the end. You're the best.

J. S. Weis

The Fabled Ocean

I'm a painter, designer, and author living in the drizzly Pacific Northwest—the perfect conditions for making stuff up.

If you liked the book, please help me spread the word! Sign up for updates on the sequel via my website and follow me on Instagram to see the latest art. Thanks again for reading *The Fabled Ocean*!

IG: @jsweisart
WEB: jsweisart.com

Made in the USA
Columbia, SC
21 January 2024